Maya Blake's hopes of becoming a writer were born when she picked up her first romance at thirteen. Little did she know her dream would come true! Does she still pinch herself every now and then to make sure it's not a dream? Yes, she does! Feel free to pinch her, too, via Twitter, Facebook or Goodreads! Happy reading!

Clare Connelly was raised in small-town Australia among a family of avid readers. She spent much of her childhood up a tree, Mills & Boon book in hand. Clare is married to her own real-life hero, and they live in a bungalow near the sea with their two children. She is frequently found staring into space—a surefire sign that she's in the world of her characters. She has a penchant for French food and ice-cold champagne, and Mills & Boon novels continue to be her favourite ever books. Writing for Modern is a long-held dream. Clare can be contacted via clareconnelly.com or at her Facebook page.

D0674728

Also by Maya Blake

The Sicilian's Banished Bride
The Commanding Italian's Challenge

Bound to the Desert King collection

Sheikh's Pregnant Cinderella

Passion in Paradise collection

Kidnapped for His Royal Heir

The Notorious Greek Billionaires miniseries

Claiming My Hidden Son
Bound by My Scandalous Pregnancy

Also by Clare Connelly

Hired by the Impossible Greek
Their Impossible Desert Match

A Billion-Dollar Singapore Christmas miniseries

An Heir Claimed by Christmas

No Strings Christmas
(Available from Mills & Boon Dare)

Signed, Sealed…Seduced collection

Cinderella's Night in Venice

Discover more at millsandboon.co.uk.

THE GREEK'S HIDDEN VOWS

MAYA BLAKE

MY FORBIDDEN ROYAL FLING

CLARE CONNELLY

MILLS & BOON

All rights reserved including the right of reproduction
in whole or in part in any form. This edition is published
by arrangement with Harlequin Books S.A.

This is a work of fiction. Names, characters, places, locations
and incidents are purely fictional and bear no relationship to
any real life individuals, living or dead, or to any actual places,
business establishments, locations, events or incidents.
Any resemblance is entirely coincidental.

This book is sold subject to the condition that it shall not,
by way of trade or otherwise, be lent, resold, hired out
or otherwise circulated without the prior consent of the publisher
in any form of binding or cover other than that in which it is published
and without a similar condition including this condition
being imposed on the subsequent purchaser.

® and TM are trademarks owned and used by the trademark owner
and/or its licensee. Trademarks marked with ® are registered with the
United Kingdom Patent Office and/or the Office for Harmonisation
in the Internal Market and in other countries.

First Published in Great Britain 2021
by Mills & Boon, an imprint of HarperCollins*Publishers* Ltd,
1 London Bridge Street, London, SE1 9GF

www.harpercollins.co.uk

HarperCollins*Publishers*
1st Floor, Watermarque Building,
Ringsend Road, Dublin 4, Ireland

The Greek's Hidden Vows © 2021 Maya Blake

My Forbidden Royal Fling © 2021 Clare Connelly

ISBN: 978-0-263-28251-1

06/21

This book is produced from independently certified FSC™ paper
to ensure responsible forest management.
For more information visit www.harpercollins.co.uk/green.

Printed and bound in Spain
by CPI, Barcelona

THE GREEK'S HIDDEN VOWS

MAYA BLAKE

MILLS & BOON

CHAPTER ONE

EAVESDROPPERS NEVER HEARD anything good about themselves. Wasn't that how the saying went? Christos Drakakis gritted his teeth at that inconvenient reminder as he stood frozen in the middle of the smaller of his two adjoining conference rooms. Except he wasn't eavesdropping per se. Both rooms had been empty when he entered five minutes ago, searing disappointment and blazing frustration colouring his perceptions.

Something that seemed to be happening with unwelcome frequency lately—

'I think we can safely assume it's reached DEFCON One around here.'

'I was thinking more along the lines of nuclear fallout, until I saw his face, then I knew we were already way past that. Apparently, it's been three years since he lost a case. I wasn't here then, but I know heads rolled on that particular case.'

The sentence was delivered with deep apprehension.

Gary Willis, one of his associates, had every right to be feeling the same sickening sensation churning Christos's guts. That was the reason he'd sidetracked to the conference room instead of continuing to his office a few dozen floors above.

Most lawyers, no matter how stellar their reputation, accepted a degree of failure in the course of their profession. Most divorce lawyers took on certain cases with the expectation of having to compromise.

Not him.

Christos never took on a case unless he'd calculated how to achieve his endgame. His first loss had jolted him enough to vow never to take his eye off the ball again. His second had been because his client was a pathological liar who couldn't speak the truth even to salvage his own divorce proceedings.

Today's loss had been…out of his control. He'd debated every scenario, investigated every piece of information and triple-checked the opposition's weak points. Everything should have gone his way. Yet somehow here he stood, disbelief shaking through his veins, with the dire reminder that the past was always there, waiting to rear its ugly head. Today's lesson had been aimed at his client and friend, Kyrios, but it was Christos who was feeling the full after-effects of losing his third case in five years.

'Are you sure it's just this case troubling our esteemed leader? We only took it on three weeks ago. He's been channelling Vlad the Impaler for the better part of two months now!'

Christos's guts turned to stone, even as his mouth twisted in acid amusement.

Vlad the Impaler was an apt description. He'd been that way ever since *the incident*. And his grandfather's increasingly pressured demands had only contributed to the… chafing that resided beneath his skin, making him excruciatingly aware that things weren't settled in his world. Or as settled as they *should* be.

He detested excuses from his subordinates. Making them for himself was even more of an anathema. Which was why his inability to have this situation sorted successfully grated so badly.

'Did something happen?' Ben Smith, another associate, asked.

'No idea,' came Willis's reply.

Yes, something happened. A moment of weakness with his executive assistant, which should've been easily dismissible, had somehow become lodged in Christos's memory and refused to budge.

A late-night dinner with his EA in the company of an unusually friendly married couple who had chosen the high road to an amicable divorce. Drinks afterwards at his private club.

Nothing seemingly out of the norm.

And yet by the end of the night, a fundamental rule had been broken. He'd stepped over his own strict, personal line. A line they'd both agreed they'd never cross.

Rich, silky hair sliding between his fingers...

Full, eager lips beneath his own...

His greedy hands exploring the mounds and valleys of her supple, curvy body...

Breathless, lust-stoking moans he continued to hear in his dreams...

Christos's blood immediately rushed south and he gritted his teeth tighter, tried harder to banish the focus-shredding thoughts from his mind. But clearly the gods weren't on his side today, because right then the subject of his thoughts entered the conversation.

'Alexis Sutton deserves sainthood for dealing with him. I don't think I've ever seen her react to him with anything but unruffled calm.'

Except for that night two months ago. His usually immaculate executive assistant had been *thoroughly* ruffled that night. And in a most delectable way that still dogged his imagination with a riling persistence.

In his more unforgiving moments, he laid the blame on his clients, who'd chosen to separate with affection instead of acrimony. Alexis had been vocal in her admiration for them during dinner, stating boldly it was what she'd prefer to do in a similar situation.

That had...*thrown* him. Enough for him to veer from professional to personal.

And so he'd succumbed to temptation and was now suffering from a peculiar inability to excise the memory. A problem, it seemed, she wasn't having.

But even while he'd been satisfied that their agreement remained in place and was unlikely to suffer further misguided bouts of temptation, a part of him remained vexed that *he* couldn't seem to move on from it. The taste of her lingered in his mouth. The soft, silky texture of her skin made the tips of his fingers vibrate whenever she was in his vicinity.

The way she'd gasped his name as he'd pinned her against his sofa echoed in his head when he least expected it.

Christos knew the confounding inability to forget those brief minutes had contributed to his disgruntlement lately. But he refused to accept it was the reason he'd lost this case.

No, part of that blame lay with his grandfather and the increasingly unreasonable demands the old man had been making for the better part of two years.

'To be on the safe side, I've called my wife and told her not to expect me home before midnight tonight.'

Willis's words broke through Christos's thoughts, bringing him back to the present.

'Oh, come on, this is ridiculous. The nuclear winter can start tomorrow. I have drinks scheduled with a hot second-year associate at that new bar across the street. It took my secretary six tries just to get a reservation. I'm not cancelling.'

Willis exhaled despondently. 'I'd probably do the same thing in your situation.'

Enough.

Christos yanked open the doors and entered the adjacent conference room. He watched with dispassionate eyes as the associates caught sight of him and turned varying shades of the rainbow.

'Willis, send your wife my apologies along with a large bouquet of her favourite flowers charged to the business expense account, because she won't be seeing you for the next *week*.' He turned to the other man, who was now visibly quailing. 'Smith, I'll let you make your apologies to your date at your own expense. You, too, will not be seeing daylight for the next week. Any active files you're working on I'll have reassigned to your colleagues. But between the two of you, I expect a preliminary report on my desk by morning as to how this case was seemingly airtight forty-eight hours ago but still ended up blowing up in our faces. I want to know how an illegitimate child was missed right under our very noses. Understood?' he asked in a deceptively calm voice.

Swift nods came his way. 'Of course, sir,' Smith replied.

'We'll get right on it, Mr Drakakis,' Willis added straightening his tie and his spine.

Christos turned to exit the room.

'Sir?'

He paused at Smith's nervous prompting, eyebrows raised.

'Umm…about what we were saying—'

'You were right. I don't like to lose. And yes, heads will roll this time too. You have one opportunity to make sure it's not yours. Use it wisely. And in the future I suggest you check you're alone before indulging in schoolyard gossip.'

Christos ignored the buzzing phone in his pocket as he left, silently cursing himself for not containing his roiling reaction to the verdict until he was back in his office. The apprehensive whispering and furtive looks that came his way from his employees as he prowled down the hallway he could withstand. Even on his best day the ruthless determination with which he attacked his punishing caseload gave the most hardened subordinate meaningful pause before they attempted to engage him.

With the news of his loss, no one would dare offer him even a benign greeting. For all intents and purposes, Christos Drakakis was an island—much like the one his grandfather was dangling frustratingly out of his reach—and not the most welcoming one at that. He didn't regret that reputation. After all, it had seen him rise through the ranks of marital law to make partner by twenty-six, and, shortly thereafter, paved the way for him to establish one of the most successful law firms in the world.

The notion that he'd been off his game because he'd come within a whisker of bedding his assistant—an incident that should've remained in his rear-view mirror—stuck in his craw like the sharpest tack.

The doors to the lift parted.

At the last moment, he bypassed the button to his office and stabbed the one for his penthouse. Only then did he reach for his phone. But it wasn't to answer the frantic messages from his client. That would come later, when he had a definitive answer as to what had gone wrong.

Instead, he sent a short, sharp message to his executive assistant, the woman who was taking up far too much real estate in his mind.

Alexis Sutton's response was equally brief. And as expected, she turned up at his penthouse door five minutes later.

'A shot of espresso or two fingers of Macallan?' She held up the choice of offerings when he opened to her knock.

Christos pulled his fisted hands from his pockets, strolling forward until he was a couple of feet from Alexis. 'If I want a drink, I'll make it myself. Did you bring the list I wanted?' he demanded. The growl in his voice was unmistakable, but the woman before him barely blinked.

Christos knew he wasn't an easy man to work for. Alexis's ability to remain unflustered was why she'd lasted this long as his assistant. It was why he'd made that proposition to her a year ago when his grandfather's subtle hints had grown into real threats.

'I won't be around forever, Christos.'

'Show me you're the right heir to Drakonisos or I'll make other arrangements.'

Costas Drakakis had forced his hand, and Christos had implemented a plan that'd proceeded smoothly for ten whole months.

Until an uncharacteristically pleasant dinner with clients and a nightcap with his assistant had lowered his inhibitions, blurring the stark professional lines he'd sworn never to cross.

'I did,' Alexis replied in that nuanced voice he'd spent far too long analysing over the past few weeks. Sometimes crisp, sometimes sharp. Always intelligent. And *always* with that huskiness that lately triggered a need to hear it wrapped in lust, moaning his name. *Again.* 'But I still think you should have a drink. You haven't had your shot of caffeine since this morning, and the whisky will mellow you out. After that, I'll give you exactly five minutes to lose your cool. Then we'll get back to business.'

Christos took another half step, his teeth clenching hard enough to make his jaw hurt. As much as he appreciated her no-nonsense approach, she was verging on insubordination. 'Who do you think you're talking to?'

She lifted her head, met his gaze with unflinching chocolate-brown eyes shot through with threads of gold that always made him think they were gathering momentum to flash pure fire at him. She didn't answer immediately, giving him an unwanted few moments to notice the silken mass of her chestnut hair, the glistening gloss of her lip balm, the pulse beating at her throat, the thin leather belt cinching her narrow waist and the floral undertones of her favourite scent.

He'd held that trim waist in his hands, knew he could

span it, easily…as he had when he'd pulled her close that night…

'I'm talking to the great Christos Drakakis, lawyer extraordinaire, the man who leaves opponents and judges alike quaking in their shoes.'

'Then you'll know that I'm in no mood to be messed around right now.'

'Yes, I know you want someone to pay for what's happened, hence the request for the list. And you're in the mood for another one of your let's-test-Alexis games today. Well, I'm not playing. So…now that we've exhausted all areas of concern, which is it to be?' She raised the coffee cup and the tumbler of whisky higher until the smell of roasted beans and aged single malt trailed into his nostrils. 'One is getting cold and the ice is melting in the other.'

Her little speech triggered equal parts vexation and calming reassurance inside him. Not everything had gone to hell. 'I want neither. The list, if you please.'

Her arms lowered. She regarded him for a resigned moment. 'I sent it to your phone before I came up. I also have several files to put together for you downstairs. Just let me know which ones you want to work on next and I'll have them ready.' She swivelled on expensive heels and started walking away, her navy pencil skirt twitching in the prim little way he'd have once laid hefty bets on fully complimenting her character.

Until he'd had a taste of the gorge-deep passion that lurked beneath the deceptively cool exterior. Christos hadn't quite made up his mind whether he resented her for that unconscious subterfuge yet.

She'd mastered the art of walking away from him before he was done with her. Increasingly in the last several weeks. Today, it was especially aggravating.

'Alexis.' The warning in his voice was enough to make her falter.

Christos was almost sure her shoulders stiffened momentarily before she relaxed them. An instant later she was walking away again, her curvy hips swaying as she headed for the coffee table in the middle of his living room. He waited until she reached it and started to bend down to place the whisky and coffee on it.

'Stop.'

She straightened, still holding the drinks. Their gazes locked. Held. After a moment he saw the merest flicker of apprehension, which absurdly pleased him. He enjoyed not being the only one unsettled before noon on what should've been a routine Monday morning.

He took his time approaching her, each step a small battle to rein in his fraying control. The unnerving sensation he'd experienced in the pit of his stomach after his phone call with his grandfather last night.

'Your cousin is now in the running...'

'I'm going to give it to you straight,' Alexis said, her voice a crisp scythe through his moody thoughts. 'If you were any other man, I'd have thought that you'd come up here to wallow in your defeat. But you're not any other man. You're Christos Drakakis.'

'Yes, I am. And you also know how much I hate sycophants.' He reached her in time to see her lips pinch for a second before, like him, she shook off her annoyance.

Christos skirted her once, then faced her. He relieved her of the tiny, expensive bone-china cup and downed the hot beverage in one swallow. Then he repeated the process with the amber liquid swirling in the crystal-cut glass.

The kick of caffeine before the calm of alcohol threw a veil of equilibrium over his senses. He released the single button to his bespoke suit and loosened his tie.

Jerking it free, he flung it on the sofa. With his gaze still on her, Christos tugged open the top three buttons of his shirt. He wasn't in the least bit ashamed of enjoying the reaction that flitted across her face.

Despite the brick wall she'd thrown up after that night in his penthouse, she wasn't immune to him. Selfishly, since his day had gone to hell so very unexpectedly, he revelled in the quickening of her breath, the flair of gold in her brown eyes, the smallest step she took away from him under the guise of straightening the coffee-table book on medieval architecture. They were the same tics she'd exhibited soon after accepting the position as his executive assistant, that he'd dreaded her acting upon, only to discover that she had no intention of doing so after three years in her role.

At first, Christos had resigned himself to waiting for the inevitable moment when Alexis, like his three prior seemingly superefficient and professional assistants, would drop the not-so-subtle hint that she would love their boss/assistant relationship to become something more.

That moment had never arrived, but he'd remained sceptical, then increasingly on edge because Alexis was his most proficient assistant, anticipating his needs and executing them sometimes even before he recognised they existed. But Christos wasn't a man who took things at face value—the harrowing events of his childhood had eroded his trust. So like the sword of Damocles hanging over his head, each interaction with her had become a watchful exercise, until it had grown into a peculiar kind of anticipation.

It had been well into the first year before he'd spotted a single sign that she was aware of him. But even that had been ruthlessly snuffed out, his assistant seemingly as capable of clamping down her responses as he was.

Until that night.

Now, he watched her gaze dart to his neck and upper chest before flicking away. But the lips that were pursed minutes ago had grown softer, parting slightly as the tempo of her breathing escalated.

'I drank the coffee and the whisky.' In truth, he'd realised he needed both the moment he'd seen her holding them. Even now, they were further calming him, creating a little distance from the unsettling after-effects of his unexpected failure. 'Now are you ready to do my bidding?'

The tip of her pink tongue darted out, touched the inner edge of her lower lip before retreating. That small act was enough to redirect the surge of fire in his chest south. To confirm that once again he was treading dangerous ground when it came to how much he enjoyed her reaction to him.

He didn't want to lose Alexis as an executive assistant or jeopardise the private agreement he had with her to secure his birthright. She'd lasted three years working with him because she was the best. But if he was to accommodate his grandfather's increasing demands, then knowing Alexis wasn't the cold wall she usually projected would come in handy.

'If that bidding involves getting Demitri on the line for you, then yes. The poor man is going out of his mind since the verdict was handed down. I told him you would return his calls within the hour,' she answered.

The reminder that beyond these walls, and the bubbling cauldron of whatever was going on between him and his assistant, there was a disaster waiting to be cleared up wasn't welcome. But he'd never shied away from challenges. Not that Demitri Kyrios would challenge him after keeping crucial information from him.

Alexis took another step back. 'Shall we say, five minutes?'

She was almost at the door, her brisk efficiency back in place like a well-worn suit of armour.

'Three,' he replied. He'd prevaricated enough. He rebuttoned his suit, reknotted his tie and crushed his frustration until it was a non-existent blip at the back of his mind.

'Make sure I have the complete transcript of today's proceedings on my desk.'

She looked over her shoulder. 'It was the first thing I did when I heard the outcome.'

He allowed a ghost of a smile to cross his lips. 'Be careful, Alexis. We don't want to get to the point where I imagine you're willing to cater to my *every* need, do we?' he challenged.

'I'm here to cater to your every *professional* need. If you don't want me to be fully efficient in that capacity, then maybe I should find another employer? I'm sure someone out there will appreciate my dedication.'

'Is that a threat?' If so, it wasn't an idle one.

A month ago, he'd come across an email from a headhunting agency offering her an impressive salary and benefits package if she jumped ship to another firm. Whether she'd left the email open deliberately for him to see because he'd been in a particularly testy mood that day, he wasn't sure. But its existence had niggled at him, prompting him to discreetly request she be given a mid-year review by HR and a thirty per cent raise.

The uncertainty that she'd still choose to leave him chafed with each passing day. The same feelings of uncertainty had dogged his formative years, although he'd hoped he'd put that period far behind him. But he could do nothing about it, not when she was instrumental in helping him secure Drakonisos, the one thing that mattered to him above all things.

Admitting it was enough to rake up his dying frustration and a few more emotions that should be buried deep enough to be dead. But weren't.

'No, sir. It's a gentle reminder that we both have options,' she answered his almost forgotten question.

'Sir?'

Her lips pursed. 'It's the correct form of address. I don't know what you have against it.'

She hadn't called him that since her initial interview, when, for some reason, the sound of it falling from her lips had spiked his temperature high enough to make him demand she never use it again.

He walked over to the door and held it open for her to walk through. 'You're not going anywhere. I'm not ready to do without you. Not just yet anyway.'

A look flitted through her eyes, gone before he could decipher it. Then her head dipped in a stiff nod as they walked together down a short corridor to the lift that would take them down to his office. 'That's good to hear. Your executive chef sent through the autumn menu today. I'd hate to be deprived of his culinary delights this side of Christmas.'

'I'm sure his ego will be boosted to know he's the only reason you're bringing yourself to remain in my employ.' He pressed the button to summon the lift, noting the reduced desire to stab at it. He didn't want to admit her presence was the reason he'd calmed down, but Christos couldn't deny it.

Her unflappability in the face of his sometimes heated Greek temperament was one he appreciated.

'I've tried to resist his cooking, but he gets me every time. I've had to up my thrice-weekly gym sessions to counterbalance the high calories.'

Christos's eyes narrowed as she preceded him into the lift. 'Is that the reason you've been absent from your desk between six and seven lately?'

She leaned past him to press the switch that closed the doors before resting her gaze on the bright green digital floor counter. 'Yep. I didn't think you noticed, though.'

His gaze drifted past her profile and down her trim body to her slim legs and heeled feet. 'I noticed both your absence, and the fact that your efforts aren't necessary.'

Their gazes met and again he experienced a split-second connection that froze time, before she raised a cool eyebrow. 'You pound your treadmill every night without fail. Are your efforts necessary?'

This time the smile that threatened stayed for longer than a second. 'Touché.'

Her gaze dropped to his mouth, lingering as her own lips curved.

Then the doors opened, and Christos was back in his true domain. In the kingdom he'd built brick by brick with one simple but solid goal in mind: to make sure people like his father never got another chance to perpetrate their despicable wrongs on helpless victims like him and his mother. And if his clients came to him already in the clutches of such vile treatment, to ensure he used the rule of law to make the perpetrators pay as high a price as possible.

Before he tackled this recent rare failure, however, he needed to safeguard the two-miles-square piece of land in the Aegean that had been his sanity and salvation as a boy. The place where the seeds of the man he was today had been sown. The only place where he'd known a semblance of acceptance. Perhaps even affection? He shrugged the question away. While he wasn't overly eager to probe the emotions tied to his need to possess Drakonisos, he wasn't prepared to sit back and let his grandfather hand it over to his cousin either.

To do that he needed to revisit his private agreement with Alexis. One that, in his moments of quiet, he'd repeatedly questioned his sanity over.

'Alexis.' The throb of...*something* in his voice stilled her.

'Yes?' Her response was a little wary. Between heartbeats, that momentary lightening of tension receded, and they were back in the tight bubble of awareness that flared up so readily between them these days. 'Did you want something else?' she tagged on when he took a moment to form the words.

'Yes. It's time to reprise your other role.'

Christos wasn't quite sure how to process her visible paling. The widening of her eyes. The decisive step she took back from him. All negative reactions when he wanted the opposite. When he'd dared hope for enthusiasm, even?

'But…it's only June. We're not supposed to travel to Greece for another two months.' Her voice held a shaky, uneven texture that spoke to how she felt. How, probably like him, she preferred to keep the entire subject at the back of her mind, calling upon it only when strictly necessary.

But again, when he should've taken her response in his stride, because this was only another clinical transaction after all, he felt…disgruntlement.

Their deal hadn't been a one-sided affair. She'd negotiated her own terms, extracted her own rewards.

Just as everyone had seen him in the key moments of his life, he'd been seen as a pawn. A means to an end.

He refused to feel guilty about stacking the deck in his own favour.

'There's been a development regarding my grandfather.' Another twist in their relationship he suspected was orchestrated by yet another greedy party.

Her eyes widened even further, another layer of tension and electric awareness arcing in the space between them. Space he closed by strolling towards her until they were a foot apart. Until he was certain he could hear her frantic heartbeat and the tiny rush of air leaving her parted lips.

'And? What exactly does that mean?'

'It means it's time for you to be my wife again, Alexis.'

CHAPTER TWO

YES, SHE WAS married to her boss, according to the pristine little document tucked in the farthest corner of her lingerie drawer that proclaimed her as Mrs Alexis Drakakis, wife of Christos Drakakis, enigmatic multimillionaire, world-renowned lawyer and rumoured heir to his grandfather's billion-euro empire.

A document she hadn't been able to glance at since the single time she'd held it in her hand, wondering if she'd made the right decision or was still caught in the ninety seconds of madness that had made her agree to her boss's preposterous proposition.

A three-year deal struck—after that brief moment of insanity had passed—when she'd believed she could fully control every outcome with the same cool, unflappable efficiency as she ran his office.

For a while, it had worked. Heck, in the beginning she'd managed to forget, for several hours at a time at least, her marital ties to the formidable man who ran his international law firm with an iron fist. Forget that underneath the marriage certificate lay a box containing a five-carat princess-cut diamond set in platinum, alongside a matching wedding ring, which he'd presented to her with firm-jawed, emotionless expediency at the sterile registrar's office in Marylebone a year ago.

Because the agreement was that she would need the rings for only two-week stretches, twice a year, when they visited Costas Drakakis in Greece, his ageing, reclusive grandfather whose demands on his grandson had compelled Christos's proposition to her.

It had all seemed so clear-cut back then—bar those

ninety seconds when she'd experienced a depth of terrifying possessiveness and increasing desire to remain in the intoxicating orbit of Christos Drakakis's success. To know she was a small but key component that made his professional life revolve with oiled smoothness.

In that moment, she'd felt…needed, not an unwanted object to be thrown away as her mother had so effortlessly done mere hours after giving birth to her. Alexis knew deep down that need was what prompted her to agree to the highly irregular proposition. That and the painful but *necessary* decision she'd made after her one devastating relationship.

She might have accepted that intimacy and marriage weren't on the cards for her, but that damning *need* to be wanted, to be *needed*, the craving to be moored to something stable and solid had never relented.

Once she'd got over those ninety seconds it had been a simple decision. With occasional bouts—deep in the night when she tossed and turned with curious restlessness—of mild astonishment at what she'd done. Thankfully, those moments always took their rightful place at the back of her mind come morning.

'Alexis, did you hear me?' came the deep, firm demand.

As if she could dismiss him that easily. As if her every sense weren't greedily attuned to his every word. As if she didn't spend every moment of every working hour steeling herself against any betrayal of what his face, his voice, his six-foot-three frame did to her equilibrium.

She'd succeeded. For the most part. Until that night two months ago. When everything had tilted and never quite righted itself again.

She cleared her throat. 'Of course I heard you. I'm still waiting for an explanation as to the change of plans though.'

A hot flame flickered through his eyes. A temperamental flash that warned her about stepping out of line, while at the same time signalling his respect for standing up to him.

It was a curious expression, that one. It made her daring. It kept her spine straight and her senses alert. It certainly didn't make things boring around here.

Not that at thirty-three, and as one of the youngest managing partners of an international law firm, Christos Drakakis had ever attracted a label like *boring*.

From the tips of his close-cropped, so-dark-it-almost-seemed-black hair to the heels of his custom-made Italian shoes, he possessed a bristling energy that encompassed anyone in his vicinity. It was an intensely magnetic force field that commanded attention, which he then held with his steel grey eyes. With that slash of hard but sensual mouth that could cut his opponent to pieces in the courtroom without raising his deep, faintly accented baritone.

Watching him strike ruthless deals across a conference table or walking in a deceptively calm but predatory stride across a courtroom had evoked near hero worship amongst lawyers and staff alike. In Alexis it had evoked a curious mix of awe and mild terror. Of quiet pride. Of an electric hum deep in her belly that she refused to acknowledge or analyse.

She tried to slow her pulse with deep, controlled breaths as he stared at her now, his nostrils flaring ever so briefly before he shoved his hands into his pockets.

'I haven't been fully apprised of the reasons. Only that my presence is required in Greece. Which means yours is too, as my wife,' he drawled.

Wife.

A term she only allowed herself to think about twice a year. A term that fired up tectonic bolts through her system. 'If you don't know for sure, then my presence may not be required—'

His headshake cut her off. 'Our deal was that you would

accompany me whenever I visited Drakonisos in return for keeping and maintaining your precious little project.'

Yes, the flip—and more important—side of her deal with Christos. Another desire to feel needed that had kept her tied to the only home she'd ever known.

Hope House.

Her need to keep it from being razed to the ground.

Christos's agreement to keep the children's home going in perpetuity in return for her agreement to act as his wife for a minimum of three years. In those restless moments deep in the night, she clung to this reason more than anything else. Because in this, she knew she'd made the right choice. Knew that she hadn't acted completely rashly when Christos had invited her for a drink in his office and confessed his need for a wife in order to secure his birthright. Hope House, she told herself, was far more important than the *intimacy* and *marriage* hopes she'd had to abandon after the emotional wringer she'd been through in her one and only relationship.

Hope House had been her single constant, a solid signpost she could cling to in a life whose beginnings had been murky.

Fresh from a phone call with the distressed director of the children's home who had taken Alexis in when she'd been abandoned in front of their high-street charity outlet, she'd blurted out her own request.

Curiously, that quid pro quo transaction had pleased Christos. As if her wanting something in return had established the true parameters of their agreement. She'd felt a peculiar sting deep in her chest that she attributed to the extreme relief she'd saved Hope House. That the spread-thin staff who manned the children's home just outside London would shelter other children, if not from the ever-present abandonment-induced heartache and fear of future rejection, then at least with a roof over their heads.

Viewing it rationally, Alexis knew she was getting the better end of the deal. Seriously, who wouldn't want a twice-yearly semi-vacation on the jaw-dropping jewel in the Aegean that was Drakonisos?

Except, she'd been unprepared for what those two weeks entailed.

Those *extras* rushed to the fore now as she stared back at Christos. As she tried, and failed, to keep her pulse under control. To keep that blaze from igniting in her belly, the rush of her blood roaring in her ears.

They would be required to share his suite. Again.

They would be required to hold hands in Costas's presence. Again.

They would be required to act, for all intents and purposes, as *husband and wife. Again.*

'Do I need to remind you of the terms?' he pressed at her silence.

'No, but…'

Things have changed, the voice in her head supplied the words she swallowed hastily.

Since that night in his Mayfair penthouse and the insanely delirious encounter on his living-room sofa. Since she'd felt Christos up close and ferociously personal; experienced the heat and taste of him, the lethal, primitive power lurking beneath his hand-stitched suits. The passionate mastery he could command at his fingertips.

'But?' he demanded, his voice a touch harder.

'You have the Kyrios case to work on. Aren't you looking at a possible new hearing?'

The reminder of the case he'd just lost tightened his features. 'It will be taken care of by the end of the week. I'll fly back to attend a hearing if need be, but I doubt it'll come to that.' His voice oozed the arrogant confidence that his opponents hungered to cut down to size but never quite succeeded in doing.

'What about the rest of your caseload?' she asked, although she knew the answer. While admittedly a few cases like the Kyrios one saw the inside of a courtroom—the Drakakis name was usually enough to get opponents to settle out of court—there were few that inevitably demanded his presence in London. It was why he was able to rule his law empire from anywhere in the world. Why he had a superyacht moored on the Greek Riviera and half a dozen luxury homes around the world at his disposal.

'Are you worried that I've forgotten how to do my job on the strength of one loss, Alexis?'

The query was edged in steel. A reminder that this man was a seasoned predator through and through, to be underestimated at one's peril.

'No, of course not. I'm just wondering if it might be wise to postpone the trip to Drakonisos for a little while.'

His head tilt resembled a hawk eyeing a hapless rabbit. 'Are you sure it's not something else bothering you?'

Electric tension ratcheted up her spine. 'What could possibly bother me?' she parried, striving for flippancy that emerged half-baked.

'Perhaps you're concerned whether your last *wifely* performance will be up to par this time around?' he suggested silkily, his gaze combing her face with narrow-eyed intensity.

She stiffened, the veiled insult striking deep. 'Excuse me?'

'I think Costas is becoming a little sceptical about our relationship.'

'What?'

He shrugged. 'We may be required to stay longer this time around. I'm merely suggesting you give your performance a little more…polish in case my suspicions are right.'

That dart burrowed deeper. 'I didn't realise you were so disappointed with my performance last time. But perhaps

I should be the one concerned here? Perhaps I'm working with limited resources.'

Her return parry was met with an arrogant twist of his lips, as if the great Christos Drakakis couldn't possibly stage a sub-par performance. That merely taking on the role of pretend husband guaranteed its success under his artistry.

And damn him, he was right in his confidence.

On their last visit to Drakonisos, the brush of his lips across her knuckles that'd felt far too natural, for instance.

The mind-altering presence of his hand in the small of her back had made her aware of every craving cell in her body.

As had the lingering touch of fingers as he passed her a piece of fruit. The heavy-lidded *faux* passion in his eyes when he offered to apply her sunscreen.

All under the watchful gaze of Costas Drakakis.

All delivered with supreme mastery.

All fake.

Yet...as she thought about repeating it now, the flames in her belly leapt wildly. Because, even fake, every act had stroked too close to that secret bubble of need inside her she kept under lock and key.

Also that episode at his place had altered things. His kisses—far removed from a sun-drenched beach on Drakonisos and from his grandfather's ever-watchful eyes—had awakened something inside her, a different kind of yearning she'd thought she'd quelled after that harrowing and humiliating period with Adrian, only to discover that she possessed a deeper vein of untapped need. One that had roused with shocking potency and persistence after a handful of minutes spent with the man who should've remained forbidden fruit to her.

With total recall, she summoned the sweet torture of his lips on her nipples, the sensation of his fingers between her thighs, skilfully strumming her to that shocking, unravelling climax that had changed the dynamic between them. *Irreparably.*

His low, derisive laugh yanked her back to the present. To the far too risqué subject under discussion.

'You think my performance was lacking?' he asked, his wry amusement implying he believed the opposite.

She forced a casual shrug. 'You're talking about something that happened more than six months ago. I don't recall the minutiae of it all.'

Alexis was aware of the red rag she was waving in front of a temperamental Greek bull. Aware of that kick of awareness and excitement triggered by her words. Just as she was acutely aware of her surroundings. Of the fact that she simply couldn't do that here. Because more than anything, she risked repeating the same mistakes she'd made with Adrian.

Sure, Christos hadn't made promises to her as Adrian had. But she'd left herself wide open to temptation. Ignored the firm warning the Hope House nuns had embedded in her. *Nothing is permanent. Don't form attachments.* She'd ignored the warning and dared to reach for the sacred promise of the one thing she desired most—to belong. To experience a semblance of the family she'd never had.

Adrian West, her erstwhile boss, had wielded that promise like a priceless treasure at the start, then slowly it had become a paring knife, stealthily slicing away her confidence, manipulating her trust until she was stripped to the bone, decimated and vulnerable, the life she'd painstakingly scraped together for herself shattered.

It was the reason she'd redoubled her efforts to keep herself free from emotional entanglements, especially in her professional life. The temp agency placement with Christos Drakakis three years ago had been the perfect environment to foster that vow, the formidable lawyer with steely eyes and forbidding aura exactly what she'd needed after Adrian's easy snake-in-the-grass smiles and cruel intentions.

Her skin grew tight and sensitive under Christos's intense gaze.

'As much as I wish to refresh your memory, this is neither the time nor place. Suffice it to say that I recall a certain…woodenness to your performance last time. One you will do well to take time to address before we return to Greece.'

Irritation rose as she frowned. 'It's not like you to wait six whole months to tell me off for something I've done wrong. I'm almost inclined to believe you're making all this up.'

One derisive eyebrow rose. 'For what purpose?' he questioned silkily.

'I don't know. Maybe you want someone to pay for what happened in court today? You haven't lost a case since I've been your assistant. Perhaps this is what happens when things don't go your way?'

Alexis watched in silent, stunned fascination as every trace of humour evaporated from his face. On some level she was relieved they were back in a more professional setting, although there was nothing comforting about the constant high-octane currents that fizzled and popped beneath her skin as his face clouded.

Existing in Christos Drakakis's orbit was like living in the eye of a tornado, armed with the certain knowledge that one risky move from that centre would be catastrophic. She knew the devastating cost of straying off that path and had barely salvaged her dignity to tell her story after making such a mistake.

'Once upon a time, perhaps I would've sought oblivion in the arms of a willing body. But I've discovered that merely postpones the inevitable victory, you see. As for your inference, I do not deflect or place blame where it's not needed in order to feel better about myself. Only the people who stand in the way of me achieving my goals or possessing what's mine will pay.'

There was a warning in there. It shivered across her skin like a ghostly feather.

'But if you want me to be specific, you proved my suspicions correct in my penthouse two months ago, Alexis.'

She swallowed a gasp, her skin flushing all over again. 'We agreed not to talk about that. Ever.'

'I don't recall making such a promise.'

'Fine, *I* said I didn't want to discuss what happened. You didn't disagree.'

'Because the situation seemed to uncharacteristically distress you.'

'Then why are you bringing it up now? Things got a little...hot and heavy when they shouldn't have, but we *both* agreed it was a mistake.' If only she'd been able to stop thinking about it. To stop secretly yearning for a repeat performance.

His lips twisted, but a hard light remained in his eyes. 'You've forced me to draw correlations. And I can't help but notice the marked difference between the mediocre performance you've been dishing out this past year when you've been pretending to be my wife and what you're truly like.'

Her whole body grew furnace hot. 'So I'm not an actress. You knew that when we agreed to this.'

'But now that I know you can do so much better, I must insist that you step up.'

'What are you saying?'

'That I want nothing less than what you showed me two months ago.'

She shook her head, wishing with every fibre in her body she'd left the subject alone. Walked out. She had a million things to be getting on with. And yet, she stayed put as he sauntered back towards her.

'Are you serious? I just said it was a mistake,' she insisted in a voice that wasn't as firm as she wished it.

His lips compressed. 'Regardless, you exhibited a side to yourself that put your previous performances to shame. Take it from me that Costas will notice anything less than a stellar delivery.'

The need to distance herself from this unnerving subject had her balling her hands behind her back, her chin coming up in challenge despite the quivering in her belly. 'You want your money's worth? Don't worry, sir. I'll deliver. I always do, don't I?'

The question lay between them, silence he seemed content to let develop growing heavy in the room.

The jarring ringing of his phone made her jump, while he barely blinked at the intrusion. Knowing she'd called him *sir* because she'd secretly wanted to rile him held her in place, wondering if she'd taken leave of her senses. Again.

'You've not let me down…so far. Let's not start now by keeping important clients waiting, shall we?' The drawl drew her attention to her stasis.

Sucking in a much-needed breath, she went to his desk and snatched up the phone as Christos settled into his chair, his fingers steepled against his lips as he watched her.

Alexis grew intently aware of the stretch of fabric over her breasts as she leaned against the desk, the wool blend of her skirt as it tightened over her bottom, the rush of air-conditioned air over her calves.

'Drakakis Law Group, how may I help you?'

She breathed through the client's brisk demand to speak to Christos, her grip on the phone easing as she held it out to her boss.

He took the receiver from her but didn't answer it immediately, his eyes pinning her in place. 'The whole team is working late, including you. So cancel any plans you have.'

Without waiting for her answer, he swung his chair away from her.

And just like that she was released from his force field; the phone call a half-time whistle giving her a much-needed reprieve. But as she exited his office, settled behind her desk and attempted to get her thoughts back to briefs and law reports and away from entangled bodies and heated kisses, Alexis couldn't help but wonder just how she'd damned herself by giving in to temptation that night on her boss's sofa.

The first few days after it happened, she'd spent every second on tenterhooks, wondering how they were going to continue working together.

The mishap had been inexcusable, one she'd vowed never to allow after that one, heart-stopping, never-to-be-repeated instant the first time she'd laid eyes on him. Then, she'd been struck dumb by the visceral potency of his presence. Having worked in a midsize law firm previously, with more than half the workforce being men with large egos who believed themselves top of the food chain, she'd thought she knew every facet of the male dynamic.

Christos Drakakis rising to his feet and watching her with his hawklike eyes and predatory stillness the moment she entered his boardroom had put paid to every preconception she'd had. To her everlasting shame, she'd stopped in her tracks, her reaction to his aura a solid punch to her solar plexus. But also in that moment, she'd wondered if she was looking at yet another downfall; whether she shouldn't cut her losses and run in the opposite direction, lest she be taken in by another callous smooth-talker.

Luckily, she'd come to her senses, her common sense further shored by her best friend, Sophie, who'd made it her business to find out everything there was to know about Alexis's potential new boss to prevent her making the same Adrian-shaped mistake again; going one step better to equip Alexis with dire stories of what had befallen Christos's previous assistants.

Stories Alexis had discovered soon after accepting the role as Christos Drakakis's assistant, and in the three years of rigid and clinical professionalism since, were absolutely true.

She'd stayed. And she'd summoned previously unmined control to withstand the sight of Christos leaning over her desk, hands planted on either side of her computer with his thick brawny forearms exposed and chiselled face filling up her vision while he grilled her about a task, using that deep, faintly accented Greek voice. She'd withstood the effect of his fiercely evocative leathery aftershave that made her want to lean up into that space between his square jaw and his collar and take a deep whiff of vibrant skin and man, the way she'd fantasised far more than was healthy.

She'd had to because, despite the outward show of calm in the face of emotional chaos, the scar tissue inside that had never healed post-Adrian still felt raw and stung deep enough to keep her awake at night, years later. Only pride and the need to draw a conclusive line between her and the greatest mistake of her life had been the catalyst that had pushed her into overcoming temptation.

She'd succeeded. For the most part.

Except in moments like five minutes ago, when Christos stared a moment too long and too deeply into her eyes, and she feared he'd seen something other than the impeccable assistant she'd striven to be. Each time he relented she felt as if she'd been saved from the jaws of death. Alexis wished those were just fanciful thoughts.

They weren't.

Up until that twenty-minute trip to the registrar's office when he'd slid a wedding ring on her finger, her position had granted her a front-row seat to his past relationships, more specifically, the fervid highs each of his new liaisons experienced when he first turned his intense grey eyes on them; the hope that blazed in their eyes that they would be the one to turn the commitment-phobic divorce lawyer into the matrimonial triumph of the decade; and their inevitable devastation when those hopes were dashed with a goodbye bouquet of flowers and an expensive trinket.

Alexis was the one who fielded frantic, tearful calls, patiently listened to wrenching, heartbroken sobs and pleas for her to intervene on their behalf. On one occasion she'd been shocked when a scorned lover had turned nasty and blamed *her* for Christos's lack of interest.

She'd been equally shocked when Christos had plucked the phone from her hand and informed the unfortunate ex that should she ever threaten his assistant again, she would be sued for everything she owned.

It had never happened again and she hadn't summoned the nerve to ask him whether the short-term liaisons that seemed to be his trademark were still ongoing. It was none of her business. Just as her personal life was none of his.

She snorted under her breath. Perhaps others would pity her that, at twenty-six, her personal life was non-existent. But she'd made the decision to keep clear of emotional entanglements.

The quiet but ever-present anguish of her abandonment topped by Adrian's betrayal had only sealed that resolution.

As usual, she felt a hollow in her stomach as she thought of the woman who'd given her baby away.

If it's possible, please name her Alexis.

Seven short words that summed up her beginning and her only connection to the mother who'd abandoned her. Before the familiar drag of anguish could squeeze her insides, she slammed that painful door shut, cringing when she realised she'd been staring into thin air for several minutes. Focusing on her email when it pinged, she stared at the message from Christos.

Demitri is calling in a minute. I want you in here with me.

She rose and re-entered his office, watched his towering six-foot-three figure stride from his window to the ringing phone on his desk, struck all over again by how effortlessly he shouldered the weight of his world.

Demitri Kyrios. The client who'd lost half of what he owned to his conniving, cheating soon-to-be ex-wife who, more importantly, had gained full custody of his legitimate child simply to spite him for the illegitimate one he'd recently acquired.

'Drakakis,' he announced into the phone with an air of unapologetic supremacy.

Alexis glanced at her tablet, determined not to watch him fold that streamlined body into his chair.

He listened for a handful of seconds, jaw set. 'No, I trusted you to leave no part of your past undocumented, including every drunken night at university when the possibility that you could've fathered a child was real.'

'But I didn't know! And how the hell did my ex find out?' Demitri wailed at the end of the phone.

Christos listened, his features tightening with each word. 'I'm going to do everything in my power to ensure you regain custody of your child.'

The depth of that promise made Alexis's heart lurch. On top of everything that had happened recently, the reminder that no one had fought for her felt too raw. While other DLG partners took on divorce cases where the welfare of the children was in question, she'd noticed very quickly that Christos rarely took those cases on himself, although he kept a ferociously keen eye on the progress. At first, she'd thought it was because he held a secret fondness for children or even harboured hopes of fatherhood.

She'd discovered otherwise when she'd heard him tersely enlighten a client that he had no intention of marrying or fathering children of his own.

And yet, when Christos took on a case where one parent was patently unfit, he'd ruthlessly gone after them.

He'd taken on Demitri Kyrios's case because they had a history. As close a friendship as she'd seen Christos accommodate. Demitri's soon-to-be ex was more interested in haute couture and basking in the adoration of her social media followers than in caring for their son. Kyrios's sin was that he'd omitted to divulge the possibility that he'd fathered another child. One whose existence he'd initially attempted to hide, despite a paternity test proving the child was his.

'Yes, you have my word,' Christos said before slamming the phone down.

A string of very dirty-sounding Greek words seared the air.

'How the hell did we miss the existence of a fifteen-year-old child in our investigation?' he bellowed, spiking a hand through his hair.

Alexis shrugged. 'Probably because not every woman crawls out of the woodwork when the man she slept with over a decade ago becomes a millionaire. According to the report the investigators unearthed this morning, she wanted to keep her child a secret, raise him on her own.'

His face clamped in a thunderous frown. 'She didn't think the father of her child deserved to know of his existence?'

'She claims she had good reasons to keep the pregnancy from him. I guess we need to respect that.'

He swore again. 'Her secret just ruined my case. Forgive me if the last thing I'm in the mood to do is *respect that*.'

Alexis nodded solemnly. 'Of course. So did you want me to stay for something specifically or just to listen to you swear in a language I don't understand?'

He glared at her. 'I believe you still owe me five minutes of a so-called wallow? And while we're at it, did we not agree that you would add learning Greek to your résumé?'

Alexis hid her relief as she rose. 'I'll get around to taking that Greek course when I'm done with the million other things on my to-do list. And since you've never wallowed in your life, I don't think you're about to start now.'

Expecting a quick reply, she was a little stunned when his face closed over a fleeting expression that looked very much like suppressed pain. A moment later, the expression, imagined or not, was gone.

'Where's the court transcript?' he demanded brusquely.

She nodded at the pile of papers on his desk. He picked it up and flicked through it, but she was willing to bet the stunning platinum bracelet he'd given her last Christmas that he already knew every word from the court case backwards.

He paused when he reached the verdict, and his jaw clenched again. Without taking his eyes off the page, he reached for his phone and hit number five on his speed dial.

Alexis winced in anticipated sympathy for the head of the firm's investigative department.

'Mr Cruz, do you have the names I requested?' He listened for a moment. 'The answer is no, your apology isn't accepted. Your team's sloppiness cost my client the custody of his child. We have a long history together. But make no mistake, you will ensure that nothing like this ever happens again or you'll be fired. Is that understood?'

The fifty-seven-year-old veteran who'd worked for DLG since its inception was in the midst of another apology when Christos slammed the phone down.

The phone immediately started ringing. He ignored it,

rising to pace to the floor-to-ceiling windows. As if to synchronise with his mood, the early afternoon views of London were gloomy and overcast, the Thames a drab grey ribbon winding itself beneath centuries-old bridges.

Alexis's gaze flicked over the view but she very quickly lost interest in favour of the man who commanded attention even in a room full of five hundred. His shoulders stretched broad and aggressively masculine beneath the bespoke Italian-made suit.

Her scrutiny dropped lower, to the trim waist framed by his jacket, then to the powerful legs planted apart in a battle stance, even though there was no opponent to decimate.

From head to toe, Christos Drakakis oozed raw power. Add his drop-dead gorgeous face and razor-sharp intelligence, and he was formidably complex enough to reduce every man, woman and child he met to a state of breathless awe without so much as lifting a finger.

She reminded herself that Adrian had been equally aware of his effect on women. On *her*. He'd preyed on it, deliberately set a trap for her. One she'd fallen into and nearly damaged her career permanently. Christos would never know, but that armour she'd been forced to build around her emotions reinforced her vow never to stumble that badly ever again.

But…lately, her foundations were getting harder to fortify.

Christos whirled around suddenly, startling her.

She schooled her features, but saw the quick glint in his eyes before his expression neutralised that hinted he might have caught her watching him. 'Wallowing over. Grab your pad and let's get to work,' he snapped.

She turned away, acutely aware that his gaze remained on her until she was out of the door. As she stopped for a moment to regroup at her desk, Alexis acknowledged to herself that what had happened with Adrian could never happen again. More importantly, what had happened at Christos's penthouse couldn't happen again.

She would play the role of convenient wife for his grandfather's sake. But not for a single moment could she drop her guard. She'd been let down, not once, but twice. Her heart couldn't afford another battering. Her soul wouldn't make it.

CHAPTER THREE

THEY WORKED LONG into the night. By the time the last, shattered-looking lawyer shuffled out of the conference room, it was almost midnight.

Alexis suppressed a sigh and just managed to stop herself from crumpling into a relieved, exhausted heap. She resisted the urge because, in contrast, Christos looked as if he could go another twenty-four hours without respite.

She rose from her seat and gathered her files. 'I'll go and type up the notes for you,' she said.

He strolled to where she stood. 'I won't be looking at them tonight. They can wait till tomorrow.'

Her eyes flicked to him, then immediately returned to the files. 'It'll only take half an hour or so. Besides, you look like...' She faltered, wondering if she should voice the observation.

'I look like what?' he drawled.

Was his voice deeper, smokier because he'd spent all day barking at his associates or was it something else? Something...sensual? Earthy? The same something that was triggering tiny fireworks beneath her skin?

'You look...the opposite of what every one of your lawyers looked like when they left the room. Whatever vitamins you take clearly work for you.'

One corner of his mouth twitched then stilled almost immediately. 'It's not vitamins that keep me going.'

'What, then?' she asked curiously. 'And don't say you like winning because this feels like something...more.'

Christos's public biography only briefly touched on a childhood spent in Southern Greece. There was hardly any mention of his parents, and Alexis had worked for him for two years before discovering his grandfather was alive, albeit living a reclusive life on a sprawling island in the Aegean. And that grandfather was Costas Drakakis, the retired shipping mogul.

'Perhaps it is,' he answered cryptically, his gaze fixed on her face.

When she realised he wasn't going to elaborate, she pursed her lips.

'Whatever it is, if you could bottle it, you'd make an absolute killing.'

'I believe it's been labelled as my pathological aversion to failure.' He shrugged. 'But if you wish to compliment me on my stamina, then by all means, have at it.'

Alexis glanced at him in time to catch him looking at her hair. She was acutely aware her bun was in the last stages of slipping its knot, and wayward tendrils had escaped about an hour ago. As for her lipstick, it had been rubbed off when they'd stopped for a hurried supper four hours ago.

Again his lips twitched.

She found she was staring at his sculpted mouth and forcibly dragged her gaze away. 'Well, this lesser human will take you up on your offer to type up the notes in the morning, if you're sure?'

'Don't put yourself down. Your fire burned almost as brightly as mine.' The compliment was countered with a slightly mocking gleam in his eye as he continued, 'Until I caught your yawn about an hour ago.'

She suppressed a grimace. She'd thought she'd hidden it well. 'Well… I—'

'I'm not going to hold it against you if that's a worry. But I don't think I've ever seen you less than immaculately put together,' he mused.

Alexis reached up to tidy her hair, but suddenly, his fingers were there, beating her to it.

Their fingers grazed, then tangled. Her breath caught,

the sharp sizzle dancing through her blood making her drop her hand as the sensation raced up her arm. With a slow, unhurried movement, he captured a tendril between his fingers and slowly caressed it. Stepping forward, he wound the strand behind her ear, then trailed his fingers down her cheek.

Her breath stalled as she stood frozen, caught between the electrifying spell and the need to flee.

Christos regarded her with an almost detached interest, his piercing grey eyes scouring every expression she attempted to hide. As if he was conducting an experiment.

'What are you doing?'

'Testing your performance levels like we talked about,' he confirmed, 'since you insist you're not tired.'

Alarmed by the excitement leaping inside her, she jerked back. 'That won't be necessary. You've given me your feedback. Allow me the courtesy of letting me work on it.'

'But how will you learn without practical experience?' he drawled.

She shrugged, a little perturbed by how quickly they'd landed in this quagmire again.

'I'm not going to discuss this with you any further. Either you trust me to do everything in my power to honour our agreement or you don't.'

His nostrils flared but he remained silent, those eyes still fixed on her.

Until his scrutiny forced her into speech. 'If that's all, goodnight—'

'It's pointless going back home tonight when I need you back here by six. You should stay in the executive suite,' he tossed out, before heading back to his seat.

The executive suite. Separated from his own private suite by a twelve-foot-long marble hallway. It wasn't a big deal under normal circumstances. She'd stayed over before when their workload had pushed their working hours deep into the night.

But somehow this felt…different. Perhaps it was all this talk of sharpening her performance. Perhaps it was the recurring recollection of what happened the last time they were near a sofa.

'It's fine. I'll get the car service to drive me home.'

'All the drivers are busy delivering the associates home.'

He picked up his phone and showed her the app that displayed their vehicle availability. Every car displayed the *in use* sign.

'I can get a cab—'

'No, I'd prefer not to spend the next hour wondering if you've become the latest victim of crime. Not when you have a perfectly adequate apartment waiting for you ten floors above.'

'Black cabs are perfectly safe,' she replied. In twenty-five minutes, she could be in her North London flat, safely away from this churning atmosphere.

A hint of steel entered his eyes, his sculpted jaw clenching for a moment before he spoke. 'I'll spare us both the tedium of throwing out crime stats when it comes to a woman travelling alone at night. I'd prefer it if you would just do as I say and stay upstairs where I can be reassured that the term *perfectly safe* will be true in this instance.'

Except she wouldn't be safe. Not when she knew temptation lay right across the hall. 'Christos—'

'Alexis?' The steel was now in his voice, a tone he usually reserved for decimating his opponents.

Their stand-off probably lasted less than a minute. It felt like an hour. 'Fine, I'll stay upstairs.' She sounded less than gracious in defeat.

The gleam in his eyes told her so as he came towards her once more, plucked up the first stack of files from the table and put them in her arms. Then he reached for the second, taller pile.

'What are you doing?' she asked, suspicious.

'Helping you out so you can go to bed quicker,' he replied blandly, settling the heavy stack against his torso as if it weighed nothing.

Her jaw dropped for a nonplussed second before she caught herself. 'Why?'

'Excuse me?'

She took a moment to absorb his mild shock at her question, then asked, 'Why are you helping me? I can easily get the file trolley to wheel them all back to the office.'

He frowned. 'You're now objecting to my assistance?'

'I'm observing you acting out of character. You've never helped me before.'

'It's been a long day for both of us, so I'll help you out. The correct response you're looking for is a smile and maybe a thank you? In whichever order you prefer to submit them.'

She opened her mouth. Then closed it.

As he'd said, the day had been long and completely out of sorts. So what if he was acting out of character by performing a menial task that was usually her remit?

'I…thanks,' she capitulated.

'You're welcome. Shall we get on with it? I need a nightcap badly to wash this regrettable day away.' The tightness to the words resonated in the room.

She nodded, and followed him out of the room, averting her eyes to keep from ogling the tightness of his buttocks as he strode purposefully for the lift.

In the office, he deposited the files on her cabinet and went into his office. She barely had five minutes to text Sophie to tell her she was staying in the executive suite and then answer her flatmate's flurry of questions before Christos returned. His eyes landed briefly on her phone as she sent the last I'm-fine-I-promise message, but said nothing as he waited for her to gather her handbag and shut down her computer.

In silence, they took the lift upstairs. The double doors to his penthouse were directly opposite the ones to the executive suite.

Swallowing around the sudden tightness in her throat, Alexis placed her hand on the handle. 'Goodnight—'

'Not yet. Come and have a drink with me.' It sounded like an order but his raised eyebrow implied it was a request.

Say no. Say. No.

'You've worked hard today. You deserve a drink too,' he added when she hesitated. 'Or are you concerned your inhibitions will be affected again?' he taunted lightly.

'I'm confident they won't,' she replied boldly, although her insides quivered.

Her last drink with him had led her down a precarious, if enthralling, path. Even without a sip of alcohol she knew he was intoxicating to her senses.

Christos's gaze grew sharper. 'So I'm assuming the company is the issue?'

She sighed. 'No, I don't have a problem with the company.' *Liar.* 'I just…' *Want a moment to regroup.*

She stared at him, noted the lines around his mouth had deepened even more. Her gaze dropped to the column of his muscular throat, the hard-packed body and the strong hand wrapped around the door handle.

Had she been given to flights of fancy, she would've concluded that he didn't want to drink alone. But he was Christos Drakakis, the man who conquered opponents with a few lethal words. Even high court judges scrambled to preside over his cases because he was a breathtaking marvel in the courtroom.

She couldn't remain standing there like a mannequin.

She opened her mouth to utter a definitive refusal but he threw the door open abruptly, and strode into his penthouse, leaving her staring slack-jawed at the open doorway.

Knowing he'd effectively tossed the ball in her court should've made her mad and go straight to her own suite.

Instead she moved towards his door. One foot inside, she paused to watch him discard his suit jacket on the velvet sofa, then fold back the sleeves of his shirt while staring out of the window.

Without acknowledging her presence, he strolled with lithe grace to the sleek cabinet that held a collection of expensive hard liquor, wine and champagne on the far side of the large living room and pulled the stopper from a Waterford crystal decanter. For a handful of seconds, the only sound was the drink hitting the glass and ice cubes plopping into the cognac.

Done, he opened the wine cooler, grabbed a bottle of chilled Chablis and fixed a white wine spritzer for her. Drinks in hand, he headed to the sofa, set the wine glass on the low coffee table, took a seat and propped one ankle over his knee.

All without looking at her.

Alexis fought several emotions. Fascination. Irritation. Envy at the effortless sophistication he exuded and the animalistic presence that captured her attention. Back to irritation at the arrogance that implied he'd known she would follow him in.

On feet that had developed a mind of their own, she crossed the living room and chose a seat at the far end of the sofa. After another throb of silence, he picked up the glass and held it out to her.

'Are you always this arrogant with the people you invite for drinks?' she said, unable to help the bite of irritation in her voice.

One corner of his lips quirked. 'Is it arrogance if I'm good at anticipating a person's needs?'

'Don't presume to know me, Christos. I may just shock you one of these days.'

His eyes darkened a shade, his gaze dropping to linger on her mouth before rising again. 'Pick another day. I've had my fill of surprises for today.'

The reminder of his loss mellowed out her irritation. Reaching out, she accepted the drink. 'Thank you,' she muttered.

He raised his glass after a beat. 'To ensuring a day like this never happens again.'

She sipped the refreshing spritzer. Then nearly choked on it when he angled his body towards her. 'This obstinate side to you is a revelation,' he observed dryly.

Why that observation pleased her, Alexis refused to contemplate. 'Like you said, it's been a challenging day.'

'Who were you texting downstairs?' he enquired suddenly.

'What?'

'When I came out of my office you were on the phone. It seemed…frantic. Who were you contacting at one o'clock in the morning?' he asked, a definite edge in his voice.

'My flatmate, Sophie. If she wakes up and I'm not there, she'll worry.'

'Just your flatmate?' he pressed. 'You weren't attached when we struck our agreement last year. That hasn't changed, has it?'

Alexis shifted in her seat, both at the directness of the question but also at the unrelenting probe of his gaze. 'I was texting Sophie. She can be a mama bear when she puts her mind to it. I have to report in on a regular basis or she worries. You probably know what I'm talking about, right?' she asked, acutely aware she was straying into prying territory.

He tensed. 'What?'

'Parents? Siblings?' *Goodness, Alexis. Just stop.* 'Special friends who harangue and make you feel as if you've committed a cardinal sin if they don't hear from you for a few days?'

The expression that flashed through his eyes was mostly bitterness but with a trace of perplexity, as if she was describing an alien concept to him.

In the long stretch of silence while her question hung between them, Alexis told herself she should've stuck to neutral topics. But then with a bite of irritation she reminded herself that *he'd* made it personal.

She was just following his lead. She sipped her drink, then cradled her glass. 'It's fine. You don't have to answer—'

'No, I don't know what it's like to have parents who worry about me, constantly or even occasionally.' The tight non-smile he tagged onto his answer was sharp enough to shatter glass.

'Oh.' *Why not?* She swallowed the question, knowing she'd stepped into unfamiliar territory the moment she'd accepted his invitation for a nightcap.

'And before you ask, no, they're not dead. They are both very much alive.'

Her breath caught at the acid-soaked tone. Looking closer, she saw that the eyes staring into his glass had darkened with shadows, and the fingers clutching his drink were white-knuckled with tension.

'I guess being estranged from one's parents isn't entirely uncommon. I'm sorry if—'

His head snapped up, cutting off her words. 'We've strayed a little from where I intended this conversation to go. This is why I'm not fond of what you English call chit-chat.'

She slicked her tongue over her lower lip, feeling a little at sea herself. 'Fine. Was there something specific you wanted to ask me?'

'Yes, but I see I should've been more direct. Are you still unattached or do you have a lover?'

For the second time in half an hour, her jaw threatened to hit the floor.

If this Christos Drakakis was the version that emerged when a case didn't go his way, she was thankful she'd been spared it so far.

Nevertheless, she wasn't about to accommodate this risky whim. 'You may dislike idle chit-chat but you haven't considered that your alternative might not suit me. Our agreement is on paper only. What makes you think I wish to discuss my private life with you?' She suppressed the inward cringe that accompanied her mild hypocrisy.

He slowly drained his drink and rolled the glass between his fingers. 'You know enough about mine. And in light of what we'll face when we go to Drakonisos, I think it's time we redressed the balance.'

'I don't agree. I think we're fine the way we are. And I only know about yours because you've made it part of my job. If you think I like dealing with the fallout from your… affairs, think again.'

A searching light flared in his eyes, chasing the shadows from the grey depths as he regarded her. 'The incident from last year hasn't happened again.' It was a statement rather than a question. She wondered whether he already knew the answer to it before she shook her head.

'No, I'm not sure how you did it, but there have been no calls since the delightful Delilah.'

'Was it that much of a problem dealing with them before?' he enquired.

Alexis wasn't sure whether to laugh or lose her temper. 'Are you serious?'

His eyes narrowed. 'Do I seem anything but?'

He didn't, which should've been astonishing but was weirdly, reassuringly not. 'Do you have any idea how disruptive it is to spend an hour, sometimes more, listening to an inconsolable stranger pour her heart out to you, while divulging personal details I really wish they'd keep to themselves?'

His head drew back and laser eyes speared into her. 'I'm fairly certain a huge percentage of those details are made-up. I'm selective as to who I share that kind of thing with.'

'Right, and the women you date don't fall into that bracket?'

'No, they don't.' The response was so weighted with certainty, Alexis experienced a twinge of pity for the women who cycled through his life, hoping to make an impression that would grant them more than the six weeks he chose to date them before losing interest.

'Be that as it may, I don't welcome whatever it is they feel I need to know about the state of their devastation.'

He remained silent for a stretch of time, digesting the information. 'I find it surprising that this task is difficult for you. You excel in every other area of your work.'

'Thank you… I think.'

'You're welcome. But I think an hour's too long to waste on those sorts of calls.'

Anger. Definitely. 'Or you can spare me the unpleasant ordeal entirely and just console your exes yourself?'

He caught the sharpness in her tone. 'It bothered you that much?' A peculiar contemplation in his gaze raised the hairs on her nape.

Alexis raised her chin. 'Frankly? Yes.'

'You should've spoken up then.'

'I considered it some sort of rite of passage. Do I take it it's over now?' she asked, a weird little bubble of hope in her chest.

He rose without answering, went to the cabinet and

poured another shot of cognac. Nursing it, he returned to the sofa but chose the seat next to her instead of the farthest.

Alexis tensed, her breath shortening as she caught a whiff of his unique aftershave. 'Consider that part of your brief nullified.'

Relief shot through her, slowly followed by another mildly damning sensation that forced her to avert her gaze from him before his sharp eyes divined it.

While playing agony aunt to his jilted lovers had been less than palatable, she'd also gained insight into how he treated his women when they were flavour of the month. She hadn't been interested in the expensive dinners and endless benefits his wealth had exposed them to. But Alexis had found herself hooked on his ex-lovers' recounts of how it had felt to dance in his arms, how they'd felt when he'd smiled at them or run his fingers through their hair. Every single one of them had confessed that being the centre of Christos Drakakis's attention had been a singularly thrilling experience. Alexis had gleaned that a large percentage of them missed that more than the red-carpet, first-class benefits of dating the world's most eligible bachelor.

'What does that mean, exactly?' she asked now. Being out of the loop was one…welcome…thing. Not knowing whether he was still dating…

Alexis wasn't sure how she felt about that. How she *wanted* to feel about it.

'You don't seem pleased,' Christos replied dryly.

'Of course I'm pleased.' She set her glass down, wisely deciding against indulging in any more alcohol. She stood, slung her handbag onto her shoulder. 'I think it's time to call it a night. Thanks for the—'

The words died in her throat when he captured her wrist. Heat from his fingers branded her skin and a gasp slipped free before Alexis could stop it.

'I never received an answer to my question.'

It took a second for her to pull her attention from the sensations dragging through her. 'What question…? Oh.' Her gaze dropped to where he held her, then to the intensity of his eyes. No. She definitely didn't like this version of Christos Drakakis. She had a feeling he was going to be lethal to her senses. 'Why do you want to know whether I have a boyfriend or not?'

'Because I want to know if there's anyone standing in my way.'

'Standing in your way of what?' she asked, her voice not as firm as she would've preferred.

'In the way of achieving my goals, of course. What else?'

'I'm not sure I follow.'

'Sit down and I'll tell you,' he said.

Slowly, Alexis reclaimed her seat, her brows knitting as mingled sensations of alarm and intrigue twisted through her.

'Costas is unwell. He's in denial about it but his condition has deteriorated over the past few weeks. Enough to necessitate a doctor's visit.'

Sympathy welled inside her. 'I'm sorry.'

He nodded, taking a moment to sip his drink, as if distancing himself from her emotions. 'I spoke to his doctor this morning.' He didn't add anything else, leaving Alexis to wonder if that had contributed to the unusual outcome in court today.

Because while Christos could be coldly ruthless in litigation, she'd been stunned at the interaction between him and his grandfather. There'd been a…guarded warmth, albeit a disgruntled one from Costas, reciprocated by his grandson.

While Christos hadn't given her the full details of why he'd needed a convenient wife to secure his birthright, Alexis had surmised it had something to do with safeguarding his relationship with his grandfather and the island he lived on. That the man who'd coldly announced that he didn't have to have a family to take that step meant that beneath his formidable exterior, Christos felt…something for his grandfather.

His words filtered through. 'The doctor told you what's wrong with your grandfather? Is he allowed to do that?'

He sent a sharp smile, then went back to contemplating the depths of his drink. 'He didn't give me the full details and Costas refused to tell me over the phone. When I insisted, he invited me to come and find out for myself if I cared enough.' His smile disappeared, a hard light entering his eyes. 'Amongst other things.'

Alexis suspected it was those other things that required her presence, not that his grandfather's health was a trivial matter. 'What other things?' He remained silent for an age, enough to raise her hackles higher. 'Christos?'

His name emerged far huskier than she'd intended, reminding her far too vividly of another night on a similar sofa a handful of miles away.

She'd used his name profusely that night. She'd moaned it. Screamed it as she unravelled.

He raised his head and their gazes clashed. The flagrant knowledge that he was recalling the same incident rendered her breathless, her blood thundering through her veins as she returned his compelling stare. It took a monumental effort to drag her gaze from his, to suck in a pulse-calming breath, her relief spiking as he spoke.

'Costas is a difficult man, as you've probably learnt from our visits.'

'I remember,' she replied. The old man had zero filter and, while she was thankful most of his views were expressed in Greek, there'd been a few times when he'd addressed her in perfect English, quizzing her about the personal history she kept close to her chest. 'When he's not terrifying me, he's deliberately baffling me by conversing with me in Greek.'

His lips quirked but his eyes remained serious. 'We've had a few…disagreements recently.'

She nodded. 'The last time we visited, he mentioned that he'd hoped you would take over his company some day.'

'I wasn't aware he'd shared that with you,' he said, a touch tersely.

'I didn't pry, if that's what you're worried about.'

'Rest easy, Alexis. It's not a secret that my decision to pursue a career in law instead of shipping isn't one he was pleased with. But the one thing we shared was a love of Drakonisos. A place he promised I would inherit. Until recently.'

Her heart kicked both at the news and the fact that he was finally choosing to share personal details with her. 'What happened?'

'My cousin, Georgios, happened.' She waited for elaboration and, after a tense moment, he continued, 'He's not satisfied with running Costas's company or the substantial benefits that come with it. He has now turned his attention towards Drakonisos.'

'He wants the island?'

Christos gave a terse nod. 'Yes.'

'Why? I mean, I imagine he's in a position to buy himself an island or three?'

He shrugged but his expression grew grimmer. 'There's been a certain resentment and rivalry—one-sided, I might add—on his part.'

'Because he was second choice?' she hazarded and received a twisted smile in confirmation.

'Exactly so. My grandfather believed I would take over his company when he stepped down. Even after I made it clear I would follow a different path, he pursued the matter. He still hasn't given up, which is why I hold voting power on his board of directors and substantial shares in Drakakis Enterprises.'

Alexis had been quietly awed to learn Drakakis Enterprises was a *Fortune 500* company worth in excess of ten billion euros. 'But Costas must know you'll never just give up being a lawyer?' Christos was too good at what he did. Was driven by an inner compulsion Alexis suspected was locked in his past. A compulsion she couldn't see him walking away from to pursue a career in shipping. But if any man on earth could straddle multiple careers, it was Christos Drakakis.

'He lives in hope, one I haven't been able to sway him from. It's also why he holds Drakonisos over my head. I had hoped that would change after you and I married, but it seems Georgios is playing an entirely different hand. One I'll need to respond to.'

'Why do you want the island so badly?'

His features shuttered, the grip of his glass tightening a fraction before he eased it. 'My reasons are my own, Alexis.'

The mild warning that she was straying too far into personal territory echoed in the room. 'You ask me whether I have a lover but I can't ask you why you want a mostly uninhabited piece of land the size of Hyde Park?'

'A question you still haven't answered. Is there a lover standing in the way of me achieving my goals?'

Alexis wasn't sure whether it was the way he said the word lover that sparked the sudden fire in her belly or if it was the effect of the churning in her stomach. Either way, she needed a few seconds to brush aside the tingling in her veins before she answered. 'No, I don't have a lover.'

He absorbed that with an unblinking stare for several seconds before giving an imperious nod. 'Good to know.'

She nodded in return. 'And since we're taking liberties, is there anything standing in my way of being able to pull off an acceptable performance as your wife?'

His eyes narrowed, glinting with a wickedly thrilling

fire before his expression turned bracingly enigmatic once more. 'I haven't taken a lover since I put a ring on your finger, Alexis.'

Before she could stop herself, a gasp left her throat. His declaration was thick, firm and low, the timbre of his voice reaching into a deep, secret place inside her and wrapping tight. It was almost as if he'd modulated his voice purely for that devastating effect. Struggling to clear her throat, she answered. 'Then I foresee nothing but success,' she said with a sangfroid she didn't feel.

'Good. With regard to the island, the only thing you need to concern yourself about is that, according to my sources, Georgios has stepped up his visits to Drakonisos. Which is a sure sign that he's attempting to encroach on what's mine.' The implacable steel in his voice suggested that would happen over his dead body. 'And Costas is allowing it.'

'That's the other reason you want to bring forward the visit?'

He nodded briskly. 'Yes. So not only will you have Costas to convince, there's a strong possibility that Georgios will be there, as well.'

Apprehension snaked through her. Pretending to be dwelling in wedded bliss under Costas's shrewd gaze was a challenge, but now there was the possibility of another audience?

Think of Hope House. Of every child you'll be helping.

'How long do you think we'll be there?'

'Prepare yourself for a few weeks, maybe a couple of months.'

She gasped. 'Months?'

His gaze turned hard. 'If I didn't know better, I'd say you were thinking of reneging on our agreement.'

Alexis was aware she had no choice. Not if she wanted to continue providing for Hope House. She'd read through the contract, knew he had a certain leeway she couldn't object to. And really, what would she be protesting against? There was no fear that this would evolve into anything beyond the clinical requirement Christos sought from her. And she… she'd given up on love or companionship long ago. It was why she'd been thankful for the black and white safety of a legal agreement. She had nothing to fear, least of all from her emotions. And yet…

She rose, ignoring the quivering in her belly as Christos watched her. 'I… I need to think about it.'

For the longest time, he stared at her, one long finger caressing the rim of his crystal glass. Then, with the litheness of a predatory cat, he rose, sauntered to the door and held it open for her. And as she passed him, he leaned in and whispered in her ear, 'Think about it if you insist. But know that anything but a *yes* will be unacceptable.'

CHAPTER FOUR

THE NEXT THREE days were hell on her nerves. She'd barely been able to sleep on Monday night. Or any night since. Christos's announcement that they were leaving for Drakonisos on Friday had merely exacerbated the unnerving sensation in her stomach. He hadn't pressed her for an answer, although announcing their impending departure suggested he fully expected her to fall in line.

That she needed to get her game face on sooner rather than later.

And it's not like you haven't had a dress rehearsal...

The snide inner voice made her cringe, and yet the truth blared starkly. She knew what unravelling in Christos's arms felt like. And it wasn't as if they'd need a full repeat performance of that episode to convince his grandfather and cousin, would they?

So why did her skin tighten with alarmed excitement each time she thought of it? Why did she hold her breath each time Christos spoke to her, anticipation beating wild wings in her stomach?

She really needed her head examined.

Hard on the heel of that thought, he materialised in front of her desk minutes before she planned to leave. As per usual this late in the day, his sleeves were folded back, displaying muscular, olive-skinned, hair-dusted forearms and those far too capable hands that occupied far too much of her attention.

To reverse the effect, she dragged her gaze upward, met steely grey eyes, which at that precise moment glinted with intense purpose.

'There's been a development. Demitri's wife has left

the family home and taken their son with her. Apparently, she's moved in with her new lover in Athens.' Again, the tight edge in his voice denoted an attachment to this case that tweaked her senses.

She rose and rounded her desk. 'Is the boy okay?'

His nostrils flared as he straightened, and she saw the tension riding his shoulders. 'No, he's not. How can he be? He's already called Demitri several times, begging to come home.'

Distress slashed through her, thankfully banking her chaotic nerves from before. 'Is there anything we can do?'

His jaw clenched for a moment before he shook his head. 'I've already instructed the partners in Athens to issue an injunction. But at the very least, the child will have to remain with his mother until after the weekend.'

The observation didn't please him one iota. And Alexis wasn't sure if his displeasure triggered something inside her. Before she could think better of it, she laid a hand on his arm. 'She's his mother. Surely she won't let any harm come to him?'

His muscles tightened beneath her hold, his eyes turning stormy as they narrowed on her. 'Her negligence where her child's concerned is well-documented. It's imperative that he's removed from her influence sooner rather than later.'

'This case means more to you than you're letting on, doesn't it?' she ventured, recalling their talk on Monday night. As much as he tried to remain aloof, Christos cared.

His gaze dropped to the hand on his arm, a peculiar expression flitting across his face before he answered. 'He's my godson.'

That was news to her, but she couldn't help probe deeper. 'Is that all?'

For the longest time she thought he wouldn't reply. He captured her hand, disengaged it from his arm but didn't release it. He held her wrist, his expression almost bleak, but still hard and unforgiving. 'I despise children being used as pawns when their parents decide they no longer wish to be together. Inevitably, it's the child that gets the raw end of the deal.'

Maybe it was the warm hold on her that weakened her resistance, but she found herself confessing. 'I know how that feels,' she muttered, then immediately wanted to take the words back.

But his laser gaze had sharpened. 'How?'

'I grew up in an orphanage. I know exactly what it feels like to be unwanted.'

Enlightenment glinted in his eyes. 'Hope House,' he surmised, his voice low and deep.

The combination of his touch, her jangling emotions and the fact that she'd divulged a huge part of her life that drew pity from most people made her pull away.

He held on, his eyes narrowing on her face for a long contemplative moment before he set her free.

But stepping away did nothing to ease the quaking inside. She felt as if a layer of her skin had been stripped away, allowing him a glimpse of something she'd rather have kept cloaked.

'Did you need anything else?'

He shoved his hand into his pocket, the motion stretching the material of his shirt across his torso and lighting even more confounding flames inside her.

'I came to tell you we might have to make a detour to Athens tomorrow if the team come up against any resistance.' His eyes narrowed on her face. 'I'm assuming you're still on board with accompanying me to Drakonisos?'

'Do I have a choice?' she asked, striving for a briskness that failed miserably.

He frowned. 'Not if you don't want to fall foul of the spirit of our agreement. Do you?'

Alexis swallowed, knowing she was caught. 'No.'

He nodded briskly. 'I'll pick you up in the morning.'

Christos hung up the phone and suppressed another curse. To say this was proving to be the week from hell was an understatement.

While Monday's loss had been a direct hit to his pride, the thought that he'd left the field open for Demitri's son to become a pawn was more visceral. It struck much too close to home for his liking.

This was why he didn't usually deal with such cases. Why the institution of marriage had been anathema to him since dragging himself from the harrowing battlefield of his parents' divorce.

But regardless of how he'd felt about his friend's too-good-to-be-true love proclamations and his subsequent rush into marriage, Christos had witnessed the genuine adoration in Demitri's face seven years ago when he'd talked about his future with the woman of his dreams. Even more astounding was that Demitri was a man who'd been previously cynical and jaded about the state of matrimony second only to Christos himself.

But even then, Christos had kept his scepticism to himself, choosing to give his friend his blessing along with the benefit of his silent doubt.

It didn't please him at all to be proven right that, beyond the first few weeks of a new liaison, all that remained were pathetic illusions waiting to turn to bitterness and acrimony.

And even then, as he was discovering lately, the initial spark of interest didn't have to progress to the bedroom for its looming demise to become patently clear.

Now the same pattern that had shattered Christos's childhood was being replayed in his best friend's marriage.

Christos swivelled his desk chair in his private jet's conference room around, but the view that met his gaze, like yesterday, remained abysmal to the point of depressing. They'd only just taken off, and while England had its charms, the weather wasn't one of them.

He didn't know whether it was talking to Kyrios that had triggered it but suddenly he yearned for the warmth and vibrancy of Drakonisos, the only place he'd truly called home. The place his greedy cousin was attempting to steal from him.

His harsh exhalation was punctuated by Alexis's entry. A different type of disturbance took hold of his chest that had nothing to do with the plane's mild turbulence, intensifying his unsettled mood. He wasn't sure exactly what had happened on Monday night in his penthouse suite. To be honest, whatever it was had started in the conference room with the tiniest display of evidence that his able and talented assistant wasn't superhuman after all.

For some absurd reason, seeing her less than perfectly put together, he'd wanted to explore that flaw. To dishevel her even more, pull her shirt tails from her tight, prim skirt, fully let down her slipping hair and mar her fading lipstick with his mouth.

The urge to push her buttons had been unstoppable. At the end of the night, once he'd put two doors between them and stood beneath a lukewarm shower, he'd relegated the aberration to the events of the day. Now, as he watched her walking across the carpet towards him, Christos wasn't so sure.

To his recollection, his assistant had never worn a trouser suit to work or any work-related function. She favoured skirt suits or classy dresses with matching jackets.

Now she looked completely different.

Christos couldn't drag his gaze from the body encased in a pair of dark blue jeans, a shimmery navy sleeveless top and waist-length leather jacket. Her hair was caught up in its usual style, but the transformation was disconcertingly visceral enough to knock the breath out of him while firing spikes of heat to parts of his body he preferred not to call attention to in public.

He'd never bothered to categorise which female body part he most favoured, but, seeing Alexis's denim-clad behind as she turned to shut the door, he was slammed with a need so acute his fist clenched on his thigh. He knew how those luscious twin globes would feel in his hands. He wanted to knead them again, leverage their delicious weight as he dragged her into his body until those breasts were pressed into his chest. He wanted to drag his nose along her sleek neck, investigate whether she'd worn that rose-scented perfume tonight or the one that made her smell like the lightest ocean breeze.

His gaze traced her skin to her wrist, the memory of her frantic pulse beating beneath her silky flesh gliding to centre stage in his mind. Now, like then, the stirring in his groin announced a new dimension to his relationship with his assistant. Because she didn't look at him with stars in her eyes, with bated breath and false promises that could never be realistically fulfilled? Because she didn't throw around words he didn't want to hear, like companionship and relationship and, heaven forbid, *love*?

Ne, perhaps that was it. His parents had uttered words like that once upon a time and look where they'd ended up. Look where *he'd* ended up, a pawn between two merciless predators, uncaring that they were tearing him to shreds.

He drew his gaze from the curve of her hip, past the slim watch and silver bracelet that circled her wrists. By the time she stopped in front of him, he'd smashed down hard on the unwanted physical reactions.

'Is there any news about Demitri's case?' She was the epitome of professionalism, with her tablet and the electronic pen and perfectly coiffed hair.

The need to see that thick, rich hair unfettered flared

through him. But a moment later, the reminder of his friend's plight caused his jaw to clench. He nodded at the chair. She sat down and crossed her shapely legs.

'I just spoke to the lawyers. They're on their way to court. We'll know in the next hour if we need to change course to Athens instead of Drakonisos.'

'Have you heard from Demitri? Is your godson all right?'

Her enquiry, though it strayed far too much into personal territory, pleased him, nonetheless. But the tightness in his chest as he answered didn't. 'The mother is refusing to let Demitri see him. Same goes for the mother of his older son. She's refusing to let him see his other son, too.' No matter how clinically he recited the facts, a part of him bristled with rage.

Alexis nodded. 'So we might be staging custody battles on two fronts instead of one?'

'Potentially, yes. But securing the return of my godson is paramount. He cannot remain in that toxic environment.'

Her lashes lifted, her eyes searching his for the reason for his caustic tone. 'When was the last time you saw him?' she asked.

A twinge of guilt snagged his gut. 'Why does it matter?'

'I have a fair grasp on your daily schedule. For all intents and purposes, we're joined at the hip. I don't recall you mentioning Demitri's son.'

A different sort of sensation attacked his lower abdomen, arrowing into his groin, the image of being attached to Alexis making his temperature rise. 'I haven't seen the boy in a…while,' he confessed, ignoring the bite of shame.

'So you didn't know that their marriage was in trouble? That all the things listed as the reason for their divorce…' She stared down at the tablet to refresh her memory, but Christos knew everything by heart.

'The infidelity? Neglect of both her husband and her child? Verbal abuse and the as yet unproved physical abuse of her child? All the usual reasons two people who shouldn't marry ignore reality and end up in these types of situations. I'm not the morality police, Alexis. My only task is to ensure the right people are saved from anguish in the fallout.'

Again, her lashes flew up, questions flitting across her expression. 'I didn't mean…of course I don't think you're the morality police…'

His teeth gritted, the knowledge that he'd revealed too much biting him hard. Alexis opened her mouth to speak but he waylaid her questions by sliding a sheet of paper across his desk. 'Contact these clients, let them know we'll be out of town for a while but that I'll let them know if there are any developments.'

She nodded, her teeth trapping her lower lip as she glanced down at the page. The sight of the plump curves glistening with the peach gloss she favoured renewed the pounding in his groin.

Her gaze darted up, caught him watching her, and her breath hitched. She raised her tablet to her chest, holding it close like armour.

Christos suppressed a grim smile, even as he clenched his fist to stop himself from tracing his knuckles across her smooth cheek. He momentarily lost track of time, his senses absorbed by the pulse racing at her throat, the susurration of her breathing and the intensifying temptation of her perfume.

His gaze dropped once again to her lips. They parted as if by command and she slicked her lower lip with the tip of her pink tongue.

The mobile phone beeped. She jumped, sending the gadget a startled look before taking a hurried step back. 'I… I'll get this done.'

He didn't answer as she rushed out. He wasn't sure he had adequate words to describe what the hell was happening. No explanations for his sudden wish to throw caution to the wind, go against his better judgement and test the depths of the blazing awareness between himself and Alexis.

Despite the rumours circulated by gossipmongers, he'd never been interested in mixing business with pleasure. It was the reason he'd sent his previous assistants packing the moment they exhibited signs of unprofessional interest.

But Alexis was different. And not because he'd struck a deal with her twelve months ago and placed a ring on her finger. Although that knowledge seemed to beat a curiously persistent drum in his blood. The kind that reeked of possession.

Her revelation about Hope House had thrown him. Granted, the first time she'd mentioned it, he'd been too preoccupied with sealing the terms of their agreement to pay attention to why a children's home meant that much to her. None of the women he'd dated in the past would've spared a thought for an orphanage past the need to look magnanimous at a fundraiser. But Alexis had reached back into her past with a helping hand. Whereas the only association he wanted with his childhood was the grim and relentless drive it gave him never to return to that helpless state.

As much as he wanted to deny it, that discovery about Alexis...affected him. Perhaps all this was because he hadn't taken a woman to bed in over a year. Even before their agreement, for some confounding reason, the thrill of the chase always seemed to end somewhere around the second course of a Michelin-starred meal or in the third act of a West End play, seeing him return to his main Mayfair residence alone.

At first he'd thought nothing of it. His workload was crushing, just the way he liked it. But then it always had been. In hindsight he recognised that the niggling dissatisfaction about the state of his transient dating had started when he'd heard Delilah Armitage threatening Alexis on the phone. The distaste and censure on his assistant's face had stayed with him long after he'd taken care of his ex. Perhaps he'd never thought he would care about being judged over the way he conducted his sex life.

But in that moment, he'd felt…less.

And that had grated.

He lunged to his feet now, unwilling to further explore the reason. Not on top of everything that had happened this week.

He had the time on Drakonisos to figure this dilemma out. And when his phone rang an hour later and he'd finished the brief conversation with his team, he registered that his stride was a little lighter, the anticipation in his belly swelling as he went in search of his assistant.

Perhaps she sensed the shift within him. Whatever. Her eyes widened as he approached her in the plane's sumptuous lounge and dropped into the seat next to her. 'I…is there news?'

'Indeed, there is. The lawyers have secured an injunction hearing first thing on Monday morning. Until then, I have a discreet security team watching that the boy doesn't come to harm.'

A warm smile curved her lips. His gut tightened and he felt himself growing hard. 'I'm glad,' she said. Then her smile wavered. 'Does that mean…?'

Sunlight broke through the grey clouds just then, bathed her stunning face in light.

And for the first time in his life, Christos accepted that, as his week had gone thus far, maybe the control he'd taken for granted was about to be turned upside down.

Unable to help himself, he trailed a hand down her cheek. 'Yes, Alexis. It means we're on our way to Drakonisos.'

CHAPTER FIVE

ALEXIS KNEW THIS trip was different the moment they landed on Drakonisos and spotted the small convoy of vehicles through the window of the plane. Her heart leapt into her throat at the sight of the old man leaning against the first SUV.

With shocking white hair and steely grey eyes, Costas Drakakis stood tall and proud despite the walking stick propped next to his right hip. His olive skin gleamed vibrant under the Greek sun. From where she sat, Alexis could detect no signs of illness or weakness. Certainly nothing that would cause his grandson to commit to spending weeks on end on this island, as idyllic as it was. 'I thought you said your grandfather was ill?'

It took a moment for Christos to respond, his eyes narrowing at the faintly accusatory note in her voice. 'One of the first lessons my grandfather taught me as a boy was never to take anything or anyone at face value. He didn't exempt himself from that assessment and I suggest you don't either.'

She bit her lip, her gaze swinging back to the unexpected welcome party as the plane finally stopped.

The moment the doors were unlocked and the steps lowered Christos rose, his hand extended to her. 'Come, Alexis.'

'If I said I wasn't ready, would it make any difference?'

The corner of his mouth tilted, but there was very little mirth in his face. 'The only reason he'd accept our tardiness is if we emerged looking like we'd just had wild sex. Is that the impression you wish to give?'

Heat stung her cheeks and she knew her face was furnace red. 'Of course not.'

His eyes darkened and those sinful lips twisted. 'Shame. I find myself in a mood to oblige.'

He was toying with her. Because that layer of tension that'd been evident in his demeanour when he'd spotted his grandfather was still there, perhaps even growing with every moment they delayed.

With very little choice but to remain on this wild roller coaster, Alexis placed her hand in his. And immediately tensed as his fingers closed firmly over hers, giving her no room to escape the electric sizzle that raced up her arm. Caught in a sensual storm, she was all but boneless when he tugged her upright, going willingly into his personal space when he nudged her closer. Then instead of walking her out as she'd expected, he simply stood there, staring down at her.

'Perhaps I should kiss you, ensure that dreamy look remains in your eyes,' he mused, his voice a rough rumble that said he was caught in whatever this maelstrom was too.

'There's no look…you're imagining things.' Her attempt to tug herself out of his hold backfired when he released her, only to slip his hands around her waist, imprisoning her against his lean, muscular body. The heat unravelling through her body intensified.

'Am I, *yineka mou*?'

She gave a soft gasp, a reminder of what those two words meant sliding through her hazy brain.

My wife.

He had every right to call her that now they'd returned once more to the location of their agreement.

Alexis swallowed, wondering why the word affected her more now than it ever had before. Love, marriage or emotional entanglements of any kind weren't on the cards for her. So why let herself imagine what it would be like if this were real? If it weren't all make-believe?

Strong, demanding fingers slid into her hair, clenching the heavy mass ever so slightly. The barest hint of his power made her hyperaware of the animal ferocity of the man holding her. Of the renewed hunger she'd experienced that night on his sofa roaring to life inside her. The expertise with which he'd delivered pleasure. How much she wanted an authentic repeat performance.

He tugged her head back, exposing her neck as his gaze dropped to her mouth. Spikes of hunger lanced her and she licked her lips.

'You want it too, don't you?' he asked, his voice a low, sexy rasp.

'Christos…'

'All you need to do is ask for it,' he encouraged throatily.

Against her belly, she felt the pressure of his shaft, the sexuality bridled beneath his suit, and the tiniest moan escaped her. Yes, she wanted this. She was human after all. A woman with needs. Needs she'd denied for years.

But with Christos Drakakis? When every single clue pointed to this being a disaster?

'Don't overthink it, Alexis.'

The hand she'd braced on his chest unfurled. Searching. Exploring. The quickening tempo of his heartbeat against her fingers made her yearn for skin-to-skin contact. For the pleasure of hearing him just as shaken as she was by their chemistry.

Even if it was pure folly? No. Because Christos wasn't Adrian. He wasn't leading her on with clever and manipulative words. He wasn't leading her on at all. If anything, he'd thrown the ball firmly in her court. And all she wanted, in this moment, was a kiss. Nothing more.

Liar.

His fingers tightened, drawing her attention back to him.

To the fevered gaze fixed on her lips. To his lowering head, the brush of his breath on her skin. 'I want to taste you again, *glykia mou.* I want to hear that little throaty sound you make when you're turned on.'

Every atom in her body leapt in giddy excitement, pulling her up onto her tiptoes. Her hand had crept around his neck almost of its own accord and the luxuriant springiness of his hair teased her fingers.

Her gaze swept up, compelled by his. Met and held. Her lips parted, her *yes* one single breath away—

'If you weren't ready to disembark, perhaps you should've instructed your pilot to circle the airspace a little while longer.'

The heavily accented rasp of the voice that evoked an image of reckless years spent smoking expensive cigars and drinking ouzo made them spring apart. Or certainly made *her* attempt to. Christos's steel-strong arm around her waist and the fingers spiked into her hair prevented her escape.

She turned, a flush creeping up her neck when she saw Costas Drakakis standing ten feet away, walking stick in hand and his eyes fixed firmly on them.

While Alexis burned with embarrassment for being caught in a melodramatic clinch, nothing in Christos's face betrayed discomfort at being discovered in a compromising position with his executive assistant.

No, not his assistant.

His wife.

Here, now, in this moment, she wasn't just his trusted employee. She was his wife. As the heavy weight of the priceless diamond and platinum rings on her finger signified.

A wave of icy realisation doused the flames of her arousal as Christos dropped his hand from her hair, his other sliding down her arm to capture her wrist after briefly lingering on the wedding ring.

'Pappous. We were on our way out. You didn't have to come up.'

The old man snorted. 'It didn't seem that way just now. It was that or burn to a crisp out there waiting for you two.'

Alexis cleared her throat and pasted a smile on her face, even as the cold thought continued to bloom inside her. 'Costas, it's lovely to see you again.'

Eyes so much like his grandson's it was eerie flicked to her. 'Is it? You could have fooled me by keeping me waiting.'

'Behave, Pappous,' Christos chided, his voice wrapped in an undeniable layer of warmth that made her curious about their relationship.

Unlike other families, they didn't move to hug and exchange exuberant greetings, but a look arced between them for several seconds, as if they spoke their own silent language.

Seconds later, the moment was over. Behind Costas, a tall man dressed in discreet medical scrubs appeared, his eyes on the older man.

Sensing his presence, Costas snorted again. 'As you can see, my guard dog is at the ready. Be kind and let's get off this tin can, *ne*?'

'Of course. After you,' Christos invited.

They exited the plane with her hand clasped firmly in his. And while she breathed a sigh of relief when Costas boarded the front vehicle and she and Christos the second, with their luggage loaded onto the third, her nerves were still all over the place as they drove away.

For the first few minutes, she stared out of the window, basking in the stunning vista of Drakonisos under the dappled light of the afternoon sun. As Greek islands went, it was one of the largest privately owned ones. It was named for its dragon-like shape as well as the craggy cliffs that lined the north of the island. Its beautiful underbelly consisted of two jaw-dropping beaches, one on the doorstep of the sprawling villa, and the other in a secluded cove half a mile away. And despite having visited twice, she knew there was far more to explore on the island. But that was a delight for later.

Nerves still jangling and knowing she couldn't keep the question firing in her brain to herself, she turned to Christos and murmured so the driver couldn't hear, 'Did you know he was boarding the plane?'

He shrugged with a carelessness that set her teeth on edge. 'I suspected he might. My grandfather isn't known for his patience.'

'And you didn't warn me?'

One eyebrow quirked up. 'So you would do what? Maintain a healthy six feet of space between us? Wasn't it better that he caught us like that? Your blushing certainly added the perfect touch.'

'I'm glad all this amuses you.'

'And I'm glad to see you're aren't blowing anything out of proportion. At all,' he said dryly.

Irritation sparked through her, thankfully blanketing some of the arousal still dancing beneath her skin.

'Are you hanging on to your annoyance in place of something else?' he enquired, after another scrutiny of her face.

'I have no idea what you're talking about.'

He gave a lopsided smile, then inclined his head. 'Take that road if you must. But for the record, I wasn't pleased that we were interrupted.'

'Because it would've played further into your hands, of course.'

His smile disappeared. 'What?' he bit out.

'It was all staged for his benefit, wasn't it?'

A harsh gleam flickered in his eyes. 'What a cynic you are.'

'I don't hear you denying it.'

'Whether it was or not doesn't matter. You're not forgetting your role, are you?' he asked quietly.

Alexis shot a glance at their driver before flicking her gaze his way. She couldn't quite settle on his face because she was a little terrified she would give herself away. 'Of course not.'

If anything, his features hardened, as if her flippant answer didn't please him. 'Then what's the problem, exactly, *glykia mou*?'

That endearment burrowed inside, seeking a vulnerable place she couldn't allow it to go. 'I don't like being blindsided.'

'Life isn't set out in perfect little boxes you can tick off at your leisure, Alexis. You need to be prepared for the odd curveball.'

She stiffened. 'What's that supposed to mean?'

'There's a reason you left your last firm, isn't there? Things didn't quite go according to plan?'

Her lungs flattened, her heart striking up a terrible hammering that attacked her ribcage. 'You know about that?'

He inclined his head with the slightest nod. *'Ne,'* he responded in his mother tongue, perhaps because they were in his homeland.

'Why haven't you asked me before?'

'Perhaps because I was attempting to be discreet. But now it's out in the open—'

'It's still not up for discussion,' she responded hurriedly, feeling blindsided.

'You're not the only one who doesn't like surprises. But I didn't go digging, if that's what you're worried about. I find gossip distasteful. I would much prefer to hear about the whole thing from you.'

A small part of her yearned to discover what he knew

and how he'd found out, while the rest shied away from knowing. 'It's nothing that affects our working relationship.'

'What about our private one? And before you say we don't have one, think again.'

She looked out of the window to buy herself some time. The last thing she wanted was to admit to the degrading humiliation of her one failed relationship. To the utterly blind error of judgement she'd made that had nearly cost her everything. Would he trust her judgement if he knew the true details? 'Can we just chalk it up to a relationship that didn't work out?' she eventually managed.

'That depends.'

'On what?'

'On whether it colours all your decisions.'

She snatched in a breath. 'Do all your relationships colour yours?'

'Very much so.'

Not the answer she expected, she reflected as she searched his face. Found it, much like many times before, an enigmatic book. But this time, within those grey depths she spotted something. Barely a glimmer but she saw it. Pain. Bitterness.

Right before he blinked and neutralised his expression. She bit her lip, torn between curiosity and reservation.

After several moments, the corners of his lips lifted. 'Not going to give in to your curiosity?'

She shrugged. 'Your past private life is your own. Much like mine is my business.'

Before he could respond, the vehicle slowed to a stop.

Alexis stepped out with relief, pulling in a long breath of fresh air in the hope of restoring the few layers of sanity she'd lost since their embrace on the plane.

The villa was set on the highest point of the island to take full advantage of the breathtaking views. Past cypress trees, perfectly pruned hibiscus bushes, bougainvillea hedges and impeccably manicured lawns, the sea glinted like a blanket of gemstones, an endless invitation for a cool reprieve out of the June heat.

From past visits, she knew the beach was less than five minutes away, that the Drakakis yacht and speedboat were moored out of sight around the cove. She'd declined an invitation to waterski with Christos on their last trip but had the stomach-fluttering experience of watching him ski with breathtaking style.

Her belly heating on that recollection, she turned towards him and saw his gaze on the far distant view. Towards the other side of the island, where the terrain was craggier. Shadows flitted through his eyes, his jaw clenching then releasing before he sucked in a long deep breath. A light breeze tossed a lock of hair across his forehead, but Alexis was certain it didn't register. He was caught in whatever memories made Drakonisos a place he wanted to possess. A place that had prompted a man with cynical views on relationships to enter a marriage of convenience with an employee. As she continued to watch him his features softened and he gave a slow exhale, the kind that came with inner contentment. Perhaps even…peace.

Sensing her regard, he turned to her. 'Shall we get out of the sun before Costas grumbles at us again?' he said evenly, but that faraway look in his eyes took another moment to dissipate.

She nodded, although her senses remained a little askew as she turned towards the villa.

Costas's home was a sprawling, multi-level whitewashed traditional Greek villa but with every modern amenity conceivable. Despite her previous visits, Alexis's breath still caught when she stepped onto the smooth terracotta tiles of the wide hallway and looked up at the large rectangular stained-glass windows that let in endless sunlight. That light glinted over light stone-coloured walls, complemented by gold-accented local Cycladic art and white furniture. Several masterpieces were dotted along the vast hallway that led to a large living room, beyond which the terracotta tiles were replicated on a sun-soaked terrace.

That was where Costas had headed and where she and Christos followed to find a long table of refreshments awaiting them. The knots that had barely loosened when she'd stepped out of the plane began to tighten again as Christos's hand landed in the small of her back.

He led her to the table and drew back a chair for her.

No reprieve, then...

'We'll have refreshments while our luggage is unpacked.'

With no option but to accept the invitation, she took a seat and smiled at the older man.

Paxos, one half of the middle-aged married couple in charge of keeping the villa and grounds in pristine condition, stepped forward and poured an ouzo-infused punch Alexis knew could be lethal if not consumed with caution. Then he served delicate pastries and sandwiches, which she helped herself to as Costas conversed in Greek with his grandson.

When a small silence fell at the table, she glanced up.

'Kalos orises spiti,' Costas rasped.

'My grandfather says welcome home.'

The old man's eyes were fixed on her, reading her every expression, her every interaction with his grandson. While she hadn't doubted Christos's emphasis that this trip was different, she'd secretly hoped it was exaggerated. Costas's laser-focused gaze confirmed Christos's assessment. This visit was different. She was being analysed. Their *relationship* was being vetted.

Acutely mindful of that, she forced a smile. *'Efkharisto,'* she replied.

A shade of warmth stole back into the old man's eyes and

she allowed herself the merest inch to relax as he turned to his grandson.

'If you're here to check on me, I suggest you instruct the staff not to unpack your luggage. I've had my fill of shameless meddlers for quite a while,' he griped in English.

Christos took his time to sip his drink before resting muscled forearms on his armrests. 'I am here to check on you,' he replied without apology. 'And we intend to stay until I'm satisfied.'

His grandfather's eyes narrowed. 'Is that the only reason?'

'Play your games all you want with me, old man. Just remember I'm not a weak opponent.'

Costas's weathered cheeks cracked the smallest smile and, within it, Alexis saw satisfaction. Anticipation.

He might project the outward appearance of a grumpy old man but, as was evidenced by his presence at the airstrip, Costas was glad his grandson was here.

They enjoyed their refreshments for a few minutes, before Christos resolutely set his napkin down. 'I would like the unvarnished report on what's going on with you.'

His grandfather's smile was pure wickedness. 'Your strong-arm tactics on my physicians didn't work?'

'We both know you made it deliberately difficult, just so I would come here and find out for myself. So enough with the suspense.'

The older man shrugged, not in the least bit unnerved by the accusation. 'It's the usual. Old age after a life well lived.'

'Details, Pappous.'

Costas's gaze flickered to Alexis before returning to his grandson. 'Now that you're here, perhaps I will give my doctors permission to speak to you. They can fill you in on all the gory details.'

Impatience vibrated from Christos, but, perhaps knowing he wouldn't gain any more headway on the subject, he nodded. 'Very well. I'll speak to them when we're done here.'

'And once that's out of the way, you might let yourself relax a little, enjoy this party your cousin has been threatening to throw in my honour.'

Christos stiffened. 'What party?'

'A birthday party, I hear. A rather large one.'

Alexis's gaze flicked to Christos to see his eyes frosting over. 'You gave Georgios permission to throw you a party without consulting me first?'

Costas shrugged. 'Your cousin insisted, even though this isn't a milestone celebration. And my grandnephew has been more…available lately. Much more than my own grandson and his new bride, who I thought would be on their way to becoming a…larger family by now,' he said, his eyes dropping blatantly to her stomach.

Alexis gasped. 'We… I…'

'You're embarrassing my wife, Costas,' Christos said, a hard edge to the softly spoken words.

That Drakakis steel entered Costas's eyes as his gaze returned to Christos. 'Perhaps a little bit of embarrassment is necessary. I'm not going to live forever, you know. And since you claim to be married but are still maintaining separate residences, I find myself wondering whether you're pulling the wool over an old man's eyes.'

Her jaw gaped. 'How—'

The words dried in her throat as Christos's firm grip found hers beneath the table. 'The intimate details of my marriage are none of your business, old man. Tell your spies to retreat if they value their skins. And if you're playing my cousin off against me—'

'What if I am? What will you do about it?' his grandfather asked brazenly, dropping any attempt at diplomacy.

Christos's jaw tightened. 'You would do that?' he asked, an enigmatic tone wrapped around the words.

The old man remained inflexible for another second before he relaxed in his seat. 'You said you're up to the game? Prove it.'

The words still echoed in Alexis's head as they finished their refreshments and Costas's nurse firmly steered the old man away for a rest.

As Alexis and Christos retreated to the suite in the left wing of the villa, she all but felt the tension vibrating off him.

The moment the door shut behind them he muttered a curse under his breath.

'He knows we don't live together,' she said. 'And he's been keeping tabs on us.' Alexis wasn't entirely sure how she felt about being under such scrutiny.

His lips pursed. 'Yes. And I'm fairly certain I know who's behind it.'

'Your cousin?'

He shrugged, clawing his fingers through his hair as he began to pace. 'We've been married for a year. If he'd known all along that we lived separately, he would've said something before now. I can only conclude that he's been fed the information recently.'

She wrapped her arms around her middle, the silken web closing over her making her shiver. 'So what are we going to do about it?'

He slowed to a stop, his laser gaze fixing on her. Whatever he read in her face made his lips thin. 'You don't need to worry that your precious Hope House will suffer because of this, Alexis.'

Hurt made her gasp. 'That was the last thing I was thinking of. If you must know, I was thinking of you!'

He tensed. 'Me?'

'I saw your face when we arrived. This place means something to you. More than a simple birthright you don't want your cousin to claim.'

For a moment, he looked poleaxed. Then his features shuttered. 'The why doesn't matter. It's the how we need to concern ourselves with.'

The hurt she felt at his shutdown was as bad as the Hope House dig. But she was determined not to show it. She was too busy grappling with the unnerving emotions she'd been unable to control all week.

'I think we can be assured the *none of your business* argument isn't going to fly with him,' Christos said, resuming his tight pacing. 'The only way to kill his suspicions is to successfully convince him that this marriage is real.'

His words steeped her deeper in the present, her pulse rattling faster as her gaze darted around the room.

Their suite was the last word in comfort and luxury. Each suite had twin dressing rooms, a sumptuous living room and private terrace.

In the past, Christos had yielded the bed to her and slept on the sofa. But, in light of the altered dynamic between them, her attention was held most of all by the four-poster bed dominating the room. Heat unfurled through her at the thought of Christos in that bed. With her.

Their bodies sliding, straining and locking together. The pleasure he'd harnessed and then detonated in her.

A small sound escaped her throat before she could stop it.

Then she watched as Christos presumably mistook the sound for distress, his eyes hardening. 'I'm not going to unleash my animalistic desires on you right this minute, if that's what you're concerned about, Alexis.'

Rather than disclose the reason for her fluster, she brazened it out. 'You said you hadn't had a woman in a year. Maybe you see this as an opportunity to scratch an itch?'

His lips curled with distaste as he stopped in front of her. 'What an unsavoury turn of phrase. I prefer the more authentic and earthy description of lust, sex and mutual satisfaction.'

She grew hot again, an alarmingly frequent occurrence every time he was within touching distance. His scent reached out and wrapped around her as he stood staring down at her.

'We're both adults, Alexis, with needs. *If* we decided on a mutually satisfactory path to pleasure, I know I can trust in your discretion.'

The very idea sent another minor earthquake through her system. 'Aren't you even a little bit worried that I might turn overly emotional if we indulge in whatever it is you're insinuating?'

His gaze grew contemplative. 'Besides your wish to secure the future of Hope House, why did you agree to my proposition?'

It was her turn to tense. 'Why does it matter?'

'You're young, attractive, with a bright future ahead of you. And yet you agreed to tie yourself down for three years. Why?'

She forced a laugh, desperate for something to break the sharp awareness zinging in the air. 'Isn't it a little too late to be asking me these questions?'

He caught a stray lock of her hair, twisting it around his finger, while his gaze remained fixed on her face. 'Why the evasion? Answer the question, Alexis.'

'Because I'm not interested in relationships. Not any more,' she confessed with an upsurge of bitterness that seared her throat. 'And the agreement we made stated specifically that there would be nothing…intimate.'

Something flickered in his eyes. A blend of satisfaction, challenge and…anticipation. 'Maybe not before, but we both know things have changed now, after what happened two months ago. You feel it with every breath. So do I.'

'That means nothing,' she argued, despite the sizzle in

her belly and the tightening of her core. 'Our agreement stays as it is.'

He curled her hair behind her ear and smiled when she shivered. 'You can hide behind the letter of the agreement if it gives you comfort. But this thing between us isn't going away, *glykia mou*. No matter how much you deny it. As for worrying about your being overly emotional, why would I? You've remained consistently unflappable in the face of every circumstance. Are you warning me that might change if I take you to bed?' The brush of his fingers over her cheek and the electric pleasure they created only emphasised his words.

'First of all, you're not taking me to bed. Second, I was being facetious since the reason you fired so many of my predecessors was because they deigned to look at you with stars in their eyes.'

'They did. And that's the difference between you and them. You just said you don't do relationships. That assures me things won't change, so we won't have a problem.'

'What about your own lines?' she challenged.

For a moment he stilled, his lashes sweeping down to hide his expression. When they lifted, the heat in his eyes seared her to the bone. 'I find you more alluring than I anticipated. What better way to work through the…situation than to immerse oneself in it? Work it out of our systems, so to speak?' he asked indolently.

She wanted to condemn him for being a calculating bastard. But could she conscientiously do so when he was only speaking his mind? Wasn't the one thing she'd despised Adrian for more than anything the lying sweet talk he'd spouted simply to manipulate her?

The mere thought of Christos sweet talking anyone brought a strained smile.

'Something amusing you, *glykia mou*?' The endearment held an edge to it.

'I had the frightening notion of you attempting to sweet talk me into your sensual web.'

'I prefer plain-speaking.'

She swallowed, his very potent vitality threatening to consume her. 'I can see that.'

'Then perhaps the time for talking is over?'

He breached the last few inches between them and took her mouth with his. The fever that had brewed just below the surface for two months now flared strong and consuming once more. They devoured each other until their breaths grew frantic, until she felt as if her whole body were a flame of desire. She'd imagined a lot during those forbidden hours in her bed when she'd allowed Christos to fill her thoughts. *This* surpassed her every fantasy. Each stroke of his tongue felt like a brush with pure bliss, as if she were touching heaven itself.

'Christos.'

'Yes. Say my name, *matia mou*.'

Dear God, what was she doing? 'Christos…stop. I have another question.'

His breath shuddered out and he held himself still for a long moment before he stepped back. 'What is it?'

She scrambled to get her thoughts together. 'What was Costas talking about? What games are you two playing?'

CHAPTER SIX

CHRISTOS STEELED HIMSELF against that firm demand. He'd hoped for a little breathing room before his grandfather went for the jugular, but no. Just like him, Costas didn't believe in beating about the bush.

He looked around him, then out of the window past the gardens to the sea, willing the serenity he usually felt when he was on this particular piece of rock to reappear. He was wealthy enough to travel to any corner of the world he desired, had acquired property in those places that pleased his senses the most. Yet he'd never experienced the sort of… grounded calm he did when he was here. Fate and souls and love and destiny weren't phenomena he set much store by, but the closest he'd come to being emotional about anything was this place. The place his grandfather was dangling from his fingertips like a snowflake over a volcano. Daring him to act. Daring him to—

'Christos?'

He wiped a hand across his jaw. He was on edge. And not just because of his grandfather. This woman whose voice flowed over him like warm silk was equally culpable. She didn't know that the sensual web she'd accused him of wielding went both ways. That the harder he tried, the more elusive his renowned iron will became.

That moments before they'd disembarked his plane had intensified his craving for her. He'd blamed their discovery on Costas but, truth be told, he'd lost all sense of time and place the moment he'd touched her.

Just like that night on his sofa.

Perhaps choosing to cut all ties with the women who

normally populated his electronic diary this last year had been a mistake.

And perhaps Costas would've discovered your sham marriage much earlier too, if you'd been seen with other women. And without help from Georgios.

His lips twisted at the grim truth, his gaze dropping to the set of engagement and wedding rings on her finger before he passed his thumb over the wide platinum band encircling his own.

Then, he inhaled deeply. 'My grandfather knows that, of everything he owns, Drakonisos is the only thing I desire.'

She frowned. 'This island?'

He nodded. 'And it seems he's determined to make me jump through the biggest of hoops to get it.'

'By pitting you against your cousin?' Her frown deepened. 'I admit I don't know him very well, but I wouldn't have thought Costas would do something like that purely for his amusement.'

He felt a peculiar pang in his chest at her astuteness. 'Nor would I. Which means either my cousin is succeeding in pouring poison into his ear or…'

'Or what?'

'Or the situation has a few more facets than I initially realised.'

Her frown evaporated to be filled by apprehension. 'You think this is part of him facing his own mortality.'

A different ache tightened his chest, and he nodded again. 'Yes.'

'What are you going to do about it?'

'I won't know until I talk to his doctor. If it's the former, I can handle it…'

'And if it's the latter?' she asked, her eyes wide on his.

He didn't answer immediately, purely because he had no answer to give. His grandfather had been a constant in his life, a formidable force to whom he'd unburdened his innermost fears as a child. In his teenage years and early adulthood, they'd been mostly at loggerheads once Christos had made it clear he was choosing his own path and not following the one his grandfather had wanted for him. But even then Costas had remained in his life. He hadn't cut him off as his parents had. Or used him as a pawn in whatever game took his fancy.

Until now.

They were Drakakis men after all, and Christos knew he didn't have to look far to see where his own father had inherited his cut-throat characteristics from.

And yet, for whatever reason, his grandfather had supported him. Hell, he'd done more than that. He'd claimed Christos as his own when his father had merely seen him as a chess piece to be used when he pleased, then set aside to gather dust.

The thought that Costas wouldn't be around for much longer, for whatever reason…

He shook his head free of that thought. 'If it's the latter, we'll discuss it.'

His grandfather's comment at the table echoed in his head, the confirmation that Costas might not believe their marriage to be real raising the hairs on his nape.

Drakanisos was his. He couldn't lose it. Couldn't lose the old man who lived on it either.

The thought burrowed deep inside him, wrapping tight around his chest until his breathing grew constricted. Until all of a sudden that one emotion he'd thought alien to him, love of the familial kind, and the possible absence of it, took on a wraithlike shape in his mind.

He whirled to face her, wishing for something…anything to distract from that harrowing possibility. Then couldn't seem to look away. *Thee mou*, had her skin always been this flawless, her brown eyes flecked with such beguiling strands of gold? He knew about the temptation of her lips, the suppleness of her hips, the delicious sensation of her warm breath over his face. The sound of her moans—

'I'm going to call the doctor. Dinner won't be served until late, so you have a few hours to yourself.'

He exited the suite before she saw the physical manifestation of his thoughts or the turbulence of his emotions, experiencing a twinge of shame for sneering at her for suspecting the churning thoughts gripping him now.

He breathed a sigh of relief when he didn't encounter any staff member before he made it to the sanctuary of his study. Still, it took a minute to summon the control to calm his thoughts and pluck his phone from his pocket.

Twenty minutes later, he had his answers. And that grip on his chest had grown into a vice. Costas had a heart condition. A long-term one he'd been ignoring and downplaying for the better part of a year. Unless he had an operation within the next three months, his prognosis would worsen irreparably.

Christos wasn't aware he'd wandered back into the suite until he arrived in front of the liquor cabinet in his private living room. His hand shook as he poured himself a stiff whisky, tipped his head back and downed it. Thrusting the glass back on the shelf, he braced his hands on the surface, attempted to calm his rioting thoughts even as the words the doctor had uttered dropped like anvils onto his shoulders.

Her scent arrived first, whispering seductively through the late-afternoon air to wrap its mingled lilac and Nag Champa tendrils around his senses. That scent had triggered a primal reaction in him the first time he'd inhaled it, and he'd had an uncharacteristic urge to discover exactly what his assistant dabbed on her skin before coming to work. A curiosity that had led to him discovering the name of her perfume and investigating the ingredients. Somehow Christos knew he would never smell Nag Champa without associating it with Alexis Sutton.

'You're back,' came her voice. He latched onto her unique blend of sultriness and firmness that evoked far too vivid thoughts of erotic intimacy. Thoughts that should've had no place here and now perhaps, but anything was better than thinking about his grandfather's state of health. About how hard he'd have to fight if the stubborn old fool refused to heed his doctor's advice.

So he pivoted to face her. And received another bolt of unwelcome sensation.

She was dressed in a thigh-skimming floral sundress, its short wispy sleeves leaving her arms bare. Unbidden, his gaze wandered down, his gut tightening as he took in her long, beautiful bare legs and pedicured feet. Further images pushed through his resistance, of those stunning legs wrapped around his waist, their grip exquisitely intimate, promising the kind of raw passion he'd found elusive in his lovers long before he'd closed his electronic black book. Dragging his gaze upward in a wild bid to overcome the heat climbing up his body and its reaction behind his fly, he bit back a curse when he found her twirling her damp, unbound hair into a rope. She'd taken a shower, stood naked beneath his shower jets and washed that sexy body in his bathroom while he'd been out.

Realising he was in extreme danger of putting his burgeoning erection on show, he dragged his mind from the bathroom to the living room.

He wondered how long she'd been standing there. Wondered what those far too perceptive eyes had seen. 'You have news.' It wasn't a question. And for a fraction of a second he wanted to be annoyed. But then wasn't this the exact trait he'd valued in her above all else? The reason his professional life ran much smoother now than it had in the years before her, when he'd suddenly seemed to attract seemingly intelligent assistants who nevertheless began to see him as a meal ticket almost as soon as they sat behind their desk?

A means to an end. That was all he'd ever been to the people who should've had his welfare at heart. And in a roundabout way, wasn't that what Alexis had extracted from him too?

Perhaps he was being disingenuous. After all, wasn't it he who'd proposed this situation? But then she hadn't exactly rejected the idea. She'd found a way to make the situation work for her. So was he really scraping the barrel to find fault with the very thing he'd orchestrated? And for a commendable goal, no less?

What was wrong with being wanted for himself, for once, with no strings attached? He sucked in a breath as the unwanted answer arrived. The only thing she'd demanded was help for her children's care home. And he…selfishly wanted that sort of care and consideration for himself.

Thee mou, was he that much of a monster? He allowed the sourness in his chest to expand. He was the recent recipient of bad news. He had a right to handle it whatever way he saw fit.

So he poured himself another drink, took a sip before he answered. And as he did, a curious little notion thrust itself into his thoughts. This was why he'd come here. Because he'd known she would ask about his grandfather. That he'd answer, and, in so doing, perhaps ease the burden of having to carry this alone.

Because that was their pattern, wasn't it? Over the years, she'd toss out questions about cases he was working on, seemingly under the guise of offhand conversation. He would answer. And before long, the conundrum would unravel itself as she waltzed out of his office, her curvy hips swinging and those long legs he was having trouble dragging his gaze from making his blood heat.

He pursed his lips, unwilling to admit to himself that

she'd become…vital. That made him dependent. Dependence led to nothing but disappointment. His father had hammered that reality home time and again. And his mother, after years of being beaten down, had given up entirely, leaving a young and helpless Christos to fend for himself.

'A heart condition,' he bit out, the need to get the words out chafing his skin. 'Any strain could lead to his condition worsening.'

Concern clouded her face. 'Shouldn't he be in hospital seeking treatment?'

His throat tightened, strangling the words. 'The only treatment is an operation. Which he's refusing, apparently.'

'But…can't you do anything?'

The very question he'd posed to his grandfather's doctor. 'I can't force him. As long as he's kept calm the decline will be slow.'

She advanced further into the room, her hand dropping from her hair after pushing the heavy, silky mass from her face. Now that he'd seen her hair loose, he was at risk of becoming absorbed with the way the chestnut waves gleamed in the sunlight.

'But he won't get better either, so what can you do?'

'He instructed his doctor to tell me that under no circumstances was I to attempt to sway him into seeking further medical help. He's taking his condition under advisement… until after his birthday, which is in two weeks.'

'What? But that's…emotional blackmail.'

A smile twisted his lips. 'Of sorts, yes.'

'What options do you have?'

'None. It looks like Costas has won this round. Until he can be convinced otherwise, he's very much in charge.'

Christos watched her eyes widen. She knew him well enough to know he didn't like operating under another's thumb.

He rotated tense shoulders. 'I need a shower. Then I need to talk to my grandfather.' It wasn't a conversation he was looking forward to having but then, when had any conversation with his family been easy? He could count on the fingers of one hand the moments of joy in his life. Most of them had happened while he was alone. All of them were tied to this island. A part of him he wasn't willing to deny any more accepted that this was why he wanted Drakonisos so badly.

Alexis nodded. Then, for the first time since she'd walked in, she looked…hesitant. As if she wanted to offer an opinion. Or an empathetic shoulder to cry on.

Christos knew which option he wanted. He wanted to forget the last forty minutes. Wanted to turn back time. To the plane? No, to that moment in his penthouse two months ago. On his sofa. That hadn't been a solitary moment. That had been an intense pleasure they'd shared. And it had felt…very good indeed.

'Can I do anything?' she said eventually, and he was hit with acute disappointment. Because he would've liked her to offer comfort of a different sort.

Aware he was reverting to his baser instincts, once more, he prowled forward. 'You know your way around, *ne*? If not, I'm sure the staff will point you in the right direction. I'll find you when I'm done.'

He walked past her. Past the evocative scent lingering on her skin. Those alluring eyes trailing after him. And even as he undressed and stepped beneath the shower, he couldn't dispel her image from his mind. The image of the lips he wanted to drown in, so he could forget his grandfather's mortality hung in the balance.

Tight-jawed after several minutes of failing to bring himself under control, he twisted the shower knob to cold, then solemnly accepted his punishment.

* * *

His grandfather, most likely alerted to Christos's conversation with his doctor, was waiting for him. And the first salvo Costas delivered sent him reeling.

'I'm sorry, can you repeat that?' Christos asked in shock.

'You're not deaf. You've known of my desire to see you married with a family of your own since you were a child, Christos. You have until the party to convince me that you're not trying to deceive me with this so-called marriage of yours, or I'll hand over Drakonisos to your cousin. He's already got a family, after all.'

Thought of a possible double loss of his grandfather and his beloved island drove a cold sweat down his spine but he refused to cower. 'Perhaps I should let you and then simply buy it off Georgios,' he countered.

'You can try. You won't succeed. Contingencies are written into my will.'

'Why are you doing this to me, Pappous?'

His grandfather's lips twisted. 'You forget that I was married for over half a century. I know what lust looks like, Christos.'

'So you want me to prove myself to you by pawing my wife in front of you?' As distasteful as the words sounded, he couldn't stop the sliver of red-hot desire that slithered through him. And as much as he wanted to despise himself for it, he couldn't quite summon the outrage.

His grandfather grimaced. 'I'm not that crass, Christos. But you didn't deny that you're living apart. And you dancing around each other only supports my impression that all this is just a production put on to placate me. I'm simply giving you an opportunity to prove me wrong.'

Christos knew that to argue with his grandfather—the man who knew him better than any other living soul—would be useless.

His only solution was to step up to the plate and deliver.

That traitorous sliver grew into a solid vein, pulsing with excitement and…anticipation.

'Where are we going?'

Christos took her hand in his—because if there were spies in England reporting his activities back to Costas, then there were spies in his grandfather's household—and led her into the living room. 'Costas is determined this party is going ahead.'

She frowned. 'You couldn't talk him out of it?'

'Since I don't relish banging my head against a brick wall, I didn't even try.'

'Okay…' Her hand trembled within his and her gaze dropped to the fingers he was slowly—unbeknownst to him—meshing with his.

'First things first, we need to prepare you for the party.'

She frowned. 'Prepare me?'

He nodded to the large TV screen. 'There are three stylists at your disposal. Choose what you need, no expense spared.'

'I have my own clothes, Christos.'

'As my assistant, you have a clothing allowance. Why should this be any different as my wife?'

Shadows crossed her eyes, gone before he could work out which expression they'd projected. A minute later, her pursed-lipped smile was contained, her nod diplomatic as she settled down on the sofa, crossed her long shapely legs and stared coolly back at him. 'Okay, let's get on with it, then,' she said.

Again that image of her in the plane returned, more forceful than before. He banished it before it could take control of his blood again, sending it streaming south. He pressed the remote and the first designer appeared on the screen.

He let the effusive greetings wash over him while he watched Alexis. His reference to work hadn't quite pleased her. Why? Because she wasn't averse to making this… personal? He shifted in his seat, the pervasive heat in his groin determined to make its presence felt despite his iron control.

Focusing his attention on the screen, he cut across the greetings. 'This isn't about me, Agatha. Save your enthusiasm for Alexis. She's the one in need of your services.'

He saw Alexis's eyes widen a touch before she regained control. 'I prefer simple lines in evening gowns,' she said, her voice a touch husky.

Agatha, after a moment of frank appraisal, nodded. 'Yes, of course.' She clicked her fingers to someone off-screen and a clothes rail appeared beside her. 'I have several here for you. Is the event black tie?'

Alexis glanced at him, one eyebrow raised. He shook his head, settled deeper into his seat and, to his eternal surprise, didn't die of boredom as the designer began displaying gown after gown for her inspection.

What he did do was observe Alexis, perhaps more keenly than he'd ever done before. And during that scrutiny, he was reminded that he didn't know much about her, save for her curious need to save a certain orphanage, the rumours about her entanglement with her previous boss and the fact that his assistant was currently single.

His *wife.*

For the duration of their time on Drakonisos, he needed to stop thinking of Alexis as his executive assistant and more as his wife. After all, if he was putting distance between himself and that truth, so would others.

He returned his attention to the clothing audition, saw the gown Agatha held. 'My wife will take that one. Add it to the pile,' he said of a turquoise gown that he was certain would look exquisite against her flawless skin.

On screen, Agatha gaped in surprise. Beside him, Alexis's breath caught.

He reclaimed her hand, meshing his fingers through hers. 'Do you like it?' he asked, voice pitched low as he nodded at the gown.

Eyes wide and a touch guarded, Alexis nodded. 'It's beautiful. I was about to add it to the collection.'

He raised their joint hands, brushed his lips over her knuckles. Felt a shiver unravel through her. 'Good. Keep going,' he instructed, settling back with her hand on his thigh.

'I…um…can I see that peach one?'

Christos curbed a smile, the wicked thought that he'd come within striking distance of ruffling Alexis's feathers pleasing him. When she attempted to extract her fingers surreptitiously a minute later, he tightened his grip.

Eight gowns later, Agatha was dispatched with instructions to courier them to Drakonisos and he was dialling the next designer. Marlene was equally effusive, just as predictably stunned when he addressed Alexis as his wife.

While he hadn't purposefully hidden his marriage from the world, his notorious need for privacy had made tabloid journalists give up on unearthing gossip about him a long time ago. It seemed he'd done too good a job if no one in his native Greece knew he was no longer single.

Twelve gowns later, Alexis determinedly pulled her fingers from his. Reluctantly, he let go. 'I think I have enough to be getting on with.'

'Of course, Mrs Drakakis. And may I offer my congratulations again on your marriage?' Marlene said.

Alexis gave a stiff nod. 'Thank you.'

Christos was busy absorbing the primitive possessiveness mushrooming through his system at hearing her addressed as *Mrs Drakakis* when Alexis clicked off the screen and turned to him. 'What are you doing?'

The arm he'd thrown over the back of the seat rested inches from her shoulder, his fingers brushing her silky hair. Unable to resist, he let the strands caress the back of his hand, mildly stunned by the sudden pulse of arousal on recalling how it had felt to bury his fingers in that glorious chestnut mass. 'Marlene is a rabid gossip. News of our marriage will be all over Athens before the hour is out. Since Georgios has been busier than I thought, we have a lot of ground to make up.'

Her lower lip disappeared between her teeth, sparking further fireworks in his blood. 'You know her well enough to trust her to be your carrier pigeon?'

He shrugged. 'We've crossed paths a few times.'

Her nostrils fluttered and her lashes swept down. 'Do I want to know?'

'Not if I want to tarnish my image as the soul of discretion. But I'm pleased you're jealous,' he teased.

She scowled. 'Don't be ridiculous. I'm not jealous. I meant do I want to know in case I have to…in case we cross paths?'

It felt like the most natural thing in the world to brush his fingers over her hot cheek. To watch her eyes turn liquid, hear her breath become a little jagged. A perfect reaction for anyone who might be watching. Regardless, the push and pull of it, the fact that Alexis wasn't falling eagerly into his arms like every woman he'd known since reaching sexual maturity, was a unique experience he was growing addicted to. 'You look a little…hot, *glykia mou*. Perhaps a swim before we get ready for dinner?' he asked.

She frowned. 'What's going on, Christos? You're acting…different.'

He shrugged. 'Perhaps it's the island air.'

When her gaze remained sceptical, his gut tightened. After several moments, she nodded. 'A swim would be nice.'

He chose the larger of the two pools at the villa because it was overlooked by his grandfather's suite. Or so he told himself twenty minutes later when they stopped beside twin loungers and he took her hand and lifted it to his lips.

He tightened his grip when she attempted to pull away. 'Stop. Costas is watching.'

She stilled, then swallowed. 'That doesn't mean you… that we have to—'

He stopped her words by passing a thumb over her lips. 'On the contrary, *yineka mou*, it means exactly that.'

'Christos—'

'I like the breathy way you say my name. I'm almost convinced you want to kiss me just as much as I want to kiss you.'

'Don't be ridiculous!'

A smile slashed his face, but Alexis noticed the slight tension around the edges. For some reason, it made her shiver in anticipation. He clearly felt it course through her, his eyes darkening in direct response.

Then every single word of protest locked in her throat as he slowly tilted her face up, as his fierce gaze combed her face, lingering with blatant sensuality on her lips. Lips that tingled with every second he held them both in suspense. In the far recesses of her mind, she knew this was just for show. But, sweet heaven, her every reaction felt real, right down to the sharp sting in her nipples, the hot need burning between her thighs. That essential urge to raise her hands, place them on his warm, virile skin, experience the sleek movement of his hard-packed muscles.

It was a need a million times more potent, more urgent than she'd felt in the distant past when she'd once believed herself in love. And that made it almost…frightening. Because if she felt like this with Christos over the mere promise of a kiss, then what—

The thought shattered as his lips brushed over hers. Once. Twice.

Then he was claiming her in a vivid, ferocious kiss that jerked her hands to his waist for fear she'd fall if...*when* her knees gave out. Because his kiss was intoxicating, that stroke of his tongue, once he'd breached her lips, the stuff of pure addiction.

A moan escaped her, triggering a grunt from him. Then he was gathering her closer, his arm banding her waist, lifting her against him until her toes left the ground, left reality. Her breasts, heavy and needy, plastered against his chest, her belly cradling his hardening arousal.

'Thee mou,' he rasped under his breath.

The raw sentiment echoed inside Alexis, a distant voice urging her to take note of the ground shifting beneath her feet, of the need to withdraw, stabilise herself before it was too late.

But then his hand was moving over her body, gripping and releasing her hip, then cupping her buttock. Alexis gasped all over again, the sound greedily swallowed into his mouth when he rolled his hips against hers, imprinting his erection in a blatant caress that fired heatwaves through her.

'As much as I like the feel of those nails of yours sinking into my skin, we're at risk of this turning scandalously graphic if we don't control ourselves,' he murmured darkly in her ear.

And by that he meant her, of course. Because she'd completely lost track of her surroundings, had only been intent on satisfying the clawing hunger inside her. But it hadn't been just that. There'd been a weighty need to...belong. To hold on to him and not let go, if only for a little while. To be a part of something good and worthy. Something she didn't have to give up, like the friends the nuns at Hope House had cautioned her against making.

This is an orphanage.

Nothing is permanent.

Don't form attachments.

Short, simple warnings that had epitomised the paucity of entanglements she'd experienced as a child. She'd made the mistake of disregarding them a few times and been rewarded with heartbreak when those fragile friendships had broken before they'd had a chance to properly kindle. And of course, once the children had left, they'd never looked back. She'd particularly felt the truth of the nuns' warnings the two times she'd come within a whisker of being adopted only to be returned to Hope House because *it didn't work out*.

'Did he make you feel like this?'

She blinked, focused back on the drop-dead gorgeous face of Christos. Of *her husband*. 'I…what?'

'West,' he said through teeth that sounded gritted. 'Did he make you tremble like this?' he demanded, his voice containing a harsh edge.

The shock of hearing Adrian's name made her push against him. She attempted to cover it up by laughing as she stepped back, distancing herself from her turbulent feelings and her body's desire to cling to him. The world hadn't quite righted itself after that kiss, so she sat down on the lounger, snatching up her glass just for something to occupy her hands with. 'Now it's my turn to ask if you're jealous.'

He didn't bat the question away with the same flippancy she'd attempted. Instead, he claimed his own seat, picked up his glass and stared into its contents. 'Your time with me has repeatedly demonstrated that you're an exemplary judge of character. Which makes me wonder what happened with him.'

She went icy cold. 'And you think I was so blinded by lust that my common sense went out the window?'

His face grew tauter, his nostrils flaring with displeasure. 'Were you?'

'Christos—'

'Did you believe yourself in love with him?' he pressed, his voice a thin blade.

That niggling shame for losing her head over such a consummate smooth-talker threatened to resurface. But she reminded herself she hadn't done anything wrong. So she raised her chin and met Christos's gaze. 'I thought we had a…connection. That I could trust him. I discovered I was wrong.'

'He betrayed you,' he stated with a conviction that stunned her.

'Yes.'

'How?' he pushed, those eyes holding her in place.

'I don't see how that's important.'

Christos's eyes stayed fixed on her face for an age, causing her senses to tingle. Making her wonder if he could see her shame. Whether he was judging her for it. 'It's important because I don't want his influence to be the yardstick you judge me by. Tell me, Alexis.'

Perhaps it was knowing she'd done exactly that that made her confess. 'He was a junior associate when we met. He needed an assistant who knew what they were doing, who was prepared to go above and beyond. He wanted to be on the fast track to making partner.'

'He spotted your talent and exploited it to his own ends.'

Her skin tightened in remembered humiliation. 'Something like that. I set aside my studies to be a paralegal to help him reach his goals. I gave him everything he asked for, told myself it didn't matter that he wanted to keep our relationship a secret from his friends and colleagues. Then in the week he made partner, I found out he had a long-term fiancée. I confronted him. And…'

'And?'

'He tried to gaslight me. Told me it'd all been in my

head. He no-hard-feelingsed his way through it. Said it'd just been a bit of fun. Nothing special.'

She chanced a furtive glance at him, her breath catching at his livid expression.

'You didn't believe him, of course,' he said.

She glanced away, the indelible reminder of her rejection at birth latching on despite his imperious declaration. 'Not all of it, no.'

He caught her chin in his hand, redirected her gaze to his. 'Believe *none* of it, Alexis. And trust me when I say users like that never amount to much. But I'm pleased that his loss was my gain.'

Far too perturbed by how his words made her feel, how very easily they went towards salving the hurt inside her, she tried to move away. His fingers encircled her wrist, holding her still.

'I must insist though that his influence on you ends here. I won't have our intimacies blemished with him.'

She huffed at his audacity. 'You're the one who brought him up. And how exactly are you going to achieve...whatever it is you're implying?'

He gave a shrewd smile and released her. 'You'll find out in due course.'

Alexis forced herself to rise and walk calmly to the edge of the swimming pool. To not give in to the dizzying sensation coursing through her stomach that warned her to flee from the dark promise in Christos's voice.

Because rather than be outraged, as she executed a perfect dive into the deliciously cool waters of the pool, all she could feel was...an electric thrill.

CHAPTER SEVEN

FAR FROM DISSIPATING with time, that sensation expanded as the afternoon drifted into evening. Fresh from blow-drying and curling her hair and on her way to the vast dressing room, Alexis stopped in her tracks at the French doors leading to the private terrace, dazzled by the play of brilliant orange and gold light over the turquoise waters.

She stepped outside, breathing in air redolent with salt, citrus and sunshine, half hoping it would calm some of the chaos raging inside her. She wasn't surprised when it didn't, but she still basked in the beauty of her surroundings for another minute before heading back inside.

Christos had disappeared after the incident by the pool, while she'd retreated to the smaller of the villa's two libraries, then walked on the beach for an hour before returning indoors.

She'd been glad for the reprieve from Christos, feeling mildly terrified of what she'd revealed. So what if she felt a little naked and vulnerable after blurting out her pain? But when it came down to it, what could he do with the information? Her emotions hadn't affected her work so far, and they wouldn't in the future either.

Alexis repeated that mantra to herself as she chose a knee-length white dress with a wide black belt and black butterfly-wing sleeves, paired with elegant monochrome platform heels and, for a splash of colour, a jade necklace and earring set she'd treated herself to at Christmas. Two dabs of perfume behind her ears and a dash of lip gloss and she was ready.

Downstairs, a maid materialised in the hallway and directed her to Costas's favourite terrace located in the east wing, directly beneath his suite. From memory, she guessed that Christos might be having his pre-dinner ouzo with his grandfather.

On the cosy little terrace, candles shone from an ornate candelabra, illuminating the exquisitely laid table and bathing its occupants in soft light. Alexis paused, unseen, at the door, the resemblance between the two men with their attention focused intently on each other catching at her.

Regardless of whatever tensions existed between them, they were family. Devoted to one another on a primal level she'd yearned for since she was old enough to know what family meant. She inhaled shakily, willing the longing away.

Even if she hadn't sworn off relationships, attempting to form one with Christos would've been foolhardy, especially in light of his unvarnished confirmation that anything that happened between them would be purely physical. Their agreement was still finite, still a quid pro quo arrangement counting down to the moment he took possession of Drakonisos.

Nevertheless, that curious little fizzing in her belly ignited as her gaze landed on him. She battled the sensation by quickly looking at his grandfather.

Costas looked much better than he had this afternoon. The lopsided half-smile so reminiscent of his grandson came easier, and there was a tranquillity about him, perhaps now he'd got what he wanted?

Knowing she risked being rude with her tardiness, she stepped onto the terrace. Christos's gaze swung to her, then conducted a slow appraisal as he rose and pulled out her chair.

'There you are. I was wondering whether I'd need to come and fetch you.'

'I dissuaded him. I couldn't risk him getting sidetracked

and finding myself once again enjoying dinner for one,' Costas tagged on dryly.

Catching his meaning, Alexis couldn't stop the heat that rushed into her face. Nor could she stop Christos from brushing his lips over one hot cheek in greeting. 'Be warned, *glykia mou*. He's in an incorrigible mood.'

Pulse racing, she forced a smile as she took her chair, struggling not to breathe in Christos's mind-scrambling masculine scent. 'Good evening, Costas. I'm sorry to have kept you waiting.'

The old man shrugged. 'I've been kept waiting a moment or two in my time. My late wife was fond of telling me that practising patience would earn me rewards. A tough lesson to start off with, but one I eventually learned to appreciate.'

'Wine? Or ouzo?' Christos offered as he retook his seat.

She wanted to say neither. The ground hadn't quite re-settled beneath her feet since this afternoon, and she was loath to further upset her equilibrium.

But, aware of two sets of stormy grey eyes staring at her, she sensed refusing might draw disapproval, maybe even offend her host. 'I'll try some ouzo, thanks.'

Costas smiled, his eyes warming further with approval as he sat back in his chair. '*Kalos.* I have an exclusive ouzo distiller two islands away. He sent this batch in today. Tell me what you think,' he said, pouring a thankfully small measure of the cloudy white drink into a crystal glass.

As she accepted the offering, she spotted the Drakonisos label in sleek blue and silver lettering, because of course Christos's grandfather would have his own brand. A small sip and the aromatic flavour of anise and cardamom burst onto her tongue.

She'd attended enough functions with Christos to have had the opportunity of sampling ouzo before. But she recognised superiority and authenticity when she tasted it. 'It's the best I've ever tried,' she said honestly.

Costas beamed, then his grandson followed suit with a slow smile that ignited flames at her feet that slowly scorched upward throughout her body.

She tried to limit herself to small sips but by the time the first course of stuffed vine leaves and roasted peppers was served, Costas was pouring her a second glass.

By unspoken agreement, she didn't mention his illness, and neither did Christos. Instead they spoke extensively about his shipping company, with Alexis noting that each time Georgios's name came up, Christos stiffened.

'Are you looking forward to your party?' she asked during their main course of moussaka with tomato and feta salad.

'It should be interesting,' Costas drawled after a contemplative moment, his deep rumbling tone indicative of what his grandson's would be like in a few decades. 'There are those who are still curious as to why my grandson chose to marry his bride in secrecy and hasn't made any attempt to introduce her to other members of his family.'

Her gaze darted to Christos, her heart thudding at the thought that she'd fallen into a trap. His lips pursed, his eyes flicking away from hers to narrow warningly on Costas. 'The most important family member has already met my bride. To everyone else, what I do is none of their business.'

Costas shrugged, a wicked gleam in his eyes. But behind it, she saw a shadow of pain. 'I'm merely relaying the family's sentiments. Especially your mother's.'

Christos visibly tensed, the hand holding his fork momentarily tightening before he eased his grip. 'My whereabouts aren't a state secret. She's known where I've been since the last time we saw each other.'

'Perhaps she didn't think she'd be welcome,' Costas parried.

Christos tossed his napkin on the table and picked up his wine glass. Unlike his grandfather, he'd stuck to a full-bodied Merlot, which he now swirled lazily despite the uneven tic in his jaw. 'If she wants advance reassurance of what her reception would be, I'm afraid she's going to be disappointed.'

Other than a mild grimace, Costas showed no outward sign of censure or disappointment at Christos's answer. 'Does the same apply to your father?'

Christos's expression grew icier. '*Ne*, very much so.'

Costas's gaze turned contemplative as he set his glass down. 'You inherited many traits from me, including my stubbornness. As much as I want to, I can't fault you for that. All I can advise is that you limit the fallout.'

'Is this your way of telling me they're both attending your party?' Christos bit out.

'Your father is my son, Christos. I cannot forbid him from attending.'

Christos raised a mocking eyebrow. 'You expect me to believe that you have no control over your own guest list?'

Costas bared his teeth, his enjoyment of the tense tussle evident. 'Maybe I do. But I despise gossip. And news that I've banned my own son from attending a birthday celebration is bound to set far too many tongues wagging.'

'You live on a private island and dictate who sets foot on it. I dare say outside gossip doesn't bother you too much.'

'But its effect on my company's share value does,' he retorted. 'And as a major shareholder, it should matter to you too.'

Alexis had to hand it to the old man for the neat counterargument. As a top-notch lawyer, Christos had a reputation steeped in solid evidence, but he also understood the power of perception. Any rumours of trouble within the Drakakis family were bound to have public repercussions.

Silence descended over the table, Christos's eyes remaining shadowed as he sipped his wine.

To her relief, the silence was broken a minute later by

the arrival of after-dinner coffee. Alexis took the opportunity to make her escape. 'I'm afraid I'll have to decline. I've already passed my two-cups-a-day tally. Another on top of the ouzo will leave me wired and wide awake for hours.'

A layer of shadow left Christos's eyes as they rose to meet hers. 'I'll be up shortly. Between us I think we can come up with a way to dissipate any nervous energy that needs expending,' he drawled, the blatant sexual intent behind his words sending a wave of heat into her face.

Costas laughed at whatever expression she'd shown as she strove for composure. 'How refreshing to see you can still make your bride blush, Christos.'

The glare she sent Christos behind her pasted-on smile earned her another heated look. 'Yes, it is indeed refreshing,' he concurred.

'I'll leave you two on this high note you seem to be having. Goodnight.'

Costas nodded at her, his smile still warm, while Christos merely watched her leave, the hyperawareness sinking into her skin telling her his gaze remained on her until she stepped through the French doors. Alexis chose to dwell on the transformation in the old man, to see it as a win, rather than on the just-for-show sexual gauntlet Christos had tossed at her.

She fully intended to be in bed, fast asleep, by the time he came up. Going on previous visits, he'd most likely retreat to his study after dinner to check on his priority cases before turning in. She hurried through her bedtime routine, slipping on her peach satin night slip before diving under the covers. She groaned as the sumptuous sheets welcomed her. But an hour later, wide-eyed and heart pounding, she hated herself for listening out for the door.

She squeezed her eyes shut when Christos turned the handle, her heartbeat roaring in her ears. For the next ten minutes she listened to him moving around his dressing room, images of him undressing infusing further heat through her bloodstream.

Perhaps it was because she was so preoccupied with calming her runaway libido that she didn't at first realise what was happening. But when the mattress suddenly shifted, she pivoted towards the man who was easing himself into bed beside her. The half-naked man, dressed in a pair of black silk pyjama bottoms and nothing else.

'What are you doing?' she semi-squeaked, the sight of him drying her throat.

Christos paused, that infernal eyebrow cocked, the slightly dishevelled hair falling over his forehead lending him a dangerously rakish look that made her fingers convulse on the covers she clutched.

'It seems fairly obvious, *yineka mou*,' he said.

'But we…you…normally sleep on the sofa when we're here,' she said, her voice curiously breathless.

Except this time, he didn't retreat to it. No, he was tossing half of his pillow mountain to the floor, then plumping one of the remaining ones, the muscles in his six-pack contracting in a way that made her fingers itch to experience that warm flesh the way she'd explored him by the pool this afternoon.

'I thought we'd established our new course of action?'

'Yes, but I didn't think you'd…invite yourself into my bed, just like that!' God, why did her tongue feel so thick in her mouth? Why was her feminine core tingling so wildly? So needily?

'Technically, this is my bed too. But you can relax, Alexis. I'm not about to pounce on you.'

I wish you would.

She nearly gasped out loud at the torrid thought. 'I should think not,' she said, inserting a sharpness into her tone that was at direct variance with the slow melting in her pelvis caused by the sight of him lying there, both arms tucked behind his head and his heavy-lidded gaze on the ceiling. Dear God, as if he didn't have a single care in the world. Whereas she was being turned inside out with intensifying cravings she feared she would never conquer.

Think practical, unsexy thoughts.

Her brain's response was to produce even more lurid images, all of them of that bronzed perfection on display. And what…*wasn't.*

She swallowed, wishing she could turn her back on him. But even that was impossible. Doing so would show weakness. Give him the impression that his overwhelmingly masculine presence threatened to shatter her control.

'Sleeping on the sofa is no longer an option. Not without giving up all the ground we made this afternoon. Besides, if knowledge serves me right, you tend to stick to your side of the bed, even when you sleep alone. My presence shouldn't have to change that.'

'Should I be worried that you know my sleeping habits?'

His teeth flashed in the semi-darkness. 'I'm extremely observant. Especially about the things that matter.'

She didn't want that melting feeling in her belly to intensify. Didn't want to take his words anywhere except at face value. Yet, she found herself turning towards him, her grip on the sheets easing when they should've been doing the opposite.

Christos Drakakis had probably never lacked for female attention since his teenage years. Beyond that, his deeply ingrained integrity assured her he wouldn't force himself where he wasn't wanted.

And that was the problem.

Alexis couldn't deny the escalating need that only seemed to swell whenever he was here. Having him here in her bed—in *their* bed—wasn't a temptation she wanted to test. But short of insisting he relocate, or relocating herself, she was left with only this option.

'You're overthinking this, *matia mou*,' he drawled, right before he tugged the sheet firmly up his torso. 'At this rate, it's not the coffee that'll keep you up but whatever thoughts are spinning through that brain of yours.'

The bed was wide enough. Hell, it could accommodate a small family at a pinch. And it was the last word in luxury and comfort. Still, she took the largest pillow she could find and wedged it between them. As if that would protect her.

As if his scent wasn't already infiltrating the space between them, curling around her senses and drawing her in.

Alexis wasn't sure how long she lay there, fighting tension in her body and wild thoughts in her head. Eventually, the sound of his deep, rhythmic breathing leached the strain from her body. She exhaled, long and slow, careful not to make a sound as she turned her head to watch him.

Sweet heaven, he was breathtaking.

A Greek god made flesh, sculpted with devotion and precision, with heaps of arrogance and elegance and mastery thrown in. Even in sleep, he remained a formidable presence, his cheekbones casting sharp shadows mitigated only by the lush sweep of his sooty lashes and soft curl of his sensual lips.

Lips she'd tasted.

Lips she wanted to taste again.

With a low moan of frustration, she turned on her side. Away from temptation.

Alexis opened her eyes what felt like minutes later to pure sunlight.

It took a moment for her to register that it was the remote-controlled parting of the curtains that had awoken her. That and the soft knock at the door.

She turned and lifted her head, a little dazed, to see Christos crossing the room. At the sight of his bare back, memories of last night flooded in, heating her body anew as he opened the door, his voice a low rumble as he let in the maid carrying a fully laden breakfast tray.

Acutely aware of her body's response, and the fact that she'd just experienced her first full night in bed with a man, albeit a non-sexual one—Adrian had always found an excuse to leave her flat before morning, presumably to return to his fiancée—she stayed frozen. Christos, still sporting decadently low-riding pyjama bottoms, and showing off his sculpted torso and designer stubble in the dazzling sunlight, thanked the maid and took possession of the tray.

Alexis looked away from the sleek synergy of muscles as he approached. Reaching her side of the bed, he paused, one eyebrow arched at her.

'You're going to have to let go of that pillow and untangle yourself from those covers if you want breakfast,' he drawled. 'Or would you prefer me to feed you?'

She glared at him, his mockery triggering another infernal blush, and slowly unclenched her fingers. 'That won't be necessary,' she snapped.

With a far too devastating smirk, he stepped forward, waited for her to sit up and tug the covers up her chest so he could settle the tray on her lap.

She managed to pour two cups of coffee without spilling it everywhere, then averted her eyes again once he'd accepted his and perched his large frame at the side of the bed. The slant of sunlight indicated the sun had risen a while ago. 'What time is it? And why aren't we having breakfast with your grandfather?'

'It's just after nine, and this—' he indicated the tray with his free hand '—is because I'd like us to be…easy with each other.'

She barely managed to stop herself from snorting. It was like asking a bird to be intimate friends with an active volcano, or a boa constrictor with a mouse. In both scenarios *she* would be the loser.

So she concentrated on the part of conversation that was least dangerous. 'Once we're done here, I'll set myself up in the study, see if there's anything urgent requiring your—'

His finger on her lips halted the rest of the words, and some of that volcanic heat she dreaded threatened to engulf her body.

'There's no need. I've already been in touch with the office. The only urgent thing is the investigator's report on Demitri's case. It'll be ready this afternoon. But the case may well conclude before the weekend is over.'

She drew back from his touch with lips tingling and a reluctance that unnerved her. 'How?'

His face tightened a fraction and his hand dropped to the bed, dangerously close to her bare thigh. 'His wife looks set to accept the financial incentive she was offered.'

Anguish caught her on the raw. 'She's accepting money to give up her own child?'

'You'd be surprised how much money and power influences parenthood.' The bitterness in his voice drew her gaze to his face. Just like last night, his gaze was shadowed, the stubble giving him an even more forbidding look.

'Is that…did your parents…?'

The cold, warning look he slanted at her made her words trail off. 'I don't wish to start our day with indigestion. What I meant to tell you was that I've cleared the calendar for the next few days, so, barring any unforeseen circumstances, you're free to use your time as you wish.'

'Oh… I…thanks.'

'You seem underwhelmed by the offer.'

She shook her head, confusion still making her hazy. 'It's not that. It's just, I haven't really had a holiday for a while. I'm not sure what to do with myself.' Her words echoed in her head and she grimaced. 'That came out much more pathetic than I wanted it to. It's just that—'

'Work has dominated your time in my employ?'

She nodded. 'Something like that.'

'You're not hinting that your boss has been a tyrant, are you?' he drawled, amusement in his tone as he bit into a plump peach.

Alexis felt butterflies dance in her belly as she watched him chew and swallow, then leant forward to pile her plate with food. 'I didn't say that.'

'Good. Eat up. You've hardly seen the island despite this being your third visit. Let's remedy that.'

At some point before she'd fallen asleep last night, she'd planned on doing exactly that. But she'd imagined doing it alone, not in the company of the most dynamic man she'd ever known. 'I can explore on my own. You don't have to accompany me.'

Slowly narrowing stormy grey eyes rested on her. 'Don't I?'

'If you're concerned about giving Costas a certain impression, you could always cite work?' she suggested, a tad desperately.

'My presence affects you that much?' A loaded question, which added another shovelful of coal to the flames burning in her belly.

'Of course not,' she denied.

'Then it's settled.'

With that final proclamation, he drew one leg onto the bed, fully facing her, then pushed her plate at her. The rest of their breakfast passed with Christos suggesting what to pack, and how long they'd be, before reaching for the bedside phone to instruct the staff on where to deliver their lunchtime picnic.

He relieved her of the tray when she was done, then sauntered back to the bed, the blaze in his eyes jangling her nerves. 'I take it there will be no further problems going forward now we've spent the night in the same bed?'

Heat rising to her face, she met his gaze. 'I…suppose not.'

'Hmm, such a rousing endorsement.' He stopped beside her, then, without warning, his fingers trailed down her cheek. 'The way you blush, *matia mou*. I'm almost tempted to test the boundaries of your innocence.'

'I'm not innocent. And I'd thank you not to toy with me.'

A mirthless smile lifted one corner of his mouth. 'Toying is the last thing on my mind.'

'Christos…'

His eyes turned turbulent, a raging storm of emotions that held her breath trapped in her lungs. Slowly, his fingers trailed to her mouth, his thumb passing over her lower lip, just like yesterday. *'Ne,'* he murmured, as if pleased with something. Before she could command herself to move away, he stepped back. 'Meet me downstairs in half an hour.'

He walked away with a long-legged stride she couldn't help but gape at.

Showering in record time, she chose a burnt-orange bikini over which she wore a white sundress and low-heeled flip-flops. After securing her hair in a ponytail, she threw on some costume jewellery. In her beach bag, she packed sunscreen, lip gloss and, on a desperate whim, her work tablet.

Christos was waiting when she emerged from the long hallway attached to the south wing.

The black golf buggy was sleek and powerful-looking. But it was the man behind the wheel who captured her attention. His slightly damp hair looked finger-combed; he'd probably showered while she was locked in her dressing room anxious about what to wear for a day of leisure with her…husband.

She looked up to find his gaze conducting an equally frank appraisal of his own. Suddenly, Alexis was super conscious of the thinness of her sundress, of the short hem brushing her thighs. Of her bare legs and the soft breeze that whispered through the cypress trees and washed over her sensitive skin.

'Get in, Alexis,' he ordered with a low, deep voice that echoed in her belly.

They headed north, towards the denser part of the island. There he pointed out the olive groves that had once supplied olive oil to the villa but now formed part of the stables for the Andalusian horses Costas kept.

Next, they headed for the craggier part where the cliffs met the sea.

'At sunset, the configuration of the cliffs and the beach gives the impression of a dragon breathing fire. Hence the name.'

'You spent time here as a boy, didn't you?'

A wry smile curved his lips. 'It's not hard to get lost in the draw of a place like this.'

She tried to imagine the picture he evoked. While it wasn't easy to picture the imposing, dynamic man beside her as a child, perhaps even a lonely one, it was easy to conjure up a boy who'd retreated to his imagination for his own entertainment. She'd done the same on countless nights in her single bed in the children's home. Dreamed of the safety and security of an imaginary family and not the loneliness that plagued her day and night.

'Did your grandfather share it with you?'

He didn't answer immediately, his eyes on the sea for several moments before he shook his head. 'Not always. He was preoccupied with my grandmother. But he insisted that I knew how to swim before he set me loose on the island, so he taught me how to swim in the pool.'

Last night's conversation and the look in his eyes this

morning almost stopped her from uttering the words. But although she risked spoiling the magic of their trip, the words tumbled out anyway. 'Where were your parents?'

His face tightened, bleakness shadowing his eyes. 'They were busy starring in the melodrama of their acrimonious divorce.'

That tight, pain-wrapped response brought stunning clarity. 'They're the reason you became a divorce lawyer, aren't they?'

He turned towards her, and even though her breath stalled at the icy contempt in his eyes, she knew it wasn't aimed at her but at his parents. 'Yes. Agios and Nadia Drakakis separated when I was five years old. I lived with my mother for a while. Then mostly with Agios. They dragged out their divorce for ten years. And when they weren't busy going for each other's throats, they used me as a pawn in their little games.'

'How?'

He gave a stiff shrug. 'My father would inform me I was changing schools halfway through a school year simply because he knew it would upset my mother. And me. My mother would suddenly take me out of my new school to go on a month-long holiday to get back at him. Then he would retaliate in another way. I once made the mistake of telling my father I was keeping my hair long because my mother liked it. He took his hair clippers out within the hour.' He paused, his lips thinning in recollection. 'They did this repeatedly, without a care as to what I wanted. Coming here to Drakonisos was my only reprieve, the one thing I looked forward to as a child.'

Sympathy filled her chest. Reaching out, she brushed her fingers over the back of his hand. 'I'm sorry.'

For a moment he looked startled, then he nodded and turned away to stare at the horizon once more. Silence reigned for a few minutes before she summoned the courage to ask what she hoped would be a less fraught question. 'Where was your grandmother?'

A flash of pain crossed his face. 'Here on Drakonisos, but she never got the chance to truly appreciate the island. Costas bought it for her after she was diagnosed with a terminal illness.'

'I'm sorry. I didn't mean to evoke painful memories for you.'

He shrugged. 'It's good that you know something about my past. It'll cause less gossip.'

Right. Their fake marriage. The reason she was here in the first place. Alexis wasn't sure why the reminder hurt.

Silence stretched between them again, longer, tauter this time. A muscle throbbed at his temple as he slowly exhaled. Alexis faced the horizon, trying to block the curious pain blooming in her chest. At least now she knew why he wanted to claim this island so badly.

Abruptly, he reached out for her hand, his gaze telling her this part of their conversation was over. 'Come. I have something else to show you.'

Before she could think about it, she placed her hand in his.

The flare of pleasure in his eyes was gone as quickly as it arrived, but she'd seen it. And deep inside felt a peculiar thrill that she'd pleased him. But even as they boarded the buggy, a niggle remained. One she suspected would grow into a chafe.

Because despite being a part of his professional life for so long, despite being his pretend wife right now, he was shutting her out. Lumping her in with everyone else he held at arm's length.

Why should you be singled out? You think you're special?

She was the one who'd always been left behind. The one discarded by her mother and lied to by her first and only lover. And as much as the reminder bruised her heart, she needed it to keep herself in check. To tell herself that this was simply a moment in time. One soon to be in her rear-view mirror.

They travelled north, and this time when they stopped, she stepped out and accompanied Christos to the edge of a steep cliff with a stunning beach below.

'Wow. That's breathtaking. Is there a way to get down there?'

He nodded, a rare softness stealing over his features. 'I dug steps into the cliff when I was fourteen.' He indicated the rock formation and the frantic waves dashing against them. 'Before that I used to climb down over the rocks.'

She blanched, staring at the jagged peaks. 'That looks incredibly dangerous.'

He shrugged. 'Danger isn't an issue when you believe you're invincible. But, yes, the steps spared my grandmother a grey hair or two.'

The fondness in his voice attracted her gaze. 'Do you miss her?'

Expecting another shrug, she was surprised when he nodded. 'Very much,' he said, then slid her a sideways glance. 'Now you know another interest of mine, in case it comes up.'

She frowned. 'I'd prefer to get to know you organically, rather than have you list interests like I'm compiling a dossier.'

His gaze turned piercingly keen. 'You believe I'm not invested in this? Is that your way of saying you require a more intimate knowledge of me?'

Her mouth dried, her heart see-sawing wildly in her chest. 'That's not what I said!'

Patrician nostrils flared, his hand rising to drag through his wind-ruffled hair. 'But perhaps you're right. Perhaps we should examine this from a different perspective.'

'What do you mean by that?' For a moment she was terrified he was about to call the whole thing off. Even more terrified that the feeling didn't stem from knowing Hope House would suffer. It was purely selfish, born of the need to not be done with this…whatever it was.

But he was speaking. And her breath caught at the words that spilled from his lips.

'Perhaps it needs full and complete authenticity. It needs for you to be my wife, in more than name only.'

CHAPTER EIGHT

IT WAS DIRECTLY because of that wild, unfettered leap in her heart that Alexis pivoted and started to walk away. Deep in her bones she knew that she would've screamed *yes* otherwise.

She stumbled to a halt when he wrapped his fingers around her arm. 'You need time to think about it—'

'No.'

He waited a beat. Two. Then his eyes narrowed. 'No?'

'I don't need to think about it. The answer is no.' Her words were firm enough, but she betrayed herself by trembling a moment after they emerged.

'You're afraid,' he observed shrewdly. 'Why?'

'Because it's absurd?'

'Or because you imagine you can protest this chemistry away?'

She wanted to hate him for hitting the nail on the head. But he'd already seen what she'd tried to hide—that she was attracted to him. Perhaps dangerously so. But the fact that he wanted to act on it didn't mean she had to give in.

Did it?

No.

'Today, tomorrow or a month from now, my answer will still be the same,' she said, glad for the firmness of her voice. Not so much for the dismay and disappointment echoing in her chest. 'I'm not interested.'

His gaze remained pinned, mildly disbelieving and faintly mocking, on her face. 'Prove it,' he taunted after a stretch of time that jangled her every nerve.

Welcome irritation stiffened her spine. 'I don't need to prove anything.'

'Not even to yourself?'

'What are you talking about?'

'If you're so confident this is no big deal to you, that you're not afraid of the power of it, then where's the harm? Haven't you wanted to put me in my place a time or two? Perhaps even a little payback for mankind in general?'

'Don't be ridiculous,' she snapped, even though a part of her wished she did. Even though a part of her wanted *someone* to pay for her hurt. 'I don't hate *all* men just because of the crimes of one.'

She knew she'd fallen into his trap the moment the words left her lips.

'I'm glad to hear it,' he said, smiling as if he knew every single chaotic dance unravelling inside her. 'Here's your chance, Alexis. Are you going to take it or run away?'

It was the smile that made her see red. That triggered a throw-caution-to-the-wind switch she feared she'd regret later. But in that moment, nothing could've stopped her from taking that step. From wrapping one arm around his waist and the other over his nape to urge his head down to hers. Nothing could've stemmed the wild need that drove her onto her toes, bringing his tantalising lips within kissing distance.

At the searing contact, she moaned, her senses already clamouring for more.

With that deep grunt she was growing shockingly addicted to, Christos tugged her closer until they were plastered together from chest to thigh.

Their exploration wasn't tentative. It was a culmination of the dance that had begun in his penthouse and matured in the time in between. Rabid for his taste, she boldly stroked his tongue, then ran hers over his bottom lip, while her nails dug into his warm skin. Pleasure and feminine power exploded through her as she felt his erection swell.

And when his hand cupped one breast, teasing her nipple, Alexis cried out.

He swallowed the sound, deepening the kiss for another minute before, forced apart by the need for oxygen, his lips trailed to her jaw and neck, tonguing her pulse before trailing hot kisses onto her collarbone.

She hazily grew aware of her spaghetti strap being lowered, of the cool breeze washing over her chest. Then his mouth was covering one nipple, drawing the needy peak into his mouth.

'Christos!'

'Hmm,' he growled against her flesh after an age of tormenting her. 'You respond so beautifully,' he said, right before he delivered the same exquisite torture to its twin.

Alexis buried her fingers in his hair, every sense tuned into the magic he was weaving, to the cavernous need demanding satiation. Dear God, this was madness. But not one she wanted to stop. Not in that moment.

'Please,' she found herself whimpering, against every shred of common sense she possessed. Straining for more even as the weight of her need terrified her.

'Yes,' he groaned, laving her expertly for another minute before lifting his head.

For the longest minute, they stared at one another, their breathing choppy. Alexis blushed when he slowly drew up her straps, the sensual glide of his tongue across his lower lip almost making her moan out loud. 'Now tell me this is a bad idea,' he rasped, the wash of colour across his sharp cheekbones making him even more alluring. His eyes blazed with an arousal he did nothing to hide and even the steady rise and fall of his chest was mesmerising.

'In my experience, mixing business with pleasure only has one unfortunate outcome.'

From languorous arousal, his face instantly hardened

into an austere mask. 'Don't judge me by another man's standards. Have I ever lied to you?'

'No,' she answered truthfully. 'But—'

He placed a finger on her lips. 'He was worthless and attempted to tarnish you with the same brush. I know your worth, Alexis.'

Deep, solemn words that shook the very root of her soul. Alexis was stunned by how much she wanted to cling to them. But...wasn't this very urge to cling what had left her devastated in the end? And once this little sexual experiment had ended, then what?

'Our agreement is for three years, Alexis, and there's still two of them left. You might grow bored of me long before then,' he said, although the light in his eyes said the contrary.

She wasn't about to stroke his ego by denying it. Maybe he assumed that because he believed she wasn't the clingy type. Or even the falling-in-love type.

Someone else might have appreciated the unspoken compliment. But his perception was a vice around her chest, a reminder that it was the same reason most families had passed her over as a child. The reason her own mother had abandoned her on a forgettable doorstep. She was unlovable. Good, it seemed, for only a brief fling and nothing more.

'I'm human, Christos. I may develop needs that go beyond just sex.'

For a nanosecond his face shuttered. Then he was back in counterargument mode. The mode he thrived in best. 'And do you intend to deny them all as a whole or will you let me take care of one, in particular? You can rest assured I won't leave you wanting in any way when it comes to sharing my bed,' he said, his voice low and throbbing with the kind of dangerous sexiness that should trigger a definite flight response from her.

Instead, the brazen and unexpected response made her roll her eyes. 'You're certainly not lacking in the sexual ego department, are you?'

His smile was pure arrogance. 'Our chemistry is remarkable. You'd be a fool to let it go to waste when we're tied to each other for the foreseeable future.'

She opened her mouth to dismiss his claim with the contempt it deserved. But slowly, her lips pressed together, that loud drumbeat in her ears warning her that this could be her only chance to experience something this spectacular.

He took the opportunity to step closer, to run his fingers down her cheek, an action he seemed particularly enamoured of. 'Take the afternoon. Think of this,' he murmured, lowering his head to brush his lips lightly over hers. 'And this.' The hand on her cheek trailed down her neck, over her shoulders, to lightly graze over her nipple, causing her to shiver wildly. Against her lips, she felt his conceited smile as his hand strayed even lower, over her belly, aiming for that hot place between her legs. She had ample time to stop him, but every last objection drained away, her senses alive with the need pounding through her, with the hunger to experience what he was offering. 'Then think of my lips here, pleasuring you for hours. Making you come over and over.'

Alexis barely stopped her knees from giving way at the thick promise. His free hand gripped her shoulder, even as the hand between her thighs splayed possessively over her hungry, feminine core. Over her clothes, his fingers boldly caressed her, unerringly finding her most responsive spot and stroking her to a frenzied arousal. Her nails dug into his skin as a delicious haze blinded her.

'Christos…' She wasn't aware she'd thrown her head back until his lips found her pulse, caressing it with lazy strokes that matched the bold ones between her thighs.

'Yes, that is exactly how you will pant my name when I'm inside you. *My* name, *matia mou*. No one else's.'

With that hard-edged edict, he caressed her one last time, then stepped back.

Alexis inhaled desperately as he took her hand and led her back to the buggy.

In the hours after that, he didn't by word or deed reference that insane moment on the cliff edge, morphing into the perfect host as they explored the rustic dwellings that had once formed part of a vineyard but was now turned into a stunning staff quarters for the caretakers of Drakonisos. Alexis was gratified to see that they lacked for nothing, that the same demanding but generous ethic she'd noted in Christos was practised by his grandfather.

She was hot and thirsty by the time Christos stopped the buggy almost three hours later under a clutch of cypress trees at a midway point between north and south.

An elaborate picnic was laid out on a checked blanket, complete with champagne, oysters and an array of mouth-watering Greek food.

'Hungry?'

'I'm starving.'

His gaze dropped to her mouth, setting it tingling. 'Come, then. Let me feed you.'

He alighted, came around to help her off the buggy. And as she dropped down to the blanket and feigned an avid interest in the spread, Alexis was terrified to note she was several degrees hotter and more bothered. And that it had nothing to do with their trek.

The possibility of everything backfiring was strong enough to allow brief moments of misgivings as Christos expertly uncorked the champagne and filled their glasses. But they were nowhere near as strong as the need that simmered beneath his skin, threatening to turn into a blaze at the smallest opportunity.

Sleeping next to Alexis last night had been a special

form of hell. He'd made an excellent job of feigning sleep until she'd stopped fretting long enough to fall asleep. Then it had been his turn to wonder what the hell he was playing at. Why he was torturing himself like this…

For Drakonisos.

For the place that had helped him hang on to a shred of humanity when everything and everyone around him had shown him that life was a hot mess of greed, pain and self-aggrandisement. In his more indulgent moods, he'd even believed the island had reached out loving arms and hugged him when he'd needed it most.

The last thing he would allow was Georgios to turn this into a hedonistic destination for his unsavoury circle of friends. *That* he wasn't prepared to stomach.

He focused on her as Alexis finished admiring the view and turned her gaze on him. That blaze flared up higher.

'This is a beautiful place. I can see why you want to hang on to it.'

He handed her a glass. 'It definitely deserves better than to have it turned into another celebrity hangout or, worse, a destination for a TV reality show.'

Her eyes grew wide. 'That's what your cousin intends to do?'

'Yes. My grandfather isn't the only one with eyes and ears.'

'Does he know?'

'No. And I don't intend to tell him.' Telling Costas to gain an unfair advantage wasn't his style.

She sipped her champagne, then flicked those magnificent eyes at him. 'Even though it might gain you an upper hand?'

'I'm confident Georgios will show his own hand before long.'

'You don't seem to think very highly of him.'

He shrugged. 'Perhaps I would if he didn't expend far

too much time and energy cursing me for advantages he seems to think I earned simply by being born Costas's grandson when he was not. What he doesn't appreciate is that it's the effort you put in, not the blood running through your veins, that matters.'

Her eyes shadowed. 'I wouldn't know, would I?'

He uttered a silent curse. 'No. And that's regrettable. But perhaps you'll take my word for it that the grass isn't always greener on the other side?'

'Is it bad to wish that I'd been given the opportunity to find out for myself?'

A twinge of shame in his chest reminded him why he was doing all of this in the first place—because while his parents had fallen far short of their duties, he'd found an outlet here on Drakonisos thanks to his grandfather. 'No, it isn't,' he found himself responding, his regret piercing deeper.

Her eyes stayed on his a moment longer, an affinity settling between them, before her long-lashed gaze lingered again on the deeper blue waters that slammed against the rocks a short distance away. 'I agree. It'll be a shame to have all this spoilt for the sake of financial gain.'

He'd already concluded that she was…unsettling to his senses. But every time she confirmed how in sync they were, the more he became certain that his plan would work. 'Unfortunately, some people can't think beyond the urge to win at all costs, regardless of how much they have or the consequences of their actions.'

The acid in his voice redirected her gaze to his. His stomach clenched, a part of him wary that she'd delve deeper into what he'd already revealed about his parents.

But again, she surprised him by holding her tongue when others would've seized the opportunity to ferret out more secrets.

They dished out small quiches, cold meats, olives and

sun-dried tomatoes. He passed on the baklava but served her a portion, watching with a compulsion he couldn't stem while she ate it.

'Well, I hope you win,' she said softly after finishing the last bite, and his breath expelled, partly in relief, and partly with an emotion he was loath to name. Because while professionally he had people on his side, personally there'd never been anyone. Even Costas had been preoccupied with his grandmother and her failing health, only granting crumbs of affection to Christos when he could. While he'd gratefully accepted those crumbs, he'd known then it wasn't enough. The hunger in his soul had demanded more. And while he hated to admit it, that lack had scarred him. Enough to put commonplace desires, like love and family, out of his mind.

But one desire he could have. One desire he craved more than anything else. His gaze dropped to her chest. Lower, over her belly to where her dress gathered in her lap. The memory of the sound of her keening arousal, the scent of her femininity, made him grow instantly hard, and he raised his eyes to clash with the liquid chocolate-brown ones he yearned to see flame with passion.

'Don't look at me like that,' she murmured, her husky voice like tinder to the flames already burning within him.

'If all it takes is a look to arouse you, perhaps you should either shore up your defences a little more…or—and this is my personal preference—give in to me.'

Her nostrils quivered. Right before her firm little chin rose in challenge. 'I'm done eating. Can we go now?'

He smiled, partly in anticipation. Partly in acceptance that she was proving unique in this too, that she wouldn't fall into his lap the way women had done so very easily in the past. He also smiled because he knew this chase would be the most thrilling of all. Because at its culmination he would gain the thing he treasured most in the world.

He rose with a peculiar lightness in his chest, and when she placed her hand in the one he held out to her that sensation intensified.

'I look forward to our little skirmish,' he murmured.

That adorable defiance remained as her gaze boldly met his. 'I wouldn't hold your breath if I were you.'

The following days became an exercise in frustration, a test of his willpower and the intensifying thrill and uncertainty that maybe he might not acquire his prey this time.

From afar, Christos watched Alexis charm the villa staff with halting Greek phrases she was determined to perfect, first when her gowns arrived and he happened upon her in the living room of their suite, trying them on with the help of a young maid. Their eyes met across the small mountain of boxes and frivolous tissues, her face flushed a delicate pink as she stood there, her curvy body lovingly outlined in a satin slip, and her bare thighs and legs delivering a fresh punch of lust into his groin.

'There are way more gowns than I remember ordering,' she said, indicating the garments strewn around her.

He leaned in the doorway, hands thrust into his pockets, another first as he basked in the previously boring exercise of watching a woman try on clothes. 'I may have let myself be talked into expanding the collection on the premise that future engagements will necessitate their use.'

'Future engagements?' she echoed.

'Costas is right. Perhaps it's time to make our union a little bit more…public.'

'What does that mean?'

'It means I intend to let the world know you're my wife when we leave here.'

Her eyes were wide and her lips parted when he walked away; she was a little perturbed to notice he was smiling.

After that he found himself watching her, increasingly

aware of and intensely absorbed by her movements around the villa. Like when he found her sunbathing by the pool, the lime-green bikini clinging to her glorious, sun-kissed skin making his entire body clench in fierce need. Her exploration on the beach, usually before sunset, when the sun cast dazzling golden light in her hair. Their meals with Costas were equally absorbing. She'd shed her shyness and indulged Costas's wicked banter with a sharp wit he found entertaining.

But the nights were the most taxing of all. To give himself a break from that battering of his libido, he waited a clear hour before joining her in their suite. Not that it helped. She might have got over her reticence on their first night but Alexis tossed and turned in her sleep for several minutes after he'd slid in beside her, making him painfully aware of her graceful limbs, of the rich thickness of her hair almost reaching out to him across the pillows, of her bewitching scent that insisted on wrapping itself around his senses and especially around his manhood, keeping him hard and on the edge of his control as she gleefully slept on.

His only consoling thought was that maybe she wasn't having a particularly easy time of it either. He called her on it four nights later, as she was about to excuse herself to let him spend a few minutes alone with his grandfather. But tonight, Costas had pleaded tiredness and retired before coffee was served, leaving them alone.

Christos caught her arm before she could make her escape. 'Wait.'

Slowly, she sat, her eyes flicking warily to his. 'What is it?'

'Are you ready to give me your answer?' he asked, unable to drag his gaze from lips she'd painted a luscious, kissable gloss.

'What makes you think it's changed?' she parried, although the faintest flush tinged her skin.

'I've seen how you grip that pillow between us. How you tuck it between your legs when you sleep, as if to alleviate a certain ache. You grow breathless around me, and I've noticed the way your eyes follow me when you think I'm not looking.'

Her mouth opened in shock. 'You're unbelievable!'

'I'm simply observant. Do you protest because it's the truth? Or because I've noticed?'

'Shut up!'

He laughed.

She gave an unladylike growl before tossing her napkin at him. He batted it away before leaning in close.

'You need an outlet? Feel free to use me instead, *matia mou*,' he offered, then had the pleasure of seeing her eyes turn that liquid chocolate he craved.

'Thanks for the offer but no, thanks. The only thing I want to do now is go to bed.' Her face flamed on the heels of her words. When he laughed again, her lips pursed. 'I meant alone…' Then at his raised eyebrow, she growled again. 'You know what I mean,' she whispered angrily.

It pleased him that, even het up, she was being discreet enough not to give the game away. Then he sobered up as sharp realisation hit him. He didn't want this to be a game. He wanted…

'What is it?' Her question held sudden tension.

He released her, snatching his thoughts away from the sudden need for the unthinkable. For things he'd never craved or wanted. Things that would eventually only spawn hatred and recrimination. He had the emotional scars to prove it after all. 'You can go.'

'That wasn't what I asked,' she replied stubbornly, standing her ground. 'What's going on in that brain of yours?'

Christos rose from the table, closed the gap between them with a single step. 'Do you really want to find out, *koukla mou*?'

She frowned. 'That one is new. What does it mean?'

He smiled, the kind that bared his deep hunger. Felt a modicum of satisfaction when she swallowed and grew slightly breathless.

Before he could taunt her some more, she stepped back. 'You know what, forget it. Goodnight.'

He didn't respond, on account of staring into the space she'd just vacated with the type of stupefaction that came from receiving a thunderbolt. Male pride at hearing her addressed as Mrs Drakakis was one thing. Her hand slipping into his in sympathy after that harrowing revelation on the cliff and salving the rawness in his soul was another.

But…he couldn't want any kind of permanence with her…could he?

He gritted his teeth, summoning every single scrap of memory he'd buried deep down, together with its attendant emotion. Anger. Desperation. Loneliness…that seared hardest.

'Your mother doesn't love you. She just hates losing to me.'

'And you, Papa? Do you love me?'

The pitying look his father had levelled at him had shrivelled every ounce of hope in his foolish boyhood heart. But it had also taught him a valuable lesson. That depending on others for his happiness was a fruitless exercise unworthy of his efforts. Accepting that simple conclusion had truly been the moment he'd known his true purpose and worth.

It was what had got him through a faceless judge deciding he needed to live with the father who didn't love him instead of a mother who, when she wasn't embroiled in bitterness, regarded him with distant affection.

Perhaps it was because of that judge's actions that he'd decided to become a lawyer. But Christos didn't go into court with hope and love in his heart. Those emotions were too flawed to be reliable. Came with too many strings to be worth the air it took to speak them.

An hour passed, or perhaps it was only a handful of minutes— he couldn't quite tell. As he strode down the hallway, Christos smiled grimly to himself.

No. There would be no permanence with Alexis.

A temporary agreement, with a side order of sex. And if everything went as planned, Drakonisos would be within his grasp. That was all he wanted.

All he would ever want.

So what if his stomach hollowed out with a quiet bleakness at his future outlook? It was only because he was yet to plan it all out.

'Where are we going?' Alexis asked as she stepped out into sunshine the next afternoon. She'd been summoned an hour ago by Christos with the instruction to pack an overnight bag. When she saw his casual state and the buggy parked at the bottom of the front steps, excitement leapt high.

'The party is in four days. I want to show you the rest of the island before the guests descend on us.'

'Why do I need an overnight bag if we're staying on the island?' The only other habitat she'd seen was the staff quarters. Unless… 'We're not going camping, are we?' She wasn't sure how she'd fare since she'd never done it.

He tossed her a wry glance. 'So many questions. It's almost as if you don't trust me.'

I don't trust anyone any more. It was a phrase she'd have unapologetically tossed at him a few weeks ago, but Alexis realised that it was no longer true.

Christos had proved himself with his generosity to Hope House, the only home she'd ever known. He trusted her professional judgement. Despite sharing a bed, he hadn't crossed any lines. As enigmatic as he sometimes was, she knew she could trust him not to betray her the way Adrian had.

The knowledge unravelled inside her, birthing a weighty, worrisome sensation. Aware of the sharp eyes watching her, she forced a casual shrug. 'Fine. I'll play along.'

His gaze combed her face, paused on her mouth long enough to make it tingle wildly. Then, with a new kind of tension vibrating off him, he stepped away.

Alexis ignored the sharp dart of disappointment and watched as her bag was placed on the small flatbed buggy next to his.

Her every nerve went on high alert as they drove off once more, this time in a westerly direction.

She told herself it was residual nerves from the past several days, but she knew it was something else. It was the ever-increasing drumbeat in her chest that urged her to stop fighting. That said this was as inevitable as her arrogant husband had stated it was.

She'd spent far too many days and nights trying to rationalise her emotions. Each subsequent mental argument veering in favour of giving in.

This was a once-in-a-lifetime opportunity. She'd known from the first day she'd walked into Christos Drakakis's office that there was no other man like him.

The brooding looks, the smouldering energy, the hunger he didn't bother to hide any more, all said he wanted her. That he wanted, even if only temporarily, to make their marriage a real one.

Adrian swayed you with words and passion too.

But that thought did Christos an injustice. He'd stated his expectations upfront. No emotions. Nothing long-term. Just a physical exploration of their chemistry. A chapter to be closed when they tired of the story.

But was it worth her career?

The fervent *no* she'd expected arrived with a question

mark. The kind that questioned the choices she'd believed were cemented in her heart. She'd seen a different facet to Christos. His care for his grandfather. For his godson even from afar. The lengths he was prepared to travel to protect the one place that meant something to him…

That already made him miles better than Adrian.

Take the leap...

She shivered, the enormity of the decision gathering strength inside her becoming a physical need as they trundled along over verdant fields and then onto a wide rocky pathway that sloped gently downwards.

'Are you cold?' Christos asked, the keen observance telling her his attention was on her despite his easy, offhand attitude.

She shook her head and tucked her hands into her lap. 'Not really.'

'We're almost there.'

The sun was due to set in about an hour, and its brilliant rays turned the water into a jewelled, breathtaking expanse as far as the eye could see. Alexis was so enthralled by the spectacular view, she didn't notice their destination until the buggy bounced onto rougher sand and gravel, then onto the powdery golden sand of a wide, hidden beach.

She stared around her, her eyes widening when she saw the yawning forty-foot opening set into the sheer rock face. 'Is…is that a cave?'

The flatbed buggy she'd watched depart a few minutes before them was parked at the cavernous entrance, the staff unloading. Christos parked and stepped out. 'Yes.'

The simple response made her glance at him. 'And? What's inside?' she asked, unable to hide her excitement.

He reached out and tucked a strand of hair behind her ear, his eyes doing that intense thing that sparked fireworks inside her. 'You'll see once we're alone in a few minutes.'

Excitement surged higher, not helped by the light breeze

that made her aware of every goosebump on her body. And the fact that she would be alone with Christos. All night long since she'd packed an overnight bag.

The bag that was currently being carried inside…

The staff emerged a few minutes later, and Christos led her in, his attention fixed on her as Alexis stepped inside the most entrancing place she'd ever seen.

Dozens of lanterns, large and small, were dotted around the living area where divans and plump futons were spread around in inviting comfort. A coffee table graced the centre, and large, thick rugs kept her bare feet cool.

Beyond the charming living area, several foldable privacy screens hand-printed with Greek hillside vistas shielded a softly lit space.

Alexis stepped around the farthest screen and stopped in her tracks, a gasp of awe leaving her lips at the sight before her.

The bed was an immense four-poster. A floaty work of art, decked from headboard to bottom in gold silk sheets, dozens of fluffy pillows and billowing muslin raining down from sturdy pegs in the cave ceiling.

In perfect complement to the gold, fat candles in lacquered lanterns were dotted all over, casting soft shadows on the ceiling and bathing the space in a seductive glow.

It was the stuff of romantic dreams. And, heaven help her, she was utterly seduced.

'This…this is more than a few minutes' work,' she breathed in stunned awe.

He drew closer, setting her senses alight with his intoxicating scent. In London, he'd worn an earthier aftershave with a sandalwood base. Since their arrival, he'd switched to bergamot and leather. Her favourite. 'They've been preparing the place since morning.'

'I…why?'

He quirked an eyebrow at her. 'Do I really need to spell it out?'

Despite the heat that flicked to life in her belly, a pang of pain reminded her of the past. 'I'm afraid you'll have to. I don't want to make assumptions.'

'I felt you needed a little more…convincing.'

Her breath shook as she exhaled. 'Convincing or seducing?'

His expressive shrug was rich in arrogance. It said whichever road she took she would end up exactly where he wanted her. Trouble was, Alexis *wanted* to be there. 'Take your pick. The outcome will be the same.'

'You're very sure of yourself, aren't you?'

'Even now, you tremble. Your lips yearn for me and your pulse is feverish with need.'

'I'm… I'm…'

'Afraid? No, you're not. Unwilling? You're not that either. What you are, Alexis, is desperate to embrace the need pounding inside you. All that's holding you back is the notion that giving in makes you weak. It doesn't. Being brave enough to grasp what you want is a strength, not a weakness.'

Heaven help her, but she lapped his words up like a starving exile offered a banquet. And when his thumb glided over her bottom lip in that indolent way he seemed to enjoy, she took that bravery one step further and flicked her tongue against his flesh.

His sharp inhale was a triumphant orchestral crescendo to her ears. He let her taste him for several thrilling seconds, before he removed his touch.

'Tell me what you want, Alexis,' he instructed thickly.

The presence of the emperor-sized bed behind her loomed large in her mind. But she managed to force back the words clamouring for release.

'Kiss me,' she said instead. 'Please.'

His chest expanded in a supremely masculine show that made her insides quiver. He cupped her nape in a firm hold and dragged her close. Before she could catch her breath, he captured her lips, his tongue delving deep in conquest, looking for a surrender she was willing to grant. The sound of her moans filled the magical space as she dared to taste him as boldly as he was devouring her. Arms tight around his neck, she felt light as a feather when he lifted her up. A few long strides and she was wedged against one cool wall.

She was being kissed by Christos in a cave on a paradise island. A surreal appetizer to a heady feast, enticing her to wrap her legs around his waist.

'Thee mou,' he muttered against her lips, then pinned her tighter, their position leaving her in no doubt as to the power and potency of his arousal. 'You feel how much I want you?' he growled.

'Yes,' she gasped, tightening her hold and making him groan.

Words evaporated as they indulged in another torrid kiss. As her core grew slicker and her breathing all but evaporated, she was at the point of begging when Christos lifted his head.

'I'd love nothing more than to toss you onto that bed and bury myself deep inside you,' he rasped, pausing to nip at her bottom lip before soothing it with his tongue, 'but we won't be alone for much longer.'

Disappointment seared her even as her imagination raged. 'Wh-what?'

'There's one last thing to be set up, and dinner to be served. But after that…' Words weren't necessary to convey his intention. His deeply smouldering gaze and the passion vibrating from his hard body told her everything.

With a clear reluctance that salved her disappointment, he stepped back and lowered her to the floor.

In silence he took her hand and led her out of the sleeping area.

As they passed the screen, she looked back at the bed. And knew without a shadow of doubt that whatever armour she'd built around her emotions was perhaps irreparably fractured.

CHAPTER NINE

SHE FOLLOWED HIM back out of the cave then once again stopped in her tracks, her jaw sagging open at yet another spectacular sight.

'Oh, my God.' Her reverent whisper was completely in line with the awe of what his staff had created for them while they'd been locked in an embrace.

She turned to Christos, to find a smug and altogether far too superior smile curving lips slightly reddened from her enthusiastic kisses. 'How did you know?'

'There was a firm-wide poll of dream activities floating around I may have taken note of.'

She frowned. 'That was two years ago. You remembered?'

'I remembered,' he said simply.

Something far too overwhelming shifted inside her, something close to what she'd imagined being special, being *treasured* felt like. Her throat tightened as she stared at the twenty-foot-high portable cinema screen and the dozens of lanterns placed strategically around it, and the wide, snow-white futon-like cushions inviting lazy relaxation. Two silver buckets with vintage champagne were set on either side of the futon with turquoise cashmere throws draped over the seats for when the weather cooled.

'Before we indulge in that though…dinner?' he asked, his voice low, deep and throbbing with the same sensation surging through her.

She turned from the pleasurable sight to see a table for two set with a white tablecloth, sterling silverware gleaming under candlelight. Beside their table stood a small buffet stand with a dozen domed dishes placed on it.

While she knew she couldn't...*shouldn't* read anything into it, Alexis couldn't stop the lump lodging in her throat, or her fingers from curling tightly around his when Christos tugged her towards the table.

It was all far too much. She wanted to step back, gather the crumbling pieces of her armour, in case she needed it later, after the magic wore away. But she suspected it was already too late.

She watched him when he moved. Stared into his face when he spoke to her. Allowed her fingers to linger on his when he passed her a glass of perfectly chilled Chablis.

And when he touched on the subject she usually never discussed, she tensed for a very brief moment before she swallowed and answered.

'Tell me how you ended up at Hope House.'

The rush of pain that came with her truth never failed to steal her breath. 'I never knew my mother. She left me on the doorstep of Hope House's high-street charity shop when I was a week old. The nuns from the orphanage took me in.'

His face froze, his eyes burning with an unholy blaze that sent agitation skittering over her skin. The blaze abated and he breathed out. 'I didn't mean to resurrect what must be a...painful memory for you.'

'You didn't know. As you can imagine, it's not information I toss into everyday conversation.'

His nod was abrupt. 'Did you ever try to find her or your father?'

She shook her head. 'All I have is a handwritten note left for whoever found me, a request that I be named Alexis, and a blanket I was wrapped in. Not much to go on.'

Incisive eyes rested on hers. 'And if you had further resources? Would you wish to probe deeper?'

Her heart lurched, then lodged in her throat. 'I've thought about it. I've never been quite able to decide if I'm better off not knowing or risking being further hurt by whatever reason she had for leaving me there.'

His sensual lips twisted and his gaze dropped to his glass before rising to meet hers again. 'Perhaps you won't see it this way, but there is a deeper pride in knowing that whatever you've become has been without either of your parents' influence.'

There was a hard edge in his voice that suggested a personal pain. One that echoed inside her but for the opposite reason. 'I guess that's where the conundrum lies. Would I prefer the choice of knowing or living with an…emptiness?'

He reached across the table, covered her hand for a moment before he sat back. 'The former might not necessarily bring the closure you wish for. Knowing my parents still left me with more questions than answers. As harsh as it seems, perhaps you're better off not knowing?'

'How did you…?' She paused because she wasn't sure he'd got over his parents' treatment of him. 'Don't you wonder how things could've turned out if you'd tried to reconcile with them?'

His lips compressed. 'No. They made their choice. I had to make mine. *If onlys* become weights that just drag you down eventually.'

'So your advice is just…live with this emptiness?'

'No, *matia mou*. My advice is to become the best version of yourself you can be so that when you find yourself in a similar position, you have better options.'

Anguish moved through her. 'I don't think I could abandon my child under any circumstances.'

Something flashed in his eyes, making her insides tighten. 'Then you're already a thousand times better than the mother who left you with no explanation,' he said, his voice gravel-rough.

That tightening moved up her chest and into her throat. Stupid tears prickled her eyes and she desperately blinked them away, registering that her pain had receded, perhaps had even shrunk smaller than ever.

'I don't know why everyone thinks you're so fearsome,' she joked, striving to lighten the atmosphere before her emotions got the better of her.

He took her cue and sent her a devastating smile that produced a much more pleasurable ache inside her. 'Fearsome has its advantages, as long as it gets me what I want.' Eyes heavy with lust watched her as she toyed with the stem of her glass.

Perhaps she knew she was straying into dangerous territory by probing, but she couldn't stop the question. 'Tell me when you last brought another woman here, to this cave. Or did any of this.' She waved her hand around the spectacular setting. The last rays of the sun tinged the sky a deep bold orange, enough to make the sea look as if it were on fire. Enough to make this the kind of paradise very few people got to experience. The kind of paradise that made foolish wishes seem attainable.

He looked almost…startled by her bold question. 'Do you want me to tell you you're special, Alexis? Is that it?'

Yes. 'Would that be so bad? I am your wife, after all,' she said, then felt something profound move deep within her.

Something echoed in his eyes too, making them widen momentarily before he reasserted his control. But she'd seen it. And, however fleeting, it had planted a seedling inside her, one she couldn't shake free.

'Not in every sense of the term. Not yet…' he drawled. They both knew he'd evaded the question, but the potential magnitude of a proper answer suddenly had her shying away from it.

But even while they returned to simpler, more benign subjects, heavy emotional undercurrents swirled until he rose and held out his hand in silent demand.

They were still there when she kicked off her stylish

mules and reclined on the wide divan set before the screen. Perhaps it was the wine that had mellowed her tongue. She couldn't resist looking up into the stars, contentment stealing over her at the sound of the waves hitting the shore.

'I can't tell you how long I've dreamed of doing this on some distant beach in the Maldives or Tahiti.'

'It would please me if you'd accept the much simpler venue of a Greek beach,' he replied, a trace of amusement in his tone.

She gave a delicate snort. 'Are you kidding me? Nowhere on my wish list was there a cave of wonders on a private island tossed in for good measure. This far surpasses everything the travel brochures promised.'

The pop of a cork refocused her attention on him. In the dancing candlelight, he was truly drop-dead gorgeous, the kind of fallen-angel masculine beauty that had the ability to stop hearts and overcome even the strongest apprehension.

Not that she had much of that left. Only the merest wisp of residue still urged her towards self-preservation. But even that was silenced when he smiled and handed her a crystal flute of vintage champagne.

When she accepted it, he aimed the remote at the projector that stood twenty feet away. Then passed her a silver bowl that made her gasp. Again.

'Caramel popcorn? Now you're scaring me a little with how much you know about me.'

That ferocious gaze raked her body, then rested blatantly on her mouth. 'I told you, I am serious about the things that are important to me.'

He meant his possession of Drakonisos. She knew that. Yet that traitorous melting sensation continued unabated. Until her every sense strained towards him, eager to please. Eager to take whatever he had to give.

She chose the movie and smiled as it flicked to life. It

was a classic she'd seen a dozen times. But here, now, in this special place, she was swept away anew.

Until she felt him wrap a strand of hair around his fingers. Until that scent of leather, bergamot and man twined insidiously around her senses, making each breath she took a tiny exercise in torture. Until her heart drummed loudly in her ears, deafening her to everything but the sound of her own need, pounding relentlessly through her.

Despite the open beach and endless sky, he invaded the space, his vitality a living force field. Vibrant and inescapable.

'Something wrong, Alexis?' he drawled, when she fidgeted one more time.

She took a gulp of her champagne just for something to do. His fingers drifted over her nape. She shivered, tried to contain herself.

'Christos.' His name was a breathless, urgent whisper in the night air.

'*Ne?* Tell me what you want and you shall have it,' he urged thickly. The designer stubble he'd cultivated over the last few days added a swagger to his already deadly good looks and when he brushed his cheek against her jaw, it drove her insane.

On the screen, the actors were caught in a melodramatic clinch; the very same one she yearned for. 'I can't wait. Please,' she whispered.

The flash of triumph in his eyes should've irritated her. But she was beyond that. So she let him tug her glass from her hand and set it aside. Let him cup her jaw, stare deep into her eyes, then slowly lean in to brush his lips over hers.

The moment she started to cling, he drew away. With leonine grace he rose to his feet and swept her up into his arms. His strides from the beach into the cave held an urgency that echoed within her.

Alexis forgot to breathe as he set her down next to the

bed, those ferociously brooding eyes watching her as he reached for the simple band that held up her hair. He gave a grunt of satisfaction as her hair tumbled free, lazily threading his fingers through the heavy mass.

'Tonight, I get to watch your glorious hair cascade over *my* pillow,' he said thickly. 'I get to claim you in the way I've craved instead of watching you from my side of the bed.'

The unabashed possessiveness in his voice sent excitement dancing over her flesh. He caught her shiver and gave a smile tinged with predatory pleasure. 'No more hugging pillows for you, *matia mou*.'

With that decree, he tugged the thin straps of her dress down her arms. The flimsy material pooled at her waist. Christos kept his gaze on her face as he reached behind her and slowly unhooked her lacy bra, flinging it away before his gaze dropped to her breasts.

She watched him swallow.

Emboldened by her effect on him, Alexis stepped forward, reached for the buttons of his white shirt, her eagerness to explore him too a heady rush that couldn't be stopped. She only managed to bare his glorious torso halfway before she slid her hands inside, gliding them over his sculpted chest. Muscles rippled beneath her touch, his hot skin a decadent invitation she wasn't going to refuse.

Alexis didn't register that she'd swayed closer until her nipples brushed his hair-dusted chest. Her aroused whimper brought another smug smile to his face.

'Perhaps you should finish what you started so you can have more of what you crave?' he suggested a touch mockingly.

On a wild whim—and perhaps because she wanted to wipe away a layer of that smugness—she grasped the edges of his shirt and pulled them apart.

For a single moment, he tensed. Then flames leapt

higher in his eyes. With an animalistic growl, Christos shrugged off the tattered remains of his shirt, then, reaching forward, yanked down her dress. She'd barely stepped out of it before he pulled her close, his lips finding hers with an urgency and fervour she wholeheartedly endorsed. With a mastery that roused every nerve ending to life, Christos stroked and teased, feasted and delivered pleasure she'd never experienced before.

When his large hands slipped into her panties and cupped her bottom, she moaned, her thighs growing slicker in readiness for his possession. Her fingers dug into his hair as their kiss grew even more frenzied, their bodies straining together in carnal need.

The rough sound of lace ripping drew another whimper, the firm tug of her destroyed panties almost making her swoon as he yanked them free and tossed them aside.

'Turnabout is fair play,' he growled. Then he was plucking her off the floor and settling her firmly in the middle of the bed.

With barely bridled patience, she watched him reach for his trousers. Heart pounding, she followed the hand lowering his zipper. Moments later he was naked.

Her mouth dried as she struggled to take in his sheer magnificence. Muscles, sleek and powerful, flowed in perfect symmetry, a body without a spare inch of flab culminating in the impressive, jaw-dropping sculpture of his aroused manhood.

One sleek lunge and he was beside her, his hand on her hip drawing her close before arranging her beneath him.

For the longest time, Christos stared down at her without speaking, that torturous caress up and down her body driving her steadily insane as his eyes pinned her to the bed.

When she tried to raise her head, eager to kiss him, he drew back.

'Not yet. A few rules first.'

She slicked her tongue over needy lips. 'Wh-what?'

'I want to see your beautiful eyes at all times, *glykia mou*,' he stated roughly, one hand cupping her breast and mercilessly torturing her nipple. 'And when I'm deep inside you, the only word from your lips will be my name. You can choose to whisper it or scream it. But I want to hear it.'

He lowered his head and flicked the tip of his tongue across her nipple, and stars burst across her vision. 'Christos…'

'*Ne*, just like that,' he growled, then sucked the tight peak into his mouth.

Pleasure arched her back, her fingers spiking through his hair to hold him close as the madness encroached further.

The hooded gaze he kept on her as he explored her flesh added a decadent edge to her pleasure. Pleasure that intensified even more when he trailed his lips down her body.

Her eyes widened and her heartbeat doubled when she realised what he meant to do. 'Christos…?'

His answer to that hesitant question was to decisively draw her thighs apart, trail his stubbled jaw over the sensitive flesh of her inner thighs, all while those infernal eyes devoured her every expression. And just when she was certain her heart would beat itself straight through her ribs, he lowered his head and delivered the most carnal of kisses.

Her sharp cry echoed in the cave, the sound lingering for an age as if to impress upon her what was happening.

'Thee mou,' he muttered roughly. 'You taste exquisite.'

Her every last thought melted away, her full attention centred on the sublime pleasure he delivered. Over and over he tortured and teased, until her vision hazed. Until she screamed as bliss smashed through her in the most sublime climax she'd ever experienced.

Her breath was still choppy and her body trembling with

aftershocks when he captured her wrists, kissed her palms, before caressing his way back up her body.

Peripherally, she saw him reach for a condom, tear it open and glide it on.

The heavy, delicious weight of him sharpened her focus, her eager gaze devouring every inch of him as he settled between her thighs.

'*Christo*, you have a body to rival Aphrodite herself,' he declared, his face a taut mask of arousal. 'I can't wait to claim you.'

'Then don't wait,' she replied, fresh hunger urging her to wind her arms around his neck, her body eager and open. He'd already introduced her to oral pleasure for the first time. Despite the faint but lingering voice of caution, she was desperate for more. To hoard as much of this experience as she could.

Because it wouldn't last? She shied away from the answer.

'Your breasts are a work of art,' he rasped huskily, before bestowing more kisses on them.

Just when she was on the verge of begging for more, he reared up onto one elbow. Alexis held her breath as his hand slid down between their bodies, and she felt his broad head brush her feminine place.

The lock of hair falling over his forehead didn't diminish the fierceness of the gaze pinning her in place as, with one sure, powerful stroke, he entered her.

'Christos!'

'Yes, *yineka mou*. My name on your lips while I take you…again and again,' he rasped, jaw locked tight as he inhaled audibly.

For the longest suspended moment, he held himself inside her. Then, when a whimper finally broke from her, he withdrew and thrust back inside.

Raw, unfettered pleasure unravelled from her core. She

was unaware her fingers dug into his shoulders until he hissed in pleasure. 'That's it, Alexis. Mark me. Show me what I do to you.'

It was as if she'd been uncaged and handed the keys to nirvana. She wrapped her legs around him, raised her head and claimed his mouth in a shockingly carnal kiss as he increased the tempo.

Dear God, she'd never felt anything like it. Suspected she never would again. But that was an issue for another day. The moment hot torrid Greek words started falling from his lips, she gave up the need to hold back. She met him thrust for thrust, his turbulent eyes and the hand locked on her hip urging her higher and higher until pleasure exploded in a shower of lights.

Her raw scream bounced off the walls before returning to wrap itself around them, as Christos locked both hands in her hair. Despite his thrusts slowing, the intensity of his lovemaking remained. She realised why when, after she'd caught half her breath back, he delivered another tongue-tangling kiss, raised his head and commanded roughly, 'Again. I want to feel you come again.'

Thee mou, she was like a drug. One he couldn't resist. Not that he wanted to in that moment.

She was an amazing revelation, even more so than he'd anticipated based on their chemistry alone.

For starters, there was that curious mixture of shy and bold, of innocence and carnal greed; it was a lit fuse to his libido. He'd seen her reaction to his pleasuring of her with his mouth, felt her quiet shock and knew she'd either never experienced it before or had found any previous attempt sorely lacking. Her subsequent reactions had given credence to this suspicion. Whatever she'd shared with previous lovers, it had not been the real thing.

He was primitive enough to enjoy that knowledge. Hell,

to even revel in the possibility that she'd never known anything like what they'd just experienced together. What they could experience while they were on Drakonisos. Perhaps even further into the future?

No.

This...peculiar and faintly overwhelming sensation was because he hadn't had a woman in over a year, nothing more. Besides, that kind of dependency was what he shied away from. It only brought chaos. Trouble. Heartache. Attachments that turned people into vicious versions of themselves.

He was past that kind of behaviour. He'd orchestrated this altered version of their agreement with his eyes wide open. He wasn't about to let emotion—however incredible and potent—cloud his judgement.

But...

While he was here, while this was happening, holding back would only be depriving himself. He pushed inside her once more and let loose the groan locked in his throat. She truly was sublime, his wife.

His *wife*...

'Christos.' Her voice was sex-soaked, wrapped in temptation, feeding his hunger.

He let go of all other thoughts. And indulged his feelings to the fullest.

And when she cried out in ecstasy once more, he was right there behind her, blinded by a unique kind of pleasure that branded his very soul. That he knew would be unforgettable once he rose from this bed and put it all behind him.

Still he gathered her close. Kissed her temple with a gentleness unlike him. And when she sighed and melted into his arms, he found himself exhaling, a curious peace settling over him.

That peace was still in place when he woke at dawn,

used the rudimentary facilities he'd had built into the cave a decade ago then gently roused the drowsing woman he'd made love to for the second time only an hour ago.

'Wake up, Alexis. There's one more experience to enjoy,' he said, trailing his lips over her smooth cheek.

She smiled without opening her eyes. 'I thought we did that last night?'

He found himself chuckling—and when was the last time he'd done that? 'This one is time sensitive.'

Drowsy chocolate-brown eyes flecked with gold opened to meet his. The soft pleasure in them caught him sharply, threatening to pierce the hard shell he deliberately kept in place. The urge to stay where he was, remain in this moment, grew stronger.

Then, vitally, he managed to remind himself of the reasons that shell couldn't be allowed to crack. After that it was easier to rise, to reach for the swim shorts he'd tossed there a few minutes ago.

'We're going swimming?' she asked, propping herself up on one elbow before gliding her fingers through her tousled hair.

Despite their very recent encounter, Christos found himself growing hard all over again.

'Eventually. What comes before that you'll have to get up now or you'll miss.' He forced himself to leave the sleeping area before he succumbed to temptation. Before all those risky little thoughts creeping in found fertile ground and sprouted roots.

He was standing on the shore, willing those same thoughts of permanence and possibilities away when he heard her behind him. The compulsion to see her, drench himself in her presence and beauty, propelled him to face her. She'd copied his style and was dressed in a sea-green-and-white striped bikini with a matching sarong, and flip-flops on her feet. Her long hair was gathered over one shoulder, and as she lifted a hand to toss the heavy strands back his gut tightened all over again, that drugging sensation threatening to steal over him again as hunger clawed through him. To counter it, he waved a hand at the small hill a short walk away.

'That's where we need to be in the next five minutes.'

She followed his gaze, then nodded. 'Okay.'

He knew it was foolish but still he held out his hand. Watched her eyes darken and her cheeks flush with pleasure as she placed hers in his.

Their walk was companionably silent, Christos again privately commending her for not filling it with chatter. But not talking meant he was even more painfully aware of how her delicate hand fitted into his, how sexily she moved and, most control-shredding of all, the distinct stamp of his scent on her body.

Primitive urges rose again. And as they crested the low hill, all he could think about was how soon he could claim her again. How indelibly he could stamp his possession on her.

He knew he hadn't done a good job of hiding his reaction when, reaching the spot he'd chosen and turning to her, he saw her eyes widen. Unable to resist, he dragged her close, slid his hands into her hair and devoured her lips for one long minute.

Only the reminder of why he'd brought her here made him stop.

Reluctantly drawing back, he dropped to the dew-dampened grass and tugged her down in front of him. She settled down between his spread thighs and as he drew her back against his chest, he secretly revelled in her jagged breathing.

Appeased that he wasn't in this madness alone, he pointed to the eastern horizon. 'Watch,' he murmured in her ear, wrapping one arm around her shoulders.

The sunrise was an exquisitely drawn-out symphony of light and colour, a slow, seductive dance of beauty and awe.

He felt her breath catch as golden light blossomed over the horizon like a hesitant flower, bathing the lush greenness of the island in vivid colour as dawn gave way to day.

'Oh, Christos. It's beautiful.'

'Ne,' he agreed, his voice gruff.

Her hands settled on his thighs as they watched the spectacular sunrise. And as the sun's heat washed over him, so did that moving sensation in his chest. The one that seemed determined to sink its profound claws into him. The one he felt almost inclined to…give in to. *Again.*

But hadn't he sat on this very hill as a child, engulfed in anguish because he'd dared give in to his emotions? Wasn't it in this very spot that he'd sworn never to allow himself to feel the vulnerability of love ever again?

The reminder was abrasive. Enough to make him tense.

'Christos?' Alexis started to twist around, to seek his gaze. 'What's wrong?'

He shook his head. 'I'm reminded why I used to come here.'

Warm fingers found his. 'Tell me.'

'I wanted to feel…something other than anger at my parents. Something other than…' He paused, feeling raw and exposed.

'Pain? Despair? Hopelessness?'

He glanced down at her, saw that kinship in her eyes once again. She understood. Of course she did, considering her situation. 'Yes,' he admitted after a stretch of silence, his fingers rubbing at the tight spot in his chest. 'It felt like this was the only place I could escape it.'

'I'm glad you could, if only for a while.'

Silence reigned again and he felt the tightness loosening, his breathing becoming freer.

'This was special. Thanks for sharing it with me.'

Somehow his lips found her temple, delivered a lingering kiss on her smooth skin. 'To answer your questions, I've never shared the cave with anyone. Nor this view of a Drakonisos sunrise. So yes, Alexis, you're special.'

He watched her inhale shakily, striving for composure. But his own admission had tilted the ground beneath him. So he rose, the beauty of the sunrise gone for him. 'Come.' He held out his hand without looking down into her face. 'One last thing before we return to the villa.'

He sensed her confusion but ignored it. The moment she stood, he led them to the edge of the hill. Reading his intention, she clamped her fingers around his.

'Wait. You're not suggesting what I think you are, are you?' she asked, peering over the edge into the swirling water below.

The smile he flashed her felt hard around the edges. 'It's barely twenty feet.'

'You go ahead, then. I'm most definitely not jumping,' she stated firmly.

'Stepping off the edge is always daunting. But the experience is all the more exhilarating for it,' he muttered against her lips. Then wondered whether the words were meant for him more than for her.

The slight widening of her eyes said she'd recognised the acuity of it too. His world tilting just that little bit more, he slid his arm around her. 'Say yes, Alexis.'

Her arms slowly trailed up his shoulders, her eyes wide and apprehensive. But then her chin lifted, and her gaze grew bold. 'Yes.'

He caught her to him, that devilish hunger demanding another taste of her. He was gratified when she fell into him, her lips clinging to his until they parted once more.

Her fingers meshed with his, her eyes growing shiny

with anticipation. Without giving her a chance to rethink, he grasped her more firmly. And jumped.

For a moment in time, every trace of anguish and disquiet from his past melted away. A fierce, incandescent joy engulfed him as the clear waters of the Aegean swallowed them both.

At first, a million bubbles obstructed his view of her. Then it cleared. He spun to his left and saw Alexis, equal joy on her face as she smiled. Keeping them submerged for a little while longer, he pulled her close, wrapped both arms around her, then stole another kiss from her smiling lips. Her legs tangled around his waist, wrapped tight, and she kissed him back with equal fervour.

The need for oxygen forced them to resurface. But Christos wasn't prepared to let her go. Arms still tight around her, he kicked towards shallower water and the large rock jutting out from the sea a short distance away.

Waves splashed around their knees as he pushed her against the smooth surface of the rock, need pummelling him.

'How was that?' he asked, as he slowly pulled on the strings of her bikini top. Her gaze dropped to his hands, and, despite the explicit way they'd devoured each other last night and this morning, a hot blush suffused her face.

'Exhilarating,' she said. Her husky voice curled around his senses and he barely suppressed a groan as he divested her of her bottoms, then yanked off his swim shorts.

The sun was already a little higher in the sky, bathing the rock and Alexis in golden light. He stepped back for a moment to savour her in this place that meant so much to him, before, sanity disappearing, he planted his hands on either side of her head.

Her moan when their bodies melded together was music to his ears. And a minute later, when her slick, warm body welcomed his groaned thrust, it spelled a certain doom he knew would alter his world irreparably.

Alexis took him inside her, and it felt as if she'd found home. A home she wanted to stay in forever. She'd suspected her heart was in danger long before last night, that it wasn't just the island weaving its magic on her. But it was last night that had sealed her doom.

The warm security she'd felt in his arms. Perhaps it was the fateful but brief conversation they'd had somewhere in the lost hours that had reinforced that belief.

'You never told me the last time you used this cave,' she'd said, her hand trailing over his chiselled chest.

'I come here every time I'm on the island, but as a child, it was my sanctuary. A place I could let my imagination run wild. Now I'll see it differently.'

'Why?'

A pause, long and deep and breath-stalling. Then, 'Because you are here.'

Four little words that had lodged a lump in her throat. That had terrified her with the need to hold them close inside the heart she suspected didn't wholly belong to her any longer. Her hand had fisted over his steadily beating heart and she'd fought back foolish tears as she'd drifted off to sleep.

And when he'd woken her a short time later and transported her to heaven once more, a very resigned part of her had accepted that the heart she'd guarded so tenaciously was no longer safe.

CHAPTER TEN

ALEXIS DRESSED FOR Costas's party with equal parts anticipation and dread. Luckily for her, the dread had been given little room to grow over the past few days, but especially in the frenzied hours leading up to the festivities.

Nevertheless, she'd caught herself in quiet moments wondering if, despite all the precautions she'd taken, she'd set herself up for a life-shattering heartache. One set to surpass the last disastrous episode, which now seemed such a non-starter compared to what she had with Christos.

And what *did* she have, exactly?

Those searing, portentous moments of dread quickly dissipated when he pulled her into his arms in their bed at night. And, as much as she knew she was sinking deeper into whatever this emotional quagmire was, she'd welcomed him. Craved his lovemaking. While clinging on to the belief that things would go back to normal when they left the island.

Except…

Normal didn't appeal any more. Normal came with a Christos-shaped hole that—

'Are you ready, *matia m*—'

She spun around at his voice, then froze at the look in Christos's eyes as he stood in the doorway to her dressing room. 'What's wrong?'

'You look…stunning,' he said, his voice hoarse and his attention…transfixed.

Alexis couldn't stop her smile or the pleasure that filled her heart. The dove grey dress edged with silvery crystals was a halter-neck design that moulded her figure from chest to thighs before dropping in an eye-catching fall of silver sequins at her feet. 'Then I guess the dress is doing its job.'

His lips twisted and he moved with a quiet urgency towards her. 'It's not the dress. It's the woman inside it.'

'I…thank you.'

His nostrils flared then, as if breathing her in. 'A woman I want to be inside right now,' he added thickly, one hand reaching out to cup her nape.

'Christos…'

He lowered his head, brushed his lips over hers. '*Thee mou*, I don't know why you do this to me,' he muttered, his voice almost bewildered.

One small part of her leapt in delight, while the other wondered where her willpower had gone. Why she continued to stand there, an open flower absorbing the power of his sun without caring if she got burned.

Because she would get burned. That note in his voice that questioned his own craving of her was a warning not to hope. But he was cupping her shoulders, drawing her to him with ruthlessly carnal intent that made her tremble from head to toe.

'I want you,' he growled against her lips.

'Christos…we need to be—'

'Nowhere but here right now. *I* need to be inside you.'

The raw words sent another hot shudder through her. And when he walked her back against the cool wall of her dressing room, she was his willing captive. When he drew up her dress and tore off her panties, she lost the ability to think. 'Hold up your dress for me, *agapita*.'

Her hands shook as she complied. And between one breath and the next, his trousers were undone, her legs were around his waist and he was driving hot and hard and mind-melting inside her.

His mouth covered hers and their tongues commenced a decadent rhythm to match the one due south. Then, their movement catching the corner of her eye, Alexis twisted her head. Christos followed her gaze and, together, they watched in the mirror as he thrust into her over and over.

But underneath the wicked hedonism of it, she caught something in her own eyes, something that went far beyond desire. Something sacred and precious she should've kept concealed but was now out in the open. So she quickly shut her eyes. When she exploded, her scream was muffled by his kiss, followed by the hoarse groan of his own release, before their urgent pants filled the room.

He lowered her to her feet and she was still coming down from the addictive high when she felt a cool touch against her throat. Her gaze dropped to see brilliant gems gleaming in his hand. Her breath caught as he fastened the diamond necklace around her neck, trailed a string of kisses along her jaw, before rasping in her ear, 'This is what I came to give you.'

With her hair up in an elaborate knot the stylist had spent almost an hour on, her neck was exposed to highlight the magnificence of the diamond choker. 'Oh, it's beautiful.' Her fingers shook as she reached up to touch it. But then the realisation of how deeply she was being drawn into this altered reality hit her hard. 'But I can't accept it. It's… it's too much.'

Displeasure hardened his eyes as he slid his semi-hard erection out of her. 'You're my wife. It will be expected.'

That hollow space inside that had never quite gone away expanded, and hurt poured in. The kind of hurt she knew she only had herself to blame for. 'Of course, how silly of me to think it would be for any other reason. Well, since you put it that way, how can I refuse?'

He heard the bite in her voice and his eyes narrowed. 'You can't.'

He remained where he stood after rearranging his clothes back into pristine sophistication, blocking out her light, filling every corner of her senses. She needed a moment…several…to recentre herself after yet another emotional roller coaster. 'Is that all?'

'Alexis—'

'We were already late before you came in. I think we're now in danger of giving fashionably late a bad rep. I need to refresh my make-up. Not to mention the underwear you ripped off.' Her face flamed as she said the last words, and she forbade herself from looking down, from giving substance to the reality of her shredded weakness.

For an eternity, he stared at her. Then he stepped back. 'I'll see you in the living room in five minutes.'

She watched him walk away, a new sensation of being in free fall with no parachute assailing her. She tried to push it out of her mind as she dug out fresh underwear, repaired her make-up and, after a few deep breaths that did nothing to restore her composure, ventured out to join Christos.

He stood with his back to the room, his gaze on the sleek yachts that had started arriving two hours ago. From the buzz around the villa, she knew they belonged to extended family and Costas's close friends. The remaining guests had started steadily arriving half an hour ago.

Christos whirled at her approach, his gaze sweeping over her. It lingered at her hips and then he nodded and wordlessly held out his arm.

He didn't speak, and she was too wrapped up in containing her dread and hurt, as they made their way downstairs and out to the west terrace where the party was under way.

The hundred-strong crowd turned in near-unison when they appeared, then the murmurs surged as, one by one, sharply suited men and their stunningly bejewelled women approached to greet Christos and his hitherto unknown bride.

Normally, Alexis trusted herself on her ability to retain names and details, but after what had happened upstairs, and the ever-intensifying sensation that she might be *falling in love* with Christos, she soon gave up any hope of recollection.

They finally reached the guest of honour and Alexis withstood his long enigmatic scrutiny with a tingling sensation before reaching down to brush a kiss on Costas's cheek. 'Happy birthday, Costas.'

He smiled when she straightened. '*Ne*, it's turning out to be,' he said cryptically, before turning to his grandson. Their conversation was conducted in Greek before he was drawn away by a small party of guests.

About to ask Christos as he handed her a glass of champagne what had just happened, she stopped when a man materialised in front of them.

He was short and stout, older by about a decade than Christos, but his sour expression nevertheless bore the Drakakis stamp. Accompanying him was a tall statuesque blonde, with overplumped lips and a bust that defied gravity. 'Ah, Christos. Kind of you to grace us with your presence. I was beginning to think Costas's mind was playing tricks on him when he said you were here.'

Outwardly, Christos remained unruffled, but the arm beneath hers stiffened. 'There's nothing wrong with his memory, Georgios,' Christos answered and only a fool would've failed to catch the sharp warning in his tone.

Georgios raised his free hand in an exaggerated show of surrender. 'Of course, of course,' he said without any hint of remorse, then he turned to Alexis. 'I'm Georgios Pantelli. This is my wife, Arianna. And this must be your elusive bride, Christos.'

Alexis held out her hand. 'I'm Alexis. Good to meet you.'

Georgios held back from taking it a fraction of a second longer, enough to make her aware of the snub, before taking her hand in his faintly clammy one. His wife's handshake was equally limp, her eyes mildly hostile as they held Alexis's.

'What a vision you are,' Georgios said. 'Were it not for my own stunning wife, I would think Christos was hiding you away because he's afraid of the competition.'

'I see you continue to set far too high a premium on your own importance, cousin,' Christos bit out.

For a flash of time, Georgios's eyes turned flinty. Then he was back to pretended suaveness and affability. He even threw in a belly laugh, attracting several gazes. 'I have missed our little banters, cousin.' He stepped closer, grabbed Christos's arm then, in a low tone, added, 'I have also not forgotten that while you may have had Costas's attention as a child, it and Drakonisos is now mine, because I have proved myself whereas you have not.'

Christos bared his teeth in a semblance of a smile as he disengaged himself, a leonine action that sent shivers down her spine. 'And how do you imagine you have done that?'

Georgios stepped back, all but preening as he adjusted his lapel. 'I see you're out of the loop yet again. Costas is craving a child or two from the next generation to run around this place. And I have a feeling the first one of us to provide him with one will get Drakonisos. And tomorrow morning, I will be proudly informing him that my wife is to bless me with a child in six months' time. So, you see, I win.'

Several things happened in the next minute.

Christos turned statue-still beside her, his face bleeding several shades of colour. At the same time, Alexis's mind spun a thousand miles an hour. Specifically, to the morning after their night in the cave. Then fast forwarded to tonight, that hedonistic episode in her dressing room.

Two occasions passion had completely engulfed them.

Two occasions they'd failed to use protection.

Grey eyes turbulent with shock and disbelief swivelled

towards her. Then his expression slowly morphed to one of dread.

Her belly fell into a steep dive, just as another man approached. The muted roar in her ears made her miss the upsurge of the crowd's murmuring. But as she fought to reassure herself nothing was wrong, that her utter foolishness couldn't…*wouldn't* be repaid with another life-altering consequence, the present arrived in a rush, and she felt Christos grow even stiffer beside her.

Alexis focused every last ounce of attention on the approaching man.

From the marked resemblance, he had to be Christos's father.

Father and son stared at one another for a tight moment before, jaw clenched tight, Christos said, 'What do you want?'

Bleakness flashed across the older man's face before it turned as neutral as his son's. 'To have a cordial conversation. It is a party, after all.'

If anything, the icy anger vibrating off Christos multiplied by a thousand. 'Cordial?' he bit out. 'I highly recommend you double-check the definition of the word before you apply it to yourself, *Pateras*.'

A tight little smile curved his father's lips. 'At least you still call me Father. I suppose that is a small blessing.' His gaze shifted to her, then back to his son. 'Are you going to introduce me?' he asked.

Tense silence fell. Then, 'No.'

His father's gaze returned to hers. 'I'm Agios.'

Once again she found herself holding out her hand to a relative of Christos's she wasn't sure she liked very much. 'Alexis… Drakakis,' she added at the last moment, the weight of it shaking through her.

This time she felt a different energy emanating from Christos. Felt his ferocious gaze on her face for one monumental second before he faced his father again. 'You've made a show of yourself to the crowd. Feel free to leave.'

A hard, combative light filled his father's eyes, then it died just as swiftly, leaving him a shadow of himself. 'Five years I've been trying to get you to talk to me. I'd hoped tonight you would spare me a few minutes.'

That bit of news surprised Alexis. Everything she'd learnt of Agios so far had suggested father and son were mutually estranged. A quick glance showed Christos's granite-hard face gave no indication of softening. 'You were wrong. Excuse us.'

The fingers linking hers were stiff, his grip tight. Reeling from the twin bombshells, she allowed Christos to march her away, her surroundings blurring as stomach-hollowing possibilities filled her mind.

Once again she found her back pressed against a wall, a short distance away from the party. But where there'd been torrid passion in his face, now there was a rabid watchfulness, as if he wanted to mine the answers from every hidden corner inside her.

'Is there something we need to talk about?' he breathed. The same energy vibrating through him, the one that felt like a mixture of earthquake, lightning and nuclear explosion held together by the thinnest rope, unravelled inside her.

Her eyes darted over the guests, attempting to find something…anything to ground her. Because the *no* that should've fallen firmly from her lips was lodged in her throat.

'Alexis.' It wasn't a question. More of a dire warning. And something else…

Something earth-shattering in its ferocity. And even though she knew it was the epitome of folly to look into his eyes in that moment, Alexis raised her gaze, met a cyclone of grey shot through with blinding, unholy light.

'I... I don't know.'

His face clenched hard before he exhaled. 'I accept that I share responsibility for this...state we find ourselves in, but I need a better answer than that.'

'That's all I can give you right now. I'm not on the pill, and my period is...erratic at best,' she confessed.

He seemed transfixed. *'Thee mou,'* he breathed. 'So you could be pregnant?'

'Not necessarily. The odds are low,' she said, mentally calculating frantically.

A look passed through his eyes, gone as quickly as it arrived. 'When will you know?'

'A week. Maybe less.'

Another eternity passed as he stared at her. Then his gaze dropped to her belly. Whatever thought went through his mind evoked a faint trembling in the fingers that raked through his hair a moment later.

'It could be nothing, Christos.'

'Or it could be...the opposite,' he countered tightly. Laughter and the clink of glasses nearby intruded on their bubble. Mouth firming, he took a step back. 'This isn't the right moment to discuss it.'

They returned to mingle with a new, jagged awareness vibrating between them. Christos barely left her side throughout the long evening. He introduced her to guests with a hand around her waist, which lingered until, the yearning it created unbearable, she found an excuse to pull away.

Because with each moment that passed, *it could be nothing* tumbled through her brain, fighting against the soul-shaking need *to be something*. And each time he touched her, each time he introduced her as his wife and those stormy grey eyes swept over her, her heart yearned harder.

As the party wound down they gravitated back to Costas, who was holding court with a small group of guests. About to take a seat, she started in surprise when Christos pulled her into his lap. It took every ounce of composure not to stiffen or show her surprise. But she blushed at the few suggestive looks that came their way.

'Relax,' he commanded quietly, his hand planted possessively on her hip.

But she couldn't relax. Besides the simple fact that she wanted nothing more than to melt into his arms, Alexis was also aware of Christos's father's frequent gaze, the regretful expression that lingered on his son when he thought no one was looking.

A nerve-shredding hour later, once a few more helicopters had taken off and overnight guests retired to their suites, she took the opportunity to make her escape. 'I'm tired, I think I'm going to head up.'

She held her breath as Christos's arm tightened momentarily before he released her. He got up and started to accompany her inside. 'I'll walk you in,' he said smoothly, his hand capturing hers.

'You don't have to—'

'Stop, Alexis. We're past that,' he interrupted.

She should've taken the hint. Instead, she paused on the first step of the sweeping staircase leading up to their wing, a different subject altogether tumbling from her lips. 'What about your father? Are you past the right moment to talk to him too?'

His eyes turned arctic. 'What?'

'Are you going to avoid him forever? Or just wait until it's too late to do anything about it?'

His eyes narrowed in warning. 'Be careful, Alexis. You tread on dangerous ground.'

'Do I?' she dared, because that need wedged tight beneath her breastbone wouldn't be silenced. The last hour had shown her the type of family she and Christos could have. The type she'd yearned for all her life. Sitting there, with the knowledge that their blind passion could have unexpected results, had only intensified that need. 'I know what he did to you was painful, but I think he regrets it. You should give him a—'

She paused, catching movement behind Christos's shoulder. A moment later, the man in question appeared.

Spotting him, Christos stiffened.

'Christos, I really must talk to you,' his father said, his voice ringed with authority she'd heard many times from his son.

Sensing he was about to refuse again, she spoke. 'Go ahead, Christos. I need to call Sophie, anyway.'

He knew it was an excuse and his lips firmed. But before she could make her escape, he caught her hand, leaned in close and brushed his lips over her temple. 'Enjoy your temporary reprieve,' he murmured in her ear before pulling away.

He strode away briskly, not sparing his father a glance. But a minute later, she heard the study door open and shut. Only then did she run upstairs, her stomach muscles weak as jelly.

All through undressing and readying for bed, the jittery feeling continued. It was as she slid into bed, the luxury comforter enclosing her body, that she accepted the truth.

She was in love with Christos.

And against all the odds, against the self-preservation she'd sworn to keep in place after Adrian, she'd arrived in a situation that now promised to deliver the very thing she'd craved her whole life.

Beneath the covers, her hand slid over her stomach, a fresh shudder—this one of quiet awe—moving within her.

Pregnant.

She could be *pregnant*.

That thought beating an ever-increasing drumbeat inside her, Alexis expected to remain awake, her senses alert for Christos's arrival.

Christos entered the study, impatience, anxiety and terror mingling in a toxic cocktail inside him. He'd thought himself immune to his father's effect on him but the moment he turned to face him he knew he wasn't. Perhaps he would never be. All the more reason to stay away from him. He started towards the door, cursing himself for listening to Alexis. 'This was a mistake—'

'Running away won't resolve this, son.'

He whirled back, righteous anger replacing the dread. 'Excuse me? How dare you!'

'That's right, get angry. I'll take that over the silence and icy indifference,' his father replied, shattered bleakness in his eyes.

'Whatever it is you're trying to achieve here, you'd better choose your words carefully,' he warned.

Agios sighed, walked over to the sofa and dropped heavily into it. 'I'm trying to say that I deserve your anger. That you have every right to feel it.'

Something attempted to crack open in his chest. He held it in place with sheer willpower. 'Thanks for the permission,' he replied sardonically.

His father's lips twisted. 'All the while I thought you'd been spared...' He paused, shook his head. 'I see you weren't. You're too much your father's son, Christos.'

Icy dread froze his spine. 'No! I'm nothing like you.' He couldn't be. Not when he'd striven to remove himself from the volatility of his upbringing. Not when he'd cut off all feeling lest he be plagued with the overabundance of the wrong type of emotion the way his parents had.

But what if he hadn't escaped?

What if the child Alexis possibly carried was doomed

because of it? The very possibility made his breath catch painfully.

'Son? What is—'

'Say what you want to say and let's be done.' He needed time to think. Time to wean himself off that traitorous swell of pure joy he'd felt when Alexis had laid the possibility that she might be pregnant at his feet. He needed to replace it with the far more acceptable reality that he couldn't do this. He had neither the tools nor the road map to make even a halfway decent attempt at fatherhood. Because of the man in front of him.

Agios sighed again. 'I want… I've wanted all these years…to ask for your forgiveness.'

That fracture returned. 'Why?'

'Because what I did to you, to your mother, was wrong. I let my bitterness get the better of me. The moment your mother threatened to leave me, I… I just…' He stopped, shook his head. 'We shouldn't have put you in the middle of our problems. I know your mother feels the same—'

'It's too late,' he snapped, because he was in danger of reverting into that little boy again, craving the affection and attention he'd sorely lacked. *But he was a grown man.* 'You're thirty years too late. You need to live with the fact that your actions created a monster.' And because of that, whatever he'd been foolishly hoping might happen with Alexis could never be. She deserved so much more. More than he could ever give her. The truth shook through him until his guts threatened to turn themselves inside out. Until his very skin was icy cold with the realisation.

'Christos—'

'Goodbye, Father.'

He walked out, an altered man from the one who'd entered.

Because all the joy was gone. And yes, it was for the best.

* * *

Alexis opened her eyes to bright sunlight and the cold, empty space beside her. Unease rapidly built inside her when, sitting up and looking around her, she spotted the two large suitcases near the doorway to Christos's dressing room.

The man himself entered from the living room a moment later. He froze, his gaze combing over her in fierce possession before he reeled himself under control. But in that split moment, she caught surprise, then resignation, which made the stone in her belly even heavier.

She clutched the sheet to her chest, trying to shake the confusion from her head.

'You didn't come to bed last night.'

Savage hunger blazed in his eyes for a nanosecond before his expression closed, his movements unhurried as he secured his favoured ultra-thin Vacheron Constantin watch on his wrist. 'No.'

When she realised he wouldn't elaborate, she pressed, 'Why are you packed? Are you…are we leaving?'

'I'm flying to Athens. Demitri's ex has agreed to the terms. He wants to secure the custody agreement before she changes her mind.'

Alexis frowned, even as she shifted to get out of bed. 'Okay, I'll start packing—'

'No. You'll stay here.'

She froze, inside and out. 'But… I'm your assistant. And I always travel with you. You'll need me to—'

'I don't need you.'

She swallowed before she could speak. 'Specifically for this? Or generally?' she forced herself to say, aware of the barbs of anguish already eviscerating her.

A muscle rippled in his jaw, and he turned away. 'I'll return once I've dealt with the matter.'

'You didn't answer me. Is this because of last night? Because I urged you to talk to your father? What did he want to talk about?' she asked, aware she was overstepping but not really caring. He was shutting her out, rejecting her in a way that was all too frighteningly familiar. What wasn't as familiar was the urge to fight this time; not to accept her lot and slink away to lick her wounds.

For the longest time, Christos remained silent. 'He stumbled his way through a mockery of an apology for how he treated me as a child. I have no intention of accepting it,' he said finally.

Cold dread closed around her throat. 'I'm assuming that didn't take all night. So why didn't you come to bed? Is it because you think I might be pregnant? Is it because you're terrified of becoming a father?'

His head went back as if he'd been stunned with a taser. 'You said the possibility of that is negligible.'

'But what if it isn't?'

His face went ashen, and while he was trying to collect himself, she ploughed on, 'You rarely take cases with children. When you do you keep a close eye on those children, to ensure they're being looked after. You're running off to fight for your godson, and yet the possibility that I might be pregnant terrifies you?'

His jaw clenched hard, but the fire in his eyes was ablaze with warning. 'You misunderstand, Alexis *mou*. I hate losing. Period. A child suffering because I haven't executed my job properly signifies a loss to me.'

'Is it really so hard to admit you care about anything, Christos? That there's a heart beating in that chest of yours? A heart that aches at the thought of loss?'

His face tightened. 'Alexis…'

'A heart that will mourn Costas at some point in the future when he's gone?' she whispered, an urgent need to see the man from the cave and not this…cold, closed-off version of him. She rose from the bed, the sheet wrapped around her.

His face clenched harder, but, like last night, the hand he lifted to rake his hair shook. The small sign of vulnerability gave her wild hope. 'Of course I'll feel his loss. As I would any fixture in my life.'

'Don't try and throw me off with that. Your grandfather is not a car. Or a well-tailored suit. Or even your beloved Drakonisos. He's flesh and blood and emotions. Just like me. Just like everything you seem hell-bent on cutting from your life.'

His hand slashed the space between them in a very Greek dismissal. 'What is this, Alexis? What exactly do you hope to achieve by riling me this way?'

'Oh, so you admit to being riled?'

He scowled. 'You wish me to show you? Is that it?'

'That you're capable of emotion? I know you are. If you're this upset when you lose a case, then you can feel. It's a specific type of emotion I'm after.'

His nostrils flared. 'Why?'

'Because I want to know that all this has been worth it! That I haven't been throwing myself on some callous altar with nothing to show for it.'

He looked stunned. Then furious. 'There was never any promise of...whatever it is you're searching for.'

'If you don't know what I'm searching for, then how do you know I can't have it?'

He cupped his nape in a gesture of pure frustration. 'Because I'm incapable of it,' he snarled. 'I lack the building blocks of your fancy emotions. I strategise. I win. That's the only fuel I need.'

'You love—'

'I don't.'

Her heart cracked, but she didn't...couldn't stop. 'Your grandfather? Did you keep the true circumstances of our marriage from him because you hate him? Or because you care about his feelings enough not to want to hurt him?'

'I care about possessing Drakonisos. That's it.'

'Why? It's just a piece of dirt. Rocks and soil and plants and water. Why go to all these lengths over this particular piece of property when there are literally hundreds more you can spend your millions on?'

'Because it's special! And it's mine! And you know how I feel about things that belong to me.'

'Do I? Yes, you like winning. But then what comes after doesn't matter to you. You're fighting too hard for this piece of land and yet I bet, once you have it, you'll never set foot on it again.' Her voice wavered and broke and she hated herself for it. 'Maybe that's why Costas wanted you to prove yourself. Maybe he wanted to see if you *cared* enough.'

'He knows I care. He knows this is the only place—' He caught himself, veered away from her as if doing so would block the emotions bristling from him.

'Say it. There's no one to hear it but me, Christos. And I won't betray you. You know I won't.'

He gave a harsh laugh. 'Does it even occur to you, up there on that little pedestal you've placed yourself on, that I don't wish to make this confession to you?'

'You can be cruel all you want. It doesn't change the fact that, after what your parents did to you, the possibility that you might become a father yourself terrifies you.'

His pallor grew more ashen. 'Enough. Stop.'

'We can make it work together, Christos,' she pressed. 'What have you got to lose?'

'Myself! Because you see too much! Because you make me—'

'I make you what?' She knew she was pushing him hard. But the need to do so was a live wire inside her, twisting with hunger.

'It's immaterial.'

'If it was, you wouldn't be leaving. And you certainly wouldn't be leaving me behind.'

He stalked towards her, cupped her jaw between his hands. Fingers shoved into her hair, his gaze ferociously turbulent as he stared down at her. 'Because you're relentless, even when you don't speak. Your eyes speak for you. And I don't like that, at every turn, they threaten to turn me inside out.'

Her breath caught. 'Christos.'

'You want to know why I can't forgive my parents? Because neither of them chose me, their son. I was merely the weapon they used to hurt each other. My mother made the error of taunting my father with wanting a divorce one too many times because she wanted his attention. Instead of taking it back—because she didn't really want to divorce him—she stood her ground. He in turn was too proud to relent once he started down that road. He decided to teach her a lesson by ripping our family apart. Everything she asked for, he refused just to see her suffer.'

'And she asked to keep you?'

'At first. But even that became too much for her. And when they tired of using me, they dumped me here. The only reprieve from being in their firing line was when I came here.'

'I'm…so sorry. But—'

'But nothing, Alexis. There is no excusing treating any child like that. And I can't risk…' He stopped, shook his head.

'He's still your father, Christos. Do you know what a treasure it is to have one at all? And one who regrets the mistakes he's made?'

His eyes shadowed, then his hands dropped. 'I don't presume to know your suffering. Don't presume to know mine.'

She was beating her head against a wall. And she was

breaking her own heart smashing it against an immovable object. 'So, what, you expect me to remain here, the obedient, possibly pregnant wife, while you go and save the world?'

He shook his head and her foolish heart leapt. Then he flayed her with, 'You haven't had a proper vacation since you've been with me. You have access to my pilot and all my properties. Go wherever you want and take whatever time you need. I only ask one thing,' he said, his face clenching with raw emotion.

She knew what was coming. 'You want to know if I'm pregnant? So you can do what, exactly? You don't want to risk your heart, so what do you have to give?' she demanded hoarsely.

His hands slid into his pockets, his shoulders rigid. 'I'll take care of you, just like I have so far.'

She frowned, unsure why the words left a hollow ache inside her. He didn't mean emotionally. No, of course he didn't. Which meant…financially. She reared back. 'You think I want your money?'

He looked alarmed for a moment. Then his lips turned down in the bitter way she was beginning to realise signified a return to old memories. 'You wanted something in exchange for marrying me. If my offer offends you, you can make whatever demands you want. Another charity patronage, perhaps?'

Her dart of hurt turned into a throbbing bruise. 'Why do I have to want something? Why can't this be a gift we both treasure? A child we can both love, together. To raise, together. *If* I am indeed pregnant?'

Again he looked…stunned. As if such an idea hadn't even occurred to him.

It was her turn to experience a quiet astonishment. 'No one has ever given you something without wanting something in return, have they?' she asked in a hushed wonder.

'Is that why you end all your liaisons with lavish gifts? Because you think it's expected of you?' She pointed to the necklace she'd placed on her bedside table. 'Is that what the diamonds are for? Because you think once you pay me off I'll have no right to make any further demands of you?'

He stared at her for a frozen moment before he turned away. 'I'm not sure when you think I signed up for psychoanalysis but, I assure you, it's becoming exceedingly boring.'

Her reply was halted by a knock on the door. Alexis snatched the robe draped at the foot of the bed, avoiding his gaze as she secured the belt.

Then he was opening the door, instructing his staff to take his cases down.

Alexis stood frozen as he turned back. 'Alexis—'

'If you're going to tell me again that I'm boring you, I don't want to hear it. I think we've said everything that needs saying, don't you?' She held on to her anger, because it kept her upright. Kept her from crumbling.

His lips moved, as if to contradict her. But after a moment, he gave a terse nod.

Then he just…walked out.

Alexis staggered to the bed, sank on it, numb. After long minutes, she heard the helicopter take off and didn't move. A knock on the door didn't stir her. When whoever it was went away, she crawled beneath the sheets once more, her eyes on the ceiling.

The sense of loss seemed unsurmountable, the swiftness with which her world had come crushing down making her nauseous. But had it even been *her* world in the first place?

What did it matter now?

She'd gambled with her heart and she'd lost. Again.

The numbness remained over the next few days, the only times she roused herself the times she spent with Costas.

She sensed his gaze on her intermittently, but he never commented on his grandson's absence. And she never volunteered information.

Before she knew it a week had passed and she was still in the dark as to whether she carried Christos's child or not. Not that it dimmed the yearning in her heart.

And when the morning came ten days later that she accepted Christos wasn't coming back, and that she might possibly need to face single motherhood alone, she packed her bags, summoned Christos's jet. And said goodbye to Drakonisos.

CHAPTER ELEVEN

IT SHOULD'VE BEEN EASY.

He'd been on an emotionally destructive path, and he'd course-corrected. The same way he'd hardened his heart to his father's stumbling apology, even though a traitorous part of him had urged him to allow it, should've been the way he dismissed Alexis's audacity to tell him there was another way forward.

He didn't deal in hope. Or require his father's regret to heal.

Why couldn't he stop thinking about Alexis's words? Or forget the pain in his father's eyes as he'd walked away from him? Why had he spent the last two weeks with the growing sensation that he'd made the worst mistake of his life?

We can make it work together, Christos.

The sweet promise of those words had terrified him more than anything else she'd flung at him, perhaps with the exception of the shocking flame of pure terrifying joy that had lit his soul at the possibility that he might be a father, even though he knew he lacked the basic tools of success.

The conviction of that lack was what had propelled him onto his helicopter and off Drakonisos. It had lasted through the court hearing that finally granted Demitri custody of one son and through the meeting that secured a custody arrangement for the other.

He tried to remain removed as he observed father and sons reunited. But he couldn't stop the clamouring in his heart that'd started the moment Alexis had confessed that she might be pregnant.

The wild panic had dulled. There'd been a peculiar kind

of serendipity in setting eyes on his father on the same day he'd learned that he might become a father too. He'd taken it as a timely reminder of his past. What he'd overcome.

But the truth was, he'd never felt as exposed, as vulnerable as he had in the hours after he'd parted ways with his father, when he'd walked the dark landscape of the only true home he'd known. He'd felt he was every inch the abomination he'd named himself, incapable of giving Alexis what she sorely needed—love. Besides that, every imaginable scenario for success required he open his heart, risk more pain. Because if he'd wanted love as a child, wouldn't his own child demand it? Wouldn't the woman who'd counter-dared him to be brave, then watched him leave with disappointment and pain in her eyes?

He'd been right to accuse her of seeing too much.

He passed his hand over his jaw, encountered the stubble and inwardly grimaced. He was supposed to be his own man, yet a simple thing such as shaving off the stubble Alexis had found so sexy had become impossible.

As impossible as the raw chasm inside him that grew wider with every minute she was absent from his life.

Two weeks. A lifetime.

She hadn't answered his emails or texts in the last five days. And before that, her responses had been perfunctory. The only reason he hadn't already hunted her down was because he was...terrified. At first because of the possibility she might be carrying his child. Then because she might not.

Once his initial terror had waned, he recalled everything she'd said to him. The hope. The sheer belief in the face of what should've been a daunting situation for her, especially after what she'd suffered.

We can make it work together, Christos.

Those words had finally driven him onto his jet then onto another helicopter ride over what he was sure was the stunning countryside of Buenos Aires. Because even as terrified as he was, the alternative—the bleak, lonely, soulless life he'd led so far—terrified him even more.

He'd allowed the hope of Alexis's words to bloom inside him when he'd finally learned her whereabouts. As the helicopter set down and he stepped out, he prayed he hadn't completely blown it.

Two things went through her mind as Alexis watched the man she wished she could hate stride towards her. The first was that she should've rushed inside, thrown on something a little more sophisticated than the flimsy yellow dress she wore, her hair windblown and her feet bare. The second was that she'd missed him with a terrifying desperation. The soul-wrenching bonus third arrived as he stopped a few feet from her.

She still loved him. Was hopelessly head over heels for him.

The heart-shredding thought made her wrap her hands around her middle, as if it would hold all that tumultuous feeling inside.

'*Kalispera*, Alexis.'

Dear God, his voice. She'd heard it far too frequently in her dreams, only to wake to empty loss. 'You should've emailed me to let me know you were coming. I would've vacated the premises.'

'Since you're the reason I'm here, that would've been counterproductive.'

She notched her chin higher. 'I have another three weeks of annual leave to take. So you're going to have to find someone else—'

'I don't want anyone else. I want you, Alexis.'

The arms she'd wrapped around her middle clenched harder, emotions threatening to spill all over the place. 'I may be the best assistant you've ever had but you don't own me, Christos. I've decided that if I return to work for you, I won't be at your beck and call twenty-four-seven any more. I deserve a life. I deserve more.'

Something harrowing flickered through his eyes but she refused to be swayed.

'But being the best assistant I've ever had meant you knew my whereabouts,' he challenged. 'You could've disappeared indefinitely. But you chose to stay here.'

Alexis knew he was right. She could've fulfilled a lifelong dream and headed for the Maldives instead. But even that had been ruined for her. Because how could she sit on a pristine beach without recalling that unforgettable night on Drakonisos?

'Don't read anything into it. Argentina is a beautiful country. It's been on my bucket list forever. And since you all but insisted that I'd earned my keep…'

'The things I said, Alexis. They were wrong. I didn't mean them.'

She froze, that precious bubble inside her threatening to burst free. 'What?'

His gaze dropped to her fingers she'd raised to toy with the cheap chain she'd bought in Buenos Aires a few days ago, a flame lighting the grey depths. A flame eerily resembling…hope. 'You're still wearing your wedding rings.'

She shrugged even as her insides quaked. She hadn't yet gathered the strength to take them off. But she wasn't going to confess that. 'I don't know your safe combination here. It seemed safer to keep them on than to leave them in a drawer somewhere.'

He winced at the barb. 'You want to hurt me. I fully deserve it.'

'What makes you think I care at all one way or the other?'

Again something resembling agony slashed his face. 'Because I'm a stubborn fool, Alexis. A stubborn fool who ran scared because he couldn't handle the possibility of accepting the one thing he craved above all else.'

A tremble started at her feet and unravelled upwards. 'And what's that?'

'To know that someone cared for me. Enough to reach out. To put me first, like my parents never did. Everything you said to me that morning, I yearned to grasp with both hands. But –'

'But experience has taught you that reaching out comes with a price. A price of rejection?'

'Exactly so. Even accepting my father's remorse felt impossible. Every second he was talking I believed there'd be a catch. That he would rip my heart out all over again. But because of you, I'm finally able to entertain the possibility that he's changed. That he regrets what he did.'

'I'm so sorry you went through that, but… Christos, I can't be around someone who clings to past pain the way you do, or anyone who throws me away like you did. *You* were the one who urged me to let go of my hang-ups about Adrian, remember? Isn't it time to take your own advice? I know I'm not that special but—'

'How can you even doubt it for a second?' he burst out, an angry edge in his tone. 'Don't you know how special you are, Alexis? That you can look forward with hope despite what you've been through? To claim your child without an iota of doubt that you'll be a much better mother than your own was to you?'

Her heart lurched as anguish returned tenfold. 'I don't… I'm not pregnant, Christos. I think you should know that before—'

His eyes shadowed but he nodded. 'I know. You would've told me by now if you were. That's the sort of person you are.'

Her heart twisted harder, the longing in her soul too

large to contain. 'Then you don't need to make any declarations.'

'But I want to. Your fierce resilience, your belief that we can do this together...be what our own parents couldn't. It's the only thing I've been able to think about.'

A flash of hurt crossed her eyes and she stepped away. 'The *only* thing?'

He groaned. 'No. I've missed you, Alexis. So damn much. I can't walk into a room without looking for you. I can't sleep, I can barely eat. Your absence cuts me like a knife.'

'And yet you managed to stay away for weeks.'

'Because I didn't think I deserved you. I still don't believe it. But you were right. I'm greedy. The things I love, I want to have close and—'

'Wait...the things...you *love*?' she echoed faintly.

Regret filmed his eyes. 'I hate that I've triggered this hesitancy in you. You should know how special you are, my beautiful Alexis. How deeply and irrevocably I love you. Long before you gave yourself to me on my beach. Long before I accepted that you were as vital to me as the air I breathe.'

Every fibre of her being shook. 'Christos...'

He cupped her cheeks, an intensity blazing in his eyes that threatened to brand her forever. 'Give me another chance. Please tell me there's a place in your future for me even though I don't deserve you.'

'You said that already,' she said, her voice a tremulous mess.

'And I'll probably say it again because... I'm nothing without you, *agapita*.'

'You...love me? Truly?' she whispered.

'With every cell in my body. Every beat of my heart. *Se agapo*, Alexis.'

She felt the sensation deep within, transforming her

with the kind of joy she'd only dreamed about. The kind she'd yearned for as a child, then searched for in the wrong place before discovering the right man.

His fingers trailed down her cheek, something close to awe filling his eyes. 'The way you look at me, Alexis. It fills my heart to the brim. Even if you don't love me—'

'Oh, Christos, I love you too!' she interjected before her heart burst wide open.

Emotion visibly shuddered through him as she saw her joy reflected in his eyes. 'Say it again, *koukla mou*.'

'I love you. So, so much.'

She fell into his arms, and they kissed. And when need built into an inferno, she dragged him to the study floor, their clothes hurriedly discarded.

'You have no idea how much I've missed this,' he confessed roughly.

Her laughter was pure delight. 'I have some idea.'

'Good, then you're prepared.'

When he surged inside her, they both froze, their eyes locked on one another as love and lust and joy spun through them.

'I love you,' he groaned. 'Marry me again, Alexis. In front of every undeserving family member I have, this time. Give me the honour of being the father of your children?'

'Yes, Christos. To all of it.'

Nine months and one week later, Christos passed shaky fingers through his hair as he paced the private hospital room.

Perhaps that was to be his fate, to tremble before the woman he loved for all eternity. As sacrifices went, it was one he would willingly perform over and over. For the gift of Alexis. And the new gift they were about to be blessed with.

'Something funny?' The wife of his heart and soul gasped, before sending a glare his way.

'No, my love.'

'Good. Now get over here. I can feel another contraction about to rip me apart.'

He did as he was told, linked his fingers with hers, pressed his lips against her temple and held on tight as she brought their child into the world.

A thankfully short hour later, their miracle was placed in their arms. Christos took one look at Diana, his baby girl, and fell head over heels in love for the second time in his life.

'Kalosorizo, glykia mou,' he rasped, his throat tight with emotion. 'Welcome.'

'Oh, Christos. She's gorgeous.'

'Almost as beautiful as her mama,' he said, unable to contain the joy moving through him.

'Come here, I want to hold both of you,' she insisted.

She made space on the bed and held out her arms. He perched beside her, his lips dropping a soft kiss on his daughter's head, before pressing a deeper kiss on his wife's lips. 'I still don't deserve you,' he murmured.

Her face creased in a smile. 'You've given me your heart, and the family of my soul. I want nothing more than to love you as you love me.'

'I do, Alexis. You have made me the happiest man on earth.'

They stared down at their baby for a few lovestruck minutes before she looked up. 'How much time do we have before Costas and your parents summon us for another visit?'

'Probably a week, maybe two. Costas believes he's found his second wind after his operation and wants to expend all his energy on his great-granddaughter.'

'I can't wait to show Diana her true home.' The home Costas had signed over to him without reservation six months ago after admitting his machinations had been to shake Christos out of his apathy and into fighting harder for the family he deserved. The place where he'd started to rebuild his relationship with his parents, thanks to Alexis's encouragement and support.

'No, *agape mou*. Home is wherever you are. Drakonisos is special because it's where we first loved each other.'

Her arms tightened, and Christos's heart sang. Because he knew, in her arms, he would always find love. And home.

* * * * *

MY FORBIDDEN ROYAL FLING

CLARE CONNELLY

MILLS & BOON

For Dan,
who I've known and loved more than half my life.

PROLOGUE

Ménage à Billionaire!

THE HEADLINE SCREAMS at me, right above the way-too-handsome face of Santiago del Almodovár, his eyes looking directly at the camera lens, so it feels as though he's staring right through me. And, even though we're separated by several countries, a shiver runs the length of my spine, a rush of apprehension. He's flanked on either side by beautiful women, one blonde, one with cherry-red hair, different in looks but no doubt interchangeable to a man like Santiago. Derision curls my lips.

'This is seriously the man you wish to get involved with?' I can't help but sniff as I address my country's Prime Minister, a man I've always thought had good judgement.

'I understand his reputation isn't particularly savoury, Your Highness…' An embarrassed laugh comes through the phone line. 'But he's well-funded and his investment has the support of the entire parliament.'

'His reputation isn't just unsavoury, Prime Minister, it's disgraceful. From my admittedly brief research, there's nothing to recommend this man except the fact he's "well-funded",' I say quietly, buying time. *His investment has the support of the entire parliament* is a sentence that speaks volumes.

I take it as the gentle warning the minister intends. This is a *fait accompli.* While technically my approval is required to sign off on the deal, I'd be going against my parliament and decades of legal precedent if I refuse. But how the hell can I let this happen? What would my parents think? That's easy. They might have died many years ago—too many—but I hear my father's voice loud and clear, his disapproval, his sadness. This is the exact opposite of what he'd want, and I swore I'd always follow in his footsteps.

I drop my head forward, catching it in the palm of my free hand, the other hand tightening my grip on the phone.

'He's offering a king's ransom for the land.'

Bleakness washes through me. There is no King now, no Queen either. There's just me, a princess, desperately trying to stave off financial ruin for the kingdom without sacrificing the culture of my people, doing everything I can to do justice to my title as my parents would have expected.

'At what price, though?' I murmur, sitting straighter, staring straight ahead. A tapestry hangs on the wall across from me, an ancient piece that I loved even as a little girl.

Out of nowhere, I hear my father's voice. *You must remember, we are Marlsdovens and, while the world knocks at our door, we must answer without being trampled. What makes us unique has to be protected at all costs.*

'My assistant will send through the contracts, Your Highness. If you could sign them—'

'I shall look at them and get back to you,' I interrupt. I hate the idea of a man like that owning such a prime piece of the city's real estate, and I loathe his plans for the site—a glitzy, gaudy casino that will turn our ancient, cultural principality into the exact opposite of my father's vision.

I'm a caretaker for this country—the throne is mine temporarily—and my duty is to look after the people as best I can. What would my father say if he knew I was allowing this to happen? *Make it worth it.* I hear his advice as surely as if he'd breathed the words into the room. Sitting straighter, I grip the phone in my hands.

'Prime Minister?'

'Yes, Your Highness?'

'I'd like to meet with him.' *Make it worth it.* What if I can get him to agree to terms that will truly make this idea worthwhile? And, if he doesn't like my suggestion, then he can simply walk away. After all, he obviously wants the land badly, so why not barter with him, ensure the deal is as advantageous as it can possibly be?

'There's no need for that.' He's scandalised by the very idea, and I can understand why. Santiago's reputation precedes him by about three thousand football fields. He's a lothario through and through, a man as famous for his hard-core partying lifestyle as for the multiple women he wines, dines, beds then moves on from.

'Are you worried I won't be able to handle him, sir?'

The Prime Minister sighs. 'He is a fierce negotiator.'

'I'll cope,' I murmur crisply, my eyes straying to the screen. 'Please arrange it as soon as possible. Thank you.'

It's only a still photo, but his eyes seem to be mocking, taunting… I shut the lid and scrape back my chair. If Santiago wants to buy this land, he can jump through a few hoops first—and, if he's not willing to do that, he can go to hell.

CHAPTER ONE

THE SUNLIGHT BATHES the palace courtyard in a pale glow. It's dappled by the surrounding birch trees so it forms a lattice effect on the ground, and across the man striding towards me.

I've been braced for this—him—for days. The security report on the Spanish tycoon was extensive and detailed—at my request. It confirmed much of what my own searching had done. He lives fast, loose, reckless, with little care for his reputation, his health or, so far as I can tell, for anyone in his orbit. Santiago del Almodovár is the kind of man I loathe.

His stride is long, courtesy of his height—easily six and a half feet—so he comes towards me too quickly. He stares at me with eyes that are a rich, pale brown, almost golden like a wolf's, enigmatic and intense, as though he can see right through me.

I paste an ice-cold smile on my face, tight and distinctly warning. He's wearing a suit—sort of. Navy trousers, a white shirt and a blazer, the shirt unbuttoned at the neck and no tie. It's a strikingly casual look for a guest here at Sölla Palace, but the security council included a note to say that Santiago has very little regard for established conventions. Privately I wonder if it's not a tool he uses to wrong-foot people from the first meeting and thus gain a hint of advantage in negotiations.

As he draws close, I wait for the trademark bow my rank generally commands. He stops two feet short of me, his own smile mocking in a way that stirs butterflies inside me to a fever pitch. His eyes probe mine and a shiver comes out of nowhere. I suppress it, ignoring his lack of protocol, extending my hand in a universal gesture.

'Mr del Almodovár, thank you for coming.'

'Princess…'

He fills my title with a husky accent, warm and spiced, like the Barcelona sun that fed his soul as a child. Another shiver threatens my equilibrium, but it's quickly overtaken by lightning as he curves his far larger hand around mine, confident and firm, his touch sending a thousand volts of electricity from my fingertips to my arm and then through my entire body. It takes every ounce of self-possession to conceal my reaction, but I pull my hand away as quickly as I can, flexing my fingers at my side.

'Please.' I gesture to the steps, swallowing to cover the hoarseness in my voice. My breath is strained and inwardly I groan. Why, of all people, at all times, do I need to develop a sudden awareness of Santiago del Almodovár's sex appeal? I'm twenty-four and I've never so much as kissed a man—it's not easy to date when you're the only surviving member of the Marlsdoven royal family. I've never met anyone that's tempted me before, either.

Perhaps it's also the knowledge that my parents have chosen my husband for me, my eventual marriage arranged before I was born. Their dearest wish had been for their daughter to wed the youngest son of their closest friends. I found out shortly after they died; perhaps that's what prevented me from getting involved with anyone. I've literally never had my head turned. I mean, I can tell when someone is objectively handsome or charming, and I enjoy spending time with nice, interesting people, but I've never met a guy and felt anything like a spark.

Why this man?

Why now?

I clamp my teeth together, reminding myself of all the reasons I need to focus. His desire to buy valuable crown land and place a casino on the riverbanks of this ancient, proud city is a threat to everything I hold dear. I have to control this.

'Nice palace,' he murmurs as we step inside the enormous golden doors, each flanked by a guard dressed in full ceremonial uniform. He pays the compliment without it sounding remotely genuine. It's a joke, if anything. I draw my brows together, surprised, because most guests to Sölla are so overwhelmed by the thousand-year-old rooms and the grandiose fittings that I have to work overtime to put them at ease before we can achieve any sensible conversation. But this man has vast personal wealth, earning more in a year than my country's GDP; I gather he's not easily impressed.

That sharpens something inside me, a curl of derision. Because wealth and luxury are one thing, but history quite another. Anyone who can stand inside this grand hall—with its ornate stone carvings made by the hands of men who lived eleven hundred years ago, its vaulted ceilings breathtakingly high, its stained-glass windows perfectly capturing the afternoon sunlight—and be immune to its beauty must surely be a philistine of the highest order.

And? What more can I expect from a man who's made his fortune by building casinos where people go to lose their livelihoods and all hope? People like my uncle, whose addiction cost him so much, ultimately his life. The thought cuts through me, and for a second I'm almost swallowed by nauseating panic. My parents hated gambling. The idea of a casino here in Marlsdoven was absolutely forbidden. What would my dad have said?

Since my parents died, all I've wanted is to make them proud, to make the decisions they'd expect me to make. Dad would have known how to get out of this; he'd have known how to dissuade the Prime Minister. I have never wished for my parents to be here more than I do now.

I squeeze my eyes shut as we walk, sucking in a shaking breath that doesn't quite reach my lungs. Stars dance against my eyelids. I see my parents and their disappointment and feel a horrible sense of failure wash over me.

Santiago makes no attempt at small talk as I lead him through the grand hall and into a narrow but no less impressive corridor—this one flanked by portraits of the royal family going back hundreds of years. My eyes stray to my parents as I pass and my heart lurches with the constant ache I feel for them even now, seven years after their shocking deaths. I can't meet my dad's eyes. I know he'd hate this; my resolution to honour their memory is in tatters.

A state room has been prepared for our meeting, but I realise the error of that as we enter, for the room is not large, and in here Santiago's presence is overwhelming. My pulse goes into overdrive as I turn to face him, so much more aware of him now. Not only is he tall but broad too, like a warrior pretending to be a businessman. I have the sense that he could tame a lion with his bare hands. I don't know where the idea comes from but it's deeply disturbing, on many levels, so I push it aside. I'd seen dozens of photos of him by now, so I'd known he was handsome, but I hadn't been expecting the effects of that in person.

Because he's not just 'handsome'. In reality, there are nuances that the cameras hadn't properly highlighted—a scar at the top of his lip that gives it a slightly angular shape, for example; and a smattering of freckles across the bridge of his nose. They're barely visible because of his dark tan, but they're there, and there's something about them that is wild, fascinating and dangerously distracting. His hair is thick and dark, with a slight curl where it's longer at the nape, and as I stare at him he lifts a hand and runs it through his hair, watching me with those lupine eyes until my stomach is in knots.

'He will seek to gain the advantage any way he can,' my closest aide, Claudia, had advised, her own preparation equal to my own. 'Be on guard.'

The memory of her words is timely. A palace staffer appears at the door and I relax, the sight of a familiar uniform and face reminding me who and where I am. This is my turf, my palace, my people, and he wants something from me: my land.

'Your Highness.' The staff member curtseys, earning another derisive half-smile from the Spanish billionaire. I grind my teeth, an inexplicable urge to somehow knock that infuriating look from his face making my palms hot. 'Are you ready for afternoon tea?'

I turn to my guest, a *frisson* of heat running through me. 'Mr del Almodovár, would you like something to eat or drink?'

'A beer,' he says without skipping a beat.

I pivot to the maid. 'A beer for our guest and tea for me, thank you.'

I can't shake the feeling he's laughing at me, so I experience a sense of pique as I gesture to the two armchairs set opposite one another in front of a floor-to-ceiling window that frames a stunning view of the Laltussen river. Usually, the river gives me calm. It is ancient and courageous, undaunted by time and man's impulses.' It is a constant in the lives of my people and I take solace from that when I look out on it. But today I am apparently not able to be calmed.

When he sits, it's exactly as you might expect—no hint of reserve or respect for the ancient room and its furnishings. He takes the chair with a dominant athleticism that speaks of a desire to run wild, his legs spread wide, elbows braced on each arm as he leans forward.

I instinctively fold myself into my own chair, knees braced, ankles together, hands clasped in my lap. We could not be more different—he is totally at ease in his own body, uncaring of where he is; he's simply himself. I have spent a lifetime learning who I must be—sometimes I wonder if I have any idea what or who 'I' really am. Who might I have been had I not been born a princess? Who might I have become had circumstance not made me the sole surviving member of the royal family at seventeen?

He's looking at me, those eyes of his overtaking me for a moment, so I forget he's here at my request, that this is my meeting to shape.

'I've had a chance to review your proposal,' I say, careful not to give away my true feelings in the tone of my voice. It won't be helpful if he knows how much I don't want his casino monstrosity here.

'So I gather,' he drawls. 'And what did you think, Princess?'

'Please, you don't have to call me that.'

'And what should I call you instead?'

I'm not one to stand on ceremony, yet with this man I hesitate to invite him to use my name as I ordinarily would. I need every boundary I can establish between us. 'Most of my guests refer to me as Your Highness,' I clip.

'Is that any different to "Princess"?' His cynical expression reaches inside my tummy and squeezes it, so I look away, flustered and warm-cheeked. The river is placid, calmly meandering past the window. I watch it for a moment.

'It's more…what I am used to,' I say, forcing myself to turn back and face him, then wishing I hadn't when I find his eyes lingering on the necklace at my throat. Or are they actually lower, on the brief hint of cleavage exposed by the neckline of my dress? My pulse goes into overdrive. There's no denying how he makes me feel. It's like being flooded with electricity. I close my eyes for a moment, needing to regain control. When I open them, he's looking right at me.

My pulse speeds up.

A knock at the door is a welcome intrusion. I jerk to my feet, uneasy and tense, striding towards it.

Another staff member is there, holding a tray. She curtseys when she sees me, but before she can come in I hold out my hands to take the tray from her. I ignore her surprise, removing the sterling silver object and turning round in one movement. The door clicks shut, leaving me alone with Santiago.

I place the tray on a side table and remove the tall glass of beer, carrying it towards him with knees that are slightly unsteady. His eyes are sardonic as he extends a hand to take it. 'Thank you, Your Highness.'

Nope. That's no better. There's still something illicit and inflammatory about his tone. He might sound as if he's being respectful, but he's not, he's teasing me.

I double back to the tray, pouring tea from the pot then lifting the saucer and cup, holding them in my hands. I don't approach my chair. It's too close to the man, and there's nowhere to look but at him. Besides, sitting doesn't match my frame of mind. Instead, I walk towards the window, looking out at the river and the city beyond.

'The project is…ambitious.' It is not, by any stretch, the

only word I can think of to describe his proposal. I hate everything about what he's planning.

'No more so than many others I've undertaken.'

'Yes.' I sip my tea. 'Your track record with this sort of thing is impressive.'

'Thank you, Your Highness.'

Another response that's lightly mocking. My spine is ramrod-straight and I cast him a look that I think barely contains my own feelings.

'It would be the first casino in Marlsdoven.'

'And you don't approve.'

Alarm bells sound in the back of my mind. Does he know about my uncle? Or is he simply hazarding a guess? 'Why do you say that?' There is a noise as he places his glass down. A cursory glance shows he's half-finished it.

'The negotiations are complete, your government ready to sign off.'

'It's crown land. The government can't sign off without my agreement.' It's a small, unthinking admission and I realise what I've said as soon as I finish.

'And for this reason you have organised a covert meeting at the eleventh hour to forestall the big, bad developer from corrupting your quaint kingdom?'

Fire spills through me. My lips part on an indignant rush of breath; I'm grateful to be holding the tea cup or I'm not sure what I might do with my hands! I cannot think that I have ever been spoken to like this, with such obvious disrespect, and such cynicism and dislike. And how can he downplay the seriousness of this? I've seen first-hand what addiction can do! I know the evils that come from places like his casinos. If there is to be one in Marlsdoven, then the benefits had better far outweigh the risks.

'This is not a covert meeting,' I respond to the first charge, too emotionally invested in the second to trust myself to speak to it sensibly. '*Nothing* about my life is covert. Your name is in my daily schedule.'

His disbelief is obvious. 'I note I was directed to come to the back gate of the palace, brought through rear doors with no photographers in attendance.'

Heat prickles beneath my skin because his observation is accurate. While it's not exactly 'covert', I did try to keep the meeting off the press's radar. Spurred onto the defensive, I respond, 'Would you have liked to be photographed, Santiago?'

I use his first name and realise I like the taste of it in my mouth. I'd started to think of him as Santiago since seeing so many photos of him during my research. I don't care. We're beyond the bounds of etiquette now, anyway.

'My comment was more about your feelings than mine,' he says, neatly turning the argument on me, studying me as though I'm a science experiment. I remember belatedly the advice in the security report: he has a savant's genius when it comes to finding what makes people tick. 'I have no issue with being ushered into the palace like a shameful secret, but I find it telling that this was your choice.'

I open my mouth to object to this characterisation but change my mind. After all, why should I be ashamed of my feelings? 'I don't see the point in advertising your intentions to my people until we're confident the development is going to proceed.'

He reaches for his beer, takes a drink then replaces the glass on the table, standing in a lithe, graceful movement, walking towards me before I can properly realise what he's doing. I have no time to brace for his proximity. He's wearing an aftershave that sends my pulses into overdrive, but not enough of it, so I have to breathe deeply to catch the intoxicating masculine aroma.

Every hormone in my body is doing a dance.

'Your Prime Minister is desperate for this to happen.'

'Naturally. You're looking at spending billions of dollars. Of *course* he's keen.'

'This doesn't sway you, though?' he asks, looking around the palace as if to emphasise the wealth at my fingertips. If only he knew! Our small country is far from prosperous. The privatisation of most of our state-owned assets shortly after my parents' death, when I'd been too young, inexperienced and grief-plagued to understand what was happening behind my back, means much of our revenue is being paid to offshore companies.

'Selling crown land is a difficult business,' I murmur, remembering the lessons I learned as a seventeen-year-old. 'Once sold, it's gone. Everything needs to be structured so the advantages to the country outweigh the loss of such an asset.'

His eyes narrow. 'You don't think the casino will do that?'

No. Casinos are dangerous. I bite back the thought, knowing how counter-productive it would be to rely on this man's compassion and comprehension. 'I think it could,' I say with a small lift of my shoulders, my heart pounding as we draw closer to the crux of my argument. Somehow, he's brought me here without my realising it. I wanted to take time to charm him, to impress him with the country's history and cultural importance, to form some kind of rapport. But he's cut through all that and found the kernel of my reservations so easily, so skilfully.

'Then let's talk, Princess. What do you need from me?'

CHAPTER TWO

WHAT DO I need from him?

My mouth goes dry as I struggle to come up with any kind of answer. My brain is clogged, completely overwhelmed by him, my body overtaking all my instincts. So, instead of focussing on the simple business of the matter at hand, I find myself aching to reach out and touch him, to feel for myself if that broadly muscled chest is as firm as I imagine it is.

What the heck is happening to me?

I have made it through my entire adult life without going gaga for a man, and yet here I stand, with exactly the man I need to keep my wits with, and I risk turning into a blathering fool.

'Shall we go over your proposal?' I suggest, the idea literally going off like a light bulb, because if we pore over contracts surely that will negate the impact he has on me?

'Isn't that what we're doing?'

'I mean properly. At a table, with the documents. It would be easier to address my concerns this way.'

'We can do that,' he agrees, and it's then that I realise how totally he's taken the upper hand in this conversation. 'But first, I'd like to hear your concerns from you. Now. In summary.'

'Are you ordering me?' I can't help but respond, lifting a brow.

'Oh, never, Your Highness,' he responds with a hint of droll amusement. 'You're the one who gives orders around here.'

My cheeks grow warm again. 'You aren't like anyone I've ever met.' The confession escapes before I can stop it.

'I can imagine.' Again, I feel scorn layered beneath the banal response, as though my comment on his uniqueness has led him to derision for my place in the palace, the country.

'Meaning?'

'That your usual visitors are probably a very carefully curated type of person.'

My gasp is audible. 'Mr del Almodovár—'

'Santiago,' he interrupts, and if I liked the taste of his name in my mouth I love the feel of it in my ears even more. He says it with such Spanish tones, all sunshine and spice. My stomach clenches in overwhelming awareness.

'I think we've got off on the wrong foot,' I say, searching for a modicum of control. 'You don't know me, and I don't know you. You're not here to get to know me, and I have no interest in knowing you. What I care about is my country, and the impact your casino mega-complex will have on the culture of the region.'

I look at him through narrowed eyes, my breath uneven. My dad flashes into my mind and I feel a stomach-clutching panic. I'm letting him down so badly. I wish there was some other way! 'So, perhaps we should avoid any personal observations whatsoever and move onto the contracts, as I suggested.'

'Are you sure avoiding personal observations is what you want?' he asks smoothly, and my whole body fires onto high alert. Heat builds low in my abdomen, spreading through me. My breasts are tingly and heavy, my nipples straining against the lace fabric of my bra. I turn away from him, afraid of how exposed I must be to someone with his experience. He's unpicking me piece by piece, stripping me raw, and I have no defence against him. More concerning, I don't know if I *want* a defence against him.

'You don't act like a man who's eager for this deal to go ahead,' I say, looking out at the river, seeking a sense of calm that won't come.

'No.'

'Why not? I thought this was important to you.'

'Oh, it is. But you are not the only one who does your research, Princess. I could walk away tomorrow and find another country to work with, many of which would be tripping over themselves to offer incentives to take my business there. But you? Could you find such an appealing investor as easily?'

I close my eyes on a wave of surrender, because he's right. Damn him. I feel actual hatred for the man then, and it's only intensified by the glorious, sensual awareness cresting through me. How dare he be the only man I've ever looked at and felt a stirring of desire for? No, not just a stirring, a total tsunami, a crushing weight of need that robs me of the ability to breathe.

'Not to put too fine a point on this, but you need me. So let's stop dancing around the issue and come to agreement. I want this concluded today.'

He's so dismissive, so infuriatingly arrogant, I whirl around to face him, all semblance of regal control dissipating completely. 'And you always get what you want, I imagine.'

His smile makes a flame flicker in my gut. 'Does that bother you?'

'You bother me,' I respond honestly.

His eyes widen with a brief glimmer of surprise, as though he wasn't expecting my answer.

'But I don't know why.' More honesty. I frown. 'We should focus on the business at hand, and then you can consider this concluded.'

The air between us sparks with lightning bolts.

'I bother you because I am the opposite of you in every way,' he says, his meaning not clear.

But that's not it. I meet people who are different from me all the time. I celebrate difference and value diversity. This is not about difference, it's about desire, and how completely threatening is my reaction to him. It's as though my body, usually a trusted ally, has defied me in every way.

'Your proposed development is bold and—'

'Ambitious, yes. You've said.'

'Mr del Almodovár—'

'Santiago.'

I grind my teeth. 'Please, let me finish my sentence.'

He eyes spark with mine and then he dips his head in terse agreement.

'We have no casinos in Marlsdoven. This would be a first.'

'One of the reasons I selected your country for this project. You're primed for this.'

'You mean my citizens are "primed" to become good little gambling lemmings?'

His eyes narrow. 'Have you ever been to a casino, Princess?'

Heat rushes my face. Before I can answer, he continues. 'Of course you haven't.'

I don't want to analyse his tone or meaning.

'Do you think if I'd been to a casino I'd be more likely to look favourably on your project? I believe the opposite is true. Seeing one of these places would likely make me refuse to sell the land to you regardless of any benefits I perceive for the country.' I suck in a shaky breath. 'But I suspect that would be cutting off my nose to spite my face, and I've no interest in doing that.'

He lifts his hand, rubbing the back of his neck, the gesture separating enough of his shirt from the waistband of his trousers to reveal an inch or so of tanned, taut abdomen. My mouth goes dry, my heart in overdrive. I stare at his chest, my stomach in knots, my brain fizzing. I've lost my train of thought completely.

'How do you know if by your own admission you have no experience?'

The challenge drags me into the conversation again, but not fully. His arm drops, and so does the shirt. The sight of his flesh is buried in my mind, yet it's not enough. I have a yearning to see him completely shirtless, to see all his chest, the entire expanse of muscled abdomen. I blink hard, trying to clear the thoughts, the vision, trying to focus. My country needs my concentration right now. I can't be distracted just because he happens to be seriously attractive.

'The land you've chosen is valuable, historic and prominent.' I return the discussion to ground I'm more comfortable with, clearing my throat, vanquishing thoughts of his chest from my mind—for now.

His accent grows thicker as he defends his plans with obvious determination. 'This land is the obvious place for this. It's perfect for such a development.'

My eyes sweep shut on a wave of sadness. My own dreams for the piece of central real estate are impossible to visualise now. The arts precinct I wanted to commission—a testament to the cultural richness of Marlsdoven history and a space where children could go and be inspired to create—was now just a once-upon-a-time fantasy.

'And your prime minister agreed to the sale.'

'I know.'

'Yet you don't agree?'

'It's irrelevant,' I say quietly. 'Isn't it? Would you consider a different location at this stage?'

'Would it make you happy if I did?'

I stare at him, not expecting the question and with no clue how to answer.

'Or wouldn't you still have the same ideological issues then that you do now? You don't want a casino at all. Right?'

'I don't think that matters.' The words are numb, resigned. 'I'm in the minority. My Prime Minister and Treasurer assure me the parliament wholeheartedly supports your investment. I have no justifiable power to overrule them.'

'It's crown land. As you said, your signature is required on the contract.'

Is he throwing me a lifeline? Reminding me that I do hold some power here? For all that I feel he's reading me like an open book, I can't understand him at all.

'I'm not in the habit of going against my parliament.'

'You're a terrible negotiator.'

My eyes widen at the criticism and then, to my surprise, he smiles, his teeth baring, his expression changing completely. His eyes crinkle at the corners and it's as if the sun is blasting into the room. I grip my tea cup more tightly, but nothing can stop my knees from wobbling.

I stare at him, so entranced by his smile that it takes a moment for his words to settle in my consciousness.

'You *can* refuse to sell to me, Princess, and that's your leverage here. So let's pretend you didn't just say that and go back to your agenda. What do you want from me?'

My heart turns over in my chest. I finish my tea, placing the saucer on a side table before fixing him with a direct stare.

'I want…' I find it impossible to finish the sentence. Focus. Focus, for the love of God. He's staring at me, waiting, and the more he looks the more my pulse fires and my brain fuzzes. 'Assurances,' I haltingly add. 'That you'll employ ninety per cent Marlsdovens, in both the construction of the development and then in the staffing once completed.' Relief that I've been able to pluck one of my talking points out of thin air spreads through me.

'I've already made assurances that fifty per cent of the contractors will be locally sourced.'

'Fifty isn't ninety,' I point out.

His eyes lock to mine as if to say, *Oh, really?* but then his lips twist with the hint of another smile and my thoughts get scattered again.

'It isn't possible to guarantee that requirement.'

'Why not?'

'I can't say that your contractors will be the best, and I'm only interested in hiring the best.'

'You think we can't offer quality workmanship?'

'The "best" encompasses many things—quality, affordability, experience. I work with a group of architects based in New York.'

'Yes, and that can be your ten per cent,' I say, glad that I spent so long analysing the details of his proposal.

'What else?'

'Is that an agreement?'

'No. But I'm interested in your list. Go on.'

He's so close to me—just a foot or two away—yet I don't move. I should. I know I should. But standing here so close to him is hypnotic and addictive. 'My biggest concerns centre on the benefits of this agreement to my people. Once I sell this land, it's gone. I need to know the choice will benefit Marlsdovens for a long time to come. Particularly if the trade-off is having a casino right over there.'

I point down the river to the banks in question, my pulse quivering as I think of my father and how devastating this would be to him. My entire life revolves around doing what my parents would have expected of me, remembering every instruction they gave me over the course of my life. I'm betraying them now, and I'm sickened by that.

'It is more than a casino. The development features restaurants and a six-star hotel as well.'

'Yes, for guests of the casino.'

'Why do you oppose this?'

'I told you, I just need to make sure—'

'No.' He shakes his head. 'It's more than that. You dislike the concept. You disapprove of the casino. Why?'

'It's just not something in our culture.'

'Gambling? I think you're wrong.'

'Gambling is everywhere, to some extent, but casinos make it so easy.'

'And that's bad?'

I stare at him. 'How can you not see that?' I shake my head, remembering what gambling did to my uncle, how his addiction led to his death. 'Of course you don't see it.'

'What's that supposed to mean?'

I realise I've gone awfully close to throwing an insult at his feet—worse, to blaming him for Uncle Richard's problem. I try to back-pedal. 'You made your fortune building casinos. Why would you stop and think about the ramifications on a society? Why would you see anything but good in these places that tempt and seduce people to fritter away their hard-earned money? How many lives have been ruined in your quest for this gambling empire?'

To his credit, he doesn't let my barb derail his argument. 'If I don't build this casino, someone else will—

perhaps not on crown land, and then your approval will not be needed.'

'I'm aware of that.' It's the only reason I dismissed the possibility of refusing to sell to him. I'm fighting a losing battle, so I might as well try to control it and get some benefits for the people of this country.

'I want to know that the income from your venture will fund health care and education for my people. I want to know there will be employment prospects for future generations. I want there to be world-class hospitality training available. Marlsdoven is haemorrhaging young citizens. They go to school here, but many then move abroad for tertiary studies and stay there. I understand the lure of your casino, Mr del Almodovár, and I understand that there are benefits. But I'm not going to stand here and pretend I'm not highly sceptical of the whole operation.'

He looks at me for several moments and I wonder if I've gone too far. I intended to improve the deal with him, not ruin it altogether. Is there a risk I've done just that?

'Your parents died seven years ago.'

It's the absolute last thing I'd expected him to say. It's like an arrow coming out of left field, spearing me with pain in my side. I blink away from him, frowning as I take in the glistening river.

'Yes.'

'You were seventeen.'

'Yes.'

'That's very young to assume such responsibilities.'

It's true. At seventeen, I felt grown up but, looking back, I was still a child. A child who'd had to grieve the loss of her parents and somehow hold together a grief-stricken nation as well. The need to be what my people required meant I never had the time or space for my own feelings.

'I managed.'

For a moment, before he dips his head in acknowledgement, I think I see sympathy in his eyes. I hate it. I don't want his sympathy—or perhaps it's more that I can't live with it. When anyone is kind to me I grow close to tears, and if this man, who came barrelling into the palace with such obvious animosity and disrespect, starts being *nice*...?

I cough to hide the fact I'm clearing my throat, not wanting him to register that I'm emotionally off-kilter.

'I can see you take your duty to the people of Marlsdoven seriously.'

I stare at him, waiting for him to make his point.

'This casino will benefit them.'

I hate that he's talking as though this is a *fait accompli,* even though I understand that it is. It must be. I can't go against the wishes of my country's Prime Minister and Treasurer. Frustration is like a whirlpool in my gut, swallowing me whole.

'Casinos benefit nobody,' I say caustically. 'Except, of course, the corporation behind the casino, which naturally stands to make gross profits from people's hope-filled gambling.'

It's the wrong thing to say. Anger flashes like a blade in his eyes, whatever sympathy I'd seen a moment ago evaporating completely. 'Yes, I profit from my casinos.'

'Not just 'profit'.' Now that I've started, I can't stop. 'You make tens and tens of billions every year. Honestly, what does someone even need with all that money? Don't you have enough? Is another casino in your empire really necessary?'

His eyes narrow.

'How do you sleep at night, Santiago, when the people who flood the floors of your casinos are living out their worst nightmare?'

'You have no idea what you're talking about.'

'Oh, yes, I do. I know damned well what places like your casinos do to families and lives.' I'm trembling with the force of my anger, Uncle Richard's haunted expression something I'll never forget. 'I hate everything about what you do. And I loathe the idea of selling this land to you.'

'What can I say, Your Highness? We do not all have the advantages of being born into this.' He gestures to the palace, and contempt is encompassed in the flat line of his mouth.

I'm so tempted to tell him that being born into royalty is many things, but 'advantaged' is not one of them.

'No, that's true,' I say instead. 'Most people aren't royal.' I aim for sarcasm. It's small-minded and rude, but I don't think I care.

A scathing twist of his lips shows, if anything, my remark has amused him. 'You want to keep "your people" in the dark ages.'

'By saving them from the lure of gambling?'

He laughs, a thick, gruff sound that sends sparks of lightning through my body. 'Do you have any idea how prim you sound?'

I gape, the disparagement unexpectedly hurtful. I spin away from him, because I need the breathing space. He's too close, too everything.

'In every pleasure, there is the potential for pain. Should alcohol be banned altogether because some people have a propensity to alcoholism? Should driving be outlawed because there are some drivers who will always speed just for the thrill of it? Of course not. You cannot protect your citizens from every possible perceived evil. Life doesn't come with any guarantee.'

'That's just the sort of reply I'd expect from someone who's never borne any personal responsibility.'

His head whips back, as though I've punched him

'With respect,' he says it in a way that makes it clear the words are empty, 'You know nothing about me or my responsibilities.'

'I know enough.'

'Because I own casinos.'

'Because you own casinos,' I agree, my anger stirred beyond usefulness. 'Because you live the life of a hedonistic bachelor intent on drinking, smoking, having debauched parties on super-yachts, all the while robbing poor people of their homes and relationships. I ask you again, how do you sleep at night?'

'Rarely alone,' he throws back, the words sparking through me, and I gasp, the image of him naked fully formed in my mind. 'But apparently you know that already, Princess.'

'This is getting out of hand.' My voice shakes, fury still ripe in my gut, disbelief at the direction our conversation has taken making my skin clammy. Or is it the reference to his sexual activities? I press fingertips to my throbbing temples, willing myself to calm down.

'You are the one who's letting a personal opinion interfere with a business proposition.'

'That's not true.'

'Then how come the way I live my life doesn't bother your Prime Minister or Treasurer?'

My eyes sweep shut at his very valid point. 'Of course it bothers them. They're men of integrity and you're… you're…'

I whirl around to face him, only to find that the Spanish billionaire has closed the distance between us. He's right behind me, his eyes latched onto mine, his face a mask of repressed emotion—but I see beyond it. I feel the fury emanating off him in waves.

'*Si?* What am I?'

'Not like them,' I finish lamely, my anger cresting and falling, being replaced by something else now, a different wave, something more dangerous and distracting. I stare up at him, my body quivering with a thousand and one things.

He's so close, though, so close, and I find myself slipping, my fingertips tingling with a need to *feel.* I clasp them together in front of me to stop myself doing something really stupid, like reaching up and running them over his chest.

I know I should move away. Take a step backward. Put some space between us. But being near him is doing something vital and addictive to my body; it's resonating through me.

I hold my ground, inches from him.

'No.' His expression is grim, his eyes piercing mine before dropping to my lips, tracing the line of my mouth until I open it on a small gasp. A gasp or a plea? I can't be certain. 'I imagine they never argue with you like this.'

I shake my head wordlessly, just the tiniest movement, for fear of dislodging his gaze from my mouth. I feel as though he's touching me. Pleasure spikes through me. I have no idea what this means—I've never seen a man and longed for him in this way. It's wrong and inappropriate, but even that knowledge makes me want him more, not less. 'No one does.'

Something like understanding flashes through his eyes. 'And do you like being argued with?'

'Of course not,' I lie, ignoring the fact that I feel more alive right now than I have in my entire life.

His soft laugh shows he understands, and it embeds itself in my nervous system. 'Then shall I leave?'

Yes. Yes, he should. This conversation is counter-productive, his presence an affront. We're never going to agree. He should absolutely leave. 'I…' The words are jammed in my throat, some invisible barrier preventing them from escaping.

Triumph crosses his expression. His eyes shift to mine, a challenge in their depths as he lifts a hand, moving it closer to my face. I hold my breath, staring at him, waiting. He touches his fingertip to my cheek, phantom-like, so I shift a little closer, pressing my cheek to his palm. What's happening to me? How can I possibly be doing this? I'm the Crown Princess of Marlsdoven and this man represents a serious threat to my country. Yet here I stand, entranced, captivated, pleasure exploding through me.

'Come to Spain with me.'

The invitation is husky, his voice deep and accented. I blink, not understanding. His finger inches lower, towards my lips. I have to swallow back a groan. 'I can't.'

'Come to see my casino there. You cannot truly form an opinion on the merits of my proposal until you have witnessed one for yourself.'

My eyes sweep shut, reality intruding on the fog of awareness that has momentarily incapacitated me. It's a timely reminder of who he is and why I have to fight this drugging attraction with everything I have. I snap out of my haze, pulling away from him, jerking backwards, trying to load anger into my eyes. 'I know enough.'

He's surprised by my rapid shift, but surprise quickly morphs into determination. 'Are you afraid to be proved wrong?'

'There's no chance of that. I'll never approve of gambling.'

'Casinos are so much more than gambling,' he insists.

'Next you'll be telling me people play with tokens and no real money is ever wagered.'

'There's no fun in that,' he drawls sardonically.

'There's no fun in people losing their money, gambling until their debts get out of control.'

'No,' he agrees. 'And we have safeguards in place to try to prevent this.' He closes the distance between us. 'Come to Spain and see for yourself.'

My heart twists, my ability to think clearly impeded once more.

'Or are you afraid of what will happen once you leave this gilded cage?'

I blink up at him. 'Afraid?'

'Just you and me, no rank, no staff—no reason to ignore what we both clearly want.'

CHAPTER THREE

HIS WORDS POUND through my mind with the force of a sledgehammer: the challenge, the assertion, the statement of intent. A *frisson* of danger and need runs down my spine. I stare at him for a long time, losing myself in the vortex he's created. I need to say something to set aside his ridiculous suggestion.

'My rank goes where I go, I'm afraid.'

'Then I'll call you "Princess" at all times.'

It's a sensual promise that does little to calm my raging bloodstream.

'Santiago…' His name is a plea, but for what?

'Your Prime Minister and Treasurer do not oppose this development because they know what you do not: this development is good for your country, your people, your future. And while, yes, there are some down sides associated with casinos, mine is probably the only casino group in the world that actively provides gambling support and interventions. But I think you're afraid to be proved wrong.'

'I'm not afraid of that,' I deny swiftly.

'Then what are you afraid of?' Has he moved closer? Our bodies are almost touching. My breath is uneven, loud in the silent room. 'Or do I even need to ask?'

'I'm not…'

Now it's my turn to stare at his lips. Of their own volition, my eyes drop to his mouth, chasing the outline, and such raw, primal need surges through me that I make a soft, gasping sound. It's as though I can will him to kiss me.

Kiss me?

Alarm spears my side.

I can't seriously want…

But, oh, I do.

'You despise me,' he says gruffly, his body position changing just enough for me to feel as though he's forming a wall around me. I like it. 'You despise my life, my choices, my business.'

I don't deny it. Not because it's true—though it is—but because I'm not capable of following A to B right now. My thought train has been completely derailed.

'But right now you wish that I would kiss you on those perfect pink lips of yours.' His eyes spark to mine, daring me to contradict him, daring me to say that's not what I want.

'So?'

A short, sharp laugh of surprise breaks between us, and then his head lowers, his face only an inch from mine. 'Come to Spain with me.'

It's the last thing he says before he kisses me—the first kiss of my life and it's with this man who, as he just pointed out, I despise.

I've seen enough movies to know what it's like to be kissed—or at least I've imagined it. But this blows every expectation way out of the water.

My stomach is in knots, looping over and over. My body is paralysed and then on fire as he lifts one hand to the back of my head, his fingers driving through my hair, holding me where I am as his mouth ravages me—there is no other word for it. His lips separate mine, his tongue lashing me, demanding answers I can't give, showing me his supremacy. I whimper into his mouth, a sound of acquiescence and surrender, a sound that hopes for more of this—him—so much more. The kiss drives down into my soul. I am in agony but an agony born of the knowledge that this kiss is not enough. My hands lift to his chest, pressing to his warmth, the rock-hard muscles just as tantalising as I'd imagined.

I curl my fingernails into the fabric of his shirt and he kisses me hard, his knee nudging my legs apart so I groan, the unexpected contact so unmistakably sexual, so hot, so raw, that I can't think or speak. I am floating high above the planet, and nothing matters besides this.

Alarm bells clang in the back of my mind. I *know* this is wrong, so wrong, but I'm powerless to stop it, held hostage by a body that has been denied any form of sensual pleasure for far too long. As a teenager I read romance novels and, oh, how I loved them. Yet that zing was never for me in the real world. I've never met anyone with the ability to set my soul on fire.

But Santiago del Almodovár, with his charismatic devil-may-care attitude, is the very last word in hot and, like the many, many women who've no doubt come before me, I have no desire to resist him.

He pulls away, just enough to break the kiss, his eyes probing mine. 'Spain. Come next week.'

'Next week,' I repeat, my mind not following.

'Stay at the casino. Experience the type of building I want to bring to Marlsdoven.'

I nod, but it's not an agreement. My brain is too fogged to think straight. Belatedly, logic starts to fall into place. 'I can't.'

'Then stay somewhere else.'

'I can't come to Spain.'

He frowns. 'Why not?'

'Because it would…arouse suspicion? I don't know.'

'Suspicion of what?'

My cheeks flame. His smile is mocking and I feel about three feet tall. I shake my head in frustration, desperately trying to re-establish a modicum of control, to put some cool between us. But his leg is between mine, his body still so close, our faces separated by only an inch. My breath burns in my lungs and my nipples tingle against the fabric of my bra. My insides feel like mush and warm heat is spreading through my abdomen. I am lost.

'It's just not like me to go somewhere on the spur of the moment.'

'This is not spur of the moment.'

'A week is… My schedule…'

'Do not make excuses.'

'I—I'm not.'

He presses a finger to my lips then steps back, separating from me with apparent ease. He is not flustered. He is not breathing as though he's just run a marathon. He looks at me with a steadiness I envy.

'This is business. You have concerns about the development? So come and see what I do. Come and experience my casino and hotel. Eat at my world-class restaurants. See for yourself what I am proposing to build here.'

I bite down on my lip, because his suggestion actually makes a lot of sense. But it would involve being in Spain with Santiago and that kiss definitely complicates things.

'I—have to think about it,' I say, not quite meeting his eyes.

'Then think.' He shrugs his shoulders with nonchalant ease. 'And let me know.' He paces towards one of the occasional tables, withdraws his wallet and leaves a card on the surface before striding towards the door. I stare at him, frowning. Is that it?

I don't want him to leave. I want…

But what I want is impossible. Or at least highly inadvisable. I need him to go so that I can start to think straight.

I hold my breath, waiting for him to turn and say something to me, to reassure me, placate me or even to walk back and kiss me all over again, but Santiago is done. He draws the door inwards and leaves the room without a backward glance.

My heart is thumping so hard I genuinely worry it could crack my ribs into tiny shards of bone.

'And? How did it go?'

I look at Claudia with a furrowed brow. Where to begin?

Claudia is my senior advisor. I've known her since I was a teenager. She's ten years older than me almost to the day, which as a teenager made her seem quite grown-up, but as I've reached my mid-twenties I think of her almost as my contemporary.

Though our life experiences are quite dramatically different. Whereas I am sheltered and, I freely admit, naïve, Claudia is worldly and sophisticated. She takes two months' holiday every year and goes back-packing all over the world, far off the beaten track. She is fearless and courageous, determined to see every pocket of the earth. A month ago she got back from Nepal and her stories of hikes and cuisine have been feathering my soul ever since.

'It was fine.' I reach for a glass of water, taking a long sip, my throat burning at the lie.

'Oh? I'm surprised.'

'Why?'

'Because he's renowned for being difficult. I would have thought you'd butt heads a bit, particularly given your reservations.'

I look at her for several seconds and then sigh. 'We *did*

butt heads.' Unconsciously, I lift my fingertips to my lips and, despite the fact he left the palace hours ago, they tingle at my touch. My body feels half-electric. I don't know when or how I'll ever feel *normal* again.

'And yet you resolved it?'

'Not exactly.'

Claudia frowns. 'I thought the contracts were to be signed today?'

'No.' I toy with my fingers. Am I letting my people down by stalling? The boost to our economy from this project would be tremendous, not to mention the flow-on effects for the tourism industry. The whole riverbank precinct would be revitalised by this development.

It's just not the kind of revitalisation I want.

I understand the economic benefits of his development, but whenever I think of my parents I shudder. This would be an enormous betrayal of their memories, and the promise I made myself right after they died. My mother used to tell me there was no blueprint for being a crown princess, but she's wrong. I have a blueprint—my parents' actions—and I want to adhere to it. But turning away Santiago when his development shows such promise for our economy? Guilt and indecision gnaw at my gut.

'So when?'

I lift my shoulders, then turn to Claudia.

'What are you not telling me?'

Too much. Yet, although I have a habit of being completely honest with Claudia, I clam up now. What happened between Santiago and me is something I need to make sense of in my own time and in my own way. I can't discuss it.

'I might have spoken too frankly with him,' I say quietly. 'I was quite forceful in my objections.'

'To the project?'

Heat marks my cheeks.

'Oh, Your Highness…' She shakes her head, her green eyes sparkling. 'Don't tell me you called the incredibly wealthy Spanish tycoon some unkind names?'

I grimace.

'I can imagine his ego wouldn't have liked that. Particularly when he's used to women tripping over themselves to fall at his feet.'

I grab onto that, my breath uneven. 'Do you think he's really such a…?' I search for the right word.

'Oh, yes. A total man-whore,' she supplies with an impish grin. 'I think he's every bit as bad as the press says, and then some. Trust me, I've known men like him before.' She wiggles her brows. 'And, while they're fun to spend time with, you definitely can't trust them as far as you might wish to throw them.'

I am not a jealous person but, illogically, I feel the blade of that emotion cutting through me.

'I don't think he's ever had a relationship that's lasted longer than one night. Probably more than one hour.' She winks, no idea how those words are tightening something in my chest. It's so stupid of me to feel like this. All those romance novels have predisposed me to ideas that make no sense. Besides, in less than a year's time my own engagement will be announced—to the man my parents dearly wanted me to marry. Never mind that I've met him only a handful of times and feel nothing for him whatsoever. That doesn't change the fact I have no business fantasising about Santiago, or being jealous of his sleazy flings.

Except…the way he kissed me is *all* I can think of. I don't care that he goes through women faster than most men do underwear. I liked the way it felt to be kissed, the way it felt to be touched, the way it felt to be spoken to as an equal.

My eyes flare wide as I realise that's a huge part of this. Santiago didn't revere me, he didn't 'ma'am' me. He ignored all the conventions and spoke to me like any other person, and I loved that.

'He wants me to go to Spain to see his casino in Barcelona.' I ponder, the idea having more weight with me than I'd allowed him to see.

'It's not a terrible idea,' Claudia responds.

'Really? I'd have thought you'd object.'

'Oh, to anyone else I'd say that if you've seen one casino you've seen them all. But you've never been inside a casino before—'

'With good reason,' I mutter.

'I know you hate the very idea.' She's sympathetic. 'But I don't think this is a fight you really want to pick; it's definitely not a fight you'll win. So why not go and see his hotel and try to talk yourself into feeling good about it all?'

Except it's not the casino that's playing on my mind so much as the way it felt to be kissed by Santiago. In a matter of months, my engagement will be announced, my marriage will take place only a few months after that and then the rest of my life will be lived according to the blueprint my parents set out. I've never questioned that fate but, for the first time in my life, I have an insatiable hunger to experience something outside of what's expected of me.

My days are always scheduled. Everything in my life is planned. Right down to who I'll spend my time with. What if this is the last chance I'll ever get to do something spontaneous and 'normal'?

The idea is seductive, almost as seductive as the thought of seeing Santiago again away from all this—the palace that reminds me at every turn of my parents and their legacy.

'I don't think it would create the right image,' I point out, almost hoping she'll contradict me and save me from myself.

'So don't let anyone know.'

I roll my eyes. 'Yeah, right. I'll just slip through the airport security unnoticed. Me, my luggage and four security agents.'

She laughs. 'The agents don't have to sit with you. As for being recognised…' She stalks to my wardrobe and returns a moment later, carrying a baseball cap. 'Try the time-honoured tradition of dressing in disguise.'

In order to keep the visit low-key, Claudia arranges everything. She alone deals with my diary secretary, booking the flights and accommodation, ensuring my schedule simply states 'personal trip'.

I wait until everything's locked in before I draw Santiago's card from where I stashed it on my bedside table, dialling his numbers with fingers that aren't quite steady. As the phone begins to dial, my stomach swoops, so I pace to the window and stare out at the banks of the river, reminding myself this is business. At least, that he doesn't know this will be a last-ditch and first ever taste of freedom for me. That the idea of escaping from my life for a few days holds an immeasurable appeal. It's nothing to do with him, really, so much as him being the first man to flirt with me so brazenly, the first man to kiss me with such obvious hunger.

As soon as he answers, his voice rolls through my body like sensual heat and honey. My knees tremble.

'Del Almodovár.' His voice is gruff, accent-spiced.

'Santiago.' I clear my throat. 'It's Freja Henriksen. From Marlsdoven.' I cringe at my own awkwardness.

A beat passes and then there's the sound of a door

closing. 'Your Highness.' His surprise is evident. 'How are you?'

My heart turns over at the question—a normal, polite, civil enquiry.

'Fine.'

'I'm glad to hear it.'

A woman's voice interrupts in the background of the call. I cannot make out what she's saying—t's too fast, her Spanish fluent, whereas mine is only passable—but I hear enough. It's a woman, it's late at night and I can only guess what I've interrupted. My heart goes into overdrive, my stomach in knots.

Claudia's appraisal of his bedroom antics plays in my mind. I'd be a fool to forget—even for a moment—what he's all about.

'Perhaps I should call back at a more appropriate time?'

I wince at my icy tone and can just imagine his smirk in response.

'Why is this not an appropriate time?'

Of *course* he'd call me out on this instead of just letting it slide. I expel a sigh. 'It doesn't matter. This won't take long.'

'Go on.'

My heart thumps. 'I've decided to take you up on your offer.'

'I see.'

'Is that a problem?'

'To clarify, which offer?'

I frown. 'To come and see your casino in Barcelona?'

A beat passes.

'You do remember suggesting that?' I prompt.

'Oh, yes, Princess. But there was another offer we discussed that afternoon, if memory serves.'

Heat spirals through me, and indignation too. Of all the

cheek! He really *is* as bad as Claudia said. To proposition me while he's with another woman! 'I don't remember that,' I respond with saccharine sweetness. 'But, rest assured, seeing your casino is *all* I'm interested in.'

His laugh is soft. 'We'll see.'

Warning bells chime.

'I'll have the presidential suite made available.'

'That's not necessary. My aide's arranged everything. Oh, And Mr del Almodovár?' I intentionally use his surname, wanting to undo any expectation he might have that this trip is about more than the casino. 'My visit is to be of a secret nature. I don't intend to tip anyone off that I'm coming and I'd appreciate it if you'd do the same.'

'You're so ashamed to be seen in one of my casinos?'

'In any casino,' I correct, wondering why I'm being so rude to him. After all, any other business contact would warrant a modicum of respect, yet with Santiago I'm deliberately baiting him.

And enjoying it.

And do you like being argued with?

'Fine. I'll ensure your privacy is respected. A car will meet you at the airport.'

'That won't be necessary.'

'When do you arrive?'

For a moment I contemplate not telling him, but that would be somewhat churlish. 'I'll have my assistant email some details. But don't worry about freeing your schedule. I won't need much of your time. After all, I'm coming to see the casino and not you.'

Another laugh, deep, short and throaty. 'I get the picture, Your Highness.'

My insides roll with unmistakable desire. I know he's doing it to mock me but the way he keeps using my title is making my pulse go nuts.

'It's just—not something I want to advertise to my—'

'Your people, I know.'

Something tightens inside me. He could never understand what it's like to live like this. The expectations and speculation, the constant fishbowl nature of my life.

'I'll see you later, then,' I say, but don't hang up.

And, interestingly, neither does he.

'Santiago?'

Oh, great. Now what am I going to say?

'*Sí*?'

Who are you with? The words tingle on the tip of my tongue but I force myself to swallow them away. His social life has nothing to do with me. The kiss we shared was a mistake, an aberration, something I won't allow to happen again. I *can't* let it happen again. There are so many reasons for this man to be off limits to me. Not least because I genuinely, chemistry aside, can't stand him!

'It doesn't matter. I'll see you soon.'

CHAPTER FOUR

IN THE END, I'm able to wangle a trip with only two security agents, and they keep a distance from me, so that as the plane lands in Barcelona and I walk down the steps, sunglasses and baseball cap in place, I feel anonymous and free. So free.

It's a warm afternoon and a light breeze lifts off the runway. I smile spontaneously, looking around before being swallowed by the milling passengers all bee-lining for the terminal. I join the crowd, happy to be absorbed by them, thrilled to have been unrecognised so far. The terminal building is air-conditioned. I flash my passport—with a brief moment of discomfort as the customs worker clearly identifies me and bows, but fortunately no one else seems to register his strange response.

Once through customs, I follow the signs to the baggage hall, taking in every detail of this pedestrian travel experience. Compared to the usual fanfare of my trips, this is low key and low stress. The noises that swirl around me are new—conversation and play, children running, adults scolding. There is none of the muted, carefully managed interaction I generally experience.

I want to remember every single detail!

In the baggage hall, I frown, not sure how to find my suitcase, but one of my agents approaches. He's also dressed casually, to blend in, and I can't help but grin at the sight of him in jeans and a T-shirt rather than the customary suit.

'This way, Your Highness.'

'Remember, Alex, I'm just Freja for the duration of this trip.'

He lifts a brow in silent scepticism then gestures with his hand. I walk alongside him but freeze. Standing at the carousel and sticking out like a sore thumb is Santiago del Almodovár.

I stop walking so abruptly that one of the children who'd been playing around bumps into my legs. I ruffle the child's hair apologetically then keep walking, my pulse in my throat, my mind in overdrive.

Santiago was not dressed particularly formally the first time we met, but now far less so, in faded black jeans and a grey shirt with the sleeves rolled up to his elbows, the hem untucked. He wears a baseball cap and a pair of aviator sunglasses. With his forearms exposed, I notice that he has tattoos. A snake on one arm spirals around and around towards his wrist, where its head appears to be biting the base of his thumb. The other bears a sentence in cursive script. I can't make out any detail from this distance.

'Would you mind getting my bag, Lars?'

'Of course, madam.'

'Madam' is a compromise I can live with. I stalk towards Santiago, my stomach doing loop-the-loops.

'What are you doing here?'

He lifts off his aviator glasses. 'Isn't it obvious?'

My heart thumps.

'I came to get you.' He pulls off his hat. 'I even brought a disguise but I can see you've got that covered.'

I stare at the hat, then him, consternation zipping through me.

'You came to get me?'

Great. I'll just parrot everything he says. That won't make me seem like an idiot at all.

'We're a six-star hotel, remember? All service.'

'I'm not… But…'

He lifts a finger to my lips and I'm instantly reminded of the way he kissed me at the palace. Possessively, with ease, as though he had every right. But he doesn't. I'm not one of his one-night stands.

I jerk my face away then step backward. 'Don't.'

His eyes glint like onyx in his handsome face.

'I have agents here.'

'And what? You're threatening to set them on me if I touch you?' he drawls and, despite everything, I laugh, shaking my head.

'That's not what I meant.'

'I know what you meant.' He leans closer and lowers his voice. 'You're fine to kiss me in a room where it's just the two of us, but not for anyone else to know you find someone like me attractive. Right?'

'I didn't have you pegged as the insecure type,' I respond, his accuracy felling me.

'Not insecure. Amused. I cannot imagine living my life with so much concern for what others thought of me.'

'Obviously,' I respond tautly.

'Your bag?'

'My agent has it.'

'And does he also have the address of the hotel?'

I nod. 'Of course.'

'Good. Then he can follow behind.'

He puts an arm on my elbow, guiding me from the crowd. I stop walking, perfectly aware that if it looks like I'm being abducted my cover will be blown in about seventeen seconds. I turn around and sure enough see my guards running towards me, one with his hand reaching for his gun.

I shake my head quickly. When they're close enough to hear, I say, 'This is Mr del Almodovár, my...host. I'm going to travel with him.'

'But Your Highness...'

Our earlier compromise about using my title is forgotten.

'It's fine,' I assure Alex. 'I trust him.'

They don't like it, but this whole trip is unorthodox enough that they grudgingly nod.

'We'll drive behind you. Where are you parked?'

He gives them directions then begins to propel me from the airport once more, and this time I let him. His fingers press into the small of my back, his touch insistent and strong.

We're crowded by others in the lift and he stands close to me, his body behind mine, his warmth enveloping me, his fragrance unmistakable. I breathe in, grateful for the anonymity of being able to close my eyes and cope with his nearness, for those few vital seconds to pull myself together before the doors ping open and his deep voice says, *'Perdóname'*, causing people to separate and make way for us.

I'm used to a degree of subservience wherever I go. People 'obey' me—I hate that term but I can't think of any other way to describe it. But the responsiveness here is all down to Santiago. Whether he's recognised as one of the country's wealthiest men, or simply exudes that air of authority wherever he goes, I see the way his words are taken as a command. Even my security agents were quick to fall in with his suggestion.

His car, naturally, is sleek and black, a beautiful sports car with heavily tinted windows, a golden badge I don't recognise on the bonnet. The headlights flash as we approach. He surprises me with his manners as he comes to the passenger door and opens it for me. When I move to step inside, he puts a hand on my arm. Every part of me goes haywire.

'I'm glad you came.'

My stomach twists. I stare at him, right back to where I was a week ago, torn between what I want and what I know I must do, how I know I must act.

My smile is tight, my body hot. 'It's a good opportunity to appraise your casino. Thank you for suggesting it.'

The suggestion of a smile plays on his lips. I feel his cynicism and slip into the car before I can say something else, drawing the seat belt into place.

He rounds his side, flaring the engine to life a moment after taking a seat. The car instantly feels smaller, his presence overpowering. I am conscious of the strain of his trousers across his thighs, his hyper-masculine fragrance, his capable hands on the wheel. He tilts me a sidelong glance, then checks his rear-view mirror. A car is approaching, black with windows tinted just as dark as these.

'Your staff?'

I flick a glance in the mirror as Alex puts down the driver window so I can identify his face. I nod. Santiago puts the car into reverse and backs out in one swift, easy motion, then accelerates forward. With every rev, I feel the car's power beneath me, thrilling and raw, just like Santiago. His hands shift the gear stick as he drives, so my eyes are drawn to his fingers, tanned and confident, and his leanly muscled forearms. At the bottom of the car park, he presses a button and the driver window lowers, allowing him to tap his phone to the boom gate. It opens in response, but he waits on the other side, conscious of the security agents, allowing them time to come through behind us before he accelerates into traffic.

I've been to Spain before, but there's something about being here like this—incognito, no official schedule of visits, no state engagements, undercover and unknown—that makes the whole outlook glisten with magic. The buildings are at first industrial, but as we draw nearer to the centre I see the hallmarks of this famed city. Baroque buildings in various states of repair are juxtaposed with modern constructions and Renaissance churches remain, their stone features beautiful, the perfect contrast to the Gaudi and Gaudi-influenced buildings we zip past in the city centre.

We drive through a restaurant precinct, the buildings close together, with red awnings and flower pots adding bursts of colour. The street is paved and narrow, so Santiago slows down, and I glimpse tables all set to face the street, the umbrellas dotted around to ward off the sun. Diners are dressed with casual elegance, and suddenly I long to be amongst them, eating tapas and drinking wine, making conversation with like-minded friends. A pang of longing assails me for the type of simple friendships most people take for granted.

'A sigh?'

I spin to face Santiago, a frown pulling at the corner of my mouth. 'Excuse me?'

He turns to look at me and my breath catches in my throat. His eyes are as golden as the Barcelona sunshine today, framed by thick, dark lashes. Those freckles on the bridge of his nose draw my attention.

'You sighed.'

'Oh.' I swallow. 'It's just—this looks so lovely.'

His eyes shift beyond me to the tables strewn with afternoon diners.

'We can come here for dinner.'

My spine jolts with warmth. It's not a dinner invitation. It's so much more intimate than that. It's a presupposition that we'll share a meal.

'I came to assess the casino,' I remind him primly, already forgetting that this is also, in part, a chance for me to kick up my heels—discreetly, of course. 'Dinner on the streets of Barcelona, while charming under different circumstances, is unnecessary.'

His eyes hold mine for a moment longer and then, with a slight smile, he turns back and continues driving. The world beyond the car has lost its ability to hold my attention. All my focus is now on Santiago.

'Is there something in your royal rule book that precludes fun?'

Despite the question, I smile. 'Sorry to disappoint you, there's no such thing as royal rule book.'

'Isn't there?'

The question is insightful. I sigh again, a soft exhalation of breath this time. 'There are…conventions and expectations,' I murmur. I don't explain to him that my life is guided by the expectations of my parents; he'd probably mock the sentiment, and I don't think I could bear that.

'And these rules mean you cannot come for dinner with me at a restaurant like this?'

'I wasn't planning on having dinner with you at all, actually.'

His laugh is a throaty sound.

'Why is that funny?'

'Because you are determined to act as though you don't want to spend time with me when we both know that is not true.'

And his hand shifts off the gear stick and towards my knee, grazing my skirt lightly so I startle, my veins immediately rushing with lava.

'I was warned about your arrogance,' I mutter, hoping I sound dismissive.

Another gruff laugh, a bark of noise. 'I'm sure you were.'

He shifts gear and my gaze flickers lower.

'You have a tattoo.' I change the subject without really meaning to. He's unnerved me by being so breathtakingly honest—and beautiful. 'Two of them.'

'I have more than two.' The look he shoots me is pure sensual invitation. My heart stammers.

'Santiago…' It's a breathless complaint. 'Listen to me. What happened between us the other day…'

'When we kissed?' he prompts, once again tilting his face to mine, a knowing look in his eyes.

'Right.' I brush it away but my lips tingle and my soul aches. 'It was a mistake.'

'Oh?' He hits the indicator then turns the car off the road, taking us towards the beach. The water shimmers like diamonds in the distance, the sun bouncing off it. He skilfully navigates a narrow one-way street then takes us across a busy road, turning one corner and then another, checking the rear-view mirror to be sure my detail is following.

'Definitely,' I murmur, toying with my fingers in my lap.

'You don't like to be kissed?'

I briefly imagine how he'd react if I told him that that was the first time I'd ever been kissed.

'It's not appropriate for *you* to kiss me.'

The only sign he's heard is that his knuckles briefly turn white as he grips the steering wheel more tightly, before sliding the car down a ramp towards an undercover car park. I notice a steel-and-glass monolith above us and my mind immediately fills in the gaps—it's his casino, the building he had designed and constructed some ten years ago when, at twenty-one, he was a self-made billionaire and already the envy of Europe.

'Why not?'

'Because.'

'That's not an answer.'

So what is an answer? That I don't have the freedom to simply kiss any man I find desirable? That I'm supposed to marry some man my parents picked out for me before they died? That I owe my country more than to become one of Santiago's lovers, a single woman in a long line of women to have graced his bed?

'Let's just chalk it up to experience and leave it at that.'

He swings the car into a parking bay right next to the lifts.

His eyes lock with mine and the air between us thickens, sparking with electricity. I feel as though I'm being sucked into a vortex of awareness, every inch of me reverberating with need.

Desire sparks like a fever in my blood, propelling me forward, but only by an inch; despite what I've just said, I want him to close the gap. My lips part, my breath is held, and my eyes are on his at first, then on his lips, tracing their outline as I remember what it felt like to be held in his hands and ravaged by him.

'You want me to kiss you right now.'

The words are a statement of fact. I contemplate denying it, but pride won't let me lie.

'What I want and what I know to be right are two different things.'

'And wanting me isn't right?'

I shake my head a little, and somehow end up closer to him, my body almost touching his now. My seat belt strains across my chest but the pleasure of that physical contact is like a placeholder for him. I imagine his hands on my thighs and at my shoulder, and shiver.

'Why not?'

In the distance, there is the banging of car doors. My security detail. Their approach makes me feel urgency.

'Because,' I hiss, my heart pounding. 'You're you, and I'm me.'

'What does that mean?'

'In a year's time I'm going to be the Queen of Marlsdoven. Even if I wanted to do what you're suggesting…' heat rushes my cheeks… 'I can't. I'm not at liberty to have meaningless affairs. My people expect more of me.'

'So how do you conduct relationships, then?' He seems genuinely interested, the look in his eyes speculative rather than sensual.

I focus on my knees. I wonder what he'd say if I told him the truth. He'd probably be shocked, then bolt out of the car faster than you could say, 'I don't sleep with virgins'. The idea has my stomach squeezing—for all that I know a relationship between us is impossible, I don't want to turn him off completely.

'You don't know what it's like,' I say after a beat. 'I'm watched *everywhere* I go. In the palace there are staff, and outside there are citizens who see me, by virtue of my birth right, as "theirs". There's an ideal of what a princess should be and all my life I've been taught to live up to it.'

'And what happens if you don't?'

The question is one I've never asked myself. 'I don't want to find out.' My expression feels heavy with regrets. I press my hand on the door handle. 'Thank you again for coming to get me.'

His eyes pierce me for several long seconds, but before I can open the door he reaches out, pressing his fingers over my knee. 'Dinner tonight. In your hotel room.'

My lips part on a rush of breath. 'No.' It's too intimate.

He reaches for my chin then, holding my face steady, our eyes latched. There is a plea in my heart, a plea for him to understand how difficult this is for me.

'*Sí.* Don't fight when you don't want to, Princesa.'

Princesa. The word heats my blood, my eyes sparking with his. His hand drops from my face and regret forms like a brick in my gut.

'I suppose it would give us a chance to go over some details of your development,' I say with a small lift of my shoulder, not meeting his eyes in case he sees the fib for what it is.

To his credit, he doesn't gloat. 'Tonight, then.'

A shiver runs down my spine, but not one of fear. No, this is a response of anticipation and warmth, a tingle of excitement at what lies ahead.

CHAPTER FIVE

WE DIDN'T ARRANGE a precise time for dinner, a fact I'm only cognisant of when eight o'clock comes and goes and there's still no sign of Santiago. I've been waiting for him for almost an hour and I feel frustrated, annoyed and more than a little disappointed.

To my chagrin, my hotel room reservation was upgraded to the presidential suite despite my insistence that it wasn't necessary, and the suite is far, far bigger than I could possibly want. Several sumptuous bedrooms, each with their own bathroom, as well as a spacious living room that features a white grand piano, marble tiles and golden curtains framing floor-to-ceiling windows. There's a fireplace as well, for those wintry nights, though it's hard to imagine Spain being cool enough to warrant such a thing when the city is as it is now—bathed in the last rays of the summer sun, warm and golden, glowing with a hint of magic.

There is a kitchen too, and a cursory inspection when I first arrived showed it to be fully stocked with Spanish delicacies. I'm contemplating making myself a little platter of olives and bread when, finally, a heavy knock sounds at the door. I know without looking that it's him, but ingrained training has me waiting right where I am. A moment later, the door opens and Alex announces Santiago's arrival.

Alex's expression is impassive yet I can't help but wonder and worry about what he might make of this turn of events.

That concern doesn't last long. The moment Santiago steps into the suite, my mouth goes dry and my mind empties of all considerations that don't revolve around him.

He's wearing a dark suit now, casual in its styling, with a crisp white shirt unbuttoned at the throat revealing a hint of dark, curling hair, just like the first day we met. He shrugs out of his jacket as he strides closer to me, discarding it over the back of a chair, revealing shirt sleeves pushed up to show his tanned forearms.

'Hi.'

I utter the greeting simply to fill the silence. My heart is thumping heavily.

His only response is to walk towards me, and I can't help but notice his taut waist as he moves, the shirt fitted to reveal his strength and raw power. I remember the way it felt to be in his arms, and the way his body had been hard and warm. Desire weakens my knees, and my determination.

I look away, but it doesn't help; he's imprinted on my mind. When he's close enough that his fragrance tickles my nostrils I turn back to face him cautiously. His eyes are heavy on my face, and a spark bursts between us as I meet his gaze.

'How was your afternoon?'

My afternoon? I have to rally myself to focus. 'I... Fine.'

'You walked through the gaming floor?'

I lift my brows. 'You're spying on me?'

'You are not the only one with security guards.'

I frown. 'You have security?'

He dips his head. 'Particularly when I'm at the casino.'

That makes sense. His net worth is stratospheric, which

must put him at risk. I just can't imagine anyone targeting Santiago—more fool them.

'And *they* spied on me?'

His lips curl in a sardonic smile. 'Actually, I advised them you were here so that they could ensure your safety.' A hand lifts, his fingers lightly brushing my cheek, robbing me of breath.

Danger sirens blare.

'It's a precaution we take with any high-value guest.'

My heart twists. I tell myself to step backward, yet stay exactly where I am.

'The point of this trip was to fly beneath the radar.' My voice is husky. 'Hence I travelled on a commercial airline, booked an ordinary room…'

'But you are not ordinary, Princesa, no matter how you try to behave. And I do not want the publicity that would result if harm were to befall you in my casino.'

Disappointment sears me, as well as a sense of foolishness at my own expectations. Of course this wasn't about me. He was only looking after his business and its reputation. 'You don't need to worry about me.' I belatedly take a step back, needing space.

He lifts his shoulders. 'As I said, it's a precaution we take with any prominent visitor.'

'Nonetheless, it's not necessary.'

He shrugs, and I know there's nothing I can say that will change his mind. 'They're discreet. You didn't notice them today, did you?'

I hadn't, but that's not the point. I can sense the futility in arguing with him, though. Besides, he's right. If he wants to waste resources having his own security guards trail me around the venue, then that's his decision.

'Fine.' I move into the kitchen, tapping my fingers on the bench top. 'Would you like a drink?'

The question is curt, my temper at risk of fraying, as it seems to be almost all the time that I'm around Santiago. I can't explain why I feel so deflated suddenly.

His face look shows a hint of mocking amusement. 'I can't have you waiting on me, Princesa. What would your people say?'

I turn to the fridge. 'Contrary to what you might think, I'm perfectly capable of pouring a glass of wine.'

'I wasn't sure if you drink,' he murmured, coming jarringly close, swinging the fridge door open and removing a dark-green bottle.

'Only when I'm not working.'

His eyes probe mine and I realise—too late—what I've just admitted. That tonight isn't about work.

My fingers twist at my sides but he doesn't make a big deal of it, simply side-steps me to remove a couple of tall-stemmed glasses from the cupboard. He pours a little into each, a very reserved amount, before handing one of the glasses over.

'What is it?'

'A Godello.'

I lift the glass to my nose first, breathing in the aromas before taking a sip, closing my eyes to fully appreciate the floral explosion, perfectly balanced with tartness and acidity.

'It's gorgeous.'

His laugh is hoarse. 'I am glad you like it. I have just enough grapes to make a small vintage each year. This is the two thousand and twelve.'

'You make the wine?'

'It's a hobby of mine.'

I blink at him in surprise.

'You didn't expect this?'

'Frankly, no.' I take another sip. Somehow the fact this

man has been involved in its creation adds even more depth to the wine, so it hums as it moves through me.

'Why not?'

'I suppose I see you as someone with more frivolous hobbies.'

One of us, or perhaps both of us, has moved closer; there's barely any gap now. The air is thick.

'You think I'm frivolous?'

'No. I think you're…' I search for a word, shaking my head in frustration when one won't come to me. 'Your lifestyle is well documented.'

'A few photographs of me on a yacht and you think you know everything about me?' The question is light in tone, his manner seeming easy and amused, but I understand the depth beneath his question, and there's a hint of something in his eyes that makes my skin prick with goose bumps.

'Is that image wrong?'

His smile is laced with tension. 'No, *querida*.' Now it's definitely Santiago who moves closer, his powerful body dwarfing me, framing me, making me feel whole and laced with adrenalin. 'I like women.' He takes a sip of his wine then places the glass on the counter top. 'I like sex.'

I gasp at the truth of that statement, and the way it sets off a chain reaction of desire all through my body. Fascination spears through me.

'I also like making wine.'

The final sentence comes to me as if from a very, very long way away. I nod, but I can barely focus.

'And what are your hobbies?' he prompts in a gravelled tone that makes me wonder if he cares what my answer is. After all, are words necessary now? Everything between us is sparking and my body is throbbing like the beating of a drum, its urgent tone pushing me forward.

'I don't have any hobbies,' I say simply.

One dark brow quirks in surprise. Somehow he moves closer, and now we're almost touching.

'I don't believe that.'

'I'm not lying to you.'

'Everyone has hobbies. Interests outside their work.'

'My work is my life,' I say softly. 'Or perhaps I should say, my life is to work?'

He *tsk*s under his breath. 'That sounds very dull.'

'Of course it's not,' I lie. 'I take my responsibilities very seriously.'

'As evidenced by your squeaky-clean reputation,' he says with a nod.

'Have you been googling me?'

'Of course.'

My heart thumps. It's been a long time since I've searched myself on the Internet but I can imagine what's written there. Nothing. No speculation about my love life, no speculation about anything, because I never, ever stray outside the lines of the palace that have been drawn for me, lines my parents stressed the importance of observing.

'You are an excellent princess, much loved by everyone.'

'Yet you sound unimpressed.'

'Because you're living a lie.'

I gasp at the statement, so certain, so hurtful.

'Am I?'

'Your life is one of calm and measure, your smile cold, your dress so formal.'

My lips part, poised to ask a question, but I never get a chance to form it.

'Yet you are not cold, you are not calm. At least, you are neither of these things when I kiss you.'

And, before I can guess his intentions, he does just that—dropping his head, his mouth claiming me, his lips pushing mine apart as our tongues clash, our bodies welded together. He kisses me until I'm everything he just said—the complete opposite of calm and cold.

My body is flushed with awareness, my nipples almost painful against the confines of my bra and my insides squirming with need, heat pooling between my legs. My feet refuse to stay on the ground; one lifts and locks behinds his legs, clamping him to me as my hands lift and intertwine behind his neck, pulling him to me. I'm half-terrified he might stop kissing me now he's made his point, and that's the very last thing I want.

His hands shift to my hips, holding me there, drawing me to him. I moan low in my throat, the power of his erection impossible to ignore, striking power and a hint of fear into me, because I've never done this before, and it's all I can think of. Kissing him is sensual and perfect but it's not enough. I want so much more.

Driven by an ancient rush of feminine power, by instincts that are an essential part of my soul, I pull up against him at the same time he lifts me, perching me on the edge of the bench. I have a vague recollection of his wine glass being somewhere nearby but I'm incapable of connecting the dots and breaking apart from him to move it. To hell with it. Other things are far more important right now. My fingers curl into the hair at his nape, pressing my breasts to his chest, and his hands at my hips find the fabric of my shirt, lifting it to reveal a bare stomach, then going higher to my bra. We separate, purely so he can rip the shirt off my head and toss it to the floor at his feet; it's a momentary, necessary pause and then his mouth is back on mine, dominating me, awakening me…

'This is who you are.' He pushes the words into my mouth at the same time he unclasps my bra, so my breasts spill out, only to be caught in the palms of his hand

There's pleasure in his possession, a thousand arrows darting through me at the intimacy of this contact. I have never been touched like this but it doesn't feel strange. On the contrary, it feels perfect and right, those same instincts removing any hint of uncertainty. *This is who you are.*

I can't analyse his statement, I can't read into the truth or otherwise of it, because I am only capable of feeling right now. But, yes, every feeling in my body convinces me of what he's said. This is who I am. I have never felt more authentic, more real, than right now, laid bare and vulnerable to this man, yet powerful too, because the fabric of an ancient ritual is overtaking my soul.

His fingers glance across my nipples and I groan, pleasure spreading through me, a desire unlike anything I've ever imagined, much less felt, eliciting a drugging sense, like the beating of a drum over and over and over again.

He drags his mouth from mine, lavishing kisses on my collar bone then shoulders, before taking a nipple in his mouth and flicking it with his tongue until my breath becomes laboured, my breathy cries filling the room. I feel him smile against me, then his stubbly jaw shifts sideways, his mouth tormenting my other nipple as his hands cup my bottom. He lifts me effortlessly from the kitchen counter and carries me through the suite, his stride long and confident. His mouth finds mine again and his kiss obliterates thought.

This is his hotel, his presidential suite; he finds his way to the master bedroom easily, shouldering open the door and crossing the plush carpet to the bed in the centre. He lays me down gently, his body coming with mine, barely breaking the kiss. It's only when he shifts to remove our clothes completely that we pull apart, but there's not enough time for reality to fully intrude. I'm glad. Reality might bring with it caution and sense, reasons to avoid this, but the truth is, I can't.

I've never known this heady rush of longing before. I've never felt desire, chemistry, sexual need. I've never felt a spark of attraction, let alone this. One day soon I'll be Queen and I'll be formally engaged to a man I barely know and certainly don't desire. My future has been laid out for me from birth with no room for deviation. A reality I have long accepted suffocates me now, and the only relief is in this tiny act of defiance, a small, inconsequential indulgence of my own needs before I assume the duties of a kingdom.

Santiago is a man who takes women to bed without much forethought. This means nothing to him, and it will mean nothing to me either. It's just sex. But it's sex with someone *I* choose. It's all my choice. Not the requirement of my country, the will of my parliament or the sensible need for a royal heir.

A spirit of revolution hardens my resolve, so I know now that wild horses couldn't draw me away from this.

As if sensing the direction of my thoughts, he hovers above me, standing. His chest has a tattoo of a bird flying just above his heart, and there's more cursive script running across his hip. His chest moves with the ragged drawing of his breath, his eyes probing mine. 'You're sure?'

'Yes.' It's a husky, hungry acceptance of what will and must be.

His eyes glitter as he spins away from me. Rustling his trousers from the floor, he flicks open his wallet and removes a condom. 'I never take chances,' he explains.

I amuse myself with what he'd say if I told him I'm a virgin, that sex with me is completely safe—before the penny drops and I realise he's alluding to children, an unintended, lifelong consequence of a reckless night of passion

'No baby del Almodovárs on the horizon for you?' I murmur as he rips open the foil square and rolls the condom over his arousal. My eyes cling to the action, and I'm jarred out of my slumberous, all-encompassing desire because of his obvious size.

His smile tilts the earth off its axis. 'Definitely not. I never intend to have children.'

I'm curious as to his reason. I have never given this issue any thought, for the simple reason that having children is yet another purpose of my existence. As a royal—the sole surviving royal of my house—I have been aware for a long time that I must have babies, and several of them. I don't know if it's what I would have chosen otherwise, but a cursory examination shows that I like the idea. I'm more excited about being a mother than I am about being a wife.

There is no more time to analyse this. He brings his body over mine, his smile gone, his expression hauntingly beautiful as his knee nudges my legs apart, his body weight on mine a pleasure in and of itself. His kiss is slow at first, his tongue languorously exploring my mouth, my breasts tingling beneath his hair-roughened chest, my fingers tracing his tattoos by memory, a question in every strike of my touch. I am lost, buried under the weight of need, full of wanting him. I'm unable to think, breathe, talk so that, when he nudges the tip of his arousal against my sex, I can only groan in the base of my throat. There is no time for anticipation or fear; he drives into me, his full, powerful length hard, strong and dynamic, pushing past the invisible barrier of my innocence, his body possessing mine for the first time.

He freezes, bracing himself on his elbows. His eyes meet mine, surprise obvious on his face, a question in his gaze.

'Freja…' My name is squeezed from between his teeth.

Is that an accusation I hear? Anger? Briefly, darkness eclipses my pleasure, but then he begins to move again and any hint of discomfort his first thrust invoked dissipates, leaving only pleasure in its path. Intense, soul-destroying pleasure.

He is skilled and intuitive, driving me to the brink of ecstasy many times before drawing me back, tormenting me with his easy mastery of my body, showing that he can control my pleasure with ease.

I don't know how long he does this for, but it's long enough for me to feel delirious with desire, a heat building inside me that is crazy for release. I plead with him over and over, his name on my lips a garbled cry until he kisses me, weaves our fingers together and finally tips me over. He drives me over the edge of awareness, heaving me from this earthly plane so that I'm in freefall, conscious only of surrender—his and mine—as his body is racked with breaths, his strength throbbing inside me. A guttural cry rents the air before he kisses me once more, murmuring Spanish words I don't understand into my mouth.

Tears burn my eyes and I can't stop them. The sheer perfection of what I just experienced defies explanation. I know people talk about sex, and I got that it's meant to be amazing, but I had no idea it could be so completely earth-shattering.

I blink to clear the tears, not wanting him to see them, needing a moment to gather myself even as he's still buried within me.

He pushes up onto his elbows to look down at me, scanning my face and, I'm sure, seeing far more than I wish to expose.

'And so the Princesa was a virgin,' he murmurs, a hint of something in his face I can't comprehend.

'Was it that obvious?'

'To me.'

My heart stammers. It occurs to me that I must have been pathetically boring after the women he's used to sleeping with. He kisses the corner of my mouth, taking my self-conscious fears with him. 'Did I hurt you?'

I shake my head. 'At first, a little. But no. That was…' I search for the right word, then smile.

'Freja.'

I blink, because it's unusual for him to use my name rather than my title. I like hearing it on his lips, in his accent. 'If I had known, I would never have pursued you.'

'Why not?'

His own features tighten. 'Because a one-night stand is a very different consideration than being someone's first lover. I have very little interest in the latter, generally.'

'Then I'm glad you made an exception for me.'

He doesn't respond to my quip.

'The reason I like one-night stands is that there are no expectations beyond great sex.'

His logic baffles me. 'Whereas the fact I'm a virgin means I must now be expecting a proposal?' I tease, smiling to show how wrong he is.

His eyes are wary. 'Or at least a relationship of sorts,' he clarifies carefully.

'I can't have relationships,' I say simply, the words hiding a pain buried deep in my heart, a pain born of jealousy for what I see as 'normal' for most of the world.

'That makes less sense to me now than when you first said it.'

'Think about it, Santiago. My life is an open book. Where would I meet someone? How would I date them? Break up with them? Heaven forbid I dated several men. My country is conservative, and the royal family is seen to be perfect, beyond reproach. I could never expose myself to that kind of gossip. I would never disgrace my parents' memory.'

'But surely behind closed doors…?'

'There are very few closed doors in my life,' I say wistfully. 'I live in a palace that has hundreds of servants. They are good people, but still people, and people gossip. If a boyfriend snuck into my apartment at night, word would quickly get out, and before long articles would appear in the press.'

'And would that be so bad?'

'It's easy for you,' I say with a sigh. 'You don't care about stuff like this. Look at the stories that are written about you! The press loves to report on your lifestyle, your over-indulgences, on the fact you're a "bad boy".' I smirk, because it's such a perfect description of this man. 'You could never understand how much I would hate that.'

'I don't love it,' he replies, surprising me with his honesty. 'But nor do I give it much thought.'

'But my job is to be the Queen my people deserve. That's incompatible with the lifestyle you're suggesting.'

'I'm not suggesting you roll from one wild party to the next, but only that you might have dated from time to time.'

'It's not possible.' If it's strange to have this conversation while our bodies are still joined together, it doesn't occur to me. 'And particularly not now.'

'Why not?'

'Because next year my coronation will take place, and directly afterwards my engagement to His Royal Highness Heydar van Anjers will be announced. It would be highly inappropriate for me to date anyone right now. So please don't think that this…' I run my fingers down his side '…is going to complicate your life in the slightest—virgin or not.'

CHAPTER SIX

'YOU'RE ENGAGED?'

It's not the reaction I'd expected, and nor is the darkening of his face; there is a look there I can't interpret.

'"Betrothed" is a more accurate description,' I explain as he pulls away, shifting to lie on the bed beside me, a frown etched on his lips.

'What is the difference?'

'Well...' I consider that a moment. 'To say we're "engaged" makes it sound like we've been dating and decided to get married. Whereas I've only met Heydar a couple of times. Our relationship isn't—and never has been—romantic.'

'Obviously.' He pushes up onto one elbow so he can see me better. His scrutiny is unnerving. 'So why the hell are you marrying him?'

'Because we're betrothed.'

'Meaning?'

'Meaning that, a long time ago, his parents and my parents, who were very dear friends, entered into a contract binding Heydar and me. The terms were crystal-clear. On my twenty-fifth birthday, our engagement would be announced, with the wedding to take place no more than three months later.'

He says something under his breath, something Spanish,

and I guess from his tone that it's a swear word. I blink up at him, unsure of his reaction.

'What is it?'

His dark eyes probe mine for several seconds.

'Frankly, I don't like the idea of having slept with another man's fiancée.'

I laugh, because it's so completely unexpected. 'I just told you, we're not engaged. It's not like that. Besides, I'm sure he's not letting our arrangement stop him from seeing other women.'

'And it's okay for him to date, but not you?'

I sigh dramatically. 'That almost sounds like there *might* be a double standard for men and women,' I observe with a fine peppering of sarcasm. 'Men are expected to have girlfriends. It's old-fashioned and it sucks, but he doesn't have the same expectations to be morally beyond reproach that I do.'

'How can you accept such restrictions so calmly? I'd want to burn the house down.'

'It's my life,' I say with a shrug.

'But it doesn't have to be.'

'A second ago you looked half-terrified I was going to latch onto you and beg you to spend the rest of your life with me, and now you're trying to talk me out of going through with my wedding?'

'I can feel both those things,' he assures me. 'This is an academic discussion; it has no bearing on what just happened between us.'

I wonder at the slight pain in my chest, as if a blade's pressing against my heart.

'So why did you sleep with me?'

The question barrels towards me like a freight train. The answer is right there, glaringly obvious, but I feel that to admit the truth to Santiago would lay me bare. I angle my head a little, pretending fascination with a painting across the room. The art work in this suite is a blend of classic and contemporary—there are pieces from the Renaissance juxtaposed with paintings featuring bold, bright colours, abstract and happy-making.

His fingers touch my shoulder lightly, sending goose bumps across my skin.

'Freja?'

My name, again. My heart slows.

'Why did *you* sleep with *me*?' I push the question back on him, angling my head to his so I can see his expression.

His eyes scan my face with indolent ease, studying me, before his lips flicker in a quick grin. 'You're sexy.' He moves his finger lower. 'And beautiful.' He draws his finger towards my belly button, then makes a circle, running his finger around it again and again. 'And I wanted you.'

I wanted you.

The words bounce around inside me, the certainty behind them filling me with surprise. 'And that's how it works, is it?'

He waits for me to continue.

'You see someone you want and what—they fall into your bed?'

'Most of the time,' he drawls jokingly, but something a lot like jealousy flashes in my gut. It's not jealousy of *him*, it's jealousy of his freedom and lifestyle. 'You didn't answer my question, Princesa.'

I nod slowly. 'I wanted you too.'

'But you must have wanted men before. Why me, now?'

I prop up onto my elbow, mirroring his body language, my fingers lifting to the bird tattooed above his heart. It's an eagle, bold and confident, watching me as though with a warning in its eyes. 'You're sexy and beautiful?' I tease.

His lips flicker in another slow smile. My heart twists.

With uncertainty slowing my words, I say, 'Actually, I haven't.' I clear my throat. 'Met anyone I wanted before, I mean.'

At the look of triumph in the depths of his eyes, I roll mine. 'Don't let your head get too big, Santiago. I didn't exactly have much of an opportunity to meet anyone.'

'You've met men before,' he points out. 'Lots of men, I'm sure. And yet I am the only one you've ever been tempted to sleep with.'

It's one hundred per cent true, but I suspect his ego doesn't need the stroking.

'Whatever.' I flick his tattoo.

He laughs, a hoarse sound that sends little arrows of desire across my spine. Silence falls between us, warm and pricked with awareness.

'I guess,' I say thoughtfully, surprised at how honest I'm prepared to be with Santiago. 'I didn't want to miss this opportunity.'

He waits for me to continue and I order my words with care.

'I don't know much about Heydar. He seems nice, and he has a good record on all the things that matter. But, the handful of times we've been in the same room, I've felt nothing. Not even curiosity. We don't have any spark whatsoever. I'll marry him because he'll be good for my country, and because it was important to my parents, but I already know that our marriage won't have chemistry.'

I shift my hand to the snake inked on his toned forearm, tracing its length.

'And then I met you, and you were so infuriating and rude and direct, and unlike anyone I've ever known,' I say with a weak smile. 'And when you kissed me I felt like part of me I didn't know existed was being brought to life: and not piece by piece, but all at once, in a huge, fiery rush. It terrified me,' I murmur. 'I didn't come to Spain expecting we'd sleep together. In fact, I came determined that we wouldn't. After all, I can't be involved with someone like you,' I point out matter-of-factly. 'The way you make me feel is both exhilarating and terrifying. But I'm going to marry a guy I feel nothing for, so don't I deserve this?'

It's a rhetorical question. I'm telling him to absolve me of a sin that I haven't really committed. I'm telling him to understand.

He mulls it over for a moment before leaning forward, brushing our lips together. 'Everyone deserves great sex in their life, Freja. I'm just sorry you're willing to walk into a lifetime without it.'

It had never really bothered me before. If anything, I'd come to the conclusion I was asexual, not remotely interested in men. But now? Having been awoken by Santiago, what will it be like to push this part of myself back into the box?

Necessary, I remind myself. My country needs this, and it was the wish of my parents.

'How long are you in Spain for?'

'Four nights. Including tonight.'

'It's not long.'

'It's long enough to appraise the casino,' I point out, reminding us both of the main reason I came to Barcelona.

His smirk pulls me apart from the inside out. 'Sure.' His accent rolls over the word, softening it. 'But perhaps not enough to make up for lost time.'

I frown. 'What does that mean?'

'That we have four nights to give you a lifetime's worth of sexual satisfaction. It's a challenge, but I think I'm up for it.'

'That's big of you.'

'If you say so.' He winks at my unintended *double entendre.*

'You seriously have an ego the size of a house.'

'Is that all?'

We're quiet. Our eyes clash. 'The thing is…' I move my hand back to his eagle tattoo, then press my palm to his chest. 'I meant what I said before. I can't date. And I especially can't date you.'

'Because if people discovered we were sleeping together, a scandal would follow?' he says speculatively.

'Well, yes.' I bite down on my lip, worried about offending him before I remember this is Santiago del Almodovár. 'With everything that's printed about you in the press, my people would be horrified.'

'I have no interest in ruining your pristine reputation, Your Highness.' For a moment, I'm reminded of his antipathy on that first afternoon we met, the silent undercurrent of disapproval that was obvious in his every remark. But then he stands, extending a hand to me, so I place my own in his and he pulls me to standing. Our bodies are so close, my hips brush his.

'Four nights in my bed, and no one will ever know.'

Something like adrenalin courses through my veins. A secret affair with Santiago del Almodovár explodes through me; wonderment fills my body. It's not what I expected when I came to Spain, but it's absolutely perfect. Why shouldn't I enjoy a fling with a bad-boy sex god before I go back to Marlsdoven and continue to act like the perfect Princess the country expects me to be?

'Isn't it technically my bed?' I ask with fluttering lashes.

'Your bed, my bed. Let's not argue over semantics.' He scoops down and lifts me easily, cradling me to his chest. 'So long as there's a bed and you're in it, I don't particularly care about anything else.'

* * *

He runs the loofah over my body, sponging me until I'm covered in soap, the warm water of the shower rinsing it off. I watch him unashamedly, fascinated by this intimacy, by his closeness, by the fact he's not intimidated by me and by the way he reveres my body, worshipping me as though there is some all-powerful energy source layered beneath my skin. When I'm clean all over, he looks up, his dark eyes hooded, his expression causing my lungs to burst with air pressure.

'How do you feel?'

Better than I've ever felt before. 'Good.' I smile shyly.

'And here?' He presses a finger to my sex so I jump, the touch unexpected and perfect.

'Good.' I thought I was shy before!

'You're sure?'

I nod but, when he presses his lips to my most intimate core, I almost jump out of my skin.

'Santiago…' It's a plea, but for what?

He flashes his eyes at me, a smile playing about his lips before he moves his tongue, flicking my sensitive cluster of nerves until stars dance behind my eyes. I lift my hands up and press them flat against the tiled wall behind me, desperate for the support. The warm water douses my naked body, cascading down my breasts as he lashes me with his tongue… Then I'm falling apart at the seams all over again, pleasure a tidal wave drowning me in desire and, though we are taught to fear drowning, I can't say I feel anything right now but ecstasy.

'Did you grow up here?' I reach for another of the Cambados oysters, their ocean-salt flavour delicious, particularly when paired with Santiago's wine.

He watches me eat then runs his hands over his jaw, as

if lost in thought…or weighing something up, perhaps. 'I grew up in the Ciutat Vella.'

'The what?'

'The Old City.'

'Ah. It sounds beautiful.'

His smile is sardonic. 'Does it?'

'Wasn't it?'

'There are parts,' he concedes.

'But not where you grew up?'

'No.'

'Why not?'

He reaches for an oyster, lifting it expertly to his lips and sliding it into his mouth, swallowing it whole. I'm transfixed, watching as his Adam's apple shifts in his stubbly throat.

'We lived in a crowded apartment building—one bedroom for the three of us. It was loud and untidy.'

My frown is reflexive. It twitches on my lips before I can stop it.

'Your parents didn't have a lot of money?' I prompt quietly.

'That is one way to say it.' He reaches for his wine and takes a sip, his eyes holding mine over the rim of the glass so bubbles of warmth spread in my veins.

'I hadn't realised. I knew that your fortune was self-made, but I presumed your parents gave you a start.'

'No.'

I nod slowly. His reluctance to expand is something I should probably respect, but curiosity fires through my belly. 'So what did?'

He waits for me to clarify.

'How did you get to have all this?' I gesture to the view of the city beneath us, the lights twinkling in the evening light. On the balcony of the presidential suite in his central casino, I feel as though the world is at his—and my—feet.

'Hard work.'

I laugh. 'That tells me nothing.'

'Doesn't it?'

Our eyes meet and I nod slowly. I can tell that he's a hard worker. Despite his party-boy reputation, I see beneath it—there is a streak of ruthless determination that convinces me Santiago will stop at nothing to achieve his ends. Even now, with hundreds of billions in the bank, he will do whatever it takes to ensure his next venture is a success.

Including sleeping with you? I push the horrible, insidious thought away before I can give it any credit. How ridiculous. Sex isn't why I'll agree to his casino proposal. It has nothing to do with it.

'I was on the brink of dropping out of school.' He surprises me by continuing, his voice raspy, as though the past is grabbing hold of him. 'I barely went anyway, not more than a few hours a week.' He casts his eyes towards the black void in the distance, at the ocean beyond the city.

'Why not? What did you do instead?'

His eyes pierce me with their intensity. 'I worked, *querida*.'

'You were just a child.'

'A teenager, and we needed the money.'

He reaches for another oyster. I shift to a horizontal position on the comfortable outdoor sofa, lying on my side so I can see him, propping my head on my palm.

'Besides, I hated school.'

'Really?'

'Doesn't everyone?'

'Oh, I loved it. Not school, but learning. In another life,

I should have been an academic. Give me a pile of text-books and a long test at the end of it, and I'm set.'

His laugh is throaty.

'No skipping classes for you?'

'No such luck. I had a tutor.'

'Of course you did.' His voice is droll, and again I'm reminded of our first meeting. His cynicism is most apparent when we touch on the trappings of my position. I push up a little and reach for my wine, taking a small sip. The breeze is warm, rustling over my hair, and I relish the sensations—cold wine, satisfied body, warm flesh. 'And of course you did not need to work to support your family,' he adds, so I feel almost a hint of guilt in my chest.

I shake my head before lying back down again. 'You didn't drop out, though?'

'No.' He studies me. 'A teacher saw me working at mechanics.'

Great. Now I have to imagine Santiago as a grease monkey, his head beneath the bonnet of a car, dressed in a white singlet and form-fitting jeans. My mouth goes dry.

'He realised I'd been ditching school to work and hauled me into his office. I was surprised he cared, at the time. The school was not known for its academic reputation, and no one had given much of a care about what I did until then.'

Something about the throwaway comment makes my heart ache for him.

'What about your parents?'

His smile is tight, cautiously dismissive. 'That's another story.'

'I'd like to hear it.'

He shakes his head once; it's obvious he doesn't intend to elaborate. 'The teacher's specialty was maths. He set me extra work. Pushed me. I had an aptitude.' His expression bears the ghosts of the past. I perceive the pain that dogs him and wonder why I didn't comprehend it at our first meeting. Because he'd come in all guns blazing, and all my instincts had been askew, thanks to the way he'd made me feel.

'About three months after he started working with me, there was a phantom-stock-market game. Do you know what this is?'

'Like playing the stock market with fake money?'

'*Si.*'

'And you were great at it?'

'I earned over a million euro in the first week,' he says. 'So, yes, you could say that.'

My eyes widen. 'Seriously?'

His head shifts in a single nod. 'I was fifteen and had never had enough money in my life. We were dirt-poor, Princesa, and suddenly I'd been given the keys to a world beyond my comprehension.'

'But that was just pretend. How did you take that and turn it into all this?'

'I found investors, charged a scaling percentage of what I earned for them. It was their money, their risk—all the up side was mine.'

I shake my head from side to side, admiration filling me.

'I was able to diversify, invest in properties then major ventures, such as this.'

'You make it sound so easy.'

'Once I was given the keys, it was.'

Pleasure has seeped through me. I am exhausted and satiated. It occurs to me that I'm happier in this moment than I've ever been.

'And now, Your Highness, I must go.'

It jerks me out of my reverie. 'What? Why?'

His smile is arrogant and hot. I don't care that I've shown how much I enjoy his company, or that my disappointment is blatantly obvious. 'I have a meeting.'

I reach for my phone, checking the time. 'It's almost midnight.'

'And, in a casino, that's prime time.'

My face probably shows what I think of that. 'It's the middle of the night.'

His laugh is laced with mocking humour. 'So prim,' he teases as he stands and walks towards me, his body brushing mine when he sits on the edge of the sofa, our hips connecting.

Pride be damned. 'Do you have to go?'

'Yes,' he says, but I don't think I'm imagining the regret in his voice now. 'Besides, it is better if I don't stay the night. Your guards might do some of that gossiping you are so afraid of.'

He's right but I don't know if I care right now. I lower my eyes, painfully aware of what a hypocrite that makes me.

'Sleep naked,' he says gruffly. 'And dream of me.'

CHAPTER SEVEN

MY PARENTS WERE close to my uncle Richard. They adored him. My father's younger brother, he'd had all the advantages of royal life and none of the pressure and expectations that had weighed down my father and which had ensured he was sensible in his life choices.

My uncle had been free to do as he wished, largely left alone by the media. My father told me, when I was only small that at one time he'd envied his brother that freedom. He'd wished he'd been born second, able to live without the scrutiny and watchfulness of the world. And, while I can understand that sentiment, it was not borne out by history.

Uncle Richard had grown up without expectations and therefore he'd never striven to meet them. And, worse, he had everything he could ever want in life, so even the basic pleasure of aspiring to achievement had been denied him. What could he do that would make a difference to anyone?

His gambling addiction had grabbed hold of him before anyone had known—the amount of money he'd lost eye-watering. I wake with my uncle in my mind and the sting of tears in my eyes, a sense of betrayal tightening around my chest.

How can I be making this deal? How can I be sleeping with the man who wants to bring a casino to my country?

It takes me a second to realise that I didn't wake up by chance. There is knocking at the door. I push the covers back, my heart racing in the hope it's Santiago. I wrap a silken robe around my body—yes, I slept naked—and pull the door inward.

A hotel staff member stands there, one of my guards at his side.

'Room service,' he offers in accented Spanish.

'Oh.' I take a step back, gesturing towards the marble-topped dining table. 'Thank you.'

It takes him a moment to wheel the trolley into position, placing it beside the table, then unstacking plate after plate of food, each covered in a golden lid. My attention drifts to the sunlit vista beyond the window, the sheer size of Barcelona fascinating me and giving me a desire to explore. In the distance, the sea glistens with shades of turquoise and aqua, so beautiful, particularly on a clear, sunny day like this. Impatience bursts through me. Impatience to be alone and free.

It's the first time in my life I've felt like this.

I nod as the waiter leaves, waiting until the door is closed to begin lifting lids off the platters. Fruit, Danish pastries, and an omelette filled with smoked salmon and drizzled with hollandaise sauce, as well as hash browns and sausages. It's too much food. There are two plates left to uncover. I pull the lid off one, frowning as I reach for what's beneath. Definitely not food. My fingers run over something soft and brown. Closer inspection reveals a chic wig. Beneath it is a brightly coloured scrap of fabric—a bikini.

Heat flushes my cheeks as I open the final lid to find a note from Santiago.

Meet me at the marina at midday. Wear the disguise. Bring the swimmers.

I stare at the bikini with a thudding heart. It's turquoise in colour and, so far as bikinis go, not too revealing. But the idea of wearing something like this…

I quickly shove it back onto the plate and replace the lid. I'm ravenous after last night—we ate only oysters and expended a lot of energy—and eat my way through the fruit and omelette, sipping orange juice and coffee, before tackling a Danish for good measure.

When I travel on official trips, my schedule is usually packed from morning to night. What a strange and pleasurable change this makes. I have nothing on the horizon, the day is my own. Or perhaps it's Santiago's…

Once more my eyes find the sea and something like excitement lifts my heart. For three days, I've escaped my normal life—no press, no intrusions, no pressure. I can do what I want, so long as no one finds out…

The car brings me to the biggest boat in the marina—naturally—a white yacht the size of several houses with tinted windows and several decks. I stare up at it from the back seat of the limousine, conscious of the wig hanging tight around my ears and the Lycra of the bikini against my skin. Naturally I'm wearing more than just the bikini—in fact, to the outside world, I look demure and business-like in a pair of cream trousers and a simple lime-green shirt tucked in at the waist. My shoes are flat, but definitely not boat shoes: in my defence, I didn't anticipate yachting as part of the trip.

My security agents scan the boat from the nearby dock and a moment later are met by members of Santiago's staff. I watch in amusement as they enter into discussion. For a moment it looks a little heated, so I step out of the car while they're distracted, approaching from behind.

'Is there a problem?'

One of my guards turns to face me, his features showing consternation. 'No, ma'am. It's just a matter of logistics.'

Santiago's staff member speaks over the top of him. 'Mr del Almodovár values his privacy and has requested your company. Alone.'

My lips twitch in amusement, even when I know I should be annoyed. After all, I've told him I don't want to draw attention to what we're doing, and that includes amongst my staff. Nonetheless, you can't make an omelette without breaking eggs and, given the level of intrusion in my life, I was probably living in a fantasy world to think I could keep things completely secret.

'I trust Mr del Almodovár,' I say firmly, surprised to realise that it's true. I do trust him. 'Go back to the hotel and wait for me there.'

'But—'

'I mean it,' I say, but gently now, smiling to soften my command. After all, I rarely give such edicts. 'I'll be fine.'

It clearly doesn't satisfy either of them, but they take a step back, signalling tacit agreement, and I expel the breath I was holding.

A moment later, I'm walking up the gang plank of the yacht, with no idea if that's actually what it's called, my pulse running away with me at the prospect of seeing Santiago again. Excitement bursts through me.

His own staff stays on the marina.

'Hello?' I call, smiling despite the fact he hasn't appeared.

The boat begins to move and I reach out, putting my hand on the railing to steady myself, my smile growing wider as I step away from the edge look for the steering wheel. Is that even what it's called on a yacht?

Santiago is standing at the front of the boat, wearing

only a pair of shorts, low-slung to reveal his toned, tanned waist, his shapely legs and strong shoulders.

Desire rushed through me.

'Is this a kidnapping?' I ask as I approach him from behind.

He casts a glance over his shoulder, his eyes locking to mine so my smile drops, the sheer heat in his look almost knocking me sideways. 'Definitely.'

A *frisson* of need runs through me. The idea of being this man's captive is unexpectedly appealing.

He deftly manoeuvres the yacht from the marina with the ease of a man who does this regularly and, once through the barrier, he sets the control in position and turns to me properly. His fingers lift, catching a hint of my dark wig, brushing it between his forefinger and thumb.

'Do you like it?'

'I thought I would.' He lifts it from my head, nodding approval at the reappearance of my blonde hair. 'But this is better.'

My heart skips a beat.

'How did you sleep?'

'Like a log.'

'And naked?'

Heat bursts through me. I don't answer.

'I imagined you naked.' He turns back to the controls, steering the boat, with no idea what his throwaway comment does to my equilibrium. I'm knocked completely sideways.

'How was your meeting?' My voice is gravelled and uneven. I come to stand to his right, staring ahead rather than looking directly at him.

'Last night?' I prompt when he doesn't answer.

'Fine.'

Out of nowhere, a blade of jealousy assails me, as the

unpleasant thought occurs to me that he'd left me to meet another woman. Memories of the phone call where a woman's voice had been audible in the background make my breath feel hot in my lungs. My envy is based on nothing but fear—I don't know Santiago that well but I somehow trust that he's not the kind of man who would go from making love to me to being with another woman all in the same night.

I move away from him on the pretence of exploring, moving across the deck and then along a railing, ducking into the main cabin and marvelling at the space—it looks like a state-of-the-art hotel, all glossy white with plush décor, sofas and an enormous television.

I'm aware that we've stopped moving and a glance through the windows shows only ocean and, in the distance, a stunning view of the city. There are no other boats that I can see, and we're far from the land—far enough to render the buildings miniature.

'There you are.' He pulls me into his arms, kissing me hard and fast, as though he's been aching to do this all his life.

My head spins. 'Hi.' The word is just a breath in my mouth.

'I'm glad you came.'

'Well, as it turns out, I didn't have anything else to do,' I tease.

His laugh is a rumble. 'Are you hungry?'

'After that breakfast? I don't know if I'll ever eat again.'

'I'm glad you have energy.' His eyes spark with mine, his meaning clear, and I laugh—but there's an undercurrent of need pulling at me, drawing me to him, so I ache for him to kiss me again.

'Where are we?'

'Drifting in the Balearic sea.'

I breathe in the salty air, letting it touch my throat. That sense of freedom is back, taunting and tempting me. Freedom is an illusion for me, but for the next little while I can pretend.

'This boat is something else.'

'Surely you're used to such things?'

'On the contrary, I could never have something so decadent. With taxpayer money? Absolutely not.'

'Says the woman who lives in a palace?'

'That belongs to the people of Marlsdoven,' I point out.

His lips quirk as though he doesn't believe me. 'And the land I'm going to buy from you?'

The remark is jarring. I pull away from him a little, a sense of heaviness in my heart assailing me out of nowhere.

'It also belongs to my people,' I murmur. 'I'm simply the legal custodian. Which is why I must be very careful with what happens to it.'

To my relief, he lets the subject drop. 'Hungry or not, I want to show you something.'

Curious, I allow his fingers to weave through mine so he can draw me through the yacht into a living area that also has a large kitchen, all gleaming white with high ceilings. He pulls a tray from the bench and walks towards me, gesturing towards it.

Rows of little chocolates sit waiting for attention.

'What are they?'

'A delicacy. Truffles flavoured with saffron and pistachio.'

I run my eyes over the pretty platter and, after a moment of hesitation, Santiago lifts one, bringing it to hover at my lips. 'Allow me.'

I open my mouth so he can slip the chocolate inside, the vour exploding in my mouth dwarfed only by the sensual awareness of the man opposite, who keeps his finger pressed to my lip as I finish the confectionery.

'Well?' His eyes probe mine.

'Delicious. Savoury and sweet at the same time.'

He nods his approval. 'They are my favourite.'

He replaces the tray on the kitchen bench then nods to the deck. 'Shall we?'

I blink. 'Shall we what?' My temperature is already sky-high.

His smile shows he understands the direction of my thoughts. 'Sunbathe, of course.' His wink is that of the bad boy I know him to be, and yet I fall into step behind him. When he gestures to a row of four sunbeds lined up at the front of the yacht, I take a middle one, relaxing as the sun wraps me in warmth.

'I don't remember the last time I did this. If ever.'

'Holidayed?'

I nod. 'Most of my trips are official, and there's barely a free moment to relax. I don't mind—if I'm going to be away from home, I'd rather use the time productively. But I've almost forgotten what it's like to simply…exist.'

He reaches out and laces our fingers together. 'You're working now too. Sort of.'

'But let's not, today.' I decide on the spur of the moment, looking at him directly. 'Let's not talk about the casino or the land. I know we have to, at some point, but it will just ruin things to do so now.'

His eyes narrow and for a moment I wonder if he's going to argue but then he shrugs indolently. 'Very well, *querida*. If you wish.'

The sun lances across him, a golden blade that invites my fingers to reach out and touch. Instead, I simply stare, my eyes drinking in the sight of him.

'You must travel often for work?' he prompts, eith

unaware of my shameless lusting or choosing not to acknowledge it.

I swallow past a constricted throat. 'Not that often, actually.' My eyes flick to his. 'Mainly in neighbouring Scandinavian countries, occasionally further afield. I went to Australia two years ago.'

'Did you like it?'

I nod. 'Oh, very much. I don't know if I've ever been to a country with such dramatic differences. One day I was in the tropics and the next in wineries shrouded in mist. There's snow and deserts, beaches filled with white sand and turquoise water—they put me in mind of the Mediterranean. And the people are so friendly.'

'Was it a work trip?'

'Of course.' I nod. 'And it was quick. I saw a lot, but my schedule was crammed full, so most of the "seeing" was done through the windows of my limousine.'

His lips twist for a moment, and again I have a sense that there's something he's not saying, but the look is gone again almost immediately.

'What work were you doing?'

'Studying their tourism industry. Marlsdoven is very small but very beautiful. We want more people to come and see it for themselves. Sadly, we're overshadowed by our more well-known neighbours.'

He nods thoughtfully, his eyes sparking with mine for a moment.

I sigh, his point, though not spoken, well taken. 'I suppose you think your casino will attract tourists.'

'Undoubtedly, but we aren't talking about that today.'

I turn my attention to the view, the beautiful glistening sea beyond the yacht, the warmth of the sun, the drama of the city in the distance. The famous spires of the Sagrada Familia, Gaudi's vision, reach towards the sky surrounded by a glow of terracotta, all golden and red. The contrast with the aqua colour of the ocean is almost too beautiful to bear.

'My government is focussing on transport infrastructure,' I say after a moment. 'We want to make it easy and cheap to come to Marlsdoven. A high-speed rail line is being designed at the moment, with the hope of bringing visitors directly from Amsterdam.'

He doesn't reply, and silence clouds around us, but it's a content silence, the gentle lapping of waves against the boat lulling me until my breathing slows and my eyes feel heavy.

'Why did you buy into casinos?'

The question is slumberous, and I don't look at him.

'You mean the dens of iniquity that make me my fortune?' he asks with a hint of mockery. I flick my gaze to him and my heart twists painfully in my chest. He is way too handsome. It's not fair.

'Potayto...potahtoe...' I say with a lift of my lips.

'You forget, *querida.* I made my fortune on the stock market. What is that if not a form of gambling?'

'It's not the same thing.' Though already I'm aware of my weakness here. I don't know enough about share trading to speak with authority.

'It is close to it. While there is a little more knowledge at play, mostly it's about spotting trends, often about following intuition. It's risky and fortunes can be lost in the blink of an eye. Sound familiar?'

'It's still different.'

'Why?'

'I don't know,' I say honestly. 'But it is.' Thinking about it a little more, I sit up straighter, no longer relaxed enough to drift away on a cloud of sleep. 'People don't generally wander into the stock market and throw away their life savings. For one thing, it's not easy to do—you have to have an account or a trader who places…bids…or whatever it's called…on your behalf. When casinos are on every street corner, then every man and his dog can wander into the lobby and spin a roulette wheel.'

'Roulette wheels are not in the lobby, and we are a strictly no-animal establishment,' he drawls.

I roll my eyes and, despite the heavy direction of our conversation, find myself smiling at his quick rejoinder. 'I'm serious. The stock market is intimidating and there are barriers to people partaking. Those barriers mean most people have a level of knowledge before they open an account. A casino has no such barriers.'

'Age isn't a barrier?'

'So you have to be eighteen to gamble. Big deal.'

'It is my turn to ask a question,' he says thoughtfully. 'Why do you hate casinos so much?'

My eyes fill with light. I swallow quickly, looking away, my family's secret like a hole in my chest. 'We've discussed that.'

'You've told me you disapprove of gambling. But why?'

'Because people lose their savings. It's damaging.' My heart is racing. 'And we said we wouldn't talk about this.' I reach out, putting a hand on his knee. 'Not today.'

His eyes war with mine, the part of Santiago that wants to win, the ruthless businessman who sniffs out the advantage and mercilessly pushes it home, finding it hard to let the matter drop. But, to my surprise and relief, he does exactly that. His smile doesn't reach his eyes, but he offers one anyway.

'We will not talk about it,' he says with a clipped nod. 'But promise me this.'

I wait, my breath held.

'Come to the casino floor with me tonight. Let me show you what it's really like.'

I stiffen at the very idea. 'I toured your casino yesterday, remember?'

My voice is unintentionally icy; I hear the tone and inwardly wince.

His expression is relaxed but I feel the intensity reverberating off him in waves. 'Did you play any of the games?'

'Games?' I respond sharply, thinking only of my uncle. 'You do realise that's part of the problem? People think it's all fun and harmless but it's not. "Games" is a misnomer, if ever I heard one.'

A muscle jerks in his jaw. 'And because of your personal animosity towards gambling you are determined to keep it from your society for ever?'

'That's not possible,' I say quietly.

'No.' We're in agreement and yet I feel like the air between us is sparking with tension. Electricity fills my fingertips. 'Perhaps at some point, but not in the twenty-first century. People travel easily, play online.'

'"Play",' I say with a shake of my head.

'What would you prefer I say? Dice with danger?'

'It would be more accurate.'

'Your hatred makes no sense.'

'Not to you perhaps.'

'So explain it to me.'

I bristle, swallowing to bring back moisture to my dry mouth. 'There's no point. It hardly seems to matter. My personal feelings on the casino are by the by. I've accepted that your development will go ahead. All I care about now is making sure my country gets the utmost financial reward from the endeavour.' Again, I hear the words, and they are laced with condemnation. I wish I could control my emotions but a hatred for gambling—and an awareness of its evils—has been drummed into me for a very long time. I cannot think of my uncle or my parents without being conscious of the enormity of this betrayal.

My breath burns in my throat.

'It is not by the by to me.' His nostrils flare with the statement and for a moment my stomach swoops with something like pleasure. His interest is flattering and dangerously addictive. I quickly remind myself that it has nothing to do with me and everything to do with Santiago: he has to understand people, things, problems. It's in his nature to know everything he can about a person.

'Tell me,' I murmur. 'When you first began trading in the phantom stock-market scenario, how did you do it?'

The conversation change annoys him. I wonder if he'll brush the question aside to return to interrogating me but he doesn't. 'I researched trends. I watched carefully. I immersed myself in everything I could on the matter. Why?'

It's just as I suspected. He has to understand everything and, right now, he's trying to understand me—but only so he can turn me to his advantage. It has nothing to do with wanting to know me, or caring about me as a person.

As a child, I was winded once when I fell off a horse. I landed on my back and all the air was drummed from my body, so I lay staring up at the clear blue sky, stars dancing on the lids of my eyes. My nanny's terrified face had hovered on the periphery of my view with me unable to offer any form of reassurance for many minutes, until slowly my lungs remembered their purpose and accepted air once more. I feel that again now, without the provocation of a fall. Several realisations slam into me at once, each on their own with the power to knock my lungs to oblivion.

I want him to care about me.

I have had no one to care about me for a very long time.

I care about him.

I feel the colour drain from my face and quickly drop my face to look at my toes. In a rare tilt of the cap to vanity, I had them painted a pearly pink before coming to Barcelona. What was that if not an admission that I'd hoped my toes might be seen by this man?

'You look as though you've seen a ghost,' he murmurs. 'Do you disapprove of my techniques? Were you hoping my answer would somehow make your argument for you?'

I'm glad for the reminder of our discussion, and even more so for the lifeline he's thrown me. 'In some ways, it does.' My voice is a little hoarse. 'You are highlighting the differences between gambling and trading, though I'm not sure it matters. I wasn't the one who drew that comparison in the first instance.'

'No, it was me. Risk and reward, the story of life. Here's another expression that is bandied about—"nothing ventured, nothing gained".'

My eyes fire to his. 'Surely it could also be, "nothing ventured, nothing lost",' I point out, my uncle heavy in my heart.

'That is a very boring way to live.'

'What you call boring, I call safe.'

'Safety from the privileged perspective of your palace is a very different consideration.'

I feel that judgement again, the same vein that had run through our first meeting and that has reared its head again here. 'You dislike the fact I'm royalty.'

His sneer shouldn't have made him more attractive, but somehow it does. 'I dislike any form of social elitism.'

'Says the man with the million-dollar yacht?'

'Bought with money I earned.'

'You don't think I earn my money?' And out of nowhere I feel rage and frustration boiling through my blood.

I stand up, needing to throw my words not only at Santiago but into the sea, the sky, to have them heard on some elemental level.

'I have given my life over to my people,' I say angrily, stalking towards the yacht's railing. 'I have no privacy, no personal life, and until twenty-four hours ago I had never taken a lover. Did you know, Santiago, that you are the first man who's ever so much as kissed me? You have no idea what I have given up because I am royal. You talk about the privilege of my position without having any idea of what I have sacrificed.'

His expression gives little away, but he stands and walks towards me, his eyes raking my face, his body moving closer to mine.

'Don't you think I live every day with a horrible resentment right here—' I press my hands to my ribs '—at what is expected of me?'

'So why do it?'

My laugh is scoffing. 'What choice do I have? I have no siblings, no cousins. There is no one to take up the mantle I wear. I cannot abdicate—that choice is not for me. And, even if it were, that's not the way it's done. Not in my family, and not by me. My parents raised me to understand my responsibilities and I would never shame them, disappoint them, by turning my back on this. I am the Crown Princess of Marlsdoven and in less than a year I will become her Queen.'

'And then you will marry the man your parents chose for you,' he says quietly, and I wonder at that same sense of pain sliding through my abdomen.

'Yes.' I tilt my chin in defiant acceptance. 'These are all the things I do because I've been born to this position. So do not talk to me about privilege when your life is not hemmed in at every turn by expectations and obligations.'

It is as though a small electrical storm is raging between us, arcs of lightning threatening to incinerate me. I suck in air, but it burns in my mouth, the acrid taste of electricity palpable all the way down.

'You have been born to your position but you are the only one allowing those expectations to define you.'

I shake my head. 'You don't understand. It's not your fault; how could you?'

His eyes narrow. 'How could I? A nobody who was born in abject poverty, do you mean?'

'Please don't do that,' I snap. 'Don't make me a snob because it suits your narrative.'

'And what narrative is that?'

Our argument has clarified everything for me. I understand now the expression I see in his eyes sometimes, and why he arrived at the palace that day with a monumental chip on his shoulder. 'The one where I somehow think I'm better than you and everyone else just because I was born a royal. I don't. If I had my way, I'd abolish the whole damned idea of royalty. But to my people, it matters. The institution matters.

'It's dehumanising and grotesque. I am not a person to anyone in my life, Santiago, I am a figurehead. Can you even imagine? My face is on tea towels and mugs and postcards, sold at corner stores and airports for tourists to snap up. My parents' faces are emblazoned across those same postcards and tacky souvenir pencils. We are not people to anyone; we are property of the Marlsdoven people. That is as it is. It has always been this way, but at one point there was more actual power and far less intrusion. Now the role involves smiling at commemorative events and never putting a foot out of line lest I am accused of being ungrateful and a freeloader. That is my life. That is my so-called privilege.'

Sympathy stirs in his expression but his response is tougher than nails. 'So fight it.'

'I can't.'

'What would happen if you started to live your life as you wish? If you dated and wore jeans and spoke out about the things that matter to you? Would you be fired?'

'I can't be fired.' I shake my head. 'It's constitutionally impossible.'

'Then you would be criticised,' he says. 'And you hate the idea of that.'

I jerk my gaze away in agreement.

'But that is *your* choice. Risk and reward. You do not take the risk and so cannot enjoy the rewards.'

'I'm not at liberty—'

'You are a human being with inherent rights and the ability to choose how to live your life.'

'You just don't get it.'

'Don't I?'

'No. Until I can forget my parents, I can never forget what they expected of me.'

His eyes lance mine. 'And that's for you to be miserable?'

'I'm not miserable,' I deny, but the words lack conviction even to my own ears.

'It is for you to marry a man you've never met, who by your own admission you feel no desire for?'

'Sex isn't important.'

His laugh is sharp. 'Careful, *querida,* or I will show you exactly how false that statement is.'

His words—and the image they evoke—make my legs feel hollowed out. I fight the tug of sensual need, though it bombards me from every direction, I'm desperately clinging to my train of thought.

'The marriage agreement was formed a long time ago. It's binding.'

'And were you part of this agreement?' he prompts, with a hint of cynicism in his tone.

'I didn't know anything about it until my parents died.'

His eyes flash. 'So they never spoke of this to you?'

'I'm sure they would have,' I respond defensively. 'When I was old enough.'

'Then how do you know this is what they wanted?'

I blink at him, confused.

'You say they made this arrangement many years ago. What if their intentions changed?'

'Then they would have torn up the contract. It was kept in the family safe with all their most important documents.'

'Isn't it possible they simply forgot?'

I shake my head. 'I don't think so.'

'So you will live your life as they dictated many years ago. But this is a decision you make. You are complicit in your fate, Freja.'

'I know that. Why do you think I'm here with you?'

His eyes pierce mine.

'Rebellion.' I answer my own question. 'A taste of freedom before I return to the palace and take on all that is expected of me.'

A muscle in his jaw flexes but he says nothing. I feel his disapproval and for the first time in my life see my decisions as exactly that—decisions *I've* made.

'What would you have done? If your parents had laid out this plan for you?'

His lips tighten into a grimace. 'Run a mile in the opposite direction.' He moves closer. 'But it's a poor comparison. I am not close to my parents and generally choose to feel the opposite to them about everything.'

'Oh.' It's enough of a revelation to pull me out of my own angst. 'Why aren't you close to them?'

His shrug is a study in indifference, but I see beneath it the harsh resolution, the determination to push me away. 'Many reasons, *querida,* all of them boring.' He holds out a hand, his eyes sparking with mine. 'And I'd much rather help you rebel.'

CHAPTER EIGHT

THE SUN IS low in the sky, a golden orb blazing across the horizon spreading purple and peach colours into the heavens.

I know that we need to go back soon, that my security will be wondering where I am, worrying about me, and yet my limbs are heavy, filled with a reluctance to leave this sanctuary. If embassies are slices outside of a country's borders then this yacht is like a fragment of life existing beyond my reality. Here time has stopped and, even though I know that's not possible, I'm almost incapable of caring about the outside world right now.

'I have a question for you.'

In the kitchen, Santiago pauses, looking at me through shuttered eyes before returning to the platter he's arranging.

'Go on.' There's hesitation in his voice and I dip my head to hide a smile. He can read me like a book yet he pushes me away at every opportunity. It's frustrating and hurtful—yes, hurtful.

'You're...how old?'

Relief lightens his eyes. 'Your question is to ask my age?'

'I'm going somewhere with this,' I warn.

'I see.' He sips his beer. 'I turned thirty-one a few months back.'

I nod thoughtfully.

'And?' he prompts, lifting a wooden board off the kitchen bench and bringing it to the coffee table in front of me. The décor in the yacht is striking. Instead of the white leather and chrome I might have imagined, the interior is stylish and minimalistic, with light timber and cream fabrics. He takes a seat beside me on the lounge, so close our knees brush and, although we've spent the afternoon in bed, my pulse goes haywire at the innocent touch.

'Well, the first time we slept together…' my cheeks spread with warmth '…you said something about always taking precautions. That you don't want children.'

He dips his head once in silent agreement but there's an inherent tension to him. He's instantly wary, as though my line of questioning is the last thing he wishes to discuss.

'Why not?' I reach for an olive. It's plump, salty and juicy, and I have to bite back a moan of pleasure as I swallow the flesh.

'You think it's strange?'

'Why are you answering my questions with a question?'

'You ask a lot of questions.'

'No, I think I've just asked one you don't want to answer.'

He weighs that up, his lips compressed in a tight line, and I wonder if he's just going to ignore me. Time drags. Tension grows inside me. Finally, he responds, the words curt. 'I have never wanted children.'

His tone leaves me in little doubt that this matter is closed, at least so far as his willingness to answer my questions. I consider pushing him, but know it would be futile. I've hit a brick wall.

'I've always known I would have to have children,' I explain. The full force of his attention is on my face, his eyes studying me intently. 'And more than one. I'm an only child and it's put a lot of pressure on me—I'm the sole surviving heir to the throne.'

'So, when you are married this will be high on your agenda?'

I nod, but the idea suddenly fills me with a drowning sensation of panic. I will need to conceive almost immediately, and that will mean having sex with my husband, a man who leaves me cold. My eyes widen as I look at Santiago and what I see on his face stills my pulse. There is a coldness in his face, a look that sends a shiver down my spine.

'And your fiancé agrees with this?'

'He's not my fiancé. I've told you.' My voice shakes a little. I take a deep breath to calm my nerves. 'And we've never discussed any of this.'

'Then what if he doesn't want children?'

'That's not an option.'

'How well do you know this man?'

'We've met a handful of times.'

'Then you know nothing about him.'

'I know that his parents—'

'And your parents were friends. But beyond this?' His disapproval is obvious, and it frustrates me now just as much as ever.

I shrug. 'I don't know if it matters.'

'That is insane.'

'Why?'

'Because you're talking about marrying the guy. Shouldn't you at least see if you're compatible?'

'Sexually?'

'*Sí,* of course, but I actually meant in any way. What if his politics differ completely to yours? What if he has a twisted sense of humour? Or wears his underpants on the outside of his clothes?'

'Like a superhero? I've always had a bit of a Lois Lane fantasy, you know.'

His eyes hold a contemplative glimmer. 'I am sure there are other ways to indulge that.'

'Oh? Such as flying off a building?'

His lips flicker in a half-smile, but he's not easily put off the conversation. 'What if you hate him?'

Anxiety trickles down my spine. 'I...won't.'

His scepticism is obvious, and makes me feel about an inch tall. 'Because your parents knew his parents?'

I swallow past a suddenly constricted throat. 'Because I *can't* hate him. I have to make it work.'

His silence speaks volumes.

'You think I'm crazy.'

'I think you obviously loved your parents very much.'

The observation is so unexpected it takes my breath away. I nod, looking away quickly.

'Losing them must have been very difficult.'

Tears threaten. I swallow quickly, then reach for a piece of cheese. 'That's an understatement.' And, even though I'm sure he knows what happened, even though I know Santiago will have done his research before coming to Marlsdoven, I say quietly, 'Their car rolled while travelling in Africa. It was a freak accident—the first of its kind to happen to the tour company. My father died instantly, my mother two days later—just long enough for me to fly to her side and be there when she took her last breath. I'll never forget what she looked like at the end. So pale and weak. It was awful.'

He says nothing, and I'm glad.

'I always find it hard to hear from people like you, people who have their parents but choose not to be close to them. I would give everything I have for one more day with my mum and dad.'

His eyes hold mine and, even though I think he reads me easily, I have no idea what he's thinking or feeling. 'It is natural you would feel this way. You view parenthood through the veil of your own experiences.'

'What are your parents like?'

There is tension in the harsh angles of his face. He's quiet again, and I wonder if he's going to ignore me, but then he offers me one curt word.

'Different.'

'To you?'

'Yes, thank Christ.' His short laugh lacks humour.

'How so?'

He expels a sharp breath, his nostrils flaring. 'Does it matter? They're not in my life. I prefer not to think of them unless I really can't avoid it.'

I reach for another piece of cheese simply to hide my face. I'm hurt. It's such a cold rejection.

But he understands, because he sighs heavily. 'Does it matter?' he repeats, but I hear the plea in his words. He doesn't want to talk about this, but he will, if I push him.

I flick a glance at him; his face gives little away. If I didn't know him as well as I do, I would say that he's the same ruthless billionaire I first met. But deep in his eyes I see sadness, and I ache for him then.

'How about just the bullet points?' I suggest as a compromise.

He stands abruptly, moving into the kitchen and bracing his palms on the counter, looking out to sea. Guilt washes over me. I'm being selfish by asking this of him.

'I'm sorry,' I say, without moving. 'I was just trying to learn more about you. But if you really don't want to tell me…'

'My parents can tell you nothing about me,' he responds with a cool voice. 'I haven't seen them in years.'

I nod thoughtfully, looking for a way to change the subject.

To my surprise, Santiago continues, almost as if the words are being dragged from him. 'My mother is a drug addict. Most of my childhood she was high, wasted or jonesing for her next fix. My father has been in and out of prison all his life. When he was home, he was aggressive and drunk. They fought constantly. He was abusive until I got big enough to fight back. Is this what you want to know?' His eyes lance mine. I'm incapable of responding. 'I left home when I was eighteen years old.'

I shiver at the brevity of his response—he's compressed eighteen years' worth of pain into a few spasmodic sentences but I feel the undercurrent of emotions beneath his words. 'You haven't seen them since?'

He turns to face me but looks right through me, the curl of derision on his lips reserved for his absent parents. 'If only that were true,' he drawls. 'Stories of my success landed in the national papers. They came knocking then.'

I frown, not understanding.

'For money,' he clarifies cynically. 'My mother figured I owed her after all the money she spent raising me.'

I draw in an indignant breath. It doesn't sound like his mother had much of a hand in raising him at all.

'I hope you said no,' I mutter.

'No, *querida.* I gave them money. I hoped they'd use it to help themselves, but they spent it on drugs, parties. I only hear from them now when they want something.'

It is a throwaway comment but it clarifies something important for me. I reach for my drink, my mind analysing this tiny piece of his puzzle. Santiago was a boy who saw his parents constantly intoxicated, ignoring him, refusing to give him the love that all children crave. They let him walk away as a teenager, and only tried to see him once he had money. Their interest in him was purely mercenary.

No one has ever loved him—not in a meaningful way—and he's spent a lifetime pushing people away. He has surface-level relationships that revolve around sex because…because why? Because he's afraid? I turn to look at him and see the beautiful strength of Santiago shimmering, showing me the boy he used to be, a boy who was rejected over and over again, who lived the kind of life I can only imagine. A mother who was always wasted or looking to score drugs. A father who was either abusive or in prison. No wonder he's so messed up when it came to relationships. No wonder he doesn't want children!

I'm moving to him before I can stop myself, anguish in my heart and sorrow on my face. He stiffens, his body language reserved and laced with rejection, but I push past that because I finally understand *why* he's so determined to push me away.

I put my hand over his heart and stare into his eyes.

'Santiago, I…' But whatever I'd been about to say is constricted in my throat. My own doubts run through me, along with the reality of my life and my situation—the duties awaiting me once I leave Spain. I flash him a smile, but it feels strained. 'I really should get back to the hotel, don't you think?'

The stars twinkle overhead like diamonds in the sky and the yacht rocks from side to side, gently, beautifully, placating me into a sense of blissful relaxation.

I didn't go back to the hotel after our conversation earlier. Instead, we swam off the back of the boat. The water was warm, the sun high overhead and afterwards I was starving. We finished the platter then shared a bowl of strawberries in the hot tub, before making love right here on the deck of the yacht, the sky our only witness, heaven above me and all around me.

'You're very good at this,' I murmur, my eyes heavy.

'At what?'

'Seduction. The whole thing. Is this what it's usually like for you?'

The moonlight slices like a silver blade across his handsome face. I push up onto my elbow so I can see him better.

'I don't have a "usual",' he says after a moment. I wonder at the erratic beating of my heart. Too fast one moment, too slow the next. 'But I can say that my experience with you is unlike anything I've ever known.'

My heart speeds up way too fast. 'Oh?'

'For one thing, you are the only princess I have slept with.' He moves closer. 'And, for another, most women do not argue with me the way you do.'

My heart rolls and tumbles. Something hard is at my side again, painful and urgent. I swallow, dropping onto my back. Superficial relationships—that's what he has. And even though I now understand why, it doesn't make it any easier to cast myself—and what we're doing—in that light.

'I imagine women generally trip over themselves for your attention.'

'Something like that.' He leans over me, his eyes flicking my face. Does he see the jealousy tearing through me? 'But not you.'

'No,' I agree, my admission a whisper in the night. 'I wanted to hate you.'

'I know.' He traces my lips with the tip of his finger. 'Because of the casino?'

'The casino. Your reputation,' I say honestly. 'Everything about you is so threatening to me. I think even before I met you I knew that you were someone who could threaten the very safe walls I've built around my life.'

'Is that what I'm doing?'

Yes. Undoubtedly. But, of course, it's not really. After this, I have to go back to Marlsdoven, to my perfectly planned life, to the man I'll one day marry, to the expectations I've always borne and which have weighed me down since my parents' deaths. As for Santiago, he doesn't want to shake the walls of my life. This is just meaningless for him. A fling, nothing more.

He moves his finger to the tip of my nose, running it over the ski-jump tip.

'At that first meeting, you were full of fire,' he says, and I blush, remembering the way we'd sparked off each other.

'You were hardly Mr Congeniality yourself.'

'I never am.' He brushes aside my remark. 'But I had expected you to be calm and agreeable. I expected you to be desperate for me to sign the contract, delighted to have the land disposed of and a project like the casino undertaken. I did not anticipate, for one minute, that you would so strenuously object.'

There's something in his eyes that makes me pause, frowning. 'And that bothers you? You're disappointed?'

His features tighten. He's doing it again—looking for ways to avoid answering me.

I sigh. 'Don't worry. Forget I asked.'

He presses a finger to my lips. 'I'm used to winning. I ordinarily take great pleasure in eviscerating anyone who gets in my way.' His accent is thick, his words raw, and my nerves tingle at the picture he paints. 'I did not expect your opposition but, once I had it…'

I wait. For some reason with breath held. 'Yes?'

But he shakes his head, not finishing the thought. I don know if he needs to. I can join the dots.

I'm his adversary in business right now, but he doesn't want to eviscerate me. He's holding back on the casino because he doesn't want to see me upset.

It's hardy a declaration of anything beyond basic courtesy—we are, after all, sleeping together—but it warms me from the inside out, regardless.

'You're different to what I expected,' he finishes with a too-casual shrug.

'Do you ever get lonely?' The question erupts before I can stop it, and only as I speak the words do I realise it's been humming inside me since we had the conversation about his parents.

'No.'

I'm glad he doesn't remind me of how busy is his social life—and by social life I mean sex life. Besides, I'm sure he's lying.

'Santiago…' I sigh, pressing a hand to his chest. 'You keep pushing me away. Is it so hard for you to be honest with me?'

'How am I not being honest?'

'Well, is there anyone in your life? Anyone who you let care about you? Anyone you care about?'

His eyes show fierce rejection of even the idea. 'My business is my life. It's all I need, *querida*.'

He sounds so certain, so confident on this score, that for a moment I wonder if I'm wrong. Perhaps my own loneliness is slanting my perception of his life. After all, I'm used to keeping almost everyone at arm's length. Claudia is probably the closest thing I have to a friend, and she works for me. Maybe I'm projecting my own feelings onto him.

Maybe I want him to tell me he *is* lonely, because in admitting that he'd be conceding he wants to make a change. And then what? Even if he were to admit he wants more in his life, it's not with me—it can't be. My own obligations prohibit that. He kisses me, and I'm glad, because the power of his kiss makes thinking almost impossible. Almost, but not quite. As he brings his body over mine, I'm acutely aware of an ache somewhere in the region of my heart.

'I love sleeping with you,' he growls in my ear, and the words send little sparks through my body. I'm flattered but afraid because, while I love sleeping with him too, there's so much more to it, and I know I can never admit that—I know he'll never feel it.

CHAPTER NINE

I'm in trouble.

I SMILE AS I send the text message, fully aware I shouldn't be so flippant. It's quite clear from the looks on my security agents' faces that they'd been about to mount an armed search for me. My disappearance was highly out of character, so I can understand their concern, but I'm not even a little sorry for it.

For the first time in my life, I've done something selfish just because I wanted to and, God, it felt good.

?

Even his reply makes me smile, because it's so business-like and to the point. I can imagine the quirk of his brow that would have accompanied it, the look of quizzical enquiry marring his symmetrical face.

Let's just say my disappearance elicited some concern.

Ah. Should I expect to be charged with kidnapping after all?

Definitely. But don't worry, I'll come see you in prison.

I should hope so.

My heart turns over in my chest. I stare at the phone, my finger hovering over the screen as I draft and redraft another message in my mind until letters are swarming incoherently through my brain. I left the yacht three hours ago and already I'm wondering when I'm going to see him again. It's just because I know I only have two more nights in Spain—and I don't want to waste a minute of them.

Are you free tonight?

His message makes my heart leap through my chest and ricochet wildly around.

What have you got in mind?

A surprise. Meet me on the roof at eight.

The roof?

I'll send a key to your room.

I was joking about the whole Lois Lane jumping off a building thing.

And I'm definitely no Superman.

At least, you wear your jocks inside your trousers.

Most of the time.

I laugh, placing my phone on the table. Half an hou[illegible] later, one of my security guards knocks on the door, wari[illegible] handing me an envelope. I rip it open, breaths coming hard and fast, and read it in front of him. It's clear and concise instructions, written in Santiago's dark, confident writing, directing me to a private lift and a roof-top helipad, as well as a key card to activate the lift.

'I'll be going out tonight,' I say without looking at the guard, my pulse a tsunami. 'Don't wait up.'

The lights of Barcelona twinkle way below us. I stare down at the vista with true pleasure and a light heart. Wherever we're going, I don't care. In this moment, I am carefree and happy.

'I feel like all the world's a tiny little snow globe.'

'And you are what? An eagle?' His accented voice crackles over the helicopter earpieces. Any answer dies on my lips when I turn to see the expert ease with which he controls the instruments. My mouth goes dry. His sleeves are pushed up to reveal his tanned forearms, the snake tattoo drawing my gaze. There is something incredibly hot about the way he commands this expensive, powerful piece of equipment.

'Where did you learn to fly?' I ask instead.

'Around the time I bought my first jet.'

My eyes are round like saucers. 'You have more than one aircraft?'

'I have one jet now, but over the years I've owned several.'

My lips form a silent 'O' of surprise or admiration.

'It seemed to make sense to me to learn how to fly, seeing as I would be trusting my life to pilots on so many occasions.'

I twist my mouth to the side, the evidence of his obsessive control obvious in the statement. 'Do you fly your own jets too?'

'Not often. From time to time, I serve as co-pilot, but it's much more comfortable in the cabin.'

I don't know why but all roads with Santiago lead back to bed, and the innocuous comment makes me think of him in the bedroom of a private plane: luxurious silk sheets, mood lighting, him handsome, naked, powerful… I turn my eyes back to the view. I'm very high yet it feels much safer to look down than to stare at the man beside me.

The pressure between us builds so that with every moment that passes all I'm aware of is him, his closeness, the proximity overwhelming me. It's a relief when the helicopter starts to descend over a significantly darker patch of land. There are still lights, but far fewer. His control is expert; I gather he knows the way very well.

'You're a nervous flyer?' he asks after touching down, mistaking my tension for something else altogether.

'Not really.'

'Then you are nervous to be here with me?'

I shake my head. 'Just…a little overwhelmed, I think.'

His brows lift and then he smiles, that rare, beautiful, soul-splitting smile.

'Don't be. This is just one night out of our lives, Freja. Nothing more.'

I love it that he uses my name. My skin lifts and, when he opens the door of the helicopter, the warm breeze rushes past me, cementing his words in my mind. *It's just one night, nothing more.*

'I figured you were right about the restaurants in Barcelona—far too likely you would be seen in a city like that. But here in Aliz it is quieter.'

Nonetheless, I lift a hand to my dark wig, glad I'd thought to wear it.

'Yes, the disguise is still good, if only because I find it impossibly sexy.' His eyes twitch at the corners and know he's teasing me. I punch his arm playfully as we stroll slowly towards a string of restaurants lined up along a cobbled path. The walk is part of the pleasure. It is a weekend and, despite his promise that this town would be quiet, the restaurants are busy, a gentle din reaching us on the street as we go.

'Aliz is famous for its seafood,' he explains as we walk. 'People come from all around to enjoy what these places have to offer.'

'And you come here often?'

'Often enough to know which restaurant is best,' he responds with another heart-stopping smile, before gesturing towards a restaurant at our side.

The frontage is made of glass, with awnings over the top, so that in the daytime I imagine the restaurant to be filled with *al fresco* diners, sunlight filtering onto them. Now the restaurant is dressed for the evening, with candles on the table-tops and a jazzy soundtrack playing.

'Santiago!' He's greeted by the *maître d'* like an old friend returning. 'It is good to see you again.'

'Enrique.' He nods, and to my surprise they embrace, before he gestures to me. 'This is a friend of mine.' His lips twitch. 'Lois.'

I lift a brow, the alias he's chosen for me causing my heart to jackhammer against my ribs. I miss only two beats before extending my own hand to Enrique. 'Pleasure.' He lifts it to his lips but, although he is also handsome, I feel nothing. Just like before. Any time in my life that I've met a man, I've never felt so much as a flicker of my pulse. But with Santiago it's as though that's all I'm capable of feeling—totally overrun by emotions and need.

He leads us to a table at the back of the restaurant. A large indoor fig with glossy green leaves partially conceals the table from view, and for added protection I take the seat against the wall, because it obscures me completely from other diners.

'Would you like to see a menu?' Santiago asks as we take our seats.

'I'm no expert at eating in restaurants, but isn't that customary?'

'I generally rely on Enrique to bring me what's best.'

It speaks volumes, given what a control freak he is. 'Then I'm sure that will be fine.'

'Is there anything you don't eat?'

His attention to detail makes me feel like the most special person in the world. Danger signs flash. That's not what this is. It's not what he wants and it's impossible for me to want it. Impossible for me to have it. I can't look beyond this slice of time.

'Lois?'

I realise he's waiting for my answer so I shake my head softly and he conveys this to Enrique in Spanish; then, we are alone.

'How did you find this place?'

'I first came here many years ago. I was looking at developing a hotel on the foreshore, just over there.' He points to a window and I lean forward, following the direction of his finger. It's dark outside, just the faint glow of pale streetlights showing the edge of the road. A beach lies beyond—we walked beside it as we arrived. The moon is shining brightly tonight, casting a silver skein across the ancient, rumbling sea.

'But you didn't?'

A waiter arrives with a bottle of champagne. He stands at the table as he removes the foil and pops the top, then tilts the glasses individually to fill them.

Both of us alone again, I run my finger over the stem of my wine glass, watching Santiago. He lifts his glass, silently gesturing to mine. I mimic the gesture, then sip. The drink is ice-cold with the slightest fizz. It tickles my tongue and dances all the way down. I close my eyes to enjoy the flavour and, when I open them again, Santiago is staring at me. My mouth goes dry despite the dousing of champagne. I blink, self-conscious and bursting with sensation.

'No.' The word is gruff and it takes me a moment to remember that we were talking about his hotel development.

'Why not?'

'In the end, it wasn't suitable.'

Now, *that's* interesting. 'No?' I sip my champagne, attempting to appear casual.

'Part of the charm of this town is that it's largely inaccessible. This means the number of tourists is limited. I realised that, in building a hotel to capitalise on the area's appeal, I'd be destroying it.'

My jaw drops. 'So you pulled out of a financially lucrative deal because it was the right thing to do?'

'It is entirely different to the Marlsdoven casino.'

I shudder to hear it described this way. 'Why?'

He leans forward and places his hand over mine. 'For one thing, the casino will be in a major European city. For another, the hotel here would not have remained lucrative once it had taken away the quaint appeal of a tiny coastal village. I feared making the coastline into a theme park—there is long-term damage in that.'

'Not a good bet?' I prompt.

His eyes glitter darkly when they meet mine. 'Exactly. The odds were not in my favour. Whereas market research shows that the scope for a casino in Marlsdoven is enormous. Believe it or not, your population responded very favourably to the prospect, in the surveys I commissioned. Additionally, thirty-five per cent of travellers returning to

Marlsdoven reported wanting a visit to a casino at some point during their trip.'

I close my eyes, a wave of nausea passing through me as I force myself to accept this reality. I already knew it was all but a done deal, but hearing these facts just show me how futile it is to keep fighting him on this.

'Why do you hate the concept so much?'

I swallow, bitterness making my throat thicken. 'I've told you—'

'Yes, you've told me,' he interrupts, but pauses as another waiter appears with a plate of food. The fragrance is unmistakably saffron. When he goes, Santiago continues. 'You've told me that you despise gambling, but you haven't told me why. And I can tell there is more to it. This is personal for you. Deeply personal.'

I stare at my hands. 'Why do you say that?'

'Because your skin grows pale whenever I bring up the casino. You look as though you've seen a ghost. This is not just business, nor is it a maternal desire to protect your citizens from the big, bad wolf of gambling. So what is it, Princesa?'

My heart stammers. I shake my head, the demurral meaningless in the face of his question. Why not tell him the truth? It is a secret I've protected all my life, which my parents valued, but I don't doubt I can trust Santiago with it.

'My uncle was a gambling addict,' I say softly, toying with the champagne flute. 'He hid it for many years. He travelled abroad, starting with poker before progressing to the casinos of Europe, where his bets grew increasingly enormous—I think in an effort to recoup some of his losses. He had a generous trust fund but he burned through it in eighteen months. His annual income from our family estates was also exceptional, but he borrowed against his share, mortgaging himself over and over until he was tied up in knots and in debt to less than savoury money lenders.'

I take a gulp of champagne, needing the liquid but also the artificial relaxation. Santiago is quiet, waiting for me to continue, and to my surprise I do. After not discussing Richard for many, many years, it feels important to speak about him. Or maybe it's just that Santiago has a unique power over me…that with him I want to be completely honest about everything.

'I think he always struggled with being the second-born son. Nothing was expected of him. He was never spoken of, never valued as more than a contingency plan if something happened to dad. He had a lot of money and fame, but no purpose. No value. And so many limitations.'

'And so he started gambling,' Santiago murmurs sympathetically.

I nod. 'My father blamed himself. He was busy with his obligations and family. They grew apart but dad always thought my uncle was happy—just living life with the kind of freedom my father would never know. If anything, I think he envied Richard a little.' I sigh.

'How did he find out the truth?'

'My uncle committed suicide.' I say the words robotically.

Santiago's brows knit closer together, his surprise evident.

I grimace. 'Nobody knew,' I explain. 'At the time, it was reported that he died after a long battle with an illness. And that's not a lie,' I hasten to add. 'Gambling addiction is exactly that.'

He dips his head in acknowledgement.

'He left a note. It revealed the extent of his losses. He ‑lt helpless. He was in a cycle of forever trying to dig himself out of trouble. He would hope for one more win, that that would be enough to start making repayments.' I shake my head sadly. 'My father felt incredibly guilty. He had money; he could have helped. But my uncle was too ashamed to ask.'

Silence falls between us.

'I'm sorry for your loss.' Santiago's voice is carefully mute of emotion, so I don't know if the story has had any impact on him.

'Thank you.' I sip my champagne. The noise of the restaurant swirls around us, but I barely hear it.

'Your family must have been devastated.'

'Yes. He hid his addiction so well, none of us had any idea until it was too late. Per Richard's wishes, the truth surrounding his death was never revealed.'

More silence, softened by reflectiveness.

'How old were you?'

'Eleven.' I close my eyes against a wave of memory. 'It killed a part of my father, you know? He loved his brother, had always felt protective of him, and losing him like that… I know he blamed himself.'

'That's futile.'

'Perhaps. But it's also unavoidable.' I offer a tight smile. 'He was different after that. My father became obsessed with duty and responsibility, with making sure I understood the importance of our role to the kingdom. I used to think when he was lecturing me that he was imagining his brother in my place, saying the things he wished he could have said to Richard.'

Santiago's expression is analytical, his eyes scanning my face. 'And you wanted to please your father,' he murmurs eventually.

I lift one shoulder in defiant acceptance of that.

'You want to please him still,' Santiago presses and, even though it's true, I feel as though it's a criticism.

'I want to make him proud,' I say eventually.

'And how do you do that, Freja? What do you need to do?'

'That's easy,' I respond tightly. 'I do exactly what I'm meant to do. What I was born to do.'

'And never deviate from what's expected of you?'

I press my teeth into my lower lip. 'No,' I agree after a moment. 'Never.' I don't know why, but admitting that aloud feels a little like cutting off something important. I turn away, but he draws my attention back.

'Freja...' he says gently, lacing our fingers together. I stare at the contrast in our skin, his dark, mine fair, the juxtaposition enchanting. 'You say your uncle grew up second best, knowing he was second best. And you are right. Gambling is an addiction. For some people it fills a void. I just wonder that, if it weren't gambling, your uncle might have relied on another crutch. Alcohol, drugs. Both of which are equally harmful.'

I lift my gaze to his, thinking of his own experience with substance abuse, parents who'd been either high or drunk his entire childhood.

'He gambled,' Santiago continues. 'But I do not know if it necessarily follows that gambling is inherently bad.'

I drop my eyes back to our hands, staring at them. 'It killed him.'

His lack of response speaks volumes, and I don't entirely disagree with him. My uncle wasn't happy. He was looking to fill a void and he found his way to gambling. The initial high of winning made him feel good, possibly for the first time in his life. Maybe if he'd tried drugs or got into binge drinking it would have been the same.

'After the funeral, I remember my father saying that

gambling is the scourge of the world…that for all that it's been around since time immemorial it should be banished, and that if he had his way it would be. He had no power over the world, but at least in Marlsdoven he could make sure the country was never touched by such a harmful practice.' My voice shakes a little. I reach for my fork, pressing it into the rice on my plate. Steam billows towards me. 'I didn't think about those words again until you made your offer.'

'And your first instinct was to reject the proposal.'

My lips tighten into something like the ghost of a smile. 'I don't really have that power. Perhaps if I asked the Prime Minister… But without an alternative that is just as beneficial to our economy…?' I shake my head sadly. 'I'm aware that I have a bias here. I know what I want is unreasonable.'

'But, if there is to be casino in Marlsdoven, you need it to be on your terms.'

My eyes widen as they lift to his. I nod. 'It has to be worth it. I don't know how I can make peace with what I owe my father, my uncle, if I don't at least try to fight this.'

He reaches for his glass and has a drink without relinquishing my hand. 'Two years ago, when I first started looking to put a casino in Marlsdoven, your government provided me with a list of land options. I chose this site because of the historic nature of the land as well as its primacy within the city—on the river bank, with easy access to the CBD. I am as convinced now as I was then that this will be the best place for the project.'

He's right. The land is ripe for development.

'Your government offered me the land,' he repeats. 'Did you know that?'

I nod. 'Every year we discuss which areas might be used and for what purpose. There has long been talk of urbanising that section of the city.'

He considers that a moment, taking a bite of his own meal. I follow suit, tasting delicate spices and butter in the rice. 'You would prefer a different kind of development.'

'Yes.'

'Such as?'

My first instinct is to tell him I've never really thought about it, but that's a lie. 'I always hoped it could be turned into a culture and arts precinct. Museums, galleries, a new theatre for ballet. Even a stadium for sporting events. I hoped we could celebrate the rich history of our arts, but the funding just isn't there.' I expel a soft sigh. 'The previous government badly mismanaged the budget and, as a result, our country's finances are in need of conservative management. It isn't the time to be investing billions of euros into a culture precinct, even though I think it would be incredibly beautiful and a great addition to our country.'

'And it would make your parents proud.'

My eyes ping to his and I nod jerkily. 'Yes.'

'Whereas, by allowing this casino to be built, you feel that you're betraying them.'

I flutter my eyes closed. 'I am betraying them. But it can't be helped.' I try to smile. 'I'm old enough to know when I'm fighting a losing battle, Santiago. I suppose the best thing to do now is focus on the positives of your development.'

I can see how unsatisfied he is with that, but he lets the conversation drop, squeezing my hand once before releasing it.

'How is your entrée?'

'Delicious,' I murmur, though I barely taste it. The conversation has filled me with emotional ambivalence. I change the subject awkwardly. 'Casinos are only a part f your business, aren't they?'

For a moment I feel as though he's going to return to our

earlier discussion but then he begins to explain that, while casinos were how he first built his fortune, he's since diversified into a wide array of interests—from hedge funds to tech companies to boutique hotels and banks. He has fingers in many pies.

The food is perfect, and as our conversation moves away from the matter of the casino he wishes to build I am blissfully content. By the time we leave, the restaurant is empty.

'Oh, my goodness, I didn't realise how late it is. I'm sorry we kept you,' I apologise to Enrique.

He smiles warmly. 'It is no problem. We are always here anyway.'

Santiago embraces him once more, in the Spanish style, then loops an arm low around my waist, guiding me into the night air. In the distance I catch the gleam of his helicopter, and by unspoken yet mutual agreement we slow down, neither of us in a rush to reach it too soon.

'Thank you for bringing me here. I've had a wonderful night. I don't want it to end.' I laugh shakily.

He stops walking altogether then, turning me to face him. For the briefest moment, he is stricken, as though fighting a war within himself. He stares down at me, through me, inside me, and then expels a soft, slow breath. He lifts a hand, tucking the brown hair of my wig behind my ear.

'No?'

I shake my head, incapable of speech.

His eyes soften and I have the distinct impression he's surrendering to something he wishes he could fight. 'Then it doesn't have to, Princesa.'

CHAPTER TEN

DAWN LIGHT SHIFTS across the bed and I reach for Santiago instinctively, my fingertips brushing the sheets in search of him. But he's not there, of course. I have no concept of what time he left, or if he tried to wake me to say goodbye, I only feel a sense of incompleteness that he's not here.

It jolts me awake, so I stare at the view revealed by my window of the sun cresting over the city, and the glistening ocean, and wonder at how he's become so important to me in such a short space of time. What happened to a secret, sexy fling? A bit of fun before I go home and pick up the mantle of my responsibilities, finally becoming Queen of Marlsdoven, and all that entails?

Except he is fun, too, even as I recognise he's become something…more…something difficult to characterise. I smile as I shower, remembering the night we shared, the way he kissed me, touched me so reverently, as though he were worshipping me…as though I completed him. Of course I don't—that's just me trying to make sense of such an intimate physical act, of the way it feels when we're together. So right.

A frown is on my face as I get ready, choosing a sunny ress and sandals for my last day in Barcelona. The thought at the edge of my mind all day, an awareness of time racing towards a finish line I no longer want to reach. What if I were to extend my trip?

Except I can't. There's a state dinner tomorrow night. That's the reason I booked my visit for these dates. I can't miss it. Not even for this.

No, I have to leave as originally planned, and then that will be the end of this.

It's late in the afternoon when my phone buzzes.

Are you free for dinner?

I roll my eyes, a smile lifting the corners of my mouth.

Who with?

Funny! I'll be back in Barcelona around six p.m. Okay?

My heart notches up a gear. Okay? It's better than okay. It's at least two hours earlier than I had expected him for dinner.

Sure. See you then.

He arrives five minutes early, carrying a large brown paper bag, and my heart races at the sight of him. He's wearing jeans and a button-down shirt with the sleeves pushed up to reveal his forearm tattoos. His skin is a golden brown, his hair pushed back from his face so the intensity of his eyes is all the more obvious. My nerves go into overdrive.

He kisses me on the cheek and my pulse throbs; it's such a normal gesture, as if we're two people who are dating, a though this isn't the last night we'll see each other. I lo away, blinking rapidly to clear the thought. This isn't the time to think about that.

'What's in the bag?' I ask, lifting up to peek in the top.

'Dinner.' He lowers it to reveal a bushy green celery top and some bulbs of garlic. 'Or it soon will be.'

My brows lift in surprise. 'You're cooking?'

He sends me a sardonic look. 'That surprises you?'

'Well, obviously!' I laugh. 'I don't think I can picture you in an apron.'

'I cook shirtless.' Even though it's obviously a joke, my breath bursts out of my lungs.

He doesn't cook shirtless, but he cooks well, as though he's often done. I watch, mesmerised, sipping wine and making conversation which, he's informed me, is my job for the evening. I don't drink much, though, just a few small sips, because I want to remember every detail just as it happened without any filter over the top.

When I take a bite of the paella he makes, my lips part on a moan of appreciation. 'This is amazing.' Saffron, olives and tomato all combine to give the dish a richness that is full-bodied yet not overpowering.

He dips his head. 'I'm glad you like it.'

'How did you learn to make this?'

'It's not rocket science.'

'I just presumed you're someone who eats out every night. I had no idea you were secretly a culinary whiz.'

He grins as he lifts a fork to his mouth. 'Paella is easy.'

'I don't believe you.' I take another bite, closing my eyes as the flavours run through me. 'How did you learn?'

'Not from my mother,' he quips with a half-smile.

Sympathy stirs through me.

'My first apartment was just above a market. I used to walk past in the evenings and see the tables groaning with fresh produce—seafood, meat, vegetables, cheeses.

I began to experiment. I would try to recreate meals I'd eaten at restaurants—most were deceptively simple—and I found I enjoyed it.'

'Like you do wine making,' I say, lifting the glass.

'*Precisamente*. It's a pleasure to create something exactly to your taste, to experiment until you have it just right.'

I nod thoughtfully.

'Do you cook?'

I grimace. 'No. I can't even make toast.'

He laughs, a rich sound that makes my stomach loop.

'You should learn,' he says after a beat. 'I think you'd enjoy it.'

'Oh? Why is that?'

He reaches across the table, lacing our fingers together. 'Cooking is an act of meditation and control. It's very satisfying. Besides, you need hobbies.' He winks then, but my heart lurches. Santiago is the first person in my life to see me as a woman, to want to encourage me to be more than my title and expectations. His ability to see many facets of my being is addictive and comforting. I feel fully formed when I'm with him, more human than royal, just an ordinary woman with the potential to be and do anything I wish.

I don't want the night to end.

I don't want to leave here.

And yet I know I must. Even without my father's voice and expectations constantly guiding my decision-making process, I understand what's expected of me.

I attempt to smile, pulling my hand away, and focus on the view beyond us. The waves roll towards the shore, towards this great, ancient city, just as they always have done. They'll continue rolling tomorrow, and the next day, when I'm no longer here to see them, just as Santiago will continue with his life once I'm gone.

I don't know if I'll ever be the same, though.

'What time is your flight?'

His finger traces invisible patterns over my bare flesh, his touch possessive and natural, as though he has every right to touch me whenever and however he wishes; as though my body belongs to him, and his to me. Despite my wish for time to stand still, my last day has arrived.

'Eleven.'

His finger pauses in its progress for a moment before re-starting the lazy exploration, charting across my stomach, towards my hip then back to circle my belly button. 'So early.'

'I have a state dinner at the palace tonight.' It was the constraint I'd had to work around when booking this trip. All my other engagements had been easy to cancel, but not this one.

'Back to being a princess?'

'I never really stopped,' I say with a lift of my shoulder.

'Yes, you did. For these last few days, you've simply been Freja.'

After my parents died, my life became the furthest from private it's ever been. My country was obsessed with how I was coping and, though their interest in me came from a good place, it was hard to bear. In order to cope with the burden I saw a therapist, and she told me to find one good thing every day and focus on that, to hold it tight to my chest in moments of panic and be grateful. Gratitude would save the day every time.

The idea of leaving Spain and Santiago stirs that same nic inside me, erupting out of nowhere and rising to-rds me like a dusk tide, so I grab hold of my gratitude.

What I've experienced with this man is something I will always cherish. Even if leaving him is going to be so much harder than I'd anticipated.

And as for Santiago? Will he think of me when this ends? Or simply move on to the next woman who catches his eye? Ice chips through me and, like a glutton for punishment, I hear myself ask, 'I suppose you'll have forgotten all about me by nightfall?'

His features are mocking, reminding me of the first time we met. He is such a contradiction; *we* are a contradiction. I feel simultaneously closer to him than I ever have another soul, but at the same time he's a constant enigma.

'You think you're so forgettable? You're the only princess I've ever slept with.'

I don't know what I want him to say; not that. 'Still just another woman in a long line of women.'

'And that bothers you?'

I feel trapped, and I don't even know why. I'm not sure why I brought this up, nor why I sound as though he's betrayed me in some way. We both knew what this was. And we both know why our relationship can never go beyond this. I have expectations on me, expectations I've carried all my life—how I'll live my life, who I'll spend it with. Marriage to a prince, children…sensible, traditional. A casual fling with a man like this would be a disgrace; my parents raised me to respect my duties, to honour the requirements of my role. This is way outside of that. But it's okay, because it's temporary, and no one will ever find out. That's the way it has to be.

So why does it feel like I want more from him? Some kind of pledge that I mean something, when I know I don't…

'I have never lied to you about my past,' he says quiet

pressing a finger to my chin, angling my face to his. Until that moment, I hadn't realised I'd been avoiding his eyes.

'I know that.' I brush aside his comment.

'Sex is a wonderful experience to share with someone.' His voice caresses me as his words turn my heart to ice. 'I've enjoyed sharing it with you. I will always feel honoured to have been your first.'

But not my last. The words he hasn't spoken hammer through me, and I feel physically ill. Out of nowhere, a desperate sense of nausea assails me. The idea of another man ever making love to me makes my heart twist painfully.

'And, after I'm gone, I'll see photos of you in the press, with all the women you share this experience with.' Despite my best intentions, the words are hollowed out. Bitterness is recognisable in the clipped remark.

'And I will see photos of your wedding,' he reminds me, but it's simply a response rather than a complaint. His words are robbed of emotion, flat, spoken with the calm delivery of someone simply making a point.

'Yes, my wedding,' I murmur throatily, trying to remind myself of the importance of my engagement, the wedding my parents planned for something I've always accepted as a necessity. 'I wonder if I'll feel differently about Heydar now.'

Santiago's eyes narrow, his lips tight as he waits for me to elaborate.

'I've never felt anything for him before, but maybe that's because I had no experience with men. Perhaps it will be different now that I understand things more. Maybe.'

I truly wonder if this is the case, but even as I say the words I'm aware I'm seeking to provoke a reaction from Santiago. I want to make him jealous because *I* am jealous. I'm jealous of him and his freedom, and I'm jealous as hell of the women who'll come after me. The women who will get to kiss him and make love to him and feel like the centre of his universe. I want to freeze time and hold on to this moment, never letting the world intrude, pushing reality away for ever more.

'You will find out when you are married. I hope the gamble pays off.'

I lift my shoulder in a slight shrug. 'I'll find out tonight, actually.'

His face remains the same, but his eyes darken, and they bore into me with the intensity of a jet engine.

'At the state dinner,' I explain. 'Heydar's on the guest list.'

'I see.'

I can't discern jealousy. It's clear that he doesn't like the idea but, at the same time, it might just be the whole concept of an arranged marriage he's opposed to. I don't know. Frustration gnaws through me.

'And so your hope is that, now you are sexually awakened, you'll desire this man you've agreed to marry?'

'I didn't agree.'

His smirk is mocking. 'You intend to go through with it, do you not?'

'Well, yes.'

'Then you have agreed.'

'I just haven't gone against my parents' wishes,' I say. 'It's a nuanced difference.'

His response is curt, the words whipping the edges of the room. 'That results in the same thing.'

'Yes.'

'And what if you feel nothing for him tonight?'

'It won't make any difference.'

His eyes flash to mine.

'What?' I demand, wondering at the fire in my belly. 'What does it matter?'

'It doesn't,' he insists, but his voice is not mute of em

tion now. I hear disapproval in every syllable, and something else too—something a lot like anger.

'Then why are you reacting like this? Why are you cross with me?'

His features show contempt. I shiver.

'What if you see him tonight and suddenly find there is chemistry between the two of you, *querida*?'

I don't know what he wants me to say. The idea disgusts me. I know that I likely won't feel anything more for Heydar that I have before. I know I won't feel anything for any man that equates to what I've shared with Santiago. I tilt my face away from his, looking towards the window.

'Then I guess that's good,' I lie, mumbling the words.

He curses in his native tongue, and I jerk my face back to his, surprised by the outburst.

'You would actually go from my bed to his?'

'Hang on a second—you're the one who was just extolling the virtues of sex and sharing sex with different partners.'

'And you're the one who is seeing her fiancé tonight, while naked beneath me.'

'He's not my fiancé,' I contradict.

'That is semantics,' he dismisses. 'You intend to marry the man. You're seeing him tonight and hoping that you feel attracted to him.'

'And what? You're jealous?'

'No,' he denies swiftly.

My breath is coming in little fits. I move my head to the side in an attempt to find sanity, then look back at him. 'I didn't mean to suggest…'

'Yes, you did.' His eyes challenge mine, so I find it hard to breathe. Guilt and shame at my childish behaviour heat my cheeks.

'I just...wish I felt for him what I do for you. That would be far more convenient,' I correct quietly.

'Because he is a suitable husband?' Santiago responds in a tone that is so quiet it roars.

My heart stammers. We stare at each other, the air between us sparking with the power of a thousand lightning bolts.

'Yes,' I say eventually. 'Because he will be my husband.'

His nostrils flare as he expels a breath. 'Tell me, Princesa, what about this man makes him suitable?'

'I... Everything.'

'By your own admission, you hardly know him.'

'I know enough.'

His eyes narrow. 'He is royal; is that your sole criterion?'

His vehemence surprises me. But hadn't I goaded him to this? Hadn't I wanted to make him jealous? It was a petty manoeuvre, to push him to reveal some kind of feeling for me—even a dark one, like envy.

'Forget I brought it up,' I say with the appearance of calm, remembering that I am a princess and I have been taught not to lose my temper. Or at least not to show that I'm losing it.

He shifts his body weight, one hand caressing my cheek. 'Do you want me to say I hate the idea?'

I blink my eyes closed, pleasure briefly feathering my heart.

'I do,' he concedes after a beat. 'I'm a regular, red-blooded man. I wouldn't be human if I didn't have some reservations about a woman I'm sleeping with moving on so quickly. Is that what you want to hear?'

Not even close. He's not jealous, he's possessive, driven by ego—there's a vital difference there.

'That seems like a double standard,' I say unevenly.

He presses a finger to my lips. 'In all this time, you are the only one who has brought others into this. You talk about the women I've slept with and the man you will marry. You say to me that you hope our relationship will make you more likely to desire him and you ask about the women I will see when you return to Marlsdoven. There are realities beyond what we share, but I am not the one making us face them.'

I flinch at his summary of the situation. Everything is so messy, and I *hate* mess.

'We have to face them, though,' I say simply, my throat thick. 'I'm marrying Heydar. Not tonight, not tomorrow, but in a few months, after my coronation. And I will never be able to see you again.'

He wouldn't want to see me again anyway. If he did he'd fight for me, of that I'm certain. Santiago is not the kind of man to lose anything or anyone he values. I mean nothing to him, and, the sooner I accept that deep in my heart, the better. It will never hurt less, but at least the knowledge will save me from making a fool of myself.

A muscle jerks at the base of his jaw, and then he kisses me hard, his lips claiming mine. It's as though he can't find the words to respond to me, so he's seeking to reply bodily, tormenting me with a desire that's eating me alive.

His kiss stirs something deep in my chest. A reality I probably already know. A sharp, dangerous knowledge that I don't want to keep hold of. I push it away resolutely, returning his kiss with all the desperation I feel—a desperation born from the fact I am leaving Spain within hours and, for the good of everyone, can never see this man again.

As pleasure floods my body, reality breaks my heart.

CHAPTER ELEVEN

HE'S QUIET BUT I don't want to read anything into that. Whatever question his silence raises, I already have the answer.

I'm leaving soon, and that will be the end of us. He doesn't look at me as he drinks his coffee, concentrating instead on the newspaper in front of him. I watch him read, marvelling at this small, ordinary action, and am struck by something unusual.

My parents used to do this.

How many mornings did I walk into the dining room to find my father reading the paper, mother opposite him? It is the most ordinary reflection of every day domesticity, and sharing it with Santiago now makes me anxious, because it's such a lie. I know I'm reading too much into it. I stand uneasily, moving towards the window. Across the room, my small suitcase is packed, stuffed with all the things I brought. Clothes that will remind me of Santiago for ever. The cap sits on top, ready for me to resume my disguise.

'We haven't talked about the casino,' I say, glancing at my wristwatch at the same time.

He lifts his gaze to my face and my heart stops beating. The golden light from behind me frames him until he shimmers. I ache for him but I know that can't happen. Like ripping off a sticking plaster, I have to go.

'We can discuss it over email,' he says quietly. 'But I see nothing in your requests that is…unreasonable.'

My eyes sweep shut. He's going to agree to my terms… Because he thinks they're fair or because we've slept together? Uneasiness grows. 'Thank you.'

The rustling of paper draws my attention back to him. He stands, walking towards me. 'I'll drive you to the airport.'

I anticipated this suggestion and have my response ready. 'I want to take a taxi. I've never done that before.'

His eyes war with mine, a challenge in their depths. 'Then I'll come with you.'

I hadn't anticipated that response, but I demur easily enough. 'It's too risky; too many people…my security guards. I'd rather say goodbye to you here. Privately.'

I wonder if he's going to overrule me, as he did with the trip here, but after a moment he nods. 'Fine.' He rakes his fingers through his thick, dark hair and I wonder if he's experiencing a similar maelstrom of emotions as I am.

I've never been with a man before. I have no experience of any of this, particularly not with saying 'goodbye', but I have bags of history when it comes to knowing what people expect of me.

This should be light-hearted. Nothing about what we've done was ever going to be serious. We both knew that coming into it. I force a bright smile to my face. 'I've had a lot of fun with you,' I say, wondering how it became so much more meaningful than just 'fun'.

'I'm glad.' He doesn't match my smile. His hand, when it cups my cheek, is gentle. 'Try to remember what you deserve, Princesa.'

Hope briefly lifts my heart. 'And what's that?'

'More than an arranged marriage.'

On this, I know we'll never see eye to eye. There's no

point discussing it further. Besides, I'm starting to worry that if we don't wrap this up quickly I might do something truly embarrassing, like crying, or begging him for one more night.

'I really have to get back.'

'Of course. Your state dinner,' he says with only the faintest hint of emotion darkening the comment.

I nod slowly.

He drops his head but, instead of the passionate kiss I crave, I receive a chaste goodbye peck on each cheek, and then he drops my hands and takes a step backwards. 'Take care of yourself, Freja.'

I watch him walk towards the door. Every inch of me wants to run after him, but I don't. I stand exactly where I am, already feeling the heavy gravitational pull of my real life and the future that awaits me.

It turns out sleeping with Santiago changed many things about me, but not this. I still feel nothing for my future husband. He is handsome and polite, well-spoken, and there's every indication he's well-read and well-educated, but if anything the idea of our marriage leaves me short of breath—in the worst possible way. I feel like my head is being pushed under water; I'm suffocating. I speak to him for longer tonight than I have before, trying to find common ground or some kind of spark, trying to find something with which to connect with him.

There's nothing.

'We should meet privately, another time, to discuss our parents' machinations,' he says, wiggling his eyebrows as though it's all some big joke. He doesn't know my heart is breaking. I'm very good at concealing such things.

'Do you want to pretend it never happened?' I ask with what I hope seems like humour, hoping he'll agree.

'I don't think that's possible. My parents would be devastated.' His eyes scan my face. 'Would you prefer to forget it, Freja?'

Hearing him say my name angers me. Not because I care about ceremony—I don't, generally—but it's an intimacy I like sharing with Santiago alone.

'I... My parents...'

He nods sympathetically. 'My parents have explained how much it meant to yours. Our marriage was their greatest wish. So let's have dinner some time between now and Christmas. We can go over the details then. Perhaps we should go away together for a weekend, get to know one another in a more private way?'

He is everything amenable and yet disgust threatens to swallow me. I nod, because I don't trust myself to respond, and excuse myself a moment later.

It's a relief when the dinner ends and I can return to my apartment, pushing Heydar from my mind gratefully and replacing him with Santiago. I lie in my bed, altered for ever by the nights spent in Barcelona, wondering what he's doing now.

I could text him, but to what end?

We shared something special—at least, it was special for me—but now it's over and I have to accept that, no matter how much it hurts.

I'm not surprised by the papers the next day. I'm single, twenty-four and in desperate need of a royal heir or three. And while the news of our betrothal is still confined to an intimate circle of fewer than ten people, Heydar is also young, single and highly eligible. A photograph of us locked in conversation runs in most of the European papers. The headlines are respectful in the more conservative papers, but in the tabloids it's all variation on a theme.

Happily Ever After! A real-life happy ending for the tragic Princess!

And in some, it was more speculative still.

Red-Hot Royal Romance!

Indeed, the photo does make us look quite intimate. Carelessly, I've leaned too close, or perhaps that's him. Our faces are only an inch or so apart, our eyes locked. I try to remember what we were discussing at that moment and draw a blank. The truth is, contrary to the image in front of me, I barely gave Heydar a tenth of my concentration. My entire mind was wrapped up in Santiago and the fact I'd flown out of Spain only hours earlier.

I throw the newspapers aside in a fit of impatience. I have just enough capacity left for rational thought to acknowledge that the photograph can be used to our advantage. When we inevitably announce our marriage, it will seem more realistic. People will believe we are in love.

I grip the wall behind me for support against the horror of that idea.

Another image floods my mind. I see Santiago as he was on the last morning, the way he'd read the newspapers from front to back, and I know there's no way on earth he hasn't seen this. Guilt rips through me and I fight an urge to message him to explain. I owe him nothing, just as he owes me nothing. If he did see the picture, only his ego will care.

I have to let it go.

A week later, at another state dinner, my heart lurches dangerously in my chest and I reach for the Prime Minister's arm, squeezing it unintentionally hard. 'What's *he* doing here?'

Henrik follows my gaze. 'Mr del Almodovár? I invited him, of course.'

'But why?' I turn to face him and am sure I must look as deranged as I feel—overjoyed and terrified all at once. It takes every ounce of will power I possess not to run across the room and throw myself into his arms.

'He's poised to invest billions of dollars into our economy. I thought it made good sense. Speaking of which, have you signed the contract yet, Your Highness?'

I think of the documents I was emailed six days ago, each condition I'd wanted spelled out in clear legalese. Why haven't I signed them? After all, I made up my mind a long time ago. I'm going to sell the land to him. The casino deal will go ahead.

Perhaps Santiago senses my questions, because at that precise moment his head lifts and his eyes pinpoint me effortlessly, slicing through me, exposing me, making me yearn, ache and fly all at once. He murmurs something to the couple he's in conversation with then begins to walk towards me. I have barely any time to brace for his proximity, or to work out how to behave. My instincts are to embrace him, to kiss him, to hold him close and never let go, but this is a very public setting and such a display would be a disaster.

I pull myself up to my full height and straighten my shoulders, aware of both the literal and figurative weight of the diamond tiara I've chosen to wear for the evening. It was my mother's favourite and it seems fitting that I should have that reminder of her tonight, when I am the closest I've ever been to wanting to disregard everything that's expected of me. The spirit of rebellion is almost impossible to tamp down.

Only two feet away from me, Santiago stops, addressing the Prime Minister first, extending a hand and shaking it as if they are old friends.

Seconds later, he turns to me, and I can't work out what's going through his mind. He looks at me and I feel a thousand and one things, but chief amongst them is relief. I thought I'd seen him for the last time, and until this moment I hadn't realised how badly I needed that not to be the case.

The week since I left Spain has been the longest of my life. I have been more isolated and lonely than ever before, more dissatisfied with my gilded cage and the limitations of my role here. Being ceremonially important—and only ceremonially important—is stultifying and infuriating.

I hold my breath, staring at Santiago—I can do nothing more. I'm frozen to the spot.

'Your Highness.' He bows low, the deference so at odds with the way he greeted me in our first meeting that a faint smile crosses my lips.

'Mr del Almodovár.' My voice shakes a little. 'Thank you for joining us tonight.'

'I was invited,' he says, flicking a glance to the Prime Minister.

'Of course, of course,' Henrik interrupts, so I want to shove him. 'I'm glad you came. Her Highness was just saying she's been meaning to sign the contract.'

'Has she?' Santiago's attention doesn't leave my face.

'I noticed you've incorporated the changes we discussed.' I hope my gratitude shows in my tone.

'I gave you my word that I would.'

My stomach tightens. 'Yes, you did.' I wish Henrik would go away. In fact, I wish everyone would. I want to be alone with Santiago so badly it hurts.

'Well, then, that's settled,' Henrik says convivially, patting Santiago's back. 'Shall we discuss the specifics of your build time?'

Santiago nods once, but his eyes stay on my face. 'However, there are some matters still to clarify with the Princess.'

'Oh?' Hope flutters in my chest. 'There are?'

'Indeed.'

'Shall we do so now?'

'Not tonight.' He gestures to the room. 'It isn't the time, and I'd hate to take you away from your adoring public.' I hear his cynicism, but it's mixed with something else too, an emotion I can't analyse. 'Does tomorrow suit?'

'I can clear my schedule,' I say eagerly—too eagerly, but fortunately Henrik is champing at the bit for this deal to be finalised, presumably so he can announce it ahead of the upcoming election and get the credit for bringing in such a valuable project. If the Prime Minister notices my willingness to meet with Santiago, it only matches his own.

A beat passes. 'You're staying in Marlsdoven tonight?'

A small smile flickers on Santiago's lips. I stare at them, mesmerised. 'If you are free to meet tomorrow, then *sí*.'

'Her Highness has already agreed to it,' Henrik says with over-the-top conviviality. 'Come, let's go and marvel at your site.'

I half-expect—and hope for—Santiago to tell Henrik to get lost. After all, he's not the kind of man to be told what to do or where to go. But he falls into step with the Prime Minister, cutting through the crowd with ease. I watch him go, perturbed and on edge.

Knowing he's here makes it impossible to concentrate. I rarely drink at events such as this—a message drummed into me when I was first conscious of alcohol and the powers it has to remove barriers—but I murmur a request for a glass of champagne to a palace staff member, grateful when a crisp, cold flute is placed in my hand a moment later.

The first sip is bliss but does little to calm my raging nerves. The evening passes in a blur. I go through the motions—making conversation, smiling, posing for photographs, remembering tidbits about each attendee's life as I have been trained to do—but all the while I'm conscious of Santiago, particularly the way he watches me. I feel his eyes on me and their possessive heat is like a glow building in my chest, burning brighter as the night wears on until finally it's over and I can escape.

All morning I've been waiting for this, yet the moment he strides into the drawing room, my breath catches in my throat and I feel as though my knees will no longer support my weight.

'Mr del Almodovár,' I murmur, for the benefit of the liveried soldiers who stand sentinel at the doors.

His eyes narrow imperceptibly and the air between us sparks with electricity. He closes the distance slowly, an agonising journey that makes me want to cry out. I force myself to remember that I'm a princess, and here in Marlsdoven I must behave like it. What we shared in Spain might as well have taken place between two different people.

But when his eyes roam my face it is as though I'm being ravaged. Heat flicks through me, slowly at first, but then with a flaming urgency burning me so my cheeks are hot and my lips part.

Finally, he reaches me, his lips twisting in a cynical half-smile. 'Your Highness.'

His voice runs down my spine like treacle and I fear my knees might actually buckle if I'm not careful. I need to sit down but I'm incapable of moving. I stand there, staring at him for a long time. The quiet clicking of the door as it closes rouses me from my stupor.

'Santiago.' Alone now, I use his name, but it's a form of torture because it reminds me of an intimacy we can never share again.

'Freja.'

My heart jolts. He's watching me carefully, his manner apparently relaxed, yet there's a tension on his face that makes me wonder if he's feeling as many emotions as I am. But of course he's not. This is Santiago del Almodovár. What we shared was earth-shattering and life-changing for me but for him? It was just another affair in a long string of affairs. I meant nothing. I force myself to remember that as I stare across at him.

'How are you?'

It's a polite question, little more than a civility, but my heart trembles when he asks it.

'Fine,' I lie. There's no sense in telling him that every moment since leaving Spain has been a form of torture… no purpose in telling him that the time we spent together has changed me in a fundamental way. 'And you?'

His response is to lift a shoulder indolently, then gesture to the chairs across the room. 'Shall we get down to business?'

My brows knit together reflexively. 'Oh,' I respond quietly. 'I— Yes. I mean, if you'd like.'

There is a coldness to him that makes me shiver. I feel his distance from me and want to shake him. 'It is why I'm here.'

It's just a statement of fact. It shouldn't bother me but I feel like I'm being pushed into a stream of lava.

'We could have dealt with this over email,' I say with quiet reserve.

'And yet you haven't.' His eyes lance mine. 'You haven't sent the contract back.'

My stomach drops to my toes. He's here for the contract; that's all. No part of this is because he wants to see me. Disappointment is like a chasm in my chest.

'Not for any reason,' I murmur, my voice halting. 'I've just been busy.'

He slices me with a look, as though he knows I'm lying, then moves towards the table set up beneath the window. The contracts have been laid out on it. I watch him from where I stand, watch his autocratic profile as he regards the documents.

'You've read them, I presume?'

I nod, but he's not looking at me.

'Yes.' I walk towards him, my stomach in knots.

'And?' He spins abruptly, pinning me with the full force of his attention so I almost lose my footing.

'Thank you for amending them so completely.' My smile wobbles. 'These terms are more than fair.'

'They're what you requested.'

'I don't think I expected you to grant them.'

'I saw no point in denying you.'

I stand opposite him, hope bursting through me, because surely he's admitting to something more? Surely he was so generous with my requests because he cares for me on some level?

'Why not?' The words rush out of me, husky and desperate.

His eyes narrow. 'Negotiating leads to delays. I want to begin construction immediately.' He looks at the papers once more. 'So, if you're ready?'

Disappointment is fierce. Of course it's business. It's always business with Santiago.

I nod jerkily, but don't reach for the pen.

'I…'

What? What was I going to say?

His eyes pierce mine. He waits. My uncertainty grows. We feel like strangers—no, not strangers. It's worse than that. There's antipathy coming from Santiago, hitting me straight in the face.

'You're angry with me,' I say, sure I'm right.

His only response is to square his jaw.

'Why?' I ask, pushing the point.

'I'm simply impatient for you to sign these documents so our business together is concluded. *Bueno?*'

Frustration slices through me. 'Why are you talking to me like a stranger?'

'Isn't that what we are now?'

My lips part. I go to deny it but pride keeps me silent. I feel the burn of tears behind my eyelids and move quickly, leaning forward and grabbing the pen, staring at the table while I flip through the contract, adding my signature at the bottom of the last page. But when that's done I stay as I am, not wanting him to see the emotion in my eyes, needing a moment to steady myself.

A single tear rolls down my cheek and thuds on the table. Embarrassed, I spin away from him, striding towards the window and staring out at the city without really seeing.

'Thank you.' For a second I think I hear something in his voice, something soft, apologetic even, but then his footsteps sound and I realise he's leaving.

I whirl round, sadness shifting to anger with lightning speed. 'So that's it?' He stops walking but doesn't turn round to face me.

Fury zips across my body. 'Is this how it goes, Santiago? You've had your fun with me and now I'm *persona non grata* to you? I had no idea this is how you treat your ex-lovers.'

At that, he whips round, his eyes like coal.

'How should I treat you, Princesa?'

I flinch at that, the weaponizing of a title he'd made so sexy and intimate now used almost as an insult.

'I'd settle for a modicum of respect—a hint of cordiality.'

A muscle jerks in his jaw. 'Respect?' He strides towards me then, his body emanating tension, his spine ramrod-straight. 'Do you think I am treating you disrespectfully? How, exactly?'

But I can't explain it. It's not anything he's done so much as what he's *not* doing. He's not smiling at me; he's not touching me. He's looking at me as though we're two strangers. He's speaking with icy civility bordering on disdain, but it's only the contrast to how he was in Spain that I resent.

'Forget it,' I say, my voice wobbling with tears. 'Just go.'

'Is that what you want?' he demands quietly.

I stare at him, frustration slicing me. It's not. But what I want isn't possible. I look around me, as if to reinforce that. I'm surrounded by ceremony. This room is one of the oldest parts of the palace. Gold wall panels meet double-height ceilings, crystal chandeliers run in a line down the centre and, at the end of the room, there's a wall of mirrors. The floor is a shining parquetry.

It's a physical reminder of who I am and what I owe my country. Across the corridor is the throne room; he would have walked past it before coming in here. Two golden thrones sit side by side, as they have done for hundreds of years, awaiting occupants.

'Or do you want this?' he asks, purposefully laying

the contract back down and rounding the table slowly, giving me time to realise his intention and to stop him if I wish to.

But I don't. Despite the impropriety and impossibility of Santiago I am stationary. Waiting, wanting, needing…

CHAPTER TWELVE

My breath burns from my lungs. I stand, waiting, my whole body on alert as he draws me into his arms and kisses me in one motion. His lips press hard against mine, his tongue an invasion, a reminder of his dominance and my surrender. And yet it is also his own surrender. I feel his body's acquiescence to mine, a reminder that there is something bigger than us, something neither can control, overpowering us both.

I groan into his mouth, my arms lifting and wrapping around his neck, my body cleaved to his as I kiss him back harder, hungrier, whimpering with desperation.

He takes a step forward, pinning me against the wall beside the window before lifting me, wrapping my legs around his waist so I feel the force of his arousal against my sex, and I cry out with a visceral, overpowering need.

'Please, Santiago!' I cry, not caring that we're here in this ancient room, not caring for anything right now but coming home again—and, yes, that's exactly what it feels like when we're together. His response is a guttural noise echoed into my throat and then he's pulling me from the wall, surrendering us both to the floor, his hands removing my pants as he pushes up my skirt. My own hands loosen his button and zipper, pushing down his waistband so I can feel his buttocks in the palm of my hand.

Even then, when passion has overtaken me so that I can't think straight, he pauses to provide protection, sheathing himself before driving his length into me so that I cry out, and would have done so longer and louder had he not kissed me, swallowing my noises, muffling my cries with his mouth as his body pleasured mine over and over; driving me to the edge of sanity and then beyond it, before dragging me back to start all over again.

My nails run over the soft fabric of his shirt then dig into his bottom until his own body is racked with pleasure. Finally, his weight collapses on top of me, our breathing rushed, the room a silent witness to something so powerful it shakes me to the core.

I don't know how long we lie there—time seems to have bent beyond recognition—but he stands eventually, turning his back on me as he zips up his trousers. Belatedly, I do the same, shifting and straightening my skirt at the same time. I can't see my panties. It takes me a second to realise he's holding them. My heart lurches.

It was an act of passion but it wasn't like what we shared in Spain. I feel further from him than I did before. I have to understand why.

'Have I done something to offend you?' I ask quietly, moving to him and putting my hand on his chest. His heart thuds, rhythmically but hard.

'No.'

I close my eyes. 'I don't understand. How can you go from making love to me to speaking like this again? I don't get it.'

'There is something I've been wondering,' he says after a beat, his tone cool.

'And that is?'

'Did you kiss him?'

I frown, not understanding what—or who—he's talking

about. 'Did you make love with him? Do you feel more for him now than you have previously?' He speaks calmly but there are dark emotions in the depths of his eyes and my pulse fires into overdrive. 'Do you have any idea how I have been tormented by that?'

It's almost conversational, and yet his words stir something deep in my soul. 'That photograph of you and your fiancé was in every newspaper,' he murmurs. 'It was easy to imagine that he'd taken you to bed. And all I could think about was undoing that—coming here and making you mine again, making you beg for me, erasing any memory of him from your mind, erasing his touch from your body.'

He pauses, allowing his words to sink in. 'I did not mean to treat you with disrespect, Freja. I was fighting my own instincts—my base, disgusting instincts to claim you as though you are a possession rather than a woman who can make her own choices. Does that make you happier?'

'Nothing about this makes me happy,' I say quickly, urgently, honestly. 'I didn't sleep with you because of Heydar. I slept with you because I wanted to more than anything in the world.'

His lips form a grim line in his face.

'Are you saying this was just…about ego for you?' I whisper, pressing a hand to my side, digging my nails into my hip.

'I hate the idea of him touching you.' He grips the back of a chair until his knuckles show white. 'I have no right. I know that. But I have been tormented, imagining his hands on your body, your voice calling out his name…'

I shake my head. 'You needn't have worried. I haven't slept with him.'

His skin pales beneath his tan.

'I haven't kissed him,' I add.

His eyes lance mine. 'The photo…'

'Just a glimpse of time. I don't even remember what we were discussing. Nothing important.'

He nods slowly, but if I'd expected relief on his features there is none.

'You still intend to marry him?'

My heart rips apart. God, how I wish things were different. I look around the room, trying to draw strength from my surroundings, but all I feel is weakened by them—weakened, vulnerable and resentful. 'Yes.'

He looks away from me, and for a second I feel as though he's fighting some kind of battle, but when he speaks it's with his trademark confidence. 'When?'

'Three months after my coronation.'

He pins me with his eyes. 'Be mine, until then.'

A shiver runs down my spine. 'What does that mean?'

'It means I want you. Until you're married, I want you to be mine.'

Nothing makes sense. I stare at him, trying to think this through, part of me elated and part of me devastated. I can't explain why I feel either emotion, just that both are overtaking me.

'It just doesn't… I don't see how…' I shake my head with frustration, trying to clarify my thoughts. 'Spain only worked because it was a secret. Here, in Marlsdoven, I'm surrounded. I can't pick up where we left off. If someone found out and it got into the press…particularly once my engagement's announced…'

His body is stiff. 'No one will find out.'

'How can you be so sure.'

He pulls a key out of his pocket, handing it to me. 'I have an apartment in the city. You can go there any time. There's an undercover parking garage. No one will ever see you.'

'And then what?' I ask, numb.

'What do you mean?'

'One day I get married and we simply stop seeing each other?'

Determination fires his voice. 'I won't sleep with another man's wife.'

My eyes sweep shut at his ability to speak with such clinical detachment. It's a skill I seem to lack where this man's concerned.

'What you're offering is very tempting.'

He stares, waiting for me to continue. I turn away, finding it impossible to think with him watching me so intently.

'But I can't do it.'

It's as though I've been struck by lightning. I understand why his offer is hurting me so much, why it's leaving me with the sense I have a hole in my heart.

'Because someone might see us together?' he responds with a dark emotion I can't interpret.

'No. Yes. Partly.' I furrow my brow. 'That would obviously be…less than ideal, and there's a risk of it happening, despite the fact your apartment has a secure garage.'

I can feel his condemnation even without turning to face him.

'I know you can't possibly understand, but the scandal would be disastrous. Particularly if it's after my engagement has been announced.'

I hear a puff of air, a sound of derision.

'Like I said, what you're suggesting is very tempting, and if I were free to do whatever I wanted then I'd probably agree. But I'm not free, Santiago. I'm not free and never will be.'

'You are martyring yourself,' he accuses coldly.

'Martyring myself? No. I'm serving my people and their needs above my own, as I always have and always will.'

'Serve them, by all means, but it's the twenty-first century. Find a way to live your own life too.'

'And what does that entail?' I demand, turning the tables on him. 'What are you suggesting? What life should I lead? Have an affair with you until you tire of me and move on—exposing me to ridicule and public sympathy as a jilted ex-lover of the great Santiago del Almodovár? Can you imagine what my parents would say?'

His eyes narrow, his face taut.

'And we both know you *will* tire of me. Because this is all you're offering, right?' I gesture towards the floor we just made love on. 'Memorable but meaningless sex—secret, shameful assignations and no future?'

'You are the one who's ashamed,' he responds quickly, then changes course. 'Do you want a future with me?'

My lips part, my brow clammy. I shake my head once, even when my heart is bursting with desperation to say, *yes, that's exactly what I want!*

'So what is the problem, then?' he demands, eyes narrowing.

I stare across at him, an ache in my chest widening into the worst pain I've ever felt.

'You have said many times that you cannot be seen with me, that no one can know about this. I get it. As ridiculous as I think that is, my ego is secure enough to not care. But if you cannot be seen with me, you sure as hell cannot marry me, so don't act as though you're holding out for a proposal.'

'I'm not,' I whisper, even as I think maybe I am. I realise it sounds ludicrous. We've known each other such a short amount of time, but none of that matters, because I *know* him. On every level I know him, and I love him, and want to spend my life with him. It's an impossible fantasy.

'But what if I wasn't going to marry Heydar?' I push

with soft determination. 'What if I was free to do what I wanted with my life? You still wouldn't be proposing to me.'

He drags a hand through his hair, pinning me with the intensity of his gaze. 'I have never wanted to marry anyone.'

I bite down on my lower lip to stop myself from reacting.

'And you have to have children. There is no hypothetical to negate the importance of that. Right?'

'Right.' I clear my throat, the chasm between us widening to an insurmountable distance. 'Which brings me back to the stupidity of continuing this. It's just going to lead to one or both of us getting really badly hurt, okay?'

'Hurt how?'

My heart breaks at that. It shows how little he cares for me that he can't even grasp what I'm getting at.

'You sleep with a lot of women. I get it. Sex is just sex for you. It means nothing.'

His brow creases.

'But I'm…not like that. You'll always be my first and, despite the fact that I know how transient this is, I care about you.'

He nods slowly, as though only just starting to comprehend. 'And you're worried you might fall in love with me?'

I close my eyes, the truth thick in my throat.

'You won't, Freja. You're too smart for that.'

I make a scoffing noise. 'Believe me, it's risky. I have to marry Heydar, and I can't do that if I'm pining for you. I need a clean break, time to get over you and move on with my life. We had fun in Spain but it needs to stay there.'

He speaks as though I haven't spoken. 'You're worried about falling in love with me, but I don't see any ris there. Not when we're both so honest about what this is and what we want.'

His calm argument is the breaking of all my resolve. 'That's just the thing, Santiago. I'm not being honest with you.'

He frowns. I suck in a breath, steeling myself to be brave. 'I'm already in love with you, and if I keep seeing you, sleeping with you, I'm terrified I won't be strong enough to walk away from you. I'm terrified that I'll love you so much I'll turn my back on everything I have to do—and I can't let that happen, okay? So just…stop arguing and let it go.'

He stares at me for several seconds, surprise on his face. Whatever hope I'd cherished that he might turn round and say he loves me too dies with every second that passes.

'Freja…' My name is a groan on his lips. Sadness engulfs me.

'You're asking me to give up everything that matters to me because your ego's been hurt by the fact I'm betrothed to another guy. I can't turn my back on my people and palace because you're not ready to let me go yet, because you like having sex with me.'

He shakes his head as if to dismiss this. 'It's more than that. It's a connection. There's chemistry between us, and it's breath-taking and urgent. That's why I don't want to let you go.' My lips part; dreaded hope returns. 'But that's not love. It's just great sex. If you had more experience, you'd understand that.'

I flinch, rejecting that with every fibre of my DNA. My voice is roughened by emotion. 'And maybe if you had a little less experience you'd be less jaded and see what's standing right in front of you. This is more than just great chemistry.'

He expels a heavy sigh. 'If you feel that way, then why

fight this? Why not enjoy what we share for a few more months? This is not complicated, Freja.'

The fact he thinks so is further evidence—as though I need any—of how little he cares for me.

'If I keep sleeping with you it will kill me. Already the idea of never seeing you again is like acid in my gut. The thought of marrying someone else and having them touch me, kiss me, make love to me, is anathema. Don't you get that?'

'You think I like the idea? Hell, that photo of the two of you together made me want to kill him, and I am not a violent person, Freja.'

A burst of heat runs the length of my spine. 'Doesn't that tell you something?'

'It tells me that I feel possessive of you, that I don't like sharing. But none of these things is love.' He drops his head, his forehead pressing to mine.

'And that's why we have to walk away.' And I do just that, taking a step back, staring at him from eyes that are smarting with unshed tears.

'Eventually, but not now.'

'It has to be now.' I press my hand to his chest, feeling the beating of his heart, wishing it were beating for me. 'I won't be strong enough later, and you're not offering me enough. This isn't enough…'

'What do you want, then?' he demands, his voice rising.

'I want all of you!' I roar back, forgetting where I am for a moment. I grind my teeth together. 'I want you to love me back. I want you to want me in your bed, not just for the next few months, but for the rest of our lives. I want you to beg me not to marry Heydar. I want you to want me like I want you.'

His eyes flare wide, his cheeks slashed with dark colour. 'That's not possible.'

'Why not?'

He makes a harsh laughing sound. 'You're the one who told me how unsuitable I am for you, how your people would react if they got wind of our affair. Have you changed your mind?'

I gape at him because he's right, and I'd forgotten momentarily. 'I'm not saying it's straightforward, but if you loved me maybe we could find a way…'

His eyes glint when they meet mine. I am on tenterhooks.

'If you loved me,' I whisper, 'Anything would be possible.'

He takes a step back, and I am reminded of all the times he pushed me away when we were in Barcelona. I gasp, because I know what's coming even before he speaks.

'I'm offering a casual relationship. An extension of what we shared in Spain, nothing more. I have no intention of asking you to do anything that would permanently change the course of your life. You've decided to marry him. It's important to you, and I accept that.'

'And that's it?' I ask quietly. 'You really don't care?'

He lifts his shoulders in a casual shrug, but every molecule of him reverberates with tension. 'I disagree with the premise of an arranged marriage…'

I wave my hand through the air. 'And that's it?' I repeat angrily.

'What more do you want me to say? Do you want me to tell you I don't love you? That I don't love anyone? That hearing you say you love me is the absolute last thing I want?'

I spin away from him, my heart in a thousand pieces. *don't love you.*

'All this time, you've accused me of living my life for er people, but at least there's a purpose to my choices.

You push everyone away because you're terrified of getting close to another soul.'

'I am not afraid.'

'Liar,' I mutter. 'You stand there and tell me you don't love me, but I don't think you even know how you feel. You're clinging to a self-protective mechanism you developed decades ago, even when it's destroying your life.'

'I'm perfectly happy in my life.'

'How can you be when you're so alone?'

'Alone is the last thing I am.'

I suck in a deep breath, his words like a sledgehammer at my side.

I spin round to face him in time to see him pick up the contract. 'You're right, Your Highness. There's no future here. You want more than I could ever give you—or anyone.'

'It's a beautiful day, Your Highness.'

I blink across at Claudia, a frown on my face.

'Sorry?'

She gestures to the window I'm sitting at, pointing at the blue sky. 'Why don't we go for a drive into the country? Have a picnic somewhere, hmm?'

My smile is tight and dismissive. 'I appreciate what you're trying to do, but it's not necessary. I'm fine.'

We haven't discussed the details of my love life. Three weeks ago, I came back to my apartment with tear-streaked cheeks and Claudia drew me into her arms and held me. Without knowing what happened—though I'm sure she's guessed some of it—she knew I was devastated. Since then, she's been a godsend, clearing my schedule as much as possible, minimising any requirements for me to go out in the world, to be seen and behave as normal.

I don't feel normal.

I feel broken in a way that must be obvious to anyone who looks at me.

'At some point, you're going to have to face this,' she says gently, propping her hips on the desk at my side, studying my face with worry.

'Face what?'

Her sigh is just audible. 'Whatever is making you feel like this. Why don't you tell me about it?'

My eyes clamp shut. I remember how certain Claudia was that Santiago was every bit as bad as his reputation, but the truth is she was wrong. He's nothing like people assume, but for me that's even worse. Loving him was too easy.

'I can't.' My voice cracks.

She sighs again. 'Then tell me what I can do to help.'

I'm tempted to respond with 'nothing', but suddenly it occurs to me that that's not true. My eyes widen as realisation starts to firm inside my chest. I rejected Santiago because of duty—a duty to my parents and my people, a wish to do them proud. Becoming another notch on Santiago's bedpost would have been insupportable. I walked away from the only man I've ever loved because it was the right thing to do. And now I have to take the next step, cementing the break between us, making it impossible for me to change my mind. He was offering sex, that's all. How could he have expected me to jeopardise my reputation for something he sees as meaningless?

I fix Claudia with a cool stare, but as I speak I feel as though my heart is turning to ice. 'Would you contact Heydar for me? I'd like to meet with him for lunch.'

CHAPTER THIRTEEN

'THANK YOU FOR meeting me,' I say quietly, nerves fluttering inside my belly.

'Of course. It would be poor form to turn down a lunch invitation from the woman I'm to marry.'

I move quickly, so the fork to my left clatters to the ground. I wince apologetically and dip down to retrieve it. Per my request, he and I are alone on the balcony, just the two of us—no staff to overhear this very private conversation and, more importantly, no chance of a photographer capturing this moment.

'That's what I wished to speak to you about.'

'The wedding?' He nods. 'I suppose it's time. Your coronation is set for three months?'

I toy with the stem of my wine glass. 'Yes.'

'And three months later, we'll tie the knot?'

A lump forms in my throat. 'I didn't know about our engagement until after they'd died.' I fix my gaze on the view beyond him. The city sprawls beneath us, elegant and ancient.

He shifts his head to the side. 'My parents told me when I was a teenager. I had been dating a girl, and they felt it fair to prepare me for my future.'

I bite down on my lower lip. 'I wish my parents had told me in person, but I suppose they thought ther wasn't a need. I would have liked a chance to discuss this with them.'

'Understandably.'

He's so *nice*, so patient. I wish more than anything that I cared for him, but I don't. At least, not enough. 'After they died, I became fixated on doing absolutely everything I could just as they would have wished. I imagined them beside me often—heard their praise, feared their disappointment and drew comfort from any opportunity that showed me clearly how they'd wish me to behave.'

My eyes bore into his. 'Marrying you is something I've never questioned, because I know how happy it would have made them. I think that in marrying you it would be a like bringing them back, in some way.' I shake my head. 'It's very hard to explain.'

'I understand,' he agrees gently.

And I really think he does. 'I want them to be proud of me, but lately I've come to realise that I can't ignore my own instincts completely.'

He sips his water, waiting for me to continue.

'Marrying you because our parents wished it doesn't make sense. Not any more.' Santiago's eyes fill my mind, giving me courage, even when I know the future I'm carving out for myself doesn't involve him.

'I've always wanted to live my life following the blueprint my parents laid out for me, but I've come to understand that doesn't entail doing everything just as they might have wished. It's about living with decency and honour, about loving this kingdom and country so much that I always work to make it better and safer, more prosperous, for our people. A blueprint isn't necessarily about ticking items off a list, but being true to a set of core values, values they drove into me since birth. But it's also about balance.'

I fold my hands in my lap. 'I'm not just a princess. I'm a person too. And while my country deserves my best it doesn't deserve all of me. I can't marry a man I don't love, Heydar. No matter how much my parents wished it. I'm sorry.'

His eyes probe mine and I hold my breath, worried he'll be angry, worried he'll try to convince me. But after a moment he smiles. 'Perhaps you'll fall in love with me over time?'

But he's joking, or at least not serious.

'I won't,' I respond firmly. 'I wish I could,' I add after a moment. 'But, as it turns out, it's not possible.'

'No?'

I shake my head, refusing to be drawn on the matter of Santiago, yet I suspect he understands what I'm not saying.

'In trying to live my life as my parents would have wished, I think I've been ignoring one of their most important lessons—to be true to myself. I can't go through with it. I'm sorry.'

'Don't apologise.' He stands and moves to the railing, looking down over the view I love so much. 'I'm surprised, of course. I fully intended our wedding to go ahead. But I respect your decision.' He turns to face me. 'I adored your parents, you know.'

My heart skips a beat.

'Your father was a frequent visitor at our palace. He was a funny, kind man.'

My smile is immediate. 'Yes, he was.'

'And I believe you're right. He would wish you to follow your heart, Freja, and it clearly isn't leading you to me.'

I shake my head silently.

'May I make one suggestion, though?'

'Yes, of course.'

'What if we become friends? I think that would have made our parents happiest of all.'

Relief bursts through me. 'I'd like that, Heydar. I really would.'

'Have you had a chance to peruse the plans yet, Your Highness?'

I blink at Henrik before shaking my head. 'I'm sorry. Plans for what?'

'The del Almodovár construction.'

'Oh.' Heat lashes me. It's been three months since I last saw Santiago and I can barely hear his name without breaking out in a sweat. I miss him in a way that defies reason and sense. I dream of him every night without fail. Well, not dream, exactly, because to dream I would have to sleep, and I find that sleep mostly eludes me. But I remember him. I impose him into my life and my bed, so that I reach for him at all hours and imagine his hands on my body. It is frustrating and soul-destroying, so each morning I wake with a deeper sense of loneliness than the day before.

I have deliberately avoided doing anything to make this harder, which includes typing his name into an Internet search browser or looking at the information I'm being bombarded with about the casino.

'You should see how the design has panned out,' my Prime Minister continues. 'I think you'll like the direction he's taken the project in.'

'I will,' I lie. 'I just haven't had a moment.'

'Of course. Your coronation preparations must be in full swing.'

I force a smile to my face.

'You will come to the ground-breaking, though?' he

asks. 'The media will be there. It's important, I think, that you are seen to support the project.'

My eyes close for a moment and then I nod. I know I can't ignore it. Henrik is right. My absence would indeed be conspicuous. 'Yes, I'll be at the ground-breaking, Henrik.'

The moment my car pulls up I see him. How can I not? Even in a crowd of faces, Santiago is impossible to miss—tall, broad-shouldered, wearing jeans, and a dark jacket in deference to the fact the temperature has turned cool. I dig my fingernails into my palms to stop myself from doing something truly stupid, such as running to him.

I want to.

I want to so badly.

But I can't.

For one thing, everything's changed between us. He hasn't called or texted since that morning in the palace three and a half months ago. I don't doubt that he's moved on, though thank God I have no confirmation of that. To see photographs of him with another woman would kill me.

The door to my car is opened and the crowd grows quiet. In the distance, there are rope garlands with people lined up behind them. I must greet them first, before I join the assembly of officials. I step out of the car and an enormous cheer erupts. Without needing to look in his direction, I feel his eyes on me, their intensity searing my soul.

Walking towards the first cluster of people, I accept a bouquet of flowers and a teddy bear. I stop and chat to an old woman, who remembers meeting my mother, then a young girl, who is dressed in a gown and tiara. She gives me a hand-written invitation to her birthday party, and as I hand it to Claudia I whisper to ask her to send cupcak as a birthday present. On and on it goes, for twenty minutes at least, before finally I'm at the end of the line and Henrik awaits.

'Your Highness…' The Prime Minister beams from ear to ear. 'How delightful to see you.'

I focus on his face, but it doesn't matter. My peripheral vision has picked up Santiago. I'm aware of his proximity and know that I must soon come face to face with him. I don't know if I have the strength for this.

Claudia, beside me, puts her hand briefly on mine, squeezing it, and I know then that she understands. She's pieced it all together. Her gesture does indeed give me some strength.

Turning to face Santiago is like being struck by lightning.

He is the same, but different. His hair has been cut shorter, and I see that what I had thought were jeans are actually the dark trousers of the suit he wears. There is no tie, but he looks so formal compared to usual garb. His dark eyes stare through me, and my heart rabbits against my ribs so hard it hurts.

'Your Highness.' He bows low. 'Thank you for coming.'

It's a perfectly respectable greeting that gives little away. I force myself to smile, but it's almost impossible. 'Naturally.'

'There's a shovel over here!' Henrik's tone is jolly, perfectly at odds with the depth of my feelings.

'I understand you are going to dig the car park?' Santiago murmurs in a light joke.

I don't smile. 'Just a ceremonial shovel, I'm afraid. No free labour today.'

'Pity. Car parks are always the most expensive part.'

I lift my eyes to him and feel as though the world has ɔed completely off its axis. I lose my footing a little but he shoots a hand out to steady me, pressing it to my elbow then releasing again just as quickly—almost as if I imagined it, as if he can't bear to touch me.

I stare at him, stricken, panic making it impossible to think straight. People are watching. Photographers are everywhere.

'Your Highness?' Claudia's voice drags me back to reality. 'This way, please.' She inserts herself between Santiago and me, gesturing towards a small timber platform that's been erected for the purpose of today.

I've done this sort of thing dozens of times in my life, yet my hands shake when I'm given the shovel.

Henrik makes a short speech about the importance of design innovation and the twenty-first century, the impressive work Del Almodovár Industries has achieved around the world and the promise for a new generation that this precinct will bring.

There is applause when he's finished, and then I do my part—smiling brightly as I wield the shovel, delicately sifting dirt around to ensure the press pool has a chance to get a decent photograph of the historic moment.

I hate to think what my father would say.

'Princesa, wait.'

His voice is low, something in the tone causing my feet to slow. I'm within sight of my car. Another minute and I'll escape.

'Freja.' He speaks my name low enough that only Claudia and I hear.

I stop walking and turn to face him, not even capable of offering a civil smile.

Up close, and almost alone with him, my legs feel completely hollowed out.

'Mr del Almodovár,' I murmur. 'What can I do for you

He’s frustrated and annoyed by that. His eyes flash to mine, irritation obvious in their depths. ‘I’d like a moment of your time.’

Panic flares in my breast. I cannot tell you how badly I want that too. I shake my head. ‘It’s not possible. I’m sorry.’

‘Then when will it be possible?’ he demands, his teeth bared.

‘Her Highness’s schedule is quite full,’ Claudia offers.

‘I believe Her Highness can speak for herself,’ Santiago responds with icy disdain.

I glare at him, then turn to Claudia. ‘It’s fine.’ I put a reassuring hand on her arm. ‘I’ll meet you in the car.’

Alone with him, I speak quietly. ‘There are people and cameras everywhere. Please remember that.’

‘Have you looked at the plans?’

This is what he wishes to discuss—the bloody plans?

I shake my head. ‘I sold the land to you, Mr del Almodovár. The nature of your casino construction is no longer of interest to me.’

He swears in Spanish, low in his throat. ‘Stop calling me that, as though I mean nothing to you, or I’ll kiss you right here to prove what a liar you are.’

I gasp, my eyes flaring wide.

‘You wouldn’t dare!’

‘Try me.’ He stares at me for several seconds then shakes his head with obvious frustration. ‘I don’t care what your plans are this afternoon. Cancel them and come to my apartment.’

I know for a fact my schedule is empty, courtesy of a vigilant Claudia, but I don’t tell him that. ‘Why?’

‘To discuss the plans, for a start. Do you still have a [illegible]?’

[illegible] shake my head. ‘I threw it away.’

I can see that angers him. I'm strangely pleased.

'Fine. Call me when you get there and I'll buzz you in.'

'It's not—'

'Seriously, Freja. Do not fight me on this. I'm not above dragging you into my car.'

CHAPTER FOURTEEN

'WHAT IS IT?'

My pulse is rushing so loudly in my ears, it's all I can hear. Alone with Santiago in his apartment, I feel the ghosts of past heartbreak and they're threatening to eat me alive.

'Please, come in.'

He gestures into the penthouse. It's nothing like I'd expected. Elegant and somehow homely. Not the blank-slate hotel décor I was imagining.

I grind my teeth together, hating that we are like strangers now, hating the distance between us, hating that I'm pretending to be angry at him when I'm actually just angry at the impossibility of our situation.

'No security guards?'

'I thought it best to keep this visit completely off the record,' I murmur.

'Heaven forbid anyone should know you came here.'

My heart stammers. 'What did you want to discuss?'

He drags a hand through his hair, pinning me with his gaze. 'Many things.'

My stomach swoops. 'I don't have long.'

His jaw clenches. 'Have a seat, Princesa.'

I startle, opening my mouth to snap back something him, but then I close it again. Fighting with him only ever leads to one thing. I move to the table and pull back a chair, settling into it with a straight spine.

He brings me a cup of coffee without actually offering one. I nod my thanks. Then he's quiet, striding the length of the table before stopping, staring at me for a second and turning on his heel, striding back. I watch, flummoxed and confused, my heart in my throat.

'Here.' He grabs something off the table and brings it to me. I recognise the papers—his logo is emblazoned on the corners.

I ignore it. 'I told you. I'm not interested in seeing your casino plans.'

He makes a noise that is a cross between a laugh and a furious grunt. 'Damn it, stop being so stubborn and look.' He opens the book in front of me, and for a few seconds I continue to stare resolutely ahead before concluding it's childish to the extreme.

'Fine,' I huff, focussing on the illustrations. I expected them to be a version of what had first passed my desk over a year ago, but these are completely different. Frowning, I look more closely.

MARLSDOVEN CROWN ARTS PRECINCT

I lift a hand to my mouth, clamping it there, tears filling my eyes. It doesn't make any sense. My fingertips tremble as I turn the page and study the drawings in more detail. Enormous glass structures to capture the river views and exquisite park-land are punctuated by tall, modern towers that spear into the sky, each housing accommodation. Two are marked as residential, one as offices and an additional two as hotels.

The glass constructions are labelled neatly: libra

performance arena, art gallery. There are several wrap-around balconies and restaurants.

My fingers trace the drawings and I shake my head. 'It's like you've reached into my mind and created a fantasy.'

'That was, more or less, the brief.'

I jerk my face to his, not understanding. 'But Santiago, why? This isn't… You're building a casino.'

His eyes burn into me with an intensity that takes my breath away. 'I no longer have any interest in casinos.'

'What do you mean?'

'I sold that part of my business.'

My jaw drops. I lift a hand to his shoulder. Despite the fact I'm sitting down, I feel like I need support, or a reminder of reality. Nothing makes sense. 'I'm sorry. I'm struggling to understand. How can that be?'

'The casinos are incredibly lucrative. It was not difficult to find a buyer.'

'But you're—they're a part of what you do. You love them.'

'I did,' he agrees with a nod. 'But not any more.'

'When did you decide this? Why didn't you tell me last time we met?'

'I hadn't arranged it then.' He stands up, moving away from me. I stare at the chair he had just occupied, my mind sluggish in the face of these revelations.

'I understand from your Prime Minister that the date of your coronation has been brought forward to April?'

'Yes,' I confirm numbly.

'I see.'

Silence falls between us, sharp and uncomfortable. I am conscious of his breathing, heavier than usual. I sense that he wishes to say something else, but he doesn't.

I fill the silence eventually. 'Your apartment's nice. Do ›u live here?'

He turns to face me, but he seems distracted. *'Sí.'*

My breath catches in my throat; it takes all my willpower to seem perfectly calm in the face of that admission. 'Since when?'

'Since a week after…we last saw one another.'

'Oh.' I stumble over the word, my mind spinning. All this time, he was within miles of my palace? When I was looking out over this city, craving him, missing him, he was right here?

'I don't understand why you did this.' I run a finger over the plans. 'But I'm…grateful, I think.'

'You think?'

'I don't know. I feel…guilty, too. That casino was your dream.'

'Not any more.'

I frown, standing and moving to his side. 'Santiago, what happened?'

'If I built that casino, you would have come to hate me.' He spears me with his eyes. 'And, every day you looked out on it, you would have hated me more. I realised I couldn't live with that.'

'I wouldn't hate you for that.'

'Of course you would. And you should. One day, someone will build a casino in Marlsdoven, Freja. I believe it's inevitable. But that person will not be me.'

I had come to terms with his damned casino; I had loved him despite it. And yet now gratitude steamrollers into love, and I feel as though I'm going to turn into a blubbering mess. I've already thrown myself at Santiago once, though, and made a fool of myself by declaring my unwanted love. For months I have lived with the pain of his rejection. I won't do it again. I have to get out of here before I say too much.

'Thank you.' I scrape the chair back abruptly, standin

and moving around the table, putting furniture between us out of desperation. He watches me with a haunted look in his eyes.

'Why did you bring the coronation forward?'

My own response is quiet. 'Why not?' I run my finger over the chair-back. 'My destiny has been plotted out for me since birth. Why delay the inevitable?'

A muscle jerks in the base of his jaw. 'I see.'

I swallow past a lump in my throat. *Leave, now.* 'Well…' I pull on the strap of my handbag, trying to smile. 'If that's everything…?' What kind of fool am I that even now I hope he'll say something, that he'll offer me what I desperately want?

But he's quiet. Watchful. His body is tense, shoulders held firm.

And, as I turn to leave, he doesn't try to stop me. Every footstep draws me further from him until my hand is on the door, turning the handle.

'Wait.' His voice is no longer commanding. It's heavy with surrender, desperate. 'Stop a moment.'

My shoulders slump because, for all that I'd been hoping he would stop me, I can't take much more of this.

'I have to go. Claudia's waiting in the car.'

He swears under his breath, so I turn to look at him. He runs a hand over the back of his neck, staring at the plans on the table. My heart twists.

'So everything is confirmed?'

I frown. 'I don't understand. With the building?'

'No, Princesa.' His features are haunted. 'With your marriage.'

All the air rushes out of me. 'I…' It hadn't even occurred to me that he wouldn't know. But why should he? My engagement to Heydar hadn't been public knowledge, and there's been no report in the press that we've broken it.

'Just tell me.' Now it's Santiago's turn to grip the back of the chair as though he needs the support. 'I appreciate that you're trying to choose the right words, but I would prefer to have the facts.'

My lips part in confusion. He sounds so wounded, as though his whole life rides on the status of my betrothal. Why?

'Will it happen soon?'

I shake my head, anguished.

'When?'

'We're not getting married.'

His head whips up to face mine. For a second, it's as though he can't speak. He stares at me, reading me, as if perhaps I'm lying—though for what purpose, I can't say.

'You're not getting married?'

'Not to Heydar,' I respond with a small shrug. 'But one day, I guess.'

'What happened?' The words rush out of him, startling me.

'Does it matter?'

'Humour me.'

I shake my head.

'Please.'

With a sigh, I pull on my handbag strap once more. 'Are you looking for more ego stroking, Santiago? Do you want to hear that it's because of you?'

'Was it?'

'Well, partly. It didn't seem very fair to marry Heydar when I was in love with someone else.'

He drags a hand through his hair so it stands up at odd angles. 'And are you still in love with me, Princesa?'

I blink at the question, my heart in my throat. I can't deny how I feel, but at the same time I'm furious with him for asking me.

'Forget I asked. I have no right. I'm sorry.'

I don't understand what's happening. I spin back to the door, but now I hear him moving, his footsteps quick. Just as I open the door, his arm reaches past me, pushing it closed again. I spin round, angry, but the look of resignation on his features silences me. His head is bent, and I know enough about agony to recognise it in someone else.

'Let me tell you something before you leave. Please.'

That word again! It's so unlike Santiago. I nod crisply but don't remove my hand from the door.

'The day at the palace…'

I groan, because I don't want to go back there. I don't want to think about the way we argued, about the way he told me he didn't love me.

'I was so angry. That photograph of the two of you was all I could think of, Freja. It tormented me and came to life inside me, so by the time I saw you I was filled with darkness. I came to Marlsdoven hoping to prove that what I felt for you was all in my head.'

I look away. 'I see.'

'No, you don't. Because, even if that was my intention, I hadn't been at the palace for more than two minutes before I realised how complicated this is. How much I'd missed you. I couldn't take my eyes off you. You were so beautiful, so regal, so incredibly confident. And I was proud of you—proud that even for a few nights I was a man you wanted to be with. But it was all an illusion—you'd never really be mine. There was always Heydar and that photo in the back of my mind.'

'It was just a picture.'

'I found it impossible to believe that.'

I breathe out slowly, dropping my hand from the doorknob.

'I don't know if this post mortem is helpful,' I say honestly. 'That morning was one of the worst of my life. I'll never forget how it felt to tell you that I loved you and have you—'

'Please don't.' He lifts a finger to my lips. 'Don't remember that morning. Not like that.'

'How should I remember it?'

'I knew you were different to anyone I'd ever been with, but since the first moment we met I've been fighting you—telling myself one more night would be enough, then another and another. And until that morning I'd never understood why I refused to see what was right in front of me.'

'But you do now?'

His smile is ghostly. 'Only because you made me understand. No one has ever loved me before. Not my parents, no one. You told me you loved me, and gave me something I wanted so much, but what if you took it away again? What if I let myself love you and you decided you were wrong? What if you married him anyway, and I could never love you? What if I had to live the rest of my life knowing you were out of my reach? I tried to convince us both that this is just sex, because sex is safe and I understand it. But it was never that with us, Freja. It was never just that.'

My knees are tingling.

'I didn't change the plans because I had any hope of winning you back. But I love you, and that means I want to make you happy—with all that I am, for the rest of my life. Even if all hope is lost.'

I shuffle backwards, pressing my spine to the door. 'You love me,' I repeat, nodding slowly, as if to commit his words to memory.

'Of course.'

There! A glimmer of his trademark arrogance shine through. I slant him a sidelong glance, but the cynicis

I'm going for is ruined by the sheen of tears in my eyes. After four months of heartbreak, I don't know if I can believe him so easily.

'Why haven't you called?'

'And say what? I thought you were getting married to him? Worse, I thought you'd brought the wedding plans forward? And what could I say? That I realised too late I'm completely in love with you? You deserve better than that. All I could hope was that you were happy, even if that was without me.'

'You're telling me this now?' I point out, my pulse ravaging my system.

'You're not engaged any more.'

I mull on that.

'I didn't deserve you then, Freja. I don't deserve you now. But at least by giving you this…' he gestures to the windows and the view of what will become his construction site '… I'm honouring you in a way that will bring you joy—the kind of joy, I hope, that those few days in Spain gave me.' He lifts his hands to cup my cheeks, staring into my eyes. 'Those days were the best of my life.'

It's too much. I lift a hand to his chest, curling my hands in his shirt for a second, tempted to drag him close—except instead I push him away. He's surprised and moves backward without much effort.

'Damn you, Santiago. Why didn't you realise this four months ago?'

He nods unevenly. 'I know. It's too late.'

'It's not that.' Again, I lift my hand to his chest, not pushing him away now. 'It's just—do you have any idea what I've been through? To love someone like I love you and think they don't feel the same way?'

'You were so brave,' he says quietly. 'To admit how you felt, even with all the obstacles we faced. You do realise nothing's changed, Freja? I'm still someone your people will be scandalised by.' He leans forward, his eyes probing mine. 'I want to be in your life, but we have to work out how to do that to avoid a scandal. I believe this apartment gives us an opportunity to see one another without anyone ever finding out.'

'No.'

His face tightens. He's afraid I'm rejecting him. And for a second I'm in awe of the power I apparently wield over this man. But I can't let him feel pain for a moment longer. 'That's not good enough. I don't want you to be some illicit secret. I'm not ashamed of you. I truly believe you are the best man in the world, and if anyone has a problem with our relationship then it's exactly that: their problem.'

His eyes widen, but he shakes his head. 'I can't let you do that. I know what your role means to you.'

All my pleasure evaporates as I realise the glaring flaw in our plan. He loves me, but he's not offering me the things I need. For a moment I'd forgotten, but I can't just have a secret boyfriend in an apartment near the city. 'For how long?' I ask quietly.

'What do you mean?'

'How long will you stay? For as long as the construction is going on?'

His brow furrows.

'Because I do need to get married one day, and have children. I know how you feel about those things, but I can't ignore all my obligations…'

'You misunderstand me—but that's my fault, not yours.' Before I realise what he's doing, Santiago del Almodovár bends down on one knee, his hand on my hip. 'The greatest privilege in my life would be marrying you and raising our children with you. I know it's an uphill journey, that my reputation will take some work to overcome, bu there is nothing I have ever wanted more. And when I want something, *querida,* I move mountains to get it.'

I laugh, a laughter born of sheer, overpowering happiness. 'I know that.'

'Wait.'

He stands quickly and walks into the kitchen, opening a drawer before returning and kneeling down once more. He holds up a small velvet box.

Despite what he's just said, this feels so much more real now. I find it hard to breathe. He lifts the lid and the most beautiful ring I've ever seen stares back at me. An enormous bright white diamond stands in the centre, surrounded by a circlet of black diamonds. 'It reminded me of you,' he says after a moment. 'It made me think about goodness overpowering darkness. It's how I've felt every day since knowing you.'

I kneel down then, ignoring the ring, despite its beauty. 'I need you to know something,' I say quietly.

'Go on.' I hear his fear, and a small sob tears through me despite my happiness.

'Please don't look like that. I will never stop loving you. There is nothing you can do, nothing you can say, that will change how I feel. I love you for who you are in here.' I press a hand to his heart. 'Because you are good and kind and thoughtful and, when I'm with you, I feel as though there's nothing in the world I can't do.' I soften my voice. 'But I will always regret implying that your reputation is something to be ashamed of. Everything you've done in life, all your choices, have made you who you are, and I am lucky beyond words that you love me as I do you. Do you understand?'

In the end, any worry about Santiago being accepted by ny country was completely unnecessary. His billion-euro vestment certainly paved the way—barely any mention of his existence before me was made. And, thanks to a few well-placed interviews, the narrative of Santiago's life had a far more accurate bearing on the truth of his character than the tabloid junk I'd seen in the past.

His reputation as a courageous fighter who overcame adversity to make his mark in the world was written about in all the papers, so too was his philanthropic endeavours. Even I didn't realise how much of his fortune he donates to child poverty and anti-hunger initiatives each year. By the time our wedding day rolls around, I know two things for sure: there is no one on earth who will make a better Queen's Consort and the people of Marlsdoven love Santiago almost more than they do me.

I have no nerves. No anxiety. Only excitement. The chapel is packed with family and friends—Heydar and his brothers sit in the front row, on my side. Santiago's parents are absent, and I didn't force the issue. It doesn't matter; the love surrounding us is palpable. Claudia serves as my Maid of Honour and is genuinely overjoyed for me. The train of my dress is almost half as long as the chapel's aisle, far heavier than any tiara I've ever worn, but I don't care. I feel weightless.

At the reception, we barely get to speak—well-wishers have come from all over the globe. I spy Heydar and Claudia dancing together and feel a spark of curiosity about the two of them—they would be very well suited!

As the night draws to a close, Santiago and I are alone, finally man and wife with the future before us—a future that I trust to be bright and long.

Seven years later

'Try not to fuss, little one.' I catch Santiago's eye and smile before turning my attention back to five-year-old Clara

'It's heavy,' she complains, lifting a hand to the delicate child's tiara.

'I know. I used to hate it too.' I wink.

'Then why did you wear it?'

'Because it's tradition,' I say. 'Tonight is a very special night and the people are excited to see you, their little Princesa.'

'And I'm excited too,' she says with a nod. 'But do I have to wear the tiara?'

Santiago settles Malthe, our four-year-old son, on the ground beside him, then crouches to Clara's height. 'How about we make a deal?' he suggests, and I smile, because Daddy always knows exactly what to say to win Clara over—just like her *mama*.

'What deal?' Clara asks, crossing her arms over her chest.

'You wear the tiara at first, just while we enter the room and photos are taken. Then you can take it off and pretend you are no longer a princess.'

Clara considers that. 'I like being a princess, just not wearing heavy things on my head.'

'Ah.' I nod wisely. 'Then let me tell you a little secret it took me far too long to learn…'

Santiago stands, putting his arm around me, drawing me close.

'What?' Clara prompts. Malthe watches us with interest.

'There is no one right way to be a princess,' I say firmly. 'Listen to your heart and all will be well, my darling.'

Clara considers that a moment, reminding me of her godfather Heydar. 'My heart is saying it doesn't like tiaras very much.'

I laugh softly.

'But I will do what Daddy suggested,' she says on a dramatic, self-sacrificing sigh. 'Particularly if there's ice-cream at the end of it.'

'You drive a hard bargain,' Santiago observes, but he grins, reaching down and tousling Malthe's hair. 'But I concede. Ice-cream it is.'

Malthe claps his hands together with enthusiasm for this idea.

'Is the baby coming?' Clara asks, slipping her small gloved hand into mine as we approach the doors.

'Sofia is only two, way too young for a New Year's Eve ball.'

Clara assumes an expression of someone far older and wiser than her years. 'Yes, you're right. Let's leave the baby to sleep.'

I meet Santiago's eyes once more and we smile, contentment wrapping around us as we contemplate the family we have made, the love we share and the life we lead.

It turns out I was wrong. Happy endings aren't just for romance books and Hollywood movies after all. They're a part of everyday life and I am living proof of it.

* * * * *

MILLS & BOON

Coming next month

THE SECRET BEHIND THE GREEK'S RETURN
Michelle Smart

Marisa opened her eyes, going from heavy sleep to full alertness in an instant.

Nikos.

He was alive.

Or had she dreamt it?

A look at her watch told her it was four in the morning.

She threw the soft blanket off and her stockinged feet sank into thick carpet.

Rubbing her eyes, she stared at the sofa. At some point while she'd slept, Nikos had put a pillow under her head, laid her flat on her side and covered her.

She hadn't dreamt him.

Heart in her throat, she found herself in the adjoining room before she even knew she'd opened the door and walked into it.

The light in there was incredibly faint, the little illumination coming from the lamp Nikos had left on for her in the living area. It was enough for her to see the shape of his body nestled under the covers, breathing deeply.

She definitely hadn't dreamt him.

Nikos was alive.

The relief was almost as overwhelming as it had been the first time, and, eyes glued to his sleeping shadowed face, she stretched out a trembling hand and lightly pressed her fingers against his cheek.

The relief was short-lived. A hand twice the size of her own flew like a rocket from under the sheet and wrapped around hers.

'What are you doing?'

Her heart jumped into her throat, the beats vibrating through her suddenly frozen body.

Nikos raised his head and blinked the sleep from his eyes, trying to clear the thickness from his just awoken brain, and stared at the motionless form standing beside him.

'Marisa?' His voice sounded thick to his own ears too.

As his eyes adjusted he saw the shock in her wide eyes before his gaze drifted down to notice the buttons of her dress around her bust had popped open in her sleep to show the swell of her breast in the black lace bra she wore.

Arousal coiled its seductive way through his bloodstream to remember the taste of her skin on his tongue and the heady scent of her musk. He tugged her closer to him, suddenly filled with the need to taste it again, taste *her* again, to hear the throaty moans of her pleasure and feel the burn of their flesh pressed together. It was a burn he'd never felt with anyone but her.

Her lips parted. Her breath hitched. Her face lowered to his…

His mouth filled with moisture, lips tingling with anticipation. He put his other hand to her neck and his arousal accelerated.

It had been so long…

Then, with her mouth hovering just inches from his, she jerked back and snatched her hand away. It fluttered to her rising chest.

'I'm sorry for waking you,' she whispered, backing away some more. 'I was just checking I hadn't dreamt you.'

Continue reading
THE SECRET BEHIND THE GREEK'S RETURN
Michelle Smart

Available next month
www.millsandboon.co.uk

Copyright ©2021 by Michelle Smart

COMING SOON!

We really hope you enjoyed reading this book. If you're looking for more romance, be sure to head to the shops when new books are available on

Thursday 8th July

To see which titles are coming soon, please visit

millsandboon.co.uk/nextmonth

MILLS & BOON

For exclusive extracts, competitions and special offers, find us online:

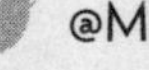

facebook.com/millsandboon

@MillsandBoon

@MillsandBoonUK

Get in touch on 01413 063232

WANT EVEN MORE

ROMANCE?

SUBSCRIBE AND SAVE TODAY!

'Mills & Boon books, the perfect way to escape for an hour or so.'

MISS W. DYER

'Excellent service, promptly delivered and very good subscription choices.'

MISS A. PEARSON

'You get fantastic special offers and the chance to get books before they hit the shops.'

MRS V. HALL

Visit millsandboon.co.uk/Subscribe and save on brand new books.

MILLS & BOON
A ROMANCE FOR EVERY READER

- **FREE** delivery direct to your door
- **EXCLUSIVE** offers every month
- **SAVE** up to 25% on pre-paid subscriptions

SUBSCRIBE AND SAVE

millsandboon.co.uk/Subscribe

MILLS & BOON

THE HEART OF ROMANCE

A ROMANCE FOR EVERY READER

ODERN

Prepare to be swept off your feet by sophisticated, sexy and seductive heroes, in some of the world's most glamourous and romantic locations, where power and passion collide.

ISTORICAL

Escape with historical heroes from time gone by. Whether your passion is for wicked Regency Rakes, muscled Vikings or rugged Highlanders, awaken the romance of the past.

EDICAL

Set your pulse racing with dedicated, delectable doctors in the high-pressure world of medicine, where emotions run high and passion, comfort and love are the best medicine.

rue Love

Celebrate true love with tender stories of heartfelt romance, from the rush of falling in love to the joy a new baby can bring, and a focus on the emotional heart of a relationship.

Desire

Indulge in secrets and scandal, intense drama and plenty of sizzling hot action with powerful and passionate heroes who have it all: wealth, status, good looks…everything but the right woman.

Experience all the excitement of a gripping thriller, with an intense romance at its heart. Resourceful, true-to-life women and strong, fearless men face danger and desire - a killer combination!

To see which titles are coming soon, please visit

millsandboon.co.uk/nextmonth

JOIN US ON SOCIAL MEDIA!

Stay up to date with our latest releases, author news and gossip, special offers and discounts, and all the behind-the-scenes action from Mills & Boon...

millsandboon

millsandboonuk

millsandboon

It might just be true love...

Unlimited access to all your favourite Mills & Boon romances!

Start your free trial now

Available at

weloveromance.com

Get the latest romance news, exclusive author interviews, story extracts and much more!

blog.millsandboon.co.uk

OUT NOW!

Payback in passion

Available at millsandboon.co.uk

MILLS & BOON

OUT NOW!

Tantalising temptation

Australian NIGHTS

SUN. SEA. SEDUCTION.

3 BOOKS IN ONE

ROBYN GRADY

NICOLA MARSH

CATHY WILLIAMS

Available at millsandboon.co.uk

MILLS & BOON